The Water's Edge

The Water's Edge

Louise Tondeur

review

An extract of this novel first appeared in *FirstHand*

First published in 2003
by REVIEW

An imprint of Headline Book Publishing

10 9 8 7 6 5 4 3 2 1

British Library Cataloguing in Publication Data
is available from the British Library

ISBN 0 7553 0140 4

Typeset in Minion by Palimpsest Book Production Limited,
Polmont, Stirlingshire
Printed and bound in Great Britain by
Clays Ltd, St Ives PLC

Headline Book Publishing
A division of Hodder Headline
338 Euston Road
London NW1 3BH

www.reviewbooks.co.uk
www.hodderheadline.com

To Sarah, whose name means Princess

Acknowledgements

Thank you to Sarah Barnsley. Thank you to my family.

Thank you to Ali Smith, Sarah Wood, Michèle Roberts, Andrew Motion and Larissa Lai. Thank you to all my friends at UEA 91–94, where it began, and 00–01, where it finished. Thank you to Hannah Griffiths and Mary-Anne Harrington. Thank you to Curtis Brown for awarding me the literary bursary in 2000. Thank you to Regency Court Holiday Flatlets for inspiration.

Thank you to Jill Hall because without you it wouldn't have been possible.

'O spirit of love, how quick and fresh art thou,
That notwithstanding thy capacity
Receiveth as the sea, nought enters there,
Of what validity and pitch soe'er,
But falls into abatement and low price,
Even in a minute!'

William Shakespeare, *Twelfth Night*

My name is Rice. My parents were big on India and China. I'm lucky I'm not called Lapsang Souchong.

My name is Esther. My great-grandmother was into the Old Testament. Lucky I'm not called Nebuchadnezzar.

My name is Beatrice. I never knew my father. He went swimming when the waves were fierce and drowned when I was just a month old.

My name is Meredith. I am secretly in love with Beatrice all the way through, but you have to wait till near the end for the kiss.

My name is Persephone. I'm a mythological figure. Don't forget. Margaret and Grace are also in the book, but they die on pages 238 and 244 and don't have time to introduce themselves. There are lots of other characters (you'll meet them as we go along) but Rice and I are the only ones who are on the beach, telling the story.

Rice

M y name is Rice. Autumn is coming, although it was warm today. The sea is calm and its white ruffles are edging their way up the sand and back. I've just driven down from London where I live. I came straight from the gallery because Meredith, Beatrice and Esther are organising a birthday party for me.

'We're organising a party,' said Beatrice on the phone a few weeks ago.

'It's the opening of my exhibition the afternoon before, so I can't drive down till the evening,' I said, looking in my diary. (Now I am a famous photographer, I have to write my appointments down.)

'Which one is this?'

'Buildings and Beaches.'

'Get here before eleven,' said Beatrice. 'I don't like to disturb the guests.'

Some important people, whose names I have forgotten, were at the opening of my exhibition this afternoon, amongst the canapés and the strawberries and champagne and orange juice. After smiling at them and shaking hands, I took some pictures of them all, so that I could think about it later. Through the viewfinder I noticed a tall woman in a thin green dress with blonde hair and a look in her eyes like something had happened to her that she had to remember before everything she said. I focused my lens on her, but she noticed and waved a hand to stop me.

'I don't like having my picture taken,' she said. She was standing in front of a photo entitled *The Photographer as a Child*. It was a blurred picture of me, aged eight, with my mother. The bottom right-hand corner was brown, like someone had held a lit match underneath until it curled. 'My mother and me outside the Houses of Parliament, 4 May 1979,' I had written for the caption. The day Margaret Thatcher became Prime Minister. I remember my mother saying something about it being important that we went and stood outside the Houses of Parliament the day after the first woman Prime Minister was elected.

'I'm sorry,' I said to the woman in the green dress, 'I should have asked.'

Next to the Houses of Parliament picture was one called *Esther's Birthday, May 1989*. The strange woman in the green dress turned to look at it and said, 'Just before the fire.'

'Yes,' I said, and then, 'How did you know about that?'

But she didn't answer, she was looking at a picture of Beatrice, taken by the thirteen-year-old me, a few weeks after I arrived there. I had called this one *Beatrice in the Hotel Kitchen, 1984*. I had looked at these pictures thousands of times before, but seeing them like this, through the eyes of the young woman, it was as if someone else had taken them. She took me by the hand and told me she had visited the Water's Edge Hotel for over sixty years because it had been so convenient for her and that she thought the photos were lovely. I knew then that she must be a nutcase. She looked no more than eighteen.

'This is just some stuff I took as a child,' I said. 'The main exhibition is through there.'

But she didn't seem interested. She leant even closer and

whispered in my ear, 'I came up for your exhibition but I've got to go back tonight. Any chance of a lift?' I looked from the picture of Beatrice to the woman standing next to me.

'Go back where?' I said, but then the manager of the gallery came up to introduce someone from Channel Four who was making a documentary about young artists. They manoeuvred their way in front of the woman in the green dress and she folded back like she was drowning into the crowd of people waiting by the buffet for summer pudding, and I couldn't see her any more.

'Rice, I'd like you to meet . . .' said the manager of the gallery.

'Who was that?' I said, looking over his shoulder.

'What? I don't know. No one important.'

At about five o'clock, I disentangled myself from the important people, grabbed my coat and a handful of cream cheese and chive sandwiches and went to find my car. I sat in the driver's seat, eating the sandwiches and thinking about the strange woman and the man from Channel Four. Then I started up the engine. It was raining that drizzly kind of rain that you only get in London and I had my windscreen wipers on, and the orange streetlights were blinking into life in the twilight and making my eyes dance, so I almost didn't see the woman in the green dress without a coat, trying to hitch a lift. She was standing in the middle of the road with her arms outstretched and cars were beeping their horns and whizzing past on either side of her. I stopped and she ran round to the passenger door and got in.

'I thought you'd gone without me,' she said, and smiled a smile that made her light up like she was immortal or something.

'My name is Delphinia,' she said, which I thought was an unusual name.

'Where are you going?' I said, hoping she wasn't really mad.

5

'The same place as you,' she said, putting on her seat belt and switching on the radio. I needn't have worried. She was a good passenger. On the way she entertained me with stories about freak weather conditions and then, when we had been going for about an hour and it was properly dark, she told me about the time she'd been chambermaid in a hotel.

'I used to work at the Water's Edge Hotel when I lived there,' I said, hoping for an explanation of what she had said at the gallery, but she didn't say anything. 'Didn't you mention that you'd stayed there?' I pressed her for an answer but she seemed to have lost interest again and was looking out of the window, watching the wet night shapes darting by. 'Maybe I misheard you,' I said.

For the rest of the journey we were silent, but it wasn't long before a sign by the roadside was welcoming us to Bournemouth.

'Where do you want to be dropped?'

'Anywhere on the beach is fine.'

'OK,' I said. It was an unusual request, seeing as it was still raining and it was nearly nine o'clock. 'Anywhere?'

'Yes,' and she smiled at me. I drove down to the part of the beach I liked the most and she looked at me and smiled like I had read her mind and this was exactly the place she wanted to get out. I parked my car by the pier and walked on to the sand. It was quite dark when we got here. It's good to breathe in the taste of salt and sand after being in London. I look up at the cliff, which runs in a shallow curve from the beach, yellow and green in the daytime, to where the old hotel used to be, and at the steps that lead from the beach to an empty space. If I half close my eyes I can see the dark outline of the old hotel standing like a proud ghost at the top of the cliff. The woman in the green dress is still sitting a little way along the sand looking out to sea, like she's waiting for something to happen. I am still standing next to the pier, wondering whether to leave her there in the rain.

I'm looking up at the space where the old hotel used to be and remembering. The story starts sixteen years ago in March 1984. I was thirteen.

My name is Persephone, only every year I change my name to something different. Without me there would be no winter, no harvest, no bonfires, no falling leaves, no ice ponds, no death and rebirth. There is Rice, looking up at the ghost hotel, her feet on the sand. I'm sitting near the sea, on the hard brown sand, which is wet underneath and packed together tightly. I'm looking out at the green sea, which is calm tonight, and at the surface of the salt water, watching for any changes, because I'm waiting for the gates to Hades to open so that I can return to the centre of the earth and autumn can begin again. Then the leaves can turn to precious metal and crumble, fragile as burnt paper. Apples can turn red and green and fall into the grass that still smells of summer, and the wheat can be gathered with thick fertile heads.

I was glad I was able to hitch a lift with Rice to the beach, because I thought I was running late, although now I'm here nothing is happening, so I'll have to wait. Rice is standing over there by the pier, wondering whether to leave me, and she's thinking about 1984, the year she arrived at the old hotel. I think she's very beautiful (like me). She's got long dark hair in a plait down her back and she's wearing a red dress because she's been at the opening of an exhibition of her photographs this afternoon. It's her thirtieth birthday tomorrow, whereas I am as old as the earth.

Each year, I arrive on the beach at Bournemouth, dizzy after my journey from the underworld. Spring always arrives with me and the season begins with a flourish of dusters and the coming of crocuses. I stay in Bournemouth from March till September. In the autumn, I wait for a sign that marks the start – usually there's a certain tree that turns first, or a dead sheep in a field – and then I return to Hades once more. What happens on the other side of the world where winter and summer are different? They have their own myths so they don't need me. There are no ceremonies these days. Demeter, my mother, has given up mourning. She just makes sure it's cold enough to keep the glove-makers happy.

My name is Rice. After my mother died, I stayed next door with an aunt, because I had no other relatives. In fact, Auntie Something wasn't a relative either. She was just a neighbour. After a week of watching me wear the same clothes and eat cereal straight from the packet, with my too-thin legs dangling from her kitchen table, Auntie Something sat me down, made me think and think of any relatives I might have overlooked, and then, after some sleuthing in my mother's address books, she phoned Beatrice Tamarack. Beatrice ran a hotel in Bournemouth, where my mother had once lived and where I was born. I stood in Auntie Something's pink hallway and listened to her saying into the phone that I needed someone to look after me and that her house wasn't big enough because she had six grandchildren to think about.

After the funeral, Auntie Something held a party in her front room and spent most of the time guarding the buffet to make sure no one had more than their fair share. I met Beatrice in front of the beef and mustard sandwiches. She turned out to be a chunky middle-aged woman with a round face, a small nose and short brown hair. When she took hold of my hand, I noticed that she was wearing sensible shoes. Then she said something about being good friends with my mother at school, and that she was sorry. I nodded my head. She said she'd be delighted for me to come and live with her, but that I must understand I'd have to help out around the hotel because she wouldn't be able to afford it otherwise, and she looked worried then, but the conversation left my head along with all the other things that people said to me that day over Auntie Something's china plates and teacups.

'I have to get back for the hotel guests,' she said, 'but you can come on Saturday.'

As I packed my things, I felt like I was getting into the red carriage of a ghost train with my suitcase and pulling the safety bar down, and even though I didn't want to I was heading into the tunnel. Auntie Something had given me a big green suitcase, but it wasn't full by the time I had finished. I had only brought a few things from the council house. My camera was the most important. Before I went I took some pictures of Auntie Something and her grandchildren in her pink hallway. I said goodbye and thank you as politely as I could. Then I got on the train to Bournemouth. It was Saturday, 31 March 1984.

It was raining on the day I arrived at the Water's Edge. The hotel stood on top of the cliff at the end of a gradually climbing road. I recognised it straight away from Beatrice's description. It was a large red brick building and the windows were at odds with each other as if most of the rooms had been added as afterthoughts. Other buildings on the road looked neater; I noted them as I went past: modern flats, a seafood restaurant and a shop selling things for the beach.

At the front of the hotel was a gravel car park and several cars were parked there already when I arrived. I got out and watched as the taxi turned left out of the drive and swept down towards the pier. Then I stood by the front door with my suitcase in my hand and my stomach felt like lumpy mashed potato. Before I could ring the doorbell, the door was opened by a girl, about my age, maybe a bit older. She didn't smile but I wanted to take her photo as soon as I saw her. She was unusual – she had green eyes and red hair. As I walked in, a young-looking woman walked out and turned to look at me and I felt like I knew her, or like I was going to know her one day, but I found out later that she was just one of the guests.

In the hotel foyer, the rest of my welcome party was waiting for me. The girl fell back behind an old woman in a wheelchair. Next to her was Beatrice. They stood in front of a large brown desk to the right of the front door, on which there was a signing-in book, a pile of hotel brochures and a small bronze bell for guests to ring when they wanted attention. The word 'Reception' hung suspended above it. On the wall behind the desk was a notice board and rows and rows of keys, bearing numbered key-rings in yellow, blue and green plastic. Next to the reception was a door marked 'Private'.

'Hello,' said Beatrice. 'This is my daughter, Esther, and this is my mother, Margaret. I'll make some tea.' She disappeared through a doorway opposite. Esther ignored me and pushed her grandmother into the guest lounge while I followed behind, feeling new and clumsy. The guest lounge had lots of old comfy chairs in it and a couple of low brown coffee tables.

'You have to work while you're here, you know,' said Esther, once we were sitting on the orange sofa.

'What?'

'You have to work while you're here, you know,' she said, a bit louder. Beatrice bustled back in. She was wearing brown trousers and she gave out cups of tea that afternoon like she was dealing cards. When she leant close to me to pass a cup, I noticed she smelt like icing sugar.

'I was telling Rice that she has to help out while she is here,' Esther said, eating cake with her mouth open. I think I protested. Esther smiled to herself and Beatrice looked awkward.

'Everyone works here,' Beatrice said, embarrassed for a second, 'I thought I told you that.' Everyone, that was, apart from Grandma Maggie, who was looking at me steadily.

10

'Dementia,' said Esther, seeing me look at her, and pronouncing all the letters carefully, through chocolate-covered teeth. After Esther had eaten three slices of cake, I stood by the door of the lounge and watched her hold a cup of tea to her grandmother's furry lips, then Beatrice told her to show me our bedroom.

'Come on,' Esther said, climbing the stairs to the attic. Those stairs became so familiar to me that I stopped noticing they were there. The first time, though, I felt each step of uncarpeted wood under my feet and saw the dust that had collected in the corners of each one. We came to the attic bedroom I was going to share with Esther. There were bunk beds, newly assembled for my arrival, in the corner, an old sofa and a record player. Esther wasn't happy about sharing her room with a stranger.

'Have you got any fags?' she said, by way of welcome.

'No.'

'Jobs,' said Esther. 'We clean on Saturdays. Normally I'm on breakfasts during the week.'

'Right,' I said, and put my bag down on the top bunk.

'We rushed through the cleaning today because you were coming. It usually takes all day on Saturday. It's the most popular day for check-in, although there aren't many people in this week. That's my bed. You're on the bottom.' I moved my bag and went over to look at the records, which were stacked up next to the record player. I bent down to pick up the top one. 'Adam Ant. "Goody Two Shoes",' it said on the front.

'Don't touch that.'

'Sorry.'

'We have to set tables for dinner,' Esther continued. 'We give them a menu card when they arrive and they choose their dinners for the week. If they haven't chosen, we give them what's left over.'

11

'Doesn't your mum pay people to do stuff like that?'

'There's one chambermaid called Sandra. Steve comes in on Saturdays, but we still have to help.'

'OK.'

Esther went over and looked out of the window and I went and stood next to her because I wanted to know what the view was like. The first thing I saw were steps leading down to the beach from the hotel garden and below them the beach and the pier. Rain was falling thickly and people were walking along the pier with umbrellas. I turned away.

'I didn't want to come here,' I said, leaning against the windowsill.

'Why did you then?'

'I don't know. This hotel stinks.'

'What of?'

'Bodies.'

'Dead bodies?'

'No. Alive ones.'

'Like feet, you mean?'

'No. Old people.'

'You get used to it.'

We stood there in silence for a while, then we descended again to the ground floor. On the way, Esther showed me which bathroom to use. It was right at the bottom of the attic stairs. After that, I followed Esther downstairs and into the kitchen, wondering if I would ever be able to find my way around on my own.

The kitchen was big. Taking up a lot of the space was a long wooden table, with chairs around it. On one side of the table was a door into another part of the hotel and on the other, a door into the garden. Half of the kitchen seemed to be designed for eating, the other for preparing food for the guests. There was an old-looking gas cooker, long steel work surfaces, and a steel sink, below a window that looked out over part of the garden. A pot full of washing-up brushes sat on the windowsill, with a jar full of different coloured sand. There was a fridge freezer, a potato peeling machine, a microwave and two big washer dryers. Spoons and pots were hanging all over the walls and there were lots of cupboards and shelves, including a row of what seemed like a hundred small silver teapots.

'This is where we have our dinner,' said Esther, pointing to the table. She opened the back door. 'You can get down to the beach from the garden,' she said. Then she turned round, opened a large cupboard and stuck her head inside. As she did so, she talked about various items of catering equipment she felt I needed to be aware of, but I stepped out into the garden and walked over to the top of the steps to the beach and looked down towards the sea, and thought about running down the steps, running into the sea and turning into a boat. It had stopped raining and people were reappearing from beach huts and fish-and-chip shops and were beginning to fill the sand. Esther hadn't noticed for the moment that I wasn't with her. I could hear her voice inside.

'We've got quite a big kitchen. You'll need to learn where everything is. Coffee pots are under there. Side plates and butter knives. The Hoovers ...' I went through the gate and sat down on the top step. When Esther realised she'd lost my interest, she came out and sat down next to me and we looked down at the beach for ages without saying anything to each other.

My name is Persephone. In 1984, I arrived at the hotel on 21 March. I had come straight from hell with my suitcase in my hand. As soon as I had climbed up the beach and dried myself in a beach hut, I heard the shoots push up from under the brown earth and the worms shifting and the sound of bluebells ringing.

The sea changed colour from dark green to light blue, and where the sky met the water there was silver light like magic. I could smell spring coming in over the waves and a fresh scent like pine needles and sea salt in the air around me. Trees came to life and put on pink blossom like calypso dancers. The daffodils began to open their yellow umbrellas, the sun got warmer and blackbirds polished their orange beaks for singing. I put on a green spring dress and shook out my blonde hair and wished for a second that I had a silver tail so that I could dive in and out of the salt water with the fish. Then I checked how I looked in the mirror my mother had given me (I am always very beautiful but a bit different every time) and I went the long way round to the old hotel, as if I wasn't used to it, up the road that leads from the pier to the top of the cliff, across the car park, through the door and into reception. Beatrice Tamarack came out from the kitchen to introduce herself, and show me to my room, even though I had seen her so many times before and had secretly watched her being born forty-two years previously in Room Fifteen.

'What are you planning to do while you're here?' Beatrice said. She asked all the guests this. It was the friendly touches that made people come back – the leaflets in the hall, giving details of forthcoming attractions and family zoos, the smiles in the corridors on the way to dinner and the joke tea towels hung behind the bar. I don't tell the mortals the truth about who I really am. I think up a different name every time. (In 1984, I called myself Diane.) And I make up an excuse, saying that I am a convalescent, I have had a nervous relapse or I need time to adjust to a family crisis. Usually I am left alone, treated as if eccentric, and brought water or tea when I incline my head to the right and frown slightly. In 1984, I told Beatrice that I had a chest infection.

'I have been unwell for a while,' I replied. 'Bronchitis. I need to take it easy.' We reached the room, which was on the first floor, at the front of the hotel.

'I hope you are able to do that while you are here,' replied Beatrice. She handed me the key. 'Breakfast is from seven until nine. From eight on Sundays.'

Esther Tamarack approached, her sleeves rolled up, a bottle of Jif in her hand.

Esther is bewitching. Each time I see her I find myself imagining that she has Wiccan ancestry, or a great-grandmother who had an unusual scar, kept a cat and grew herbs in her garden. She fitted into the old hotel like she was born out of one of the walls. She knew its routines like a mantra and hated anyone who tried to break its rules. No breakfast before eight on a Sunday. No guests' washing accepted after five. The management is not responsible for possessions left in the dining room. She is elflike, magical, watery and elegant. Her head is a map of things to do in Bournemouth and rooms and pipes and sinks and bath plugs. The old hotel wombed her and made her its child as much as she was Beatrice's. When Rice arrived she was nearly fourteen.

'Ten and eleven are ready,' she said, as I went into my room.

'Twenty are complaining because they don't have any soap,' Beatrice replied. 'Have you done the pillowcases . . . ?'

I closed my door. Then I went and opened the window, moving aside a purple curtain, and looked down at the sea. I listened to the sounds of the hotel going on around me. I could hear the front door swinging shut behind a newly arrived couple. I could hear the guests shuffling in the room next door to mine, saying, 'It looks like rain again,' and as I watched, spring rain began to fall from the big belly of the sky and large drops of water blew in through the window.

Ten days into my stay in 1984, I was lying on my bed with

my hands behind my head, when I heard Esther and Beatrice approaching my room. They spoke to each other in raised voices.

'As long as she's going to take over some of the cleaning, I don't mind her being here,' Esther was saying.

'For God's sake, Esther, the girl's mother has just died.'

'But why can't she stay in Fifteen?'

'Because I'm using it for storage. Anyway, I want you to be friends.'

'Why does she have to live with us?'

'I was friends with her mother at school. She doesn't have anywhere else to go.'

'I've never met her before and you want me to share a room with her.'

'Yes.'

'And you want me to sleep in a bunk bed.'

'I don't want you to sleep in a bunk bed, Esther. But I don't have any more single beds free at the moment.'

'So let her sleep in the bunk beds on her own and I'll keep my bed.'

'I can't waste beds by leaving three in your room. If you have the bunk beds, then I can put your bed in Twenty and make it into a family room. Have you done the curtains in Room Four?'

'Yes. What time is she getting here?'

'Any minute.'

Their conversation ended as they both headed off in different directions. It was raining again so I decided to go for a walk because I like being on the beach in the rain. I was ready and about to leave when I heard a taxi pulling up in the driveway. A minute later I heard Esther calling to Beatrice from the bottom of the stairs.

'Rice is here.'

16

I hadn't seen Rice since she was a baby, and I remember thinking how good it would be to watch her again. I opened the door to my room and saw Beatrice move swiftly along the corridor and down the stairs, so I followed her.

I made sure I went out of the door as Rice came in so that she would turn and look at me for a second. I looked back and held eye contact with her but I didn't say anything. It was time for her to meet Esther, Beatrice and Maggie, not me. Rice made her way nervously into the hotel and I heard Beatrice say something about tea and cake as the door closed behind me and I was off across the car park and into the street. Rice was dressed in tight black jeans and a T-shirt that said 'Sisters of Mercy' in big white letters. I wondered for a second if she had become a nun, and then discounted it as unlikely. She had grey eyes, like her mother, which reminded me of home. The dead have grey eyes too.

Now here I am sixteen years later, sitting on the beach in the rain, waiting for autumn to start. I'm looking out to sea, but there is no sign yet. The trees are still leafy and the combine harvesters haven't started up their engines. The mouth of Hades is still closed. I am impatient to get back to my love and to let the first frost creep slowly up walls and gardens and across the sand. My hair and clothes are getting wetter and wetter and it looks as though I've been swimming. On the day Rice arrived at the old hotel all those years ago, it was raining hard too. My clothes got wet as soon as I stepped outside. I remember striding off down the hill towards the pier, taking the long way so I could stop at the ice-cream booth. I had already extracted enough money from my purse and I was clutching it in my hand. When I reached the ice-cream seller, I was ready.

'Ninety-nine, please.'

'There you go.' I remember the man looking surprised to have such an eager customer, as I smiled at him and held out my warm wet coins. Then I went to find a deck chair. The rain was splashing into my ice cream as I walked across the sand and sat down. I was excited because now Rice had met Beatrice, Esther and Maggie, and I would be able to watch their stories unfold like bits of paper in front of me. Maggie, Beatrice's mother, was the daughter of Tom and Grace, the origin of this line of hotel queens and princesses. She was nearly six feet tall at the height of her womanhood and was very beautiful during the war. She wore dark brown curls and dewdrop eyelids, had pink lips and smooth creamy skin. Maggie was bearer of the hotel's history, which Rice had come to find out about, although she didn't know it yet. I looked out to sea and rainwater ran down my face and down my neck and into my clothes and I shivered with pleasure because I could feel the season beginning.

Rice and Esther were sitting at the top of the beach steps. Maybe they saw me down on the beach, in my deck chair, taking my shoes off. The rain stopped and the sun was shining and people started to come out of hiding and to take off their coats and sit on them. I didn't want to sit on the beach any longer, so I went to buy some postcards to send to the underworld, because Hades misses me during the summer. I wrote, 'Wish I was there' on each one and then went down to the water's edge, held up my skirt and waded up to my ankles – to all the world it looked like I was paddling, carefree and innocent, shoes in my left hand, bag over my shoulder. I cast the postcards into the water. There were ten of them. I always send a few, because some get eaten by fish and don't make it. Then I went back up the sand and walked up the familiar steps, barefoot, to the hotel. I passed Rice and Esther at the top as they sat and looked down at the tourists slowly gathering below with their towels.

My name is Rice. I'm on the beach where the rain is making

thousands of tiny footprints in the sand. (I've got an umbrella out of the car.) If I look carefully enough, I can see the outline of Esther and me, sitting at the top of the beach steps in 1984. Soon they will go inside, because eventually Esther will look at her watch and say, 'Time for dinner,' and I will follow her into the kitchen.

When we got to the kitchen, Esther closed the door and locked it behind her.

'My grandma never had a lock fitted on that door,' Beatrice said to me by way of introduction to her kitchen. 'It didn't have a lock till the seventies.' Beatrice was standing next to her shiny new microwave, opening a catering-size tin of beef stroganoff with red wine sauce.

'Esther, can you do the potatoes and carrots?' she said. 'We're behind schedule. They'll be down in a minute. It's melon to start. Rice, be a darling, it's in the fridge.' I went and found the packets of pre-sliced melon and stood looking at them, wondering what to do next. Esther was emptying a vat of carrots into a microwave dish and Beatrice was still struggling with the stroganoff, so I left my melon on the side and went to examine the potato peeling machine in the corner and the rack of serving spoons hanging from the wall. The biggest one had a bowl the size of my hand.

'Where are those melons?' I heard Beatrice say. I turned round. 'Esther, can you show the poor girl what to do?'

Esther glared at me. 'The dishes are in the cupboard over there,' she said. 'Cherries are in under here. Cocktail sticks are on the side.' I stood looking helpless.

'Hurry up,' said Beatrice. 'I can hear them coming in.'

'I'll do it,' said Esther, and she seized the cocktail sticks from my hand and I watched her cherrying each of the starters. She was a professional.

19

'I'm taking these out now,' she said, and she went into the dining room laden with melon, where expectant guests were already sitting at the tables.

'You're in the way there, dear.' It was Beatrice trying to get through the door with fruit juices. 'Why don't you go and sit with Grandma Maggie in the lounge?' So I followed her out into the dining room. As I went through the door, I felt the guests' eyes resting on me and I suddenly felt conscious of my clothes. I hadn't thought about how untidy I looked till now, in jeans and a T-shirt. I hadn't been thinking about how I looked very much at all.

'What are you doing?' said Esther under her breath. 'You're not supposed to be out here.'

'But Beatrice said to go and sit in the lounge.'

'Go round the back way where they can't see you.' And she ushered me back into the kitchen and through two other doors and into the lounge. There I sat, out of their way, watching a television quiz show with Grandma Maggie. She eyed me suspiciously from her wheelchair but didn't say anything. Later, after the guests had left the dining room, wiping their mouths, we had what Beatrice called Proper Dinner, and she fed Grandma Maggie bits of boiled ham, mashed potato and onion.

Esther

It was the next day when I had my first good look round the hotel. I woke up in the unfamiliar attic room with where-am-I swords waiting to spear me out of sleep. Esther had also slept in late.

'How are you settling in, Rice?' said Beatrice, handing Esther and me a Sunday morning cup of tea.

'When you're ready,' Beatrice said to Esther, 'Twenty needs doing, if they're out. Sandra's gone home with a headache. Take Rice with you, you can show her the ropes.'

I didn't want to help with the cleaning, but I was curious enough to be enticed by the offer of a guided tour, and I found Esther intriguing. So Esther showed me round the hotel on that second day, with the air of someone who had much more important things to do. The corridors seemed impossibly twisted, rooms were hidden in alcoves and cupboards tucked in next to fire doors. I felt like I was inside a gigantic crossword puzzle. As we went I wondered about all the things that had happened in this new place I had come to live in and whether I would ever find out about them.

We started off downstairs with Maggie and Beatrice's rooms, which were long and thin, because they were stretched out next to the kitchen and under the stairs. In Beatrice's room, there was a bookshelf and on one shelf I noticed some big blue photo albums. But I couldn't stop to look around because Esther was heading out into the hall again.

'That's the bar,' said Esther, waving at the room next to the guest lounge. I poked my head in. It smelt vaguely of peanuts, but there was no time to stop. Esther was already climbing up the stairs. I followed her.

'Only my mum and Grandma Maggie sleep downstairs,' she said when we got to the top. 'Rooms Two to Twelve are on this floor and Twelve A. We can't have a thirteen, because some guests are suspicious.'

'You mean superstitious.'

Esther ignored me and went round the corridor and up more stairs, saying, 'Those are the storage cupboards,' as she went. I had to jump up the stairs two at a time to keep up with her.

'Rooms Fourteen to Twenty. My mum stores her stuff in Room Fifteen,' she said as we went past it. 'It used to be Grandma Maggie's room.' I wanted to go and look but Esther was heading off down the corridor. She had a magic key that got her into all of the bedrooms. We went into a couple of empty rooms to start with. Room Seventeen was the first.

'Duvets,' said Esther, pulling back the bedspread like she was uncovering the crown jewels. 'Grandma Maggie bought them when she was in charge. She resisted them at first because her mother was a traditionalist, but you have to move with the times.' There were pink frills around the lampshade that danced like tiny fingers in the breeze from the open window.

'Tea and coffee,' said Esther, pointing to a kettle. I walked over to it. The light shade, wallpaper, bed and carpet were all reflected in the shiny silver kettle, like another room in miniature. I bent to look closer and the room was replaced by my face, bulbous and onion-like.

22

'There's no bathroom in this one. They have to use the one on the landing.' Esther was already walking off down the corridor.

'Eighteen is en suite.' She stopped outside the door. 'It's hard to hoover in here, because the nearest socket's in the hall,' Esther said as we went in. 'Don't do that,' she said, because I had sat down on the bed, bored already. 'That bed's been made.' So I went and sat on the windowsill instead. Esther glared at me.

'That rug can go in the washing machine but don't put anything else in with it,' she said, and opened the bathroom door. 'This one always smells funny, so we open the window on Saturdays so the guests don't complain when they arrive. Then they think it's them and don't say anything.' I stayed where I was, kicking my heels against the skirting board and listening to Esther's voice sounding echoey and strange from inside the bathroom.

'Always put two toilet rolls in, the same colour as the tiles. This one's green. Come and look, because I need to show you what to do.' She sounded annoyed. I got up and walked as slowly as possible over to the bathroom. Esther was standing by the sink. She pulled back the curtain around the cubicle and I peered inside.

'Use lots of bleach,' she said. I looked at her, about to tell her that I wasn't going to be using any bleach at all but then I noticed (again) how unusual her eyes were. They were green and almost see-through at the same time. They made me gasp inside my head. I closed my mouth and didn't say anything. She carried on instructing me and I went along with it because of her interesting eyes.

'If you can't get the brown marks off, cover them with a bath mat and give them extra shampoo sachets. You just have to hope that will pacify them. If not, we usually move them down to Room Eleven. It's slightly smaller, but the shower's spotless. We never say, "Mrs Brown wants kippers." We say, "Room Nineteen wants kippers."' With that, she made her way back out into the corridor and we moved on to Room Twenty.

'There's people in here but I'll show you round if they're out.' She knocked and there was no answer, so she used her magic key again.

'We might as well do it now,' she said, and I wondered if she really thought I was going to help her shift other people's mess like I was cleaning out a rabbit hutch. It turned out that she did. We stepped inside. Small purple flowers crowded the wallpaper like spectators at a football match. I noticed that the bedspread was purple too. The rug next to the door was orange, although the carpet was mustard yellow. There was a faint stale smell of morning farts and coffee, mixed with Lambert and Butler. Damp towels had been thrown all over the unmade bed, along with a copy of the *Mirror* and a bottle of Tesco's sun screen. The ashtray was full and a dress hung from the outside of the wardrobe. Underneath it there was a pair of new-looking flip-flops. Esther went over to open the window, while I stood by the bed and examined a half-eaten packet of ginger nuts and a leaflet about Bournemouth Gardens.

Then we went into the bathroom, where the smell of the guests intensified and where two tired-looking toothbrushes were peering over the top of the toothbrush holder. There was a trickle of family-size shampoo running down between the taps and a stubborn stool floating in the toilet pan.

Esther sniffed. 'When they're here,' she said, 'we do ashtrays, beds, towels, bins and tea and coffee. Not bathrooms.' She closed the bathroom door and started to pull the duvet about. 'Unless the toilet roll's run out, of course. Do the bin first,' she ordered. The bin consisted of a small metal pot with large pink roses embossed on the front. It contained a hair ball, an empty Tampax box, and a couple of the biscuits. I stood staring at it reluctantly.

'Bin bags, and tea and coffee in the cupboard opposite Room Seven, down the stairs. Here.' She threw me the key and I sloped off to follow her instructions because I couldn't think of anything else to do. That was the first room we cleaned together. I did as little as possible. After I had made a half-hearted attempt to wipe down the windowsills, Esther told me to move out of the way so that she could do it properly, and I sat down sullenly on the bed. Following much the same pattern, we cleaned the sink, made the bed, replenished the tea and coffee, and straightened the curtains.

Next she worked her way along the corridors methodically, emptying bins, then retowelling and toilet-rolling each empty room, and I followed, reluctantly carrying the Jif.

'It's all I can trust you to do,' said Esther, flicking her duster at an imaginary cobweb. That day Esther taught me to fold toilet roll ends into points and how to aim the air freshener at the ceiling. I discovered that the bulging white bin bags went inside one large black bin bag – the black bin bags went outside, round the side of the hotel – and I learnt how many towels could be stuffed into the wide and friendly mouth of the washing machine. I went along with it, but I made sure I did as little as I could.

'I'd have been better off without you helping,' Esther said as she removed the last spot of dust from a bedside cabinet and replaced an ashtray. I wrapped a J-cloth around my wrist and yawned and pretended not to care.

I stayed out of the way for the rest of the day, ignoring Beatrice's worried attempts to get me to drink cups of tea and thinking about how unfair it was that they expected me to work. Mostly, I kept Grandma Maggie company in the guest lounge and Esther carried on as if I wasn't there. Later, she came to take Grandma Maggie into the bathroom to wash her hair with specially formulated shampoo, but she didn't speak to me.

The next day I woke up early – it must have been about seven o'clock – but even so, Esther was already up. (She got up early almost every day.) Her duvet was thrown back untidily and yesterday's clothes were still lying on the floor. There was no sign of Beatrice with tea today and I felt hungry, so I went downstairs barefoot and in my pyjamas, ignoring the smiles and good mornings from stray guests on the way. I made my way through the reception and into the kitchen, by the back way this time, hoping to pick up breakfast. The kitchen was full of activity and the air smelt of bacon. Beatrice and a woman I took to be Sandra were passing in and out of the door to the dining room, issuing instructions to each other as they went.

'Nineteen says no egg.'

'Have you got the extra tea for Room Three yet?'

'Oh, hello, Rice, what are you doing down here in your pyjamas?' said Beatrice, on her way into the dining room.

Esther was standing on the far side of the kitchen making hundreds of pieces of toast. She had her back to me and didn't react to my arrival. I wove my way round everybody towards her and took a piece of toast from the pile. She turned round.

'Oh my God,' she said, looking at me as if I were an alien, just sprung out of one of the teapots, 'don't touch that.' But I was back over the other side of the kitchen, extracting a cup of coffee from a tray by the door. I sat down at the long wooden table and ignored her.

'Mum!' Esther said, pointing in my direction when Beatrice came back in through the swing doors. Esther turned back

26

round and carried on buttering toast furiously. I looked at her hair. It was red, a deep kind of red, not ginger. The sort of red that's called plum and comes in a packet from Boots. It was very shiny and clean. Thinking about it now, mine must have looked a mess, first thing in the morning and unwashed for a week. Beatrice took in my untidy form, sitting eating toast in her kitchen.

'I think you should get dressed before you come down, dear,' she said. 'Why don't you take that upstairs, have a bath and come down when you're ready?' She disappeared into the dining room with a plate of scrambled egg, but I didn't move. I wasn't too keen on having a bath and didn't see what the big deal was about me eating breakfast.

'Are you deaf or something? Go upstairs and get dressed,' Esther said, still frantically buttering. 'Or maybe you're just stupid.' She added the last bit under her breath.

I untangled myself from the table. 'What is wrong with you?' I said.

She turned round. 'Don't take the guests' toast and coffee,' she said, 'and don't come into the kitchen like that. It's unhygienic.'

'OK,' I said, and looked at her to see if she was going to say anything else. Then, leaving my half-chewed toast and lukewarm coffee on the table, I climbed the stairs, went back to bed, and fell asleep under the covers, because maybe I would wake up and discover that none of this had happened and I hadn't come to live in the hotel after all.

I got up again at about two o'clock and Beatrice told me that Esther had gone to school. I wasn't starting at school until after the holidays. It was to do with the grieving process that I heard Auntie Something talking to Beatrice about on the phone.

27

'She's got school today and tomorrow, then she breaks up for Easter,' Beatrice said. 'I'm putting the sheets in the tumble dryer. Make yourself a ham sandwich if you like.'

After the ham sandwich, I went upstairs and looked all the way through Esther's record collection, even though I knew that she would be angry if she found out. I counted up the records. She had fifty-seven and they were all arranged by artist. I closed my eyes and thought about what would happen if all the records started to play at once. When I opened my eyes again I felt sad, so I reached under my bed and pulled out my suitcase. I opened up the lid and there was my camera. It was the first time I had looked at it since I had arrived at the hotel and it was good to pick it up and feel the weight of it in my hands again. I took off the cover and breathed in its dusty reassuring smell. Then I lifted it to my eyes and looked at the attic room through the viewfinder and suddenly it all seemed very far away, like an island that I was watching through a telescope.

I took a few pictures of the garden from the window and tidied the records away again as neatly as I could – they looked much nicer than they had before – took my camera and went down to the second floor.

Two corridors stretched out from the bottom of the attic stairs, one to my left through a fire door, the other to my right. I decided to go left first, through the fire door, and after making sure Beatrice and Sandra weren't around, I went along the corridor, trying out the handles of each of the doors. Just one room, Fourteen, was unlocked, and when I put my head inside there was a guest sitting on the bed and another, a man, hanging something up in a cupboard. They looked at me expectantly.

'Sorry,' I said, and closed the door. There were no more doors to try so I went back the way I had come, through the fire door and along the other corridor. I was most interested in Rooms Fifteen and Sixteen, because I knew they would be facing the beach. I tried the handle of Sixteen and the door was unlocked. This time there were no guests inside. I went over to the window. The beach was nearer now, because I was further down. It would be nice, I thought, to pretend to be a seagull taking a picture from the air, so I opened the window and leant out as far as I could, with my camera in front of my face.

After that I went back out into the corridor and I remembered Esther telling me Room Fifteen was where Beatrice stored her things, so I tried the handle. The door opened. The inside was full of boxes, so many that it was difficult to get through the door. Room Fifteen was small and smelt dusty. It had a sloping ceiling and a pink carpet. There were rolled-up rugs, a velvet curtain, some candles in a box, a dismantled single bed, a cot, a few crates of books and some chairs stacked up in the corner, but most of the space was taken up by a pile of mattresses, with blankets and duvets on top, which almost obscured the window. I made my way over to them and found that if I stood on a dusty red chair and gripped the side of one of the mattresses, I could pull myself up. When I tried sitting upright, I had to bend down slightly to stop my head connecting with the ceiling, so I lay down on my stomach instead with my camera towards the window, feeling like the princess with the pea.

I stayed in the room with the mattresses for the rest of the afternoon, until I heard Beatrice shouting, 'Rice, where are you?' in a worried kind of voice, and I carefully lowered myself off the pile of mattresses and slipped out of the door. 'Rice.'

I ran back up to the attic room, hid my camera again and went downstairs. I met Esther on the second-floor landing.

'What have you been doing all day?' she said suspiciously.

29

'Nothing,' I said.

'You better not have touched my stuff,' she said. 'My mum is looking for you.' She headed up to her bedroom. Ten minutes later she came running down the stairs and into the kitchen, where Beatrice had made me a cup of tea.

'She's been listening to my records,' she said to Beatrice, pointing at me, as if we were playing Cluedo and she had just discovered who the murderer was.

'Esther, calm down.'

'I didn't play them. I just looked at them.'

'Don't look at them and don't touch them. Don't touch any of my stuff. OK?'

'Esther, don't be so selfish. Sit down and have some tea.'

'I don't want any tea. I don't see why you had to come here anyway.'

'Esther,' said Beatrice more sharply.

'Tell her not to touch my stuff.' And she went out into the garden and slammed the door behind her.

'Rice, it's probably better not to play Esther's records till she gets a bit more used to you being here.'

'I didn't play them. I was just looking.'

'OK, dear. Now maybe you could take your tea and go and watch television in the other room until it's time for Proper Dinner.'

Esther came back in from the garden and did the mixed veg for the guests and for us, but she didn't speak to me again all evening, not even when we climbed the attic stairs together. She just got into bed quickly and turned to face the wall.

Esther came home from school at lunchtime on Tuesday, 3 April 1984 and I had only just got out of bed. I had been eating Rice Krispies in the guest lounge (I liked them because my name was on the packet) and had walked into the hall, about to go

30

and lie on the mattresses in Room Fifteen again, when Esther came through the front door. She was covered in flour, with a plastic bag full of Easter eggs from her friends slung over her shoulder.

'Why are you covered in flour?' I asked her.

'It's the end of term,' said Esther. 'Why are you wearing your pyjamas?' She was still angry with me about the records.

'Don't the teachers mind you throwing flour around?' said Beatrice, coming out from behind reception and taking Esther's bag of chocolate eggs from her. I looked at them enviously, because they meant that she had a lot of friends.

'No.'

'Meredith phoned,' Beatrice said. 'She's getting back in a couple of days.'

Esther's face suddenly changed. She looked like a little girl for a second. 'Meredith,' she said. I could see she was very impressed.

'I've invited her for Sunday lunch.' Beatrice and Esther looked at each other as if they knew a secret thing that I didn't and they were very excited about it.

'Is she bringing her guitar?' said Esther, who could have been a ghost haunting the hotel, she was so white with flour.

'Who's Meredith?' I said, but Beatrice and Esther didn't hear me, because Beatrice was trying to brush the flour from her daughter's coat, making it look as though they were standing inside a cloud.

'I don't know about the guitar,' Beatrice said when she'd stopped brushing.

'Will you call her and check?' Esther asked.

'Do you know how much it costs to phone India? Wait till she gets back.'

'Please.'

31

'No. Go and have a bath or something.'

'She needs a bath more than I do,' said Esther, pointing to me.

'Be quiet, Esther,' said Beatrice. But still, Esther went upstairs with a big grin on her face because three weeks of holiday stretched out in front of her like an open road and someone called Meredith was coming to lunch, who Beatrice and Esther liked very much (I could tell by their eyes).

Some guests came in through the door and Beatrice said, 'Go and get dressed, dear,' to me, and then went to help them with their bags. I heard the water running through the pipes and imagined Esther pouring lavender bath oil into our bath on the second floor, a bath that I hadn't actually ventured into yet. I wandered upstairs and got dressed quickly before Esther got out of the bath. I remember wondering vaguely if Beatrice minded me looking untidy and whether that was why Esther wanted me to stay out of sight. Since my mum had got really bad I had forgotten how many baths I had had, but it wasn't many. No wonder Auntie Something had been so keen to get rid of me.

I didn't feel like taking pictures any more so I went back into the guest lounge and watched TV with Grandma Maggie.

'Pea soup and apples,' she said as I went into the guest lounge.

'It's not teatime yet,' I said, trying to be friendly, but underneath I was frightened by her dark mad eyes.

'That man wants to see his baby,' said Grandma Maggie carefully, as if she were explaining a secret to me, but I didn't understand her. She closed her mouth and was silent again. We sat quietly like accomplices, with the TV turned up too loudly.

Later on that afternoon, Beatrice came and told me that she

and Esther had to go on an emergency trip to the cash-and-carry, and could she show me how to lay the tables? She laid out one table for me to copy, with the glass, cutlery and side plate all in their correct places.

'Do you think you'll be all right?' she said.

'Yes.'

'Sandra's on reception.' So I set about preparing the tables for dinner, carefully laying out glasses, table numbers, serviettes, bread baskets and plastic flowers, one after the other. It was steak and kidney pie and runner beans or beetroot salad followed by apricot crumble and custard. Doing the tables was like playing patience and I started to enjoy myself. Then I looked up at the wall and saw some photographs in a big frame that I hadn't noticed before. The frame had different-sized holes for the photos, which were all black-and-white. There were two or three featuring the hotel in the old days, which looked much newer and not as shabby as it was in 1984. Then there was a photo of people sunbathing on the beach next to some barbed wire, which I thought was strange, and in the bottom left-hand corner, a small picture of two women. One looked about forty, the other was in her late teens or early twenties. The older woman looked very much like Beatrice but I realised that it couldn't be her because this photo was too old. Pictures of dead people, I thought, and that made me think of my mother, so I went all the way up to the attic room and got my picture of my mother and me out of my suitcase. It had been taken five years before, outside the Houses of Parliament and was the only one I had of her. My mother didn't like pictures of people, she used to tell me.

'Where are you going?' said Sandra as I went past reception.

'Upstairs.'

'Have you finished the tables?'

33

'Not yet.'

When I came downstairs again, Sandra was on a cigarette break in the garden. Somehow the enjoyment had gone from the knives and forks so after only a few minutes I ended up going to sit in the guest lounge instead and I started to think about the funeral again. The memories squeezed themselves out like toothpaste, so that when Beatrice and Esther came back they found me crying silently in front of *Family Fortunes* with a bread basket in my hand, and the dining room only half ready.

'Esther, go and finish off the tables,' Beatrice said, her arms still full of carrier bags. Esther hesitated for a moment, then disappeared. Beatrice sat down next to me and handed me a hankie out of her anorak pocket.

'I'm OK,' I said, and stared at the television. Then I looked at her. 'I'm sorry about the tables.'

'Don't worry, Esther's doing it,' said Beatrice. I could hear Esther sighing and clunking glasses and side plates noisily in the other room. 'Shall I make you some hot chocolate?'

'If you want.'

'Right.' And she picked up her carrier bags and went off into the kitchen.

As soon as she had left the room, I got up, went out of the front door and round the side of the hotel and into the garden by the side gate. I went quickly down the steps to the beach, so quickly I was almost stumbling, and down to the water's edge. I picked up some stones and threw them into the sea.

After a few minutes, I heard someone on the steps behind me. It was Esther, but I pretended not to notice her.

'My mum made me come and see if you were OK,' she said, after an awkward minute had passed. 'I didn't want to but she made me.'

I carried on throwing my stones.

'Are you coming back up or what? I'm cold,' she said when she didn't get a response.

'I want to stay here.'

'My mum won't let you.'

'She's not my mum.'

'I'm going back,' Esther said, but she hesitated.

'Go on then.' She turned and began to trudge back to the hotel. 'Your mother's still alive,' I shouted after her, making her turn round to face me again.

'So?' She shrugged as she said it. Then Esther walked back up the steps and I followed her slowly. We went inside to where Sandra was helping Beatrice with dinner and Beatrice sighed and hummed and buzzed around the kitchen, making drinks, and tried to tell me off for going to the beach when it looked like it might rain. I drank my hot chocolate sitting at the long wooden table and didn't say anything.

'Leave her alone,' I heard Beatrice say to Esther later. 'She needs time to get over it.'

For the rest of the week Esther and Beatrice buzzed around the hotel like wasps, but I tried to stay invisible. I don't think I even unpacked in that first week. Each day I stayed in bed with my head under the covers until I couldn't hear anything, then I got dressed quickly, put my camera round my neck and went to find new views of the beach from unlocked rooms. Every day it was different. The sea might be flat one day and churning about like it had indigestion the next. The sand was always shaped differently too. Sometimes it was smooth with no debris at all. Other times there was seaweed or shingle and pieces of wood or dead things. Often the seagulls sat and waited on the sand with their necks collapsed and their heads resting on their bodies.

I especially liked to take my photos in Room Fifteen, and lying on top of the mattresses became my favourite position. I liked Room Fifteen because it had a ghostly feeling, as if all the people who had once slept in there had left a bit of themselves behind to haunt it, like the smell of soap, or a purple sock, a half-smoked cigar, or a stain on the wallpaper. Most of all Room Fifteen was haunted by Beatrice, because of all the objects from her past. I would climb over boxes and piles of Beatrice's things each time I went in, feeling all the time like an explorer. I found clocks, and old kitchen utensils and trunks full of clothes. I even had a rummage through one or two of the small boxes one afternoon, until I felt guilty, like I was reading her diary. Afterwards, I would retreat back to the attic room and hide my camera in my suitcase and then go downstairs and watch TV with Grandma Maggie in the guest lounge.

The second time I went down to the beach by myself was on Friday. We were having stew and potatoes for Proper Dinner around the brown table in the kitchen, but it wasn't ready yet so I went and sat on the bottom step and thought about how much I hated the hotel and all the people in it. I lined them up in my head. The stupid guests with round holiday faces with smiles if it was sunny and frowns if it was raining, like the barometer where the man and woman come out of their huts but they never meet each other. Then there was Grandma Maggie: I thought she had a nice soft face, but I still hated her because she smelt of feet and talcum powder. I hated Beatrice for saying I had to work at the hotel, like I was a chambermaid, but without getting paid. And I hated Esther most of all, even though she was very beautiful and I sometimes thought she might be magic. I lined them all up in my head and imagined them falling over at the bottom of the steps flat on their faces and then the sand burying them like when children bury people on the beach, or like the Egyptian slaves who got buried alive in the pyramids. Then I felt bad that

I had left them there and I imagined them sitting up again and spitting sand out of their mouths and shaking it out of their hair. I wondered if there were any other people buried in the sand apart from the hotel people, and I thought that maybe all the people who had ever sat on the beach might still be there, under the surface, like demolished sandcastles, still there but just a different shape, waiting for the salt water to cover them slowly at night-time.

I was born in Bournemouth, though I don't remember it. My mother told me that we came to the beach when I was a baby and she made me a castle with a moat and I smashed it with my hands. I wondered whether the sand my mother made the castle out of was still there somewhere. I stood up and looked in one direction and then the other, and as far as I could see there was yellow beach. There was enough sand to bury hundreds of people and their castles, I thought. My mother wouldn't feel the yellow grains next to her face where she was buried because she was inside a coffin and she wasn't buried at the seaside. I imagined her inside with her grey-blue face like it wasn't made of skin any more, like I had seen her in the hospital. It would be nice to be buried by the seaside, because it smells of salt water and fish and chips, but Auntie Something said that she couldn't think or feel any more so it didn't matter how cold or hot it was. I imagined her sleepy grey face was under the sand instead and that made me cry a little bit – or maybe it was the wind blowing the sea water into my eyes, or maybe I was buried too and under the surface the world was the same as it is up here only yellow and scratchy, like when you get sand in your socks.

When my mother first got ill, I thought it was the normal kind of ill, like when I had chickenpox. It's bad, itchy, spotty, pukey and someone tells you that people used to die of it once,

37

but nowadays people go to the doctor and buy calamine lotion from the chemists and are OK in two weeks. When two weeks had gone by, I asked her when she would get better. She said she was feeling better now and got out of bed and I thought it was all over. We went to the shops and bought ice cream and sausage rolls and a box of lollies, but later she was sick again on the carpet in the lounge. Then I found out that my mother's ill was different. She got ill for two weeks, then better for two weeks. But soon, the time she was better got shorter, until there were just good and bad days. On good days she would get out of bed and tell me she had to get everything done, like hoovering, phoning the dentist or washing up, until eventually I'd feel sad and say, 'I'll do it, Mum.' She'd mutter to herself, 'Don't treat me like a bloody invalid,' but she would sink down into an armchair anyway, relieved. On bad days, I had to get cold flannels from the bathroom and a bowl for beside the bed. I brought her water in a mug or sometimes soup, because the doctor said quietly, 'Try to help her keep something down,' as if I were grown up already.

There were other things I hated, I thought, which could be buried under the sand. My new room, which I shared with Esther, the new school uniform Auntie Something had bought me, the food we ate at the hotel after the guests had eaten theirs and the paper serviettes that they wiped their mouths on. I thought about all the rooms and the corridors that went from one to the other and in one door and out of the other. For a test, I tried to remember off by heart all the rooms and which ones had bathrooms and which ones didn't. It was difficult, like maths.

Then I thought about how old the hotel was and how Grandma Maggie had lived there her whole life. She had been born there (Beatrice told me) and I started to think maybe she had never been outside. I wondered what it would be like never to go outside and to be locked inside the same house all of your life, even if it was an interesting house with lots of places to explore. What would it be like to see somewhere only from the inside? If I could see myself from the inside there would be blood and muscles and bones and my dinner in my stomach, and all the thoughts in my head written on pieces of paper and other things like apple crumble, which was my secret favourite food. I could think I was a film star with long ginger hair in curls and a big smile, and as long as I never looked in the mirror I wouldn't ever know if I was right or not, and only the apple crumble and the paper with things written on would matter and the blood and bones as well.

When I climbed back up to the kitchen, Beatrice was sitting at the end of the table, although Grandma Maggie was still in the lounge.

'She's watching TV,' said Beatrice. 'Esther can take her some stew later.' I sat down opposite Esther.

'Where have you been?' said Esther.

'Nowhere.'

'You've been to the beach again.'

'So?'

'You're stupid.'

'Esther!' said Beatrice. Esther began to dollop spoonfuls of stew on to our plates.

'What are we having when Meredith comes?' she said, scowling at me when her mother wasn't looking.

'Roast chicken,' said Beatrice.

'Who's Meredith?' I asked, for the second time. I felt left out. Esther looked at me as if my life had, up to this point, been incomplete. Perhaps Meredith was some sort of prophet.

'We were school friends,' said Beatrice, in a strange voice, like she didn't want to talk about it, 'me, your mother and Meredith. I'm surprised your mum never mentioned her.' But my mother didn't talk about the past much. She used to say that it didn't exist any more. I sunk down into my chair.

'Meredith lives in Poole but she plays the cello so she's away a lot,' Beatrice said. Her strange voice had gone again. 'It's very exciting.' Esther put our plates down in front of us, got up and left the room quickly through the door to Beatrice's bedroom.

'Where's she going?' said Beatrice to herself, but then she saw I was looking upset again. She tried to cheer me up by telling me all about Meredith and where she lived.

'You'd like her flat, Rice. It's very pretty,' she said. Poole is the town next to Bournemouth and her parents had given it to her when her dad retired from the army and they moved Up North somewhere. I don't know where. Beatrice told me that Meredith didn't speak to her parents very much after she joined the CND, although I didn't know about any of that when I was aged thirteen, and was sitting at the long wooden table stirring my stew and potatoes with a fork.

Esther came back into the kitchen. She had a photo in her hand.

'Have you been in my room?' Beatrice said, pretending to be annoyed.

'Yes. That's Meredith. The blonde one,' Esther said. She held it out for me to look at.

'From my photo album?' asked Beatrice.

'Yes,' said Esther.

The picture contained a young-looking Beatrice, someone else's arm and a blonde spiky-haired woman, who was too close to the camera. She had bright blue eyes that shone, even out of focus, and she had an easy, open kind of face.

Beatrice took the picture from Esther and gazed at it with the lopsided smile she saved for looking at the past. Then she passed it to me, but Esther snatched it back before I had looked at it for long enough and propped it up next to her plate using the salt and pepper pots.

After we had had Bakewell tart and custard for pudding, Beatrice ran the water for the washing-up but then the bell rang in reception and she went off to find out who it was. Esther began to prepare a special cut-up version of steak and gravy, dumplings, potatoes and carrots, which I knew was for Grandma Maggie (no one else had false teeth), but I stayed where I was. I looked at the photo on the table again. Even though I had guessed already, I picked it up and turned it over to see if there was anything written on the other side. It said, in neat green ink: 'Beatrice and Meredith (and Suzie's arm!)' with an exclamation mark to explain away the bad photography that had left most of my mother out of the photo. There was a date too: January 1970. I remember wondering who took the photo. Maybe it was Grandma Maggie, I thought. I quickly put the photo into my pocket while Esther had her back to me, so I could think about it later. I was just in time, because she turned round to issue instructions.

'You're supposed to help with the clearing-up after dinner, you know,' she said. 'Take this to Grandma Maggie. She's in the lounge. Give her a spoon.'

I knew this was Esther's job and Beatrice wouldn't approve but I said OK anyway. I got up and she handed me the dinner on a tray.

I found Grandma Maggie comforting, especially when the old hotel was still strange and new. She had a velvet quilt face and I felt warmed by her. When I had been living there for a few years, I could see how she had let the hotel mould her and fold her into its arms. Grandma Maggie could walk with her sticks from the bedroom to the bathroom and sometimes into the kitchen, but so slowly, she usually used her wheelchair instead. Sometimes Beatrice scrubbed and polished her mother and her wheelchair until she smelt of lavender. Sometimes Grandma Maggie would shout 'Piss' and a dark water mark would spread from under her skirt. Sometimes she thought she saw a man standing in the corner of the room. On the day of the stew, I was still getting used to her. I walked nervously towards the lounge with the tray. I was frightened by the happy way I had seen her eat before, as if she had forgotten where her mouth was. I manoeuvred through the door, and found Grandma Maggie examining a television news programme from the safety of her wheelchair.

'Tell him to go away,' Grandma Maggie said when she saw me. I didn't reply. I put the tray on her lap and the spoon in her hand, then I sat down and took out the photo, because I only half wanted to see it when she missed her mouth. Half of me wanted to close my eyes and imagine her eating a banquet like a princess with silver knives and forks.

'Who are you?' said Grandma Maggie, as I sat down.

'Rice.'

'How did you get into my house?'

'I live here,' I said, putting the picture down on the table.

'Who gave you the key?'

'No one.'

'I never married.'

'Oh.'

'Are you a nurse?'

'No. I'm Rice.'

'Rice? Potatoes. He's dead, Mother.'

'Oh.'

'Dead as a doornail. Bang them in hard, Mother. Who are you?'

'My name is Rice.' Then there was silence as I gave in and watched Maggie aim her spoon wildly at her mouth and dribble thick onion gravy down her chin. I imagined the throbbing purple circles of madness inside Maggie's head, opening and closing like new universes, and I thought about the story of her life packed up inside her like the boxes in Room Fifteen.

Jonathan Kagel

My name is Persephone and I have goddess eyes. I have known Grandma Maggie since she was a child and called only Margaret and nothing else. Being a goddess, I can see into her head and into the places where her stories are kept. The stories are about cooking and hands and pumpkins and witches, and start one Hallowe'en with Thomas Tamarack saying goodbye to his wife and his daughter.

On 3 September 1939 King George VI spoke to the nation and World War Two began, but Thomas Tamarack didn't leave until 31 October. In the autumn of 1939 I watched from the underworld as the stories unfolded above me. The trees started to cast off their leaves like old clothes and went naked in the cold and people lit candles on their mantelpieces. I watched through clay and sand and water, and through the walls of the hotel and I saw Thomas Tamarack go. Margaret was nineteen years old.

After he left, I saw Grace working in the kitchen long into the night. She couldn't sleep, she said, so she put her hands to work, leaning over the long wooden table in the kitchen, chopping vegetables and kneading dough. Grace believed in walking spirits so she had already positioned her pumpkins around the kitchen, each with a solitary light flickering behind the mouths she had carved. Margaret could smell the yeast as she fell asleep, or maybe she heard her mother throwing the dough on to the table and thumping it into shape. That night Grace made bread and pumpkin soup, and November slipped in through a crack and ghost October slipped out and the air became colder and smelt like frying sausages, gunpowder, bonfires, rain, rotting leaves and Margaret thought she heard fire spitting. November came in and lay down next to her as she slept and wrapped her thick arms round her belly. The next day, as Margaret sat down to breakfast, the kitchen smelt of bread and the oven was still hot. She thought about how dangerous everything was, now her father had left. It was the first time in her life that Thomas Tamarack hadn't sat at the end of the wooden table at breakfast time, buttering his toast. The Tamaracks had their breakfast early, before the guests came. I watched Margaret and Grace on that first morning they were alone at breakfast together, as Grace broke the loaf into rough pieces and Margaret took some from her, and I looked into Margaret's head and saw that she was thinking that the bread tasted of her mother's hands and of her salt.

A few months later, in January 1940, some serious-looking men came to see Grace and they talked to her for an hour at the kitchen table. Grace came out of the kitchen with a red face and wild-looking eyes.

'We've been requisitioned,' she said proudly to Margaret, who was waiting in the guest lounge to find out what would happen next. 'For Mr Churchill,' said Grace, when her daughter didn't reply. 'I told them I'm not leaving and they said good because they need a housekeeper.' So Grace and Margaret were officially enlisted for the war effort. After that the gate at the bottom of the hotel garden, which had always stood slightly ajar, was kept locked shut and there was barbed wire at the bottom of the beach steps.

In July some more serious-looking men came and packed

explosives under the pier and blew a hole at the end near the shore.

'To stop the enemy landing,' Grace said.

Margaret watched from the window of Room Fifteen and thought about the people who had paraded up and down with umbrellas and sunhats without a thought for anything at all until only a few months before. The pier, detached from the land, looked like a lost child at a funfair and the pillars that moored the pier to the sand were eerie and unfriendly. If anyone wanted to walk on the pier now, Margaret thought, they would have to act like Jesus and walk on water.

There were two types of soldier at the hotel during the war: soldiers who had been wounded and were sent for a kind of holiday after they had recovered, and soldiers on leave from the nearby base in Wimborne, who had no family to go to. When the soldiers arrived, they swarmed round the hotel like insects, digging into each part of it, hiding under the stairs, putting their feet on the chairs, leaving forgotten cigarettes on a table in the guest lounge. The serious-looking men moved in as well and set up an office in Room Nineteen and issued instructions to Grace about who was coming and who was going.

Margaret liked to come downstairs early in the morning from Room Fifteen where she slept and watch through the window above the sink as the sun filled the garden. She liked to stand and think or talk to Thomas Tamarack in her head, and sometimes she would do jobs like making stock from yesterday's bones or mixing up the oats for porridge so that while her mother would stay up into the night cooking, Margaret preferred the early morning and kept up her meditations in the kitchen every day right the way through the war. Margaret Tamarack enjoyed her time in the kitchen on her own, looking out at the garden, and down to the gate where the beach steps started.

From the beginning of 1940, until the end of 1945, there were no guests allowed at the hotel because of the soldiers, so I had to make adjustments to my disguise. I came back for five summers as a seasonal chambermaid. During the 1940s, I kept a secret tweed suit in a suitcase and a hat in my beach hut and after I was washed up on the sand, being careful of the barbed wire, I got changed and I curled my hair in paper rollers before I walked up to the hotel. I settled into my work with a spring in my step. I am naturally tidy and I love cleaning. I knew every part of the hotel back to front and inside out, so nothing could surprise me.

In 1941 I was called Delilah. As soon as I arrived, the sun came out and the grass turned greener. Tulips lifted up their pink hands in the garden, and in the old ivy-covered tree in the corner brown-freckled starlings sat and watched us. I fitted in very well and made Grace smile by talking about the things I knew she loved to talk about, like making bread and gardening (each year I was a chambermaid I proved to be even neater and tidier than myself-as-someone-else the year before me). I made sure that the bedspreads were just so and that there were no stains on the sinks or dust on the windowledges. Grace put her hand on my arm and said she wished her husband could see me work, and I had to pretend that I had never met her husband and I asked her about him.

'He is a kind man,' Grace said, and smiled at me for asking. After that I was invited to eat at the long wooden table in the kitchen with the guests, and with Grace and Margaret, and Sammy, the other chambermaid, who said she didn't like my fancy ways with the duster.

'Hard work takes time,' she said once, suspiciously, after I had finished Room Ten and had asked her to inspect it. I like my work to be praised. I was good at my job because I could see into people's heads and through the walls, and I knew when a room needed cleaning or when someone was about to check out, ahead of time. I could see into Margaret's head too and found it was full of butterflies and apple juice in those days, unlike in 1984, when the purple circles grew wilder every day.

Before the war, Grace was already a good gardener, with home-grown produce on the hotel menu almost every day, but as soon as she heard on the radio that all over Britain people were growing vegetables for Winston Churchill, she rolled up her sleeves and doubled her efforts. She pulled up her beautiful but useless flowers and, in their place, rows of carrots and turnips and lettuces and onions and potatoes and peas and pumpkins sprung up. They came from cuttings and seeds Grace had begged from people at church and from next-door neighbours. Once Grace found me out in the garden talking in my head to the plants, telling them to grow big and strong for Grace and Margaret. After that she asked me to help and Grace told all the soldiers that would listen about how green my fingers were. Soon I was spending half the day on bedrooms and half the day outside, and on days when it rained and we couldn't work because the garden was turned to mud, I would help with the cooking and Grace would tell me stories about her mother, who had died of influenza, over cups of peppermint tea.

'Anyone would think we were all vegetarians,' Grace laughed as she served up another vegetable broth.

'No meat at the butcher's today,' she said, passing round the bread, but the soldiers dug their spoons into the broth hungrily and complimented Grace on her cooking.

The first time Margaret met Jonathan, it was summer 1941 and she was sitting in the hotel garden reading a book and breathing in the lavender. It was hot and there was a gentle salty breeze.

Margaret was wearing a pretty dress, which was blowing against her legs. I was outside, gardening.

'Nice, isn't it?' Jonathan Kagel said, coming through the kitchen door and out into the sun. Margaret looked up from her book. 'The lavender,' he said, going over to it and stroking it with his hand so that when he smelt his palm the memory of it would still be there like a fading photograph.

'Yes,' said Margaret.

'Are you Mrs Tamarack's daughter?' he said.

'Yes,' said Margaret again.

That hot day was Jonathan's first at the hotel. He had come back from fighting in France a year ago, which was why he had only one hand. The Germans blew the other one right off, he said, and showed her the bandage.

'I lost a lot of blood,' he said. 'I went white like a ghost. The doctor told me.' She shuddered, but he took out a cigarette and although, Margaret discovered later, he had learnt to light his cigarettes expertly with one hand, he let her light it for him and they both laughed with relief. Although she wanted to know, Margaret didn't ask him what it was like in France because Grace had told her that there are some things Mr Churchill doesn't want us to talk about, and God would know, even if she whispered her questions so that Grace couldn't hear.

'Think about your father,' Grace said, stirring her vegetable soup. 'Don't be a knowbody', it said on a banner in Bournemouth town centre. 'Gossip is dangerous.'

The next time Margaret saw him was in the garden again. It was Tuesday and she had finished cleaning up in the kitchen and was looking over the gate and down the beach steps. The sea shone brightly back at her and the sun was hot on her face, but the barbed wire made the beach look like an assault course. I was weeding the turnips.

49

'Not a pretty view,' said Jonathan, making her jump, because suddenly there he was, sitting on the little stone wall around one of the beds that had recently been converted for potatoes, smiling at her as she turned round.

'What are those white flowers called?' he said, pointing into a vegetable patch. She walked over towards him to look where he was indicating.

'Those are weeds,' I said, but Margaret and Jonathan ignored me, so I looked into their heads instead, to see what they were thinking. They both liked each other and Jonathan already had a picture of Margaret, walking down the aisle towards him, dressed in white.

'They're just weeds.'

'I like them,' he said, 'I'd like to learn the proper names of things.'

'I don't know what they are called.'

'You should get a book,' he said.

'It's so hot today,' said Margaret. Then Jonathan lit a cigarette, one-handed, as if he had special powers, Margaret thought. He held the cigarette in his mouth, his Zippo in his palm, and flicked it alight with his one remaining thumb, the corners of his eyes screwed up, as if he was trying to work out a puzzle. He had a curious face, Margaret thought, as though someone had taken a knife and cut lines into it.

'I got a new one each time I opened my eyes in the morning,' said Jonathan, when she asked him about the lines. He was half joking.

'In France?' Margaret said.

'Yes,' said Jonathan and he looked at her as though he was trying to make her understand something without saying anything. His eyes were sea blue – like blue paint, Margaret thought – and they didn't go with the rest of his face, so that

when he turned to look at her it was a surprise that they were
still that colour and that she hadn't imagined it. They were the
colour you'd get if you dived down under the water when you
were swimming in the sea, Margaret thought, and you forced
yourself to open your eyes to look at the bottom. That taste
of salt at the back of your throat, they were a colour like that.
Jonathan reached down suddenly and pulled one of the white
flowers out of the ground, roots and all, and gave it to her.

'I told you. That's a weed,' Margaret laughed, but she took the
white flower anyway, with its muddy roots, like witches' pubic
hair, and sat down next to him.

'I like it,' Jonathan said, and tipped his head on one side and
looked at her, and she had to turn away so that he couldn't see
her cheeks going red. But Margaret crossed her legs all the same
and tucked her hair behind one ear and smiled.

That Sunday morning, when Grace had gone to church, leaving
her daughter in charge of lunch, the sun was still burning up the
world below it, and Jonathan and Margaret went for a walk.
Margaret made sure she stood on his left side, the good side
he called it, so that if he had wanted to hold her hand he could
have done, but he stuck his hand in one pocket and the end
of his bandaged arm in the other, so they didn't hold hands
after all.

'I don't have a sweetheart,' he said when they got back. 'Let's
have our picture taken.'

'I've got to do the cabbage,' said Margaret, but he didn't listen
and got one of his friends, who had a camera, to take their picture
in the garden.

The next day was sticky with heat once more and there was
Jonathan in the garden again when Grace and I went out to start
work. Margaret was next to him, reading a book about names of
flowers.

'Margaret, there's peas that need shelling in the kitchen,' Grace said, and Margaret got up and went inside.

'In the garden again?' said Grace Tamarack to Jonathan Kagel, sticking her spade into the soil to dig up more carrots. I was on my knees weeding the lavender and the rosemary.

'It's very relaxing, Mrs Tamarack,' said Jonathan, crossing his legs and looking over to where we were working.

'For some, Mr Kagel,' said Grace, lifting the spade into the air and shifting the clump of earth and carrots into a pile.

'Would you like some help?' said Jonathan, standing up and coming over to us.

'There,' said Grace, and she passed him the shovel and dusted off her hands, 'I have cooking to do.' She went to join her daughter.

From then on, during that long summer, Jonathan and I did the garden together. He was good at working one-handed, and gentle with the roots when he planted a sapling in the ground or teased aside the soil for a new row of cabbages. Margaret sat reading in the garden when she wasn't working and she started to miss Jonathan's curious face when he wasn't there too, and hoped that she would meet him by accident on the stairs and that he would smile his generous smile at her.

Once I came down to the kitchen early because I couldn't sleep, and Margaret was looking out of the window at the morning coming in over the sea and Jonathan was there with her. That was the first time I saw them holding hands. On other days too, when I woke early and couldn't get back to sleep, I heard Margaret's footsteps on the stairs and heavier footsteps behind them.

'Maybe we could go to the pictures?' I heard Jonathan say to Margaret casually one day while they were reading together. Margaret went to ask her mother, who said that she needed her to help now her father had gone to war, and that Margaret had a duty to the hotel.

'I was married too young,' she said, sighing and looking out of the window. 'What would my mother have thought of me being here on my own? I'm glad she's in her grave.' Then: 'Perhaps Mr Kagel would like to come to church,' she added as an afterthought.

So Grace washed his uniform for him and he shone his shoes and the three of them went to church and sung hymns and said prayers on Sunday. Margaret looked at Jonathan Kagel proudly, as he stood next to her, hymn book held in his good hand, singing slightly out of tune at the top of his voice, because to Jonathan every song said thank Jesus that the Germans had taken his hand away and he wasn't in France any more. All the same, it was the only time they went to church together.

Grace did soup for lunch. 'Because there is no time now for a proper dinner,' she said.

Jonathan tried to take Margaret into town one more time.

'Would you like to go dancing, Margaret?'

'My mother wouldn't let me,' said Margaret, shyly. So Jonathan Kagel asked Sammy, the other chambermaid, instead, who came up to Margaret on the day before they went and said that she was proud to be seen with one of the boys, even though he'd been wounded and she should be ashamed of herself for being so hoity-toity, what with the war and the hotels getting bombed and there being not many men around to choose from anyway. Jonathan stopped asking Margaret after that – although he still watched her sometimes with his blue-as-paint eyes as they sat in the garden together – until he left the hotel, in the middle of August, and went to a job with the army in Wales.

Just before Jonathan Kagel left for Wales in August 1941, Grace got her husband's camera out and took a photo of

53

the soldiers around one of the vegetable patches in the garden.

'A keepsake,' she said.

A few days later, Henry Duffle arrived at the Water's Edge Hotel. I was sweeping the stairs when he came in through the front door with his bag.

'I don't have any family to visit. They are all dead,' I heard him tell Grace as he checked in. 'I'm on leave.'

Henry's reputation had gone before him. He had won prizes for survival, Grace told Maggie, and the test had included living in a jungle for a week and swimming in the sea for three miles.

'Delilah,' Grace said. I looked up from my dustpan, 'show Mr Duffle to his room. Room Sixteen.'

'Lieutenant,' said Henry Duffle.

'Lieutenant Duffle,' said one of the serious men, coming downstairs from Room Nineteen. 'On leave?'

'Yes,' said Henry Duffle, and followed me up the stairs.

Timothy Mackintosh

You know my name by now. I am still here on the sand reminiscing. I think Beatrice thought it was better to leave me alone while there wasn't much work to do, but I couldn't keep my disappearing act up for long because the day after the photo of the arm, a week after I first arrived, it was Saturday again.

'Rice.' Beatrice was banging on the door. I picked up my watch from the floor by my bed. It was ten o'clock. 'Rice. Wake up, dear. We need your help.' She opened the door. Esther was hopping from one foot to the other behind her.

'It's Saturday, dear,' said Beatrice, as if this were significant.

'So? Leave me alone,' and I turned to face the wall.

Beatrice sat down on my bed and put her mouth close to where she supposed my ear was under all that untidy hair.

'Rice, you are going to have to help us out today. Steve is off with his feet and Sandra can't do beds today because of her back. I can't afford to phone the agency when you're here doing nothing.' And I knew then that I had been defeated. Beatrice expected me to work. On that, my first full Saturday, I hated her for it, but eventually I worked her out like a puzzle. The old hotel was the best therapy I could have wanted.

Reluctantly, I emerged from my bed, got dressed without having a shower, much to Esther's disgust, and tied a fluorescent green band round my hair and the apron she gave me around my waist. So Esther had another chance to instruct me. At five o'clock, I retired to the guest lounge and sat with my feet on a table, exhausted. Then Esther came in, looking thin and beautiful in her grey apron. She fixed her green eyes on me.

'What are you doing?'

'Having a rest.'

'The stairs need hoovering.'

'Why can't you do it?'

'I've got a difficult carpet stain in Seventeen. Anyway, you're not supposed to put your feet on the tables in the guest lounge. It's a good job none of them are in here.'

I had just started to hoover the stairs when two guests came through the front door and approached reception. They put down their bags, rang the bell and looked at me expectantly, but then Beatrice came out from the door marked 'Private' and went behind the reception desk. She opened the big blue book where she wrote the names of the guests. It was hard to hear what she was saying above the sound of the hoover. Then the phone began to ring and Beatrice waved at me but I didn't know why. I carried on working my way down step by step. Esther appeared at the top of the stairs.

'Oh my God,' she said, and she ran down and pressed the off button.

'What did you do that for?' I said.

'Don't hoover in front of the guests.'

'Thank goodness for that,' said Beatrice, putting her hand over the receiver and smiling, 'I couldn't hear myself think. Esther, can you show Room Two where to go?' Esther went and picked up Room Two's bags, grabbed the key and pushed past me, the two guests following behind her. When Beatrice put the phone down, she inspected the stairs. She said that I had done a very good job

56

on my first day and that I could leave the rest and so we took our aprons off and went to sit in the lounge, so that she could listen out for guests arriving and watch TV at the same time. Grandma Maggie was engrossed in a football report.

'The atmosphere is electric at Anfield this afternoon,' said the TV. 'Weren't Liverpool magnificent, Brian? Six goals in ninety minutes. West Ham didn't get a look-in.'

'Everyone's here apart from Eleven,' said Esther, coming back from Room Two.

'Good. That was Meredith on the phone just now,' Beatrice said to her.

'What time is she getting here?' said Esther.

'One o'clock.'

'Tomorrow?' I said.

'Yes,' said Esther.

'It's nearly time to start dinner,' Beatrice said. She and Esther went off towards the kitchen together, I heard the dining-room door close behind them and I was left alone in the guest lounge with Grandma Maggie, who had begun to bang a teaspoon on the side of her wheelchair in time to the voices coming from the TV. The photo of the arm was still on the table where I had left it the day before. I sat kicking my feet against the sofa for a few minutes, listening to the television and to Maggie's tap-tap-tapping.

'And of course on Wednesday Dinamo Bucharest are on their way to Merseyside in the next round of the European Cup. How do you rate their chances after today's performance, Brian?'

Then I picked up the photo again, but I wasn't satisfied with it. I heard the guests trooping into the dining room, and snatches of their conversation, the door swinging shut in between each one: 'I'm going back for my cardigan.' 'We had to eat the chips inside when it started raining.' 'Nigel wanted a tattoo, but I said no.' 'Now he's spending the money on Easter eggs, so that's a good thing.'

I knew Beatrice and Esther would be busy, so I was safe for a while. I got up quickly, ran to Beatrice's room and turned on the light. I went over to the shelf where I had seen the photo albums the first time Esther showed me round, reached up and pulled one of them out. Then I decided that I didn't care about being discovered any more. I just wanted to see my mother again, so I took the album back into the guest lounge. I had at least forty-five minutes until the rush was over, anyway. It was bangers and mash, which was very popular – Esther had told me so earlier.

The photo album was a long blue plastic folder, and was a bit tattered at the corners. Inside the front cover was the same neat handwriting that had appeared on the photo of the arm; this time it said: 'B. Now I have a camera, I will take all my pictures for you. T.M.' I turned the cardboard first page and underneath were the clear plastic leaves into which Beatrice had slipped her memories, all grouped around dates. '1969,' the first page said on a white label at the top, and there was my mother as I had never seen her before (she didn't keep any photo albums on her shelves) with a man with a beard on one side of her and Beatrice on the other, their arms around each other's shoulders. I lifted the picture out of its sleeve. It was a good photo for a snapshot, I thought to myself. (Even in those days I found myself weighing up the composition, and the sharpness of the colours.) Then I realised that big tears were falling into my lap so I wiped my eyes with the back of my hand but I carried on looking.

On the back of the picture was different handwriting – Beatrice's, I knew, because I had seen it in the blue hotel book that she kept in reception. It said, 'The Isle of Wight Festival'. My mother was wearing an orange and brown dress with beads stitched at the neck and a scarf tied around her head.

She had long straight hair and I could feel her smile coming out of the photo at me from fifteen years previously. It climbed into my fingers where I was touching the picture of her face and up into my arm and into my chest. They were standing in a field and the sun was shining. Behind them was a tent. The man in the picture had a brown beard, with a feather on a string around his neck, and he was wearing brown drawstring trousers and a leather waistcoat. Beatrice was just as small as usual, but a bit thinner. She was wearing a green and blue dress and had curly hair down to her shoulders. My mother was holding a can of something and a cigarette in one hand. That photo was like a window into the bit of my head where my mother was – like I had always known she was there in a 1969 picture with her friends, but up until now I hadn't been able to see her.

I put it back and carried on looking through the album. There were more photos of the three of them at the festival plus some with the blonde out-of-focus woman in, who Esther said was Meredith. There was one of Beatrice with no top on waving her arms, with her eyes closed, presumably to some music I couldn't hear. When I saw it I felt like maybe I shouldn't be looking at all, but I carried on anyway. I found the hole where the photo of the arm belonged and I slid it back in and turned the page to find a picture of the man on his own, a green band tied around his head. On the back Beatrice had written: 'Timothy Mackintosh'. I played with the name in my head, wanting to remember it so that I could ask Esther about it later. Timothy Mackintosh. I liked it because it sounded like a tambourine. I put it back and turned the page.

This time it said, 'May 1970'. And there was Esther, new and round, with a crunched-up red face, surrounded by white wool. Beatrice had inscribed this one too. It said: 'Esther. Born 10 May 1970'. And there was Beatrice in the next one, smiling, holding

Esther in her arms. All the 1970 pictures were of Beatrice and Esther in different poses, with different hats on, in different kinds of weather. Esther on the beach, crushing handfuls of sand in her fat fists. Esther and Beatrice in front of the hotel on Christmas Day. One or two had Grandma Maggie in them, upright and not yet mad. I glanced over at the 1984 version, who was now tapping the theme tune to the news and then the first headline, something about unemployment, typewriter-like. Then I heard the dining-room door swing and there was Beatrice in front of me. I snapped the album shut and sniffed loudly. I had been caught but I didn't care. I kicked my feet into the sofa again and looked at the floor.

'Oh,' she said, 'you found my photos then?'

'I was just looking.'

'Esther needs a hand with the sponge puddings.'

'OK.' I didn't move for a moment. Beatrice took the teaspoon from Maggie's hand and silence filled the space where the tapping had been. Then she got a tissue from the side and passed it to me so I could blow my nose and she took the blue photo album from my lap.

'I'll show you the rest of them later if you like,' she said.

'OK.' I got up and went to pour molten strawberry jam on to the little puddings that Esther was turning out of plastic pots. Then I was in charge of custard and the yellow mixed with the hot red jam and it looked like little sunsets had fallen into each of the bowls. Esther puddinged the guests and then came out to help me scrape the insides of the pudding moulds, and all the while I was thinking of fifteen years previously and the photo of my mother's arm and of Beatrice, Timothy Mackintosh and my mother on the Isle of Wight.

After we had had cold sausages and beans and warmed-up mash for Proper Dinner that evening, Beatrice brought her photo albums into the kitchen. She sat down at the long wooden table with Esther on one side of her and me on the other, and went through them page by page. Esther had seen the pictures before but she was fascinated by them because of the secret stories they hid inside themselves. Also, she loved looking at photos of herself, even the ones where she was inside Beatrice's tummy.

'This is me, just before Esther was born,' said Beatrice, showing us a picture of herself in a dress with big brown flowers on it, looking fat with red cheeks. She had had her hair cut into a bob, but it was still very curly. With each picture we got to, I felt like climbing inside to find out what the people in it were looking at, but I couldn't. Soon we got on to the second album.

'This is Meredith in Room Nineteen,' said Beatrice, and she pointed out a photo of Meredith in an apron. 'She came to work here when I was looking after Esther.' Meredith was holding a pillow. She wasn't smiling but her blue eyes looked like bits of sky. Beatrice paused and looked at one of the silver saucepans hanging on the wall in front of her.

'This is one I took of her when she started playing in the orchestra,' she said, indicating a picture of Meredith, concentrating hard, cello between her legs. 'She was always good at music,' Beatrice added, looking at the photo and smiling her lopsided smile again.

She turned the pages and got to 1973, and there outside a church somewhere was Sandra the chambermaid, in a big white wedding dress, with Beatrice and Meredith. Underneath were some of the reception. There was my mother and ('That's you!' Beatrice said) there I was sitting next to her. I must have been nearly three years old.

'Sandra's wedding,' said Esther. 'That's boring.'

'You're in this picture as well,' said Beatrice, pointing herself and Esther out. They were sitting at a different table.

61

'I know,' said Esther. 'I've seen it before.'

'Here's a better picture of you,' said Beatrice, to keep her happy, and she showed Esther one of her and Grandma Maggie outside the church. Then there was another picture of Esther aged seven or eight, with a duster in Room Five. I noticed how the man with the name like a tambourine had been missing from the later photos we'd looked at.

'Who's Timothy Mackintosh?' I asked.

Beatrice was about to answer, but Esther looked up quickly and said, 'My dad.'

Beatrice closed the album. 'When Esther's dad left me,' Beatrice said, using her strange voice again, 'he took his camera with him, so I didn't take any more pictures for a while.'

Meredith

The next day, which was Sunday, 8 April 1984, Meredith arrived just in time for lunch. Esther had been in the guest lounge since ten o'clock, pretending she wasn't watching for Meredith's car. I remember thinking that Esther was right about how glamorous Meredith was. She stood in the hotel reception with her sunglasses balanced on top of her head, looking like someone I knew from television or from a film, although I couldn't say who. She was the same as she was in the photos, only with thin lines around her eyes and mouth. She had short blonde hair and was wearing a denim jacket with three little badges on the collar: one was Duran Duran, one said 'Keep Music Live' and one was green and looked like an upside down tree with three branches. If I close my eyes and think about the first time I saw her, I can still see the badges and I can still see her white shirt and blue jeans and the green silk scarf around her neck. Her eyes looked much wider than they had in the photos and even bluer. She put down her bag and gave Beatrice a hug. Then she looked at me very seriously and said, 'And you're Suzie's daughter.'

I didn't say anything so she glanced at Beatrice for confirmation, then she stretched out a hand towards me.

'Very pleased to meet you,' she said in her earnest voice, as

63

she shook hands with me and tried without success to get me to look her in the face. 'So sorry not to be at the funeral.' I knew at once why Esther liked her so much. She had a way of speaking to me as if I mattered most to her in the whole world. She spoke to everyone like that.

Lunch was roast chicken, potatoes, carrots, peas, stuffing and gravy. It was Esther's second favourite.

'Meredith eats only fish or chicken,' said Esther as she sat down next to her at the long table in the kitchen.

'And vegetables,' said Meredith, smiling widely and sticking her knife into a potato. She talked for a while about where she had played her cello since she had last been to visit, and about India and how she hadn't spent enough time there and would like to go back.

She had brought four silk scarves for Beatrice, Grandma Maggie, Esther and me. Mine was brown and gold, like a leaf. I put it on straight away.

'My dad's in India,' said Esther suddenly.

'Esther!' said Beatrice. She sounded alarmed.

'I don't think anyone's sure where he is,' said Meredith kindly and then she looked straight at me. I was concentrating on stabbing peas with my fork.

'Rice, I'm longing to find out more about you,' she said, and Esther regarded me jealously. 'But first tell me about your mother. We were all so devastated to hear.' I went on stabbing my peas. 'You know we were friends at school?' I think I nodded because she carried on. 'Such a shame that we all lost contact,' she said and looked at Beatrice thoughtfully. 'How old are you now?'

'She's thirteen,' said Esther, when I didn't answer, 'I'm a year older than her.'

'Not quite a year,' said Beatrice, looking at me. 'Only a few months.'

'How did you manage to get in touch with Beatrice again?' Meredith asked.

I muttered something about my next-door neighbour through a mouthful of chicken.

'More stuffing, Meredith?' said Beatrice, trying to change the subject.

'Oh, yes, please,' she said, taking a big spoonful. 'So when did it happen?' she asked, posing the most direct question anyone could have asked me. Only Meredith could have asked it. I looked up.

'I didn't think she wants to talk about it, Merry,' said Beatrice quietly.

'Oh, rubbish, of course she does.'

'She died on the twenty-first of March,' I said, looking into Meredith's big blue eyes for the first time. Everyone stopped eating and looked at me, apart from Grandma Maggie, who was taking big slurps of her orange juice.

'In hospital?'

'Yes.'

'I hear she was ill for a long time.'

'It was really bad for about a year.'

'Did you look after her?'

'Yes.' Then I realised that it felt good to talk about her, and I felt excited because Meredith had seen through me. It was like she'd seen my dead mother underneath my skin and she was making her come back to life a little bit with each word, and I wanted all my words to tumble out of my mouth and not stop. I wanted to tell Meredith that I kept thinking about the colour of her hair on the day she died, that it was still that auburn brown colour it had always been, and I wanted to tell her about the time we walked across a bridge together and she held my hand, or that time I was ill in the middle of the night and she made me a hot-water bottle even though she was ill herself. But I couldn't say anything. I helped myself to more peas instead. Then it was chocolate sponge pudding and ice cream.

'When do you go back to school?' said Meredith, turning first to Esther and then to me.

'The twenty-fourth of April,' said Esther.

'How long are you back here for?' said Beatrice.

'I've got a weekend in Austria coming up. Then we go on a tour of Europe in the summer and Canada for Christmas,' Meredith replied.

I looked at her with my mouth open. I thought it must be wonderful to go to so many places. I was about to ask her about it, but Esther interrupted.

'Tell me about India,' Esther said, frowning at me because she wanted Meredith to herself. But I only heard some of the conversation after that anyway because I was feeling pleased about Meredith and my mum and all the places Meredith went to. I smiled at Grandma Maggie, who had chocolate pudding round her mouth, and I looked at her for a while and wondered if she had a mother under her skin too.

After lunch we went into the guest lounge. Room Three were sitting silently in armchairs in the corner by the window. I didn't know what their names were. They were watching the television. It was Brian Walden on a podium with Arthur Scargill. Mrs Room Three had a black and red dress on and her legs were crossed. Her hair was backcombed on top and looked like it was held together by hairspray. Mr Room Three was wearing a green jumper, which was neat and tidy like the rest of him.

'Hello,' said Beatrice. 'Mind if we join you?'

'Hello,' said Mr Room Three.

'No,' said Mrs Room Three. Esther sat down as far away from them as possible and when I sat down next to her, she moved her chair away from me but I ignored her and watched Beatrice push her mother into position in front of the TV. She made sure Room Three could still see.

'Not on the beach today?' Beatrice asked them.

'No,' said Mr Room Three.

'Too cold,' said Mrs Room Three.

'Hopefully the sun will come out tomorrow for you,' Beatrice said. She pushed down the brakes on her mother's wheelchair, left then right.

'Esther, take Rice and go and make some coffee, will you, dear?' said Beatrice, so Esther and I went back into the kitchen and I heard Beatrice say, 'She's thirteen years old and she's just lost her mother,' as we went through the swing door to the dining room.

Once we were in the kitchen, Esther started clunking cups and saucers and issuing orders.

'Put the kettle on and get the milk out,' she said. 'Get the sugar. No. In the cupboard, stupid. The bowls are under there.' We went back into the guest lounge, laden with coffee.

'Happy Easter,' said Grandma Maggie eagerly and looked up at the TV as if she expected it to turn into an Easter egg. Grandma Maggie loved chocolate. There was still chocolate pudding around her mouth, so she looked like a chocolate monster, soft and sweet and dangerous. Maybe she had had her fangs removed when the dentist fitted her false teeth, I thought. And I turned Grandma Maggie into a monster inside my head, raging around the hotel in her wheelchair, slavering at the mouth.

For the rest of my second week at the hotel, Beatrice gave me small tasks to complete, like replacing soap in the shared bathrooms or topping up the big bowls of cereal before breakfast. On Wednesday, Esther went to the cinema with her friends. I thought Beatrice would tell her to let me go too but she didn't. She seemed to be thinking about something, like she was looking into a big barrel of water and couldn't see the bottom properly. Her forehead had been wrinkled since Meredith had phoned that morning, and even though Esther asked her, she wouldn't tell us what she had said.

I sat in the bar with Beatrice, who was still being quiet, instead of going out. There were some guests in the corner, laughing and chatting loudly to each other, and Beatrice had served them all with Cokes and bitter lemons before she sat down. I was drinking a lemonade when Meredith arrived.

She stood in the door for a second and they looked at each other and then Beatrice said: 'Can you go and give Sandra a hand, Rice?'

I hadn't finished my lemonade. 'Sandra doesn't need any help. I asked her,' I said.

'Oh. Well, pillowcases then,' said Beatrice. Meredith came in and sat down. I could see she was waiting for me to leave. 'They're in a basket outside Room Fifteen,' said Beatrice. 'Can you put them in the cupboard? Sandra will show you.'

'OK,' I said. I gulped my lemonade down so quickly that I felt like I had bubbles coming out of my mouth.

As I was going up the stairs, a handful of the laughing guests came out of the bar and I wondered if Beatrice had asked them to leave too. As the door swung open and then closed again, I heard a little bit of Meredith and Beatrice's conversation.

'I can't tell her,' said Beatrice.

'Why not?'

'Because I don't want to upset her.' I wondered what they were talking about. It sounded like something big and important, like a murder mystery. I sat on the stairs and listened carefully, but could only hear mumbles now the door was closed. Then the final laughing guest came out, and Beatrice said in an annoyed voice: 'I don't want to think about him any more,' but that was all.

I was about to get up and go, when two more guests, a man and a woman, made their way towards the bar from the dining room, but instead of going in they stood in the doorway and had an argument. In between their argument, when their voices didn't get muddled up, I could hear Beatrice and Meredith talking. When they remembered, they spoke quietly so the guests wouldn't hear them, but then they started to argue too and their voices got bigger, so I could listen again, although sometimes the man and the woman drowned them out altogether.

'Do we have to drink in here all the time?' the woman said, through her teeth. 'Why can't we go to the pub?'

'You go to the pub. I'm stopping here,' said the man.

'Well?' said Meredith from inside.

'Not yet. When they're older,' said Beatrice. When who's older? I thought and I felt like I was in *Bergerac* on TV, or *The Dukes of Hazzard*, finding out about a secret plan. It had to be important because Beatrice didn't usually talk about herself when the guests were around. Sometimes I forgot about the rules for when I was supposed to talk about serious things. Sometimes words came out of my mouth when I didn't want them to and I felt like stuffing them back in again. Like sometimes when I spoke to Esther, when I wished I hadn't started to talk but once I'd started I couldn't stop. Maybe Beatrice had forgotten and that was why she was saying things in the bar.

'Oh, and do you have to tell the kids that they can have a Lilo?' said the woman guest loudly as if she wanted people upstairs to know how dangerous Lilos were.

'What's wrong with that? I want them to have some fun.'

'What if they got swept out to sea on it? Whose fault would that be?' The woman tapped her foot and the man folded his arms. They stared at each other, like they were fed up of being on holiday and wanted to go back to what they usually did. The woman sounded like she might be a bus driver. I imagined giving her a pound and getting into trouble for not having the right change and not knowing which stop I wanted.

'I don't know who my father was.' It was Beatrice again and this time she sounded sad. I felt shocked because I didn't know about Beatrice not knowing her father before. She was just like Esther, I thought, and like me. Then I got muddled up with the Lilos that the guests were arguing about and I thought about Beatrice's father getting swept out to sea as far as the horizon and she was standing on the beach and couldn't see him any more.

'Anyway I don't want to go to the beach tomorrow,' said the woman.

'Well, I want to go to the beach,' said the man.

'You can go to the beach. I want to go shopping.'

'Are you coming in here for a drink or what?' said the man. The two guests went through the door and it shut behind them so I couldn't hear any more. I had forgotten all about the pillowcases. I got up to go, so I could lie on my bed and think about Beatrice's dad on the Lilo and the secret she didn't want Meredith to tell someone. I got up to the first landing before I heard the door to the bar opening again. I looked over the railings and saw Meredith come out. She didn't turn round and shout goodbye to Beatrice again like the last time. She pulled on her denim jacket in a hurry and drove off fast, like she was late for the dentist.

The days merged into one another and soon it was Saturday again, checking-out day, and time to start cleaning rooms. I was on towels, bins and toilet rolls once more. Esther helped Sandra with the beds and Steve, the Saturday boy, cleaned the kitchen and washed dishes and stuffed sheets in the washing machines. I emptied all the bins, colour co-ordinated my towels and toilet rolls and delivered Esther's yellow linen basket to her. At the end of the afternoon, I had just turned off the Hoover after doing the stairs, and was winding the cord up around the back of the handle, when two new guests arrived, a man and a woman. I glanced around. There was no one on reception. I took off my apron and went through the brown door marked 'Private'.

'Can I help you?' I said, pretending to be Beatrice.

'We've booked a double room under the name of Brown,' said the man, putting down his suitcase. I looked in the blue book, which I had seen Beatrice writing into with a stubby pencil when the guests phoned.

'Room Eleven,' I said, looking for the key on the wall behind me. 'If you'd like to sign in, please. And choose your dinners . . .' The man took up the pen I offered him and filled in their names. Then he studied the menu card carefully. He had a black beard and looked very solemn.

'Where's Beatrice?' said the woman suspiciously. 'We usually see Beatrice.' They had been before.

'Yes, um, there's your key, Room Eleven is upstairs some-where,' I said. Mr and Mrs Brown looked bewildered, but I ignored them and pretended to be making important entries in my blue book. Just then Beatrice came bustling out of the guest lounge.

'Mr and Mrs Brown,' she said, smiling all over. 'Can I take your bags?' And they were off up the stairs. 'Dinner's at seven as usual,' I could hear her saying as she whisked them up to their room. I stayed at my station behind the reception desk, pleased with my new status.

Esther appeared, to find out what was going on. 'What are you doing?' She glared at me. I was getting used to her saying this to me by now and I sighed.

71

'I'm welcoming the guests,' I said, waving a hand in the general direction of the front door.

'You're supposed to be cleaning the stairs,' she said. 'Where's Sandra?'

'I don't know.'

Someone else was arriving. It was a small man with a neat blue bag.

'Do you have any vacancies?' he said.

'Certainly, sir,' I began, looking carefully at the blue book. 'Room Four. Could I have your name, please?'

'Yes, it's—'

Esther was getting angry. 'Room Four isn't free, I'm afraid, sir,' she said, moving me out of the way. She picked up one of the cards that had to be filled in when new guests arrived and I leant back sulkily against the wall. 'And it does really depend on how long you'd like to stay for.'

'A week,' said the man, putting down his bag.

'I can do you a standard double. It has got a sink and a nice view of the beach.' Esther knew the words to say very well.

'I'll take it.'

'Will you be having dinner here?'

'No.'

'OK. Room Twelve. If you'd like to sign here, sir,' she said, 'I'll show you to your room.' I went and sat on the stairs and was determined that soon I would check a guest in all by myself without her interfering. I just had to wait for my chance.

'Room Four have decided to stay for another week,' Esther hissed at me, when she came back downstairs.

'How was I supposed to know?'

'You weren't supposed to be on reception.'

Sandra had returned from her cigarette break and was telling an old lady with a dog that pets weren't welcome because of the hair.

Then the phone rang and Sandra put her hand over the receiver like a secret agent and said, 'Get your mother,' to Esther.

When we had found Beatrice and she had taken the phone from Sandra, she told us to go and lay the tables, so Esther and I did so, in silence. Afterwards, Beatrice came into the dining room with Steve, the Saturday boy, and said that he could leave early because he had done such a good job.

'His granddad used to work here as a porter,' said Beatrice, when he'd gone. I think she was trying not to talk about the phone conversation. 'It was a long time ago,' she said, 'but he tells me he wants to be a nurse.'

'Who was on the phone?' said Esther.

'Meredith.'

'Have you had an argument?' said Esther, because her mother wasn't smiling like she usually did when she spoke to Meredith, but Beatrice didn't answer.

The first time I went to see Meredith's flat was a few days later, after she phoned again and had another conversation with Beatrice, who said 'Yes' and 'No' and 'OK' a lot with her mouth in a straight line. Part of the reason she was calling was to suggest that I have guitar lessons. I wasn't happy about having to learn the guitar but I was invited over for tea as well and I was excited because I was going to see Meredith all by myself. Esther wasn't invited and, even though she had been before, she was angry. I heard Beatrice telling her that it was because of my mother and I wondered whether Meredith was going to tell me that it had all been a trick and my mother hadn't really died in the hospital and maybe she was going to be there on Meredith's sofa when I went round to see her and I could go back to how I was and everything

73

would be the same again. But my mother wasn't there. Instead, Meredith looked at me with her worried blue eyes.

'Sit down,' she said, 'I'll make some tea.' And she disappeared through a door. I sat on the edge of the white sofa. Above the fireplace there was a big line drawing in a black frame of a naked woman with her back to me. Meredith had pretend zebra cushions on the floor and black and white rugs. On the table next to me there was a pile of colourful drinks mats and a picture of an interesting shell. I looked over to where Meredith's guitar was leaning against the piano and I felt nervous. Then I heard some plates banging in the kitchen and cupboards opening. Through the door, I could see Meredith with a kettle in the white-tiled kitchen. It was taking her a long time, I thought, and I wondered if she was used to making tea for people.

'I won't be long,' Meredith said when she saw me looking. I could see pots on shelves with pictures of vegetables and French words on them. There was pasta in jars, packets of tea and chocolate and chopping boards. Later, when I went into the toilet, I found pictures of seahorses and some real shells round the sink that were big enough to cover the whole of my ear when I listened to them. The walls in there were deep ocean blue, but in the front room they were white and it was light because of the big window and shiny, like an angel's room, I thought. Her cello was leaning against one wall near the piano and guitar, and there was music on a stand and scattered around the floor. Above the piano there was another picture. It was a woman with red and white hair and funny make-up sniffing a rose. It had a red frame. After I had looked at it, I went over to the window, lifted up the silver blind and stood inside it. In the distance I could see tiny triangles of colour as the boats rode over the grey waves in Poole Harbour.

Meredith came back in with a tray so I untangled myself from

74

the blind and sat back down on the sofa. She poured the tea out of a teapot although it wasn't real tea. It smelt of flowers and a little bit of honey. I sipped it carefully. She had made crumbly flapjacks with sultanas and cherries and slices of toast with jam on them. I ate with my plate held under my chin in case I dropped any crumbs on Meredith's sofa.

'Meredith,' I said, with my mouth full, still fascinated by how shiny her flat was.

'Yes?'

'How long have you lived here?'

'Since I left home, mostly.'

'I bet it cost a lot of money.'

'No. It was free. My parents gave it to me when they moved.'

'I know. Beatrice told me. Are your parents rich?'

'No. Not rich. My dad was in the army.'

'Did he kill anyone?'

'I don't think so. Have another flapjack,' Meredith said. 'Beatrice says you like taking photos.'

'Yes.'

'Will you show me your camera sometime?'

'OK.'

'How are you and Esther getting on?'

'OK,' I said, surprised.

'And how are you feeling?' She looked worried. I thought then that maybe Beatrice had told her I wasn't very well because I liked to wear my pyjamas for most of the day and because I spent lots of time by myself or watching TV.

'OK,' I said again. I looked at the picture of the shell on the table next to me. It was white and yellow with little ridges like tiny riverbeds down the side. Maybe the surface of the moon was the same, I thought, but it would be dusty as well. I couldn't tell Meredith how I was feeling because it was like when you cut yourself really badly and then you get a scar and when you touch it you can't feel anything. Like when you touch your teeth with your fingernails. But sometimes the place where you cut yourself comes back to life again and you can feel it, only worse, like it is being cut open again with scissors. I couldn't tell Meredith all of the stuff about scars because it was a secret. Like the secret where I hated everyone at the hotel and the one where I liked apple crumble the best. It was written on a piece of paper inside me. Or maybe I had to keep all the words inside me like the game I played once where you have to keep all the marshmallows in your mouth and not let any of them out. Meredith was looking at me with big eyes because I hadn't answered her question so I just told her the bit about the scissors instead.

'It feels like scissors.'

She nodded. 'Do you wish she was still here?'

'Yes.' Then I told Meredith that Auntie Something had said that because I knew that my mother was very ill and was probably going to die it was easier because I had already been feeling sad about it for a long time. I said that I thought Auntie Something was stupid and that I hated her and that I never wanted to go back there.

'So you like living at the hotel then?'

'It's all right,' I said. I thought guiltily about sitting on the beach and pretending to bury the hotel people all in the sand. I was glad that I had brought them back to life in my head, but I wanted to talk about something different.

'Meredith.'

'Yes?'

'Do you earn a lot of money from playing in the orchestra?'

'Not loads. That's why I give music lessons, but I get to travel to lots of places.'

76

'Oh.' I hadn't thought about Meredith teaching the guitar to anyone apart from me.

'Don't worry. You get your lessons for free.'

'Do you teach the violin and the piano and the cello or just the guitar?'

'All of them.' Things were different now I had to share Meredith's flat with all the other people who had been there for lessons. I imagined them all crammed into the room like they were waiting for a bus in the cold.

'How many people have you taught?'

'Oh. I've lost count.'

'Wow,' I said, and I imagined even more people crowded into the front room. Some of them were thin with big hands, and one of them was very tall so he had to bend down to stop himself from banging his head on the ceiling.

'Am I the only free one?'

'Yes.' I was pleased and stored up the crowded bus stop to think about later.

'When are you going to Austria?'

'In a couple of weeks.'

'Which town?'

'Innsbruck.'

'Good. I'll look it up in the atlas.'

'I'll bring you some chocolate if you like.'

'Now,' said Meredith, when she had put the tea away, and got her guitar out of its case. I still wasn't very sure about the idea of learning. Meredith showed me how to hold it and told me to press my fingers down on the strings at one end and to strum it with my other hand. It was hard to hold and the strings hurt my fingers and I found it difficult to get them into the right shapes.

'Don't worry,' said Meredith. 'It's your first go.' I tried hard because I wanted Meredith to be impressed, but I didn't enjoy it. By the end of my half an hour I had little dents on the end of three fingers on my left hand from where I had been pressing the strings to make a chord. Then we heard Beatrice drive up outside and beep her horn. Meredith went over to the window and pulled up the blind with the string, but she didn't wave.

'Can I bring my camera next time?' I said, looking out of the window and across the bay.

'OK,' she said. Then before she said goodbye, she put her hands on my shoulders and looked at me and said in a serious voice, 'Rice, there's something I want to tell you.' But then Beatrice beeped her horn again and she didn't say what it was. Maybe Meredith had a secret thing too, I thought, like the scissors.

I got into the car.

'Aren't you going to go in and say hello to Meredith?' I said to Beatrice. She wasn't smiling.

'No, I've got to get back for dinners.'

'We had flapjacks.'

'Very nice.' I showed her the dents on my fingers and then we drove back to the hotel.

Grandma Maggie

Esther had decided that she wanted to be a beautician when she was older, and one Saturday evening early on in my time at the Water's Edge she got out her comb and rollers and said that we were going to do Grandma Maggie's hair. I protested that I didn't know what to do but she told me not to be stupid, all I had to do was hold the towel. Although Esther washed her grandmother's hair once a week, this was the first time I had been allowed to help.

'Clean and beautiful,' said Grandma Maggie, as Esther wheeled her into the bathroom. I followed behind.

'You're not having a bath, Grandma. We're going to wash your hair.'

'Shampoo and set.'

'That's right,' Esther replied, and pushed the wheelchair as far under the sink as possible.

'Who's she?' said Grandma Maggie, turning round and fixing her fierce eyes on me.

'She's going to help,' said Esther, not answering the question. I wanted to say: 'My name is Rice. I told you that before, don't you remember?' But I just stood there nervously, fiddling with the towels, as Grandma Maggie looked me up and down for a couple of seconds before deciding I was safe.

'Shampoo and set,' she repeated.

Esther removed her grandmother's creamy blouse, revealing her breasts, clutched in a musty-coloured bra, which had been made comfortable through years of use and had moulded to fit her shape. At the right moment, I passed Esther the raggedy old blue towel that she used when she performed her hair-washing duties. Grandma Maggie was used to having her hair washed and immediately the towel was put around her shoulders she bent over the sink, as if she were about to be decapitated and was waiting patiently for the axe.

'Are you ready?' said Esther. There was no reply, so she carefully tipped the first jug full of water over Grandma Maggie's head like she was baptising her, and waggled a hand towards me for another towel, which she used to wipe the water from her grandmother's eyes. Then she rubbed No Tears shampoo into her downy hair. After she had finished, Esther put her hands on Grandma Maggie's shoulders and lifted her upright again and said, 'All done now,' like she was talking to a sweet but deaf client in the hair salon she had begun to carry around with her in her head.

Esther moved out of the way and motioned me forward. 'Right. Dry her hair. Not totally. Just so it doesn't drip.' I took the blue towel from around her shoulders and began to rub Grandma Maggie's head awkwardly.

'Be careful, stupid!' said Esther, and I thought then that maybe she had only asked me to help so that she could tell me what to do.

'You'll tangle it up if you do that,' said Grandma Maggie, and I stopped. She looked at me in the mirror above the sink. 'Tell that man to stay away from me,' she said sternly.

'She sees things sometimes,' said Esther, comb in hand, and wheeled her back into the lounge. There weren't many guests around so Esther said it was OK to do things in there. She already had most of her implements set out. She put the comb down next to the hair spray. The pink rollers were heating up in the corner.

'My mum said I could as long as I didn't burn her head,' Esther said.

Grandma Maggie looked suspiciously from Esther to me, and back again. I decided to leave Esther to it so I went into the kitchen to make us all a cup of tea and to open a tin of gingerbread. Dinner hadn't started yet. Beatrice and Sandra were in the bar, talking about cleaning rotas. I took my time. I enjoyed being in the kitchen on my own when it was completely quiet. The spoons hung on the wall innocently like they hadn't seen all the things they had, reflected upside down in their big silver bowls. When Beatrice and Sandra came in to start making the salads, I went back into the lounge with a tray.

'What took you so long?' said Esther, as she took a bite out of her gingerbread.

Grandma Maggie had bendy pink rollers in her hair. Later, when Esther took them out, Grandma Maggie looked like a princess, with beautifully curled hair, which Esther twisted gently around her brush. She tucked her into her blanket and turned up the television so that she could listen to the comforting sound of the football results being read out.

After a while, Beatrice came in from the kitchen to admire her mother's new hairstyle. Sandra was waitressing by herself as most of the guests had gone for fish and chips and only a few had turned up for haddock salad and butter beans. After that it was *Dr Who* and *Jim'll Fix It*. While the others watched TV, I sat and looked at Grandma Maggie and I wondered about her hair and all the hairstyles she had had. It was too hard to imagine her looking different and she ended up with brown princess curls again. I wondered whether, when I was sixty-four, I would have lots of hairstyles inside me, one on top of the other, like she did. I thought about how much time it had taken me to grow my hair as long as it was. I used to be able to tell people that I had never had it cut but then when I was ten my mother made me sit on the floor while she cut it short because she said it was a mess and that she couldn't put up with it any longer. It took me three and a bit years to grow it back to how it is now, I thought, half watching *Dr Who*. Then I wondered about Grandma Maggie's face and how she came to have so many lines. Maybe there were lots of Grandma Maggie's folded up inside her when she was a baby, waiting, and lots of days inside her too.

'Sixty-four isn't very old,' Beatrice had told me, when I asked her, 'but she is the same age as the hotel, which makes her special.'

I closed my eyes and thought about the hotel when it was new and shiny and Grandma Maggie crying in a cot when she was new and shiny too. I closed my eyes and in my head I picked up the crying baby Margaret and carried her out to the kitchen and showed her her face upside down in the bowl of one of the big spoons. Then I showed her the huge saucepans and the old oven and I gave her some of the gingerbread to eat, which made her stop crying and look up at me with baby eyes.

'It's gingerbread, like a witch's house is made of,' I said. Underneath the red bricks, in between the inside wall and the outside wall, I thought that maybe the hotel could be made of gingerbread. Only I knew about it and baby Margaret, who was laughing now with a toothless mouth and waving her arms. I sat down at the kitchen table and rocked her gently, whispering to her about how she was special because she was the same age as the hotel and probably made of gingerbread too. Then *Dr Who* ended and the *Jim'll Fix It* music came on. I opened my eyes and Esther was staring at me.

'What are you doing, Rice?'

'Thinking.'

'Can you only think with your eyes closed?'

'No.'

'Leave her alone, Esther,' said Beatrice.

On the TV, Jim was talking about all the impossible letters he had had about things he couldn't fix. 'Dear Jim,' said one, 'please can you fix it for me to go to the moon?'

My name is Persephone. The water teases the sand and looks different every time I see it. On a summer's day it is flat and hemmed with white lace like a giant tablecloth that someone standing on the horizon is shaking out. Being a goddess, I could hear through the walls of the old hotel and see things the mortal guests couldn't see. I liked to hide in corners and to watch people talking. I liked to know their secrets.

I had been coming to the hotel since Thomas Tamarack first stood by the front door to welcome his guests, so I knew about all its secret places. I can still walk around the hotel in my head: through the kitchen, into the dining room and out into the hall. Then into the lounge, where the guests would relax on comfy chairs, and over to the window, which looked out over the hotel car park. There was a TV in the corner. Next stop the bar, where there were small tables, and behind the long white counter there was another (portable) television. Opposite the door to the bar, next to the door to the dining room, was the reception, and on the other side of the reception was a door marked 'Private'. Through the door was the bathroom (straight on), and on the left were Beatrice and Maggie's rooms. At the end of the little passageway to the bedrooms there was a door into the kitchen.

Out into the hallway again and up the stairs, which curled round to the first-floor landing. My room was always on the first floor. Room Five. Up some more stairs to the second floor, where there were more rooms and two bathrooms – one, the biggest, was at the bottom of the stairs up to the attic.

I first stayed at the old hotel because it was the closest to the beach when it opened, and then as I stayed there year after year, I listened to its stories and I grew more and more fascinated by it and the people who lived there. Looking up at where the hotel used to be, I feel sad that its stories are lost and have sunk into the earth. I can see hell underneath everyday things. I have X-ray vision, and my hearing is supersonic. From below the earth, I can hear a snowdrop opening; I know when my time is coming to return into the world, to bring spring with me. When I stayed at the hotel, I could hear it speaking. I would listen to the building's stories, put my hand on the red walls and feel them breathing. I could hear them saying: 'Listen. Listen to the story of Persephone. Listen to the sea coming in, going out, across the sand of Bournemouth beach.' Stories would come up through the earth with the flowers in the garden. They came down the drainpipes with the dirty bath water and were served up on a plate in the dining room. There were stories in the signing-in book in the reception. They skirted over the gravel in the hotel car park when a new guest arrived and were ushered in through the front door with a flourish. 'Here is your key Mrs Brown,' Beatrice would say. 'You're Number Eleven. Up the stairs turn right, past the picture of the pink and white flowers, next to the fire extinguisher, you can't miss it, breakfast is from seven until nine.' Stories were poured into glasses in the hotel bar and gurgled round the toilet bowls when someone flushed away the contents of their bowels, washing another day's dirtiness into the sea. Stories rushed through each corridor, through open doors and tumbled headlong out into the street and into the air. I could hear them like no one else could. I am omnipresent and omnipotent, after all.

I liked listening to the history of the people at the hotel and the people who belonged to them. I used to stroke the walls in my room and listen and this is what I would hear. Beatrice and Paul were married in the first spring of the new century, when Queen Victoria was still on the throne and their daughter Grace was born a year later. Alexandra and Thomas were married in January 1901 and the week after their wedding Queen Victoria died and the country went into mourning. At that point the old hotel hadn't even been built. In 1902, their only son, Thomas Tamarack, was born, fourteen years before his father was killed in the Great War, ten years before the *Titanic* sunk and eleven years before Emily Davison was killed at the Epsom Derby. In June 1913, Emily ran out into the path of King George's horse. Her skull was broken and she died and people said she was mad to die like Humpty Dumpty for the vote. None of this happened here, it's just that it was inside the heads of the people who lived at the hotel. Grace's mother never did get to vote because in 1918 she and her husband, Paul, died of influenza, and Grace was left on her own, ready to fall into the arms of Thomas Tamarack. Meanwhile, the foundations for the Water's Edge Hotel were being laid.

Thomas Tamarack was interested in the art of photography. When he joined the *Bournemouth Evening Echo* as an apprentice, he went to interview the owner of the new Water's Edge Hotel. When Thomas told the man about his camera, he asked him to take a photograph of the grand opening, early in 1920.

The owner of the hotel was a middle-aged businessman, and he needed a cook so Grace and Tom got married and Grace got the job as the cook, even though she was pregnant with Margaret.

The attic was turned into a bedroom for Thomas Tamarack and his wife. When Margaret was born later on that year, Grace kept her cradle in the kitchen while she cooked for the guests, so that she could watch her sleep and rock her when she cried.

When they moved in, Grace Tamarack kept a ginger cat called Barnabus in the attic room, and guests who were allergic sneezed their way through their holidays, thinking it was the feathers in the pillows. On the day they got there, Grace smuggled Barnabus up to the attic room under her coat, so that the owner wouldn't know. Barnabus was scared, being in the dark under Grace's coat, and somewhere in his head there was a second-hand memory about kittens being drowned in a big brown sack but, all the same, Grace had got to the top of the second flight of stairs before he scratched her across the chest, and bounded away from her. They found him later under the bed in Room Twenty and Grace had a scar across her chest for the rest of her life. Sadly Barnabus passed away in 1926, on the day Houdini died after being punched in the stomach in a pub by a man who thought he'd won the bet (I don't know if they hanged him afterwards), and the allergic guests stopped sneezing. It was the same year that Gertrude Ederle became the first woman to swim the English Channel. Grace still saw Barnabus's ghost prowling around after dark sometimes, snapping at spiders and swiping at the air with his paw.

Nearly sixty years after Barnabus died, one afternoon in the spring of 1984, when I knew no one would be there, I climbed up to the attic room to gaze down at the view. It had the best view in the whole hotel. Looking out of the window I could see the hotel garden spread out below, like a square on a quilt pattern, with a path running down the middle, leading to a small gate in the wall, which opened on to the steps to the beach. Below that I could see the beach, a long yellow strip of sand leading to Hengistbury

Head in one direction and the Purbecks and Old Harry Rocks in the other. There are two piers in Bournemouth. To the west is Boscombe Pier and in the distance, also to the west, forty-five minutes' walk away, is Bournemouth Pier. I could see the beach huts and people sitting on towels and eating sandwiches. Standing looking out of the window of the attic room was like finding a map that had come alive. Miniature people down below unfolded deck chairs and threw balls to their dogs and didn't know about me watching them silently, like the sun, from the top of the hotel. It all looked so wonderful that I felt like flinging the window open and letting the air play with my face, and then running down on to the beach and into the sea until I was up to my neck in it and swimming. And I would have done it if I hadn't been frightened about being sucked back into hell too early and bringing on autumn too soon.

When Grace was twenty-four, Thomas was twenty-three and Margaret was just five, the owner of the Water's Edge got ill and Thomas became the manager. Then in 1936, four years after Amelia Earhart became the first woman to fly solo across the Atlantic, the owner of the hotel died and, as he had no relatives, he left Thomas and Grace the hotel in his will, although, six months later, Thomas joined up, leaving Grace in charge, while he got himself fit and used to a gun in case there was another war.

Back in the spring of 1984, I stood in the attic room and looked at the beach for a while, and then I went back down the stairs to the second floor, past the bathrooms and the toilet and the storage cupboards and all the way down to the kitchen. There was no one about, so I had a look round. I wandered amongst the giant saucepans on the wall and the red spaghetti measurer and the teapots, and then I went over to the far wall and ran my fingers over the marks underneath the wallpaper that only I can see, with my goddess eyes, because in the kitchen, under the wallpaper, there was a door into the cellar, which Beatrice didn't know about. She was a new-born baby lying in a cot in Room Fifteen when her grandmother, Grace, sealed up the door, in 1942. Her mother, Maggie, was sitting at the kitchen table, mixing a little bit of tea with some dust from the dustpan. I could see the cracks behind the wallpaper but no one else could.

Grace inherited her superstitions from her own mother, and as soon as Thomas took charge of the hotel she made him change the name of Room Thirteen to Room Twelve A, because she said she had seen the ghost of a crying man in the corner, next to the high-backed chair, and she didn't want to encourage the spirits with numbers. Thomas didn't believe her – like his biblical counterpart he was a doubter – but he changed the name of the room anyway. Grace really had seen the crying man, but she started to doubt it herself until she saw him again, sitting on the stairs. After that she expected to see ghosts behind every door and in every cupboard, and sometimes she did.

So this is the story of Thomas and Grace and of Margaret and how she went mad, and of Beatrice and her daughter. But most of all this is the story of Rice and how she fell for the Water's Edge Hotel and the people in it. Slowly, without her noticing the change, like people who fall asleep on the beach don't notice the creeping tide, Rice became intrigued by Grandma Maggie's history and the hotel people and the things they carried round with them. Sometimes I think that Rice dived into the hotel like it was the sea and went under the surface in a white line beneath the blue water. She wanted to look inside each cupboard and climb into the walls to see the people who had been there before her, and she began to fall for Esther most of all, because Esther looked as though she had witch ancestors and like she might cast spells with her eyes. Later Rice looked at Esther through the lens of her camera and thought she could capture her story, but they were only just beginning together. They were beginning together in a love story that tasted sweet like raspberries and strange like the taste of the sea at the back of your mouth. They were beginning in a love story that twisted and turned like a maze at a stately home or a bindweed that curls around roses and rosemary bushes. The ending was surprising and not what they expected. The middle of the maze or the heart of the story was strange and beautiful, like bare volcanic islands that dip and rise in mountainous stretches and plunge towards the sea.

The Man in the Frankie Says Relax T-Shirt

My name is Rice and I'm still here. The night after I visited Meredith's flat for the first time, I had a dream that my mother was a guest at the hotel, but the hotel was different. There were shiny crystal chandeliers and the guests had big bells on the ends of pieces of rope in their rooms that they could pull if they wanted food. One guest kept pulling his bell and ordering fish and chips and sandwiches until his room was so full of food that he was buried underneath it all and then the hotel turned into an office block and I couldn't find my way out, and I couldn't find the room where the man was buried in food although I wanted to help him. I woke up and I didn't want to sleep any more. It was morning anyway, only it was very early and the air smelt new, so I got out of bed quietly so I wouldn't wake Esther, picked up my camera, and went to lie on the mattresses in Room Fifteen.

Once I was there, I thought about the people who had stayed at the hotel and the bits of them that hung in the spaces around the place, in the cupboards, under the stairs, in the dining room. Even though they had been gone a long time, they were all still there in a way, hundreds of them eating their dinner, sleeping in late, arranging their toiletries around the sinks. Sometimes I thought I heard the guests from previous years, their forks scraping the edge of a plate, but when I looked the chair was unoccupied. Sometimes I went into an empty room and it seemed crowded, full of smells, the body odours that happen when people are jammed together, legs, arms, heads, hair, faces. They were packed in like on the tube train I had been on with my mother once, under the bed, in the wardrobe, in the chest of draws, inside the kettle, in the baths in the en-suite bathrooms. I found myself wondering, lying on the mattresses that morning, where they would all go if the hotel ever stopped being there. Into the ground, or maybe out to sea, I thought, as I watched a pleasure boat go past the pier. They could go out to sea in a big boat, but if the boat wasn't big enough, some of them would sink into the sea and down into the sand and would never be seen again. Then I imagined that some of the older ones, guests who came in 1920 when the hotel first opened and had come back again over and over for years afterwards, were living in the walls, and I stared at the wallpaper till my eyes went funny and thought about them underneath, biding their time and watching the coming and going. Maybe some of them were fed up and had had enough of a holiday. They were packing their cases to leave, I thought, jamming their hats on their heads and kissing each other goodbye.

From my spot on the mattresses, I had an excellent view. I took secret photos of the sand and sea, although I would have needed a special lens to take close-up pictures from where I was, high above the beach. I knew because I had seen a programme. I held up my thumb and finger to my eye in a circle, like I had seen a woman on the programme do, to see what I could take a picture of. I could see early-morning beachgoers laying out their blankets and sandwiches, discarded drinks cans and orange Frisbees, and I was enjoying myself when I heard Esther coming down the stairs from our bedroom. Too late I realised I had left the door ajar.

'Rice, are you in there?' she said from the bottom of the stairs. 'What are you doing, Rice?'

I decided to come clean. 'Taking photos.'

'What?' Esther's face appeared round the door. She clambered over the boxes and stood looking out of the window for a while.

'Where did you get that camera from?'

'My mum gave it to me. Someone gave it to her just before I was born so it's very old.'

'Oh. I've got to go and do breakfasts now. You have to come and put cereal out.'

'OK.'

'Get dressed first,' she said, and when she'd gone I noticed that there was a hole where she'd been and that I liked being in the same house as her even if she was prickly like a hedgehog. I looked out to sea at the clouds that were touching the horizon and smiled and I thought that maybe I liked being at the hotel after all.

When I finally got to the kitchen, dressed but still holding my camera, Esther was at her usual station, buttering toast, and Beatrice and Sandra were moving here and there, plates of food in their hands.

'Eighteen is vegetarian,' said Sandra, returning from the dining room with a rejected sausage sandwich. 'He says he told you no sausages.'

'Tell him he can have cheese on toast. Hello, Rice,' said Beatrice.

'And Twelve has gone to the beach. He wants scrambled egg when he gets back.' Sandra opened up the sausage sandwich and started to spread it with ketchup so that she could eat it herself.

'I thought you were going to do the cereal,' Beatrice said. 'I had to get Esther to do it instead.'

'Sorry. I was getting dressed,' I said. Beatrice looked from me to Esther and back. I think she was worried because we weren't making friends.

'Esther, Sandra and I will finish off. Why don't you and Rice have breakfast together?' Then she went over to Esther and took the butter knife out of her hand. 'Go on,' she said, and glanced at me. I was sipping a stolen cup of coffee. 'Get some croissants out of the cupboard.' I knew that croissants were a treat and that Esther loved them because I had heard her say so to Sandra. She left the toast buttering and got the croissants without saying anything. Then she went to open the door to the garden.

'Come on then,' she said, and I got up and followed her out, cup in hand. We went through the gate at the end of the garden and sat on the top of the beach steps. It had been raining earlier but now the sun had come out. It was a warm morning and the garden smelt sweet.

We both chewed on our croissants, then Esther took out a packet of Benson and Hedges. She took off the plastic wrapper and the gold foil inside and offered me one. When I declined, she extracted a cigarette for herself with her long white fingers, took out matches from the other pocket, lit the cigarette, and inhaled deeply. I watched her perform the whole sequence from start to finish, surprising myself with my fascination.

'I do smoke actually. Sometimes,' I said.

'Have one then.' She held up the packet and I took one. 'I'm giving up anyway,' she added, taking in another lungful.

I lit my cigarette thoughtfully. 'Doesn't your mum mind?' I said, glancing towards the kitchen.

'Who cares? She can't see and, anyway, she knows I'm giving up.'

'Oh.' We watched the man from Room Twelve on the beach

93

below. He took off his trousers, revealing his swimming trunks underneath, folded his clothes neatly and headed for the sea.

'Will you take my picture?' Esther said. Her green eyes lit up, just for a second.

I took another gulp of my coffee and got up. 'If you want.' I took off my lens cap. Esther went and stood by the ivy-covered tree in the corner of the garden. I looked through the viewfinder and moved the lens round. She came in and out of focus.

'Esther?' It was Beatrice calling from the kitchen. As Esther turned her head to respond, she looked just right, like a proper portrait in a Sunday magazine, I thought. I pressed the shutter release.

'I wasn't ready,' she said. 'You should have waited till I was ready.'

'Taking photos?' said Beatrice, coming out into the garden.

'Yes,' I said.

'Esther, can you do the teapots? Room Six have just complained about their bathroom and Sandra's had to go and investigate.'

Esther went into the kitchen, annoyed that I hadn't given her a chance to smile. I went inside too and took a picture of Beatrice in the kitchen.

Later, when they thought I was upstairs in the attic room, I overheard Esther asking Beatrice if she could go into town the next day.

'Yes, and you can take Rice with you to cheer her up.'

'Why can't you take her?'

'Because I want you two to get to know each other.'

'Do I have to?' Then Beatrice told her that if she took me out, she'd meet us and buy us lunch for a treat. I knew Esther liked going out for lunch because I'd heard her talk about it, and even if she had to bring me along, it would be worth it. When I heard Beatrice get up to go, I went up the stairs as quietly as I could so they wouldn't know that I'd been listening.

That night, as we lay in bed and started to smell of sleep, Esther leant over the side of the bunk bed and said, 'My mum says I've got to take you into Bournemouth.'

'Why?' I said, turning over in bed to face her, pretending not to know.

'Because I've got to show you round. I wanted to go on my own but she won't let me.'

'I'm not that bothered,' I said, but secretly I was quite pleased, because there was something about Esther that made me want to look through every room in the hotel to find her if I didn't know where she was, even though I wouldn't have done it in those first few weeks and I knew she wouldn't want me to find her anyway. But all the same, when we were doing jobs, I tried to make sure that I knew where Esther was, because she had a magnet in her that made me want to look at her and talk to her and ask her questions.

'My mum says I've got to show you round in the morning and she'll meet up with us at lunch time.'

'OK.'

'I don't want to share my room with you but I have to,' she said, and then when I didn't answer: 'Do you like amusement arcades?'

'No.'

'Tough because that's where I hang out and you better not wear anything embarrassing in case anyone sees us.'

I rolled back over again and closed my eyes.

The Water's Edge was near to Boscombe Pier, which was little more than a walkway and some deck chairs. Bournemouth Pier was in the town centre at the bottom of the flower gardens. It had shops that sold rock, honeycomb and postcards, and an ice-cream booth, a bar, and an amusement arcade round the entrance, which was called the Pier Approach. On the pier itself there was a clairvoyant and a music-hall theatre. I hadn't been to Bournemouth town centre before, apart from when I was a baby, so Esther led the way. We got off the bus outside Boots and walked past Debenhams, under the subway, through the gardens, past the Pavilion Café and the teddy bear raffle, under the bridge and eventually we got to Pier Approach. Esther had her hands in her pockets and she didn't say much. I noticed, as we walked, that she was carrying a little bit of the hotel with her, like she was walking in a bubble. She wasn't vulnerable to the tourists with their jacket potatoes in polystyrene boxes and white sunhats.

'Let's go in the arcade,' she said, and showed me inside her pockets. They were full of two-pence pieces from Beatrice's kitchen kitty. The kitty was for emergency items, like toilet roll, milk, soap or eggs, which might need to be purchased at the last minute.

'I'll pay it back, anyway,' Esther said, 'when I win. I might win a hundred pounds.'

We went past the 'Over Sixteen Only' sign and made our way between straggles of people standing absorbed in front of game consoles of various kinds, most of which had flashing orange and blue lights. The carpet was green and cigarette-stained and the machines were playing tinny tunes over and over. There was a booth marked 'Change' in the middle of the arcade where a middle-aged woman stood wearing a yellow sweater and a peaked cap that both also said 'Change' in red letters. But we didn't need her. We had our change already. Esther sauntered over to a machine, one of the ones where two pences teetered on the edge of a moving shelf, waiting to be pushed. Esther started feeding the machine with the kitty money. I soon got bored watching.

'Let me have a go,' I said.

'No.'

'I'm bored,' I said. Esther looked around her. The security guard was standing by the door a few metres away with his back to us. When he turned to talk to someone, I saw that he was wearing a Frankie Says Relax T-shirt.

'OK,' she said, 'but you can only have a few because you haven't done it before.' Esther doled out a handful of coppers. I moved on to another similar machine. I tried putting them in slowly at first, then quickly. The two pences were like people with round faces and flat bodies, I thought, queuing up to jump off a cliff and into the sea. After I had used up nearly all of my money, a coin landed in just the right place and sent four two-pence pieces rolling off the edge of the shelf. I think I shouted something. I was reaching my hand inside excitedly when I heard a voice behind me.

'You again.' I grabbed my winnings and turned round to see Esther being addressed by the security man. 'Under sixteens are not allowed.' To my amazement, Esther conceded.

'OK. I'm going,' she said.

'And you,' he said, pointing at me. I hurried after Esther.

'He chucked me out for leaning on a machine once, and now he's on my case,' said Esther, once we were outside. 'I look sixteen anyway.'

'Oh,' I said.

'It's your fault,' she went on. 'Why did you shout?'

'I won. Look,' I said, holding out my eight pence winnings.

'I shouldn't have brought you,' she said, and went to sit at the top of the slope a few metres away that led down to the sand. It was where the trendy kids with fluorescent socks, body warmers and McDonald's milkshakes sat to smoke. I saw Esther get out a cigarette too and light it. She ignored me, so I stood leaning on the railings next to the pier, looking along the beach at the people and the colours, as the waves stroked the sand with their long fingers, until Esther got up and said, 'Are you coming or what?' and we made our way back through Bournemouth to meet Beatrice and explain about her two-pence pieces.

Esther's Friends

We had come to the end of the Easter holidays and, on 24 April 1984, I was cut out and pinned up, uniformed and ironed, straightened and sprayed down, squeezed and scribbled, and I started my new school. (Esther was in the year above me and she and her friends were superior.) My life changed again. Now it was lessons during the day and the hotel at evenings and weekends. The weather changed too and the days got warmer and bluer.

I tried to make myself as invisible as possible at school and it worked. The teachers were only interested in the bright kids and the naughty kids. Being average and quiet was the best way of avoiding unnecessary attention. I even managed to stay off the register in PE for the whole of the summer term by sitting in the library on the first lesson. Because I was new I got away with it and my name didn't make its way to the PE teacher's list until September. Sometimes in that first term I would turn up for games because I thought I should, and stand in the field breathing in the smell of the grass with the sun on my neck. (I never went when it was raining.) The teacher would look at me oddly and tell me to be referee or to hit tennis balls against the wall or clean out the cupboard where the hockey sticks and javelins were kept. She would ask my name but she'd forget it again the week after, so usually I stayed in the library and did my homework. Handing in work on time was another way of not being noticed.

Esther at school was different from Esther at the hotel. She hung out with her friends at lunch times and sometimes went into the toilets with them to smoke and draw on the walls during history lessons because, she said, the teacher didn't care. She still carried around a bit of the hotel with her, which marked her out from everyone else, but only I could see it. Although she wasn't friendly towards me (sometimes she changed direction if she saw me coming down the corridor and she wouldn't speak to me at lunch time or meet me at 3.30 unless Beatrice was picking us up) there was an understanding amongst the other kids that they wouldn't get me into trouble like they usually did with new girls because Esther had a reputation. Mostly, my classmates left me alone. They said hello, goodbye, how are you, did you see Boy George on *Top of the Pops* last night, I like your hair, but nothing more than that.

Lots of people in my class lived in hotels. We weren't unusual. They carried bits of their hotel with them too. If you touched their sleeve or sat on the edge of their desk you could see a little bit of the things they took around with them – dancing guests and egg on toast and cocktails with umbrellas and washing machines that went round and round all the time. I often gazed at my books in class on the warmest days of the summer term and pretended to be studying hard when really I was trying to read between the pages and pages of empty lines in my exercise books and to see out the other side to the world beyond, wondering what I would become when I was old enough to become something.

Esther always managed to get home from school before me. It was probably because I hung behind in the classroom and packed my bag carefully, not having anyone to go and meet,

100

and I almost always missed the first bus, which was crowded with kids from other schools anyway. According to Esther, there were times when the driver had to stop the bus to intervene in the fights. Esther always got a seat. She would untuck her shirt and push the younger kids out of the way and go and sit upstairs with the girls from her class, where they would talk about Madonna, their mouths all full of bubble gum. She told me that once she wrote 'Esther' in black marker pen on the back of one of the seats, and everyone laughed. I looked for her name on lots of yellow buses after that, but I never found it. The later bus was quieter and cooler because there were fewer people on board. The bus ride and the twenty-minute walk back to the hotel gave me time to think, but it meant that every evening when I walked into the kitchen, threw my bag in a corner and put an apron over my new uniform, Esther was already waiting for me impatiently with a spoon or a table mat in her hand and would greet me with instructions like: 'Do the bread baskets. I thought you'd be back ages ago.' Or: 'Wash up some more forks. I've been back for an hour.'

I hadn't forgotten that I was supposed to be having guitar lessons with Meredith. I remember going one afternoon after school when the hot weather had broken and it felt like a thunderstorm was coming. To get there, I had to take a yellow bus to the town centre, then a red bus. When I went up the stairs to the flat, a boy with blue National Health glasses and brown hair came downstairs with his father behind him, carrying his violin.

'Hello,' said Meredith. Then we had little lemon cakes that Meredith had just taken out of the oven and toast with honey. The cakes were so hot that they burnt our mouths.

'How are you?' Meredith said as she handed me my cup of flowery tea.

I had my mouth full of cake but I answered anyway. 'Esther doesn't like me.'

'Why do you think that?'

'She says things. I like her, though.'

'Good,' said Meredith.

'I brought my camera,' I said, but I kept it inside my bag because I wanted to ask a question first. 'Beatrice said you went to Greenham Common and slept in a sleeping bag. Is it true?' I imagined Meredith in the mouth of a tent, like I had seen on the news.

Meredith looked surprised. 'Yes,' she said, 'that's me in the picture.' I looked at a picture on the mantelpiece, which I hadn't seen last time. Meredith was standing with a few other women. She was wearing a pink hat and had her guitar strapped over her back.

'It was last year,' she said.

'Why did you come back?'

'Well. I would have lost my job with the orchestra if I hadn't.'

'Oh,' I said, but I had another question to ask. 'What was it you wanted to tell me?' I said.

'When?'

'When Beatrice came to pick me up last time.'

'Oh, you remembered.'

'Yes.'

'Something you'll find out when you are older.'

'Tell me now.'

'I can't. Beatrice doesn't want me to.'

'Oh. Is it to do with my mother?'

'No. More tea?' She got up quickly and went into the kitchen with the pot. We drank lots of flower-flavoured tea and then my lesson started. I thought I had upset her by talking about

102

Greenham Common and I was unhappy about pressing my fingers into the guitar strings after that because I was wondering what Meredith's secret thing was. I tried hard to get my hand into the right shape but it didn't work.

'I don't think I want to learn the guitar any more,' I said, taking Meredith's guitar from round my neck.

'This is only your second lesson.' Meredith picked up the guitar and started to pluck at it absent-mindedly. Her fingers moved like sea anemone fingers over the strings and the music sounded pretty, like the sea coming in. She smiled at me.

'Do you want me to call Beatrice to take me home early?' I said. I wasn't sure if I was allowed to stay if I didn't want to play like Meredith.

'Not yet,' said Meredith, leaning her guitar against the sofa. 'Now, what did you do with your camera?'

I pulled my camera from my bag, took it out of its case carefully and showed it to her.

'Can you teach me how to use it?' she said. I got up and went over to the window. I focused the lens on one of the little boats in the harbour, with a sail like an orange flag. It was coming in to port before the rain started. Meredith came over to see what I was looking at. Then I gave her the camera and told her what to do.

'Adjust the aperture and press the black button,' I said, pretending to be an expert. She pressed the black button and took a picture of the sailing boat, with the white water splashing up its sides.

'Let's take some more,' Meredith said, and we took pictures of the harbour until the film ran out and then nearly-summer rain started falling thickly on the windowpane, so we ate more honey on toast, until the butter ran down my chin. After that, Beatrice drove up outside with her windscreen wipers going backwards

103

and forwards. She didn't get out of the car. She beeped her horn like last time.

'Thanks for the lesson,' said Meredith. I felt suddenly pleased that I had taught her something she didn't know. I had even forgotten about Meredith's secret although I remembered it when she opened the door for me. But I decided not to mention it again in case it meant she would get angry with me.

'Bye then,' she said.

'Don't you want to come down and see Beatrice?'

'Another time maybe.'

'Aren't you friends at the moment?'

'We had a bit of an argument.'

'Why don't you make up?'

'Oh, we haven't fallen out really. We're just cooling off.'

'Like cakes?' I said.

'Yes,' she said, and smiled.

The guitar looked at me from the sofa.

'Um. Sorry about the guitar lessons,' I said.

'It's OK. Come and see me again and we'll take some more pictures.'

That night I lay in bed in the attic room and listened to the storm pass overhead and go out to sea. The lightning came through the window and the thunder sounded like an angry giant growling. Eventually the storm blew itself out and I fell asleep, dreaming of giants. By the next morning the sky had been washed clean and blue again and the sun looked new and fresh.

When we were doing breakfasts, Beatrice said she didn't see why I had to keep going to visit when I wasn't learning the guitar any more, but after that, I went to see Meredith quite a lot, because I knew Beatrice was only pretending to be annoyed with me. She started to ask me questions about what Meredith was doing and what she'd said when I got back, like she was missing her.

When I visited in those days, I often saw small musicians, carrying music and instruments in cases, either going down the stairs as I arrived or coming up the stairs as I left: a girl with a long black plait and a handful of piano music or a boy with a serious face and a three-quarter-size violin. A few times I came early while a lesson was in progress and sat and drank camomile tea in the kitchen with music coming through the walls. Once or twice a mum or a dad was there too and I made them tea and we sat and looked at each other in silence whilst the tunes went on next door.

Sometimes Meredith would go away for weeks at a time to countries that I would look up in Beatrice's atlas or the one at school until I could put my thumb on the town where she was staying and find out the names of the rivers nearby. When she came back she brought souvenirs, like pens and sweets and soap, and once a T-Shirt from Marseilles. She would give me presents to give to Beatrice, Grandma Maggie and Esther too, so I knew that she still wanted to be friends with them really, whatever it was she and Beatrice had argued about.

Gradually, I got used to helping out at the hotel. In fact I started to get into a routine and I tried to impress Esther by remembering what to do. Saturdays were always our busiest days. Sometimes we worked from the top of the hotel downwards and sometimes we worked from the bottom of the hotel upwards, depending on who checked out first. My work always had to suffer Esther's inspection afterwards, because I was never as much of a perfectionist as she was. I think she enjoyed hoovering the corners I had missed, just to show me that the hotel still belonged to her, but even so, the old hotel accepted me like I'd always been there. On other days we were often called upon to help with

105

breakfasts or prepare tables for dinner. I began to love the smell of the bathroom in Room Eighteen and the sound of my feet on the stairs as I ran down in the morning, late for cereal duty.

In July my first term at my new school ended in a few weeks when everyone got fed up of studying and we went on trips to galleries and ancient settlements and listened to speakers. Then the summer holidays started and I could spend all my time at the hotel again. Summer that year was made up of hot days on the beach, when I felt that I would melt and turn into a puddle like a melted ice lolly, and other days full of warm rain, when the guests would look out of their windows and sigh. Sometimes we had lunch on the beach and watched the sea stretched out flat like a gigantic pancake in front of us. There were tiny white waves, like unicorns dancing, and the sun was hot on my neck and my face. I thought that maybe I was in a frying pan, being cooked. Some days it was so hot we couldn't do anything. The garden smelt of lavender and bees swam around in the watery air, like lazy synchronised swimmers. The first time I put on my costume and ran down the beach steps and across the sand to the sea, I went in slowly, even though Esther and her friends laughed at me and called me stupid, because the water felt so cold at first against my red-hot legs. Esther ran in fast and dived under the surface. She came up laughing, with her hair flat against her head. If she had her friends with her she usually ignored me. They went off to smoke or to have swimming races while I sat on the bottom step and looked at all the tiny grains of sand stuck to my feet. When I was older, I learnt to run in quickly too, because it always feels beautiful once you have dived underneath and you are swimming through the green water with your eyes closed.

When the summer holidays were over, we went back to school looking neat and tidy, Esther to the fourth year, me to the third. On the first day back, it seemed so exciting to be older and wiser, but I soon found out that we were learning the usual kind of stuff about long shore drift and Shakespeare. To me, school didn't matter as much as the hotel and Esther, Beatrice and Grandma Maggie. Even though Esther didn't want to make friends, I wanted to be with her and find out about her stories. I felt like we had pieces of string tying us together, because we both shared the same secret. We lived at the Water's Edge Hotel. She got annoyed with me when I went to look for her on the beach or in the attic room or in the kitchen when we weren't working. Even though I had no excuse and had to say I don't know when she asked me what I wanted, I started to feel like I wanted to stand in the September rain with her and look up at the sky and let the rain run into the corners of my mouth. I only thought it when I was half in and half out of my head, looking out of the window, or lying on my bed or on the mattresses in Room Fifteen.

I knew it was really autumn on my fourteenth birthday. The air got colder and we put on our jumpers and turned up the heating. Beatrice bought me a big photograph album and the leaves on the trees turned red and brown. A month later it was the end of October and we'd forgotten how the sea and the sky were the same colour blue in the summer, instead of grey, and how hot it was on the beach at lunch time. Our heads were full of rain and clouds like angry fists.

'Your first Hallowe'en at the hotel, Rice,' said Beatrice, and she made pumpkin soup and put a cut-out pumpkin face in the kitchen.

'My grandmother's recipe,' said Beatrice, stirring the soup. We decorated the whole hotel with pumpkins and I took lots of pictures of their strange faces. Beatrice made soup in four giant saucepans so that there would be enough for all the guests. There were hot dogs and onions, chips and beans on the menu.

Next we had Bonfire Night and fireworks by the pier. I used up a whole film trying to take pictures of the sky as it was lit up for a few seconds at a time.

Then the weather got really cold. I went down to the beach one morning in November and it was full of mist that looked like smoke. The sea was flat and cold and the colour of washing-up water. The rain blew horizontally into my face and made it hard to walk. The sand was stony and wrinkled, like it had spent too long in the bath, and there was no one else there. I could stretch out my arms and run along the beach with the wind behind me and nobody would see me. I stood and looked at the place where I had swum in the summer and the bit of beach where I had rubbed myself dry and shaken my hair like a dog. It was like two different places. It was too cold to stay there for long, though, and soon I went back up the steps to the garden and quickly inside to ask Beatrice if I could have some hot chocolate.

On the last day of term, just before Christmas, Esther was going to see *Ghostbusters* with some of her friends. She had been planning it for a couple of weeks and I wanted to go too (although I hadn't told her) because I heard there was green slime and real ghosts and I wanted to know how they caught them. I secretly bought the 'Ghostbusters' single from W H Smith's with my pocket money, and I played it on Esther's record player when she wasn't there. I was very surprised when, on the day of the trip, Esther cornered me in the dining room where I was setting out the seasonal table decorations and asked me if I wanted to come.

'I heard you singing the song when we were doing the bedrooms on Saturday, and I thought you might want to go but you don't have to,' she said.

'Did your mum tell you to invite me?' I said warily.

'Yes,' she said, but I didn't let that put me off.

'OK then, I'll come.'

'Don't embarrass me and don't speak too much.'

'OK.'

'And you can wear my second-best jeans and the jumper I got from Top Shop because you haven't got any nice stuff.'

'OK.'

'I'm doing the mashed potato, so we'll leave after dinner.' One or two guests started to arrive and sit down at the tables. Esther's friends were meeting us at eight at the Wimpy so I had no time to lose. I got rid of the last of the seasonal table decorations and ran upstairs to get ready. In the bath, I thought about the trailer I had seen for the film, where the librarians find a ghost in the library and all the books fly off the shelves, and I wondered if there were any real ghosts in the hotel and how we'd catch them if there were. Then I got dressed in Esther's clothes. It was a nice feeling being inside them. Her jeans and jumper still held her shape and as I slipped in my legs and arms it was like I was getting inside her.

I smelt of lavender bath oil and of Esther when I came downstairs, feeling new and excited. Esther wasn't around but Sandra was sitting in the bar with her feet on a chair, smoking and drinking a tonic water. I had heard Beatrice say to Esther that Sandra was going through a divorce. Her husband worked for the AA, had to wear a yellow jacket all the time and did difficult hours.

'Where's Esther?' I asked her.

'Friends now, are you?' Sandra said, flicking her ash expertly into an ashtray with her nail-varnished fingers.

'I don't know.'

'She's washing up, because I'm resting my back.' Then someone rang the bell in reception. Sandra sighed melodramatically.

'I'll do it if you want,' I said, but she laughed.

'It's OK, love,' she said. She carefully stubbed out her cigarette, got up and made her way slowly behind the reception desk. I stood in the hallway and watched. I still wanted to learn what to do so that I could check in the guests properly.

'We've decided to stay in Bournemouth for another week, but our hotel was fully booked,' the guest was saying. She shifted her handbag on to a different shoulder.

'All right for some,' said Sandra. She picked up the booking card and filled it in as she spoke. 'Twelve A. Double room. En suite without a view. Colour TV.'

'Thank you.'

'Sign here. You want dinner?'

'Yes, please.'

'Tick what you want.' Sandra handed her a menu card.

'Er, can't I choose later?'

'Have it your way, but you'll have to have chicken pie tonight,' said Sandra, taking the card back and putting a tick by 'Chicken pie, sprouts and mashed potatoes'. Storing this lesson in my head to think about later, I went into the kitchen.

'Are we still going?' I said to Esther.

Esther looked at Beatrice accusingly. 'I'm washing up.'

'You look nice, dear. Don't worry, I'll run you both down in a minute,' said Beatrice.

'I'll help,' I said, and picked up a tea towel. Esther didn't speak so we stood in silence, washing and drying, until all the pots were shiny and beautiful again.

'Shall we go then?' Beatrice said, and we went and got into her brown car. Before we got out, Beatrice gave Esther some money for the tickets and for Wimpy.

Esther's friends were already there. There were three of them, all older than me. One had pink and blue eye shadow, one was tall and had bangles like Madonna and one had a denim jacket,

110

with a badge on the back shaped like a heart that said 'True Love' inside it. I suddenly felt like I was too small and Esther's jumper was too big. It was very cold and we stood stamping our feet to keep warm.

'What took you so long?' the tall one said.

'Had to do dinners and washing-up.'

'We've been to the arcade.'

'Yeah. We got chucked out when the security guy caught us by the cigarette machine.'

'He's a fascist.'

'He's probably gay.'

'Why is she wearing your jeans?'

'I said she could.'

'She doesn't say much.'

'What year are you in?' said the pink and blue one, trying to be friendly. I looked at her eyes. They looked like those tropical fish you could get to keep in an aquarium, only maybe they were yellow. All the same, her eyes looked like a fish flicking its tail.

'I'm in the third year. My name is Rice,' I said. I started to say more but the girl in the denim jacket interrupted me.

'Funny name,' she said.

'Come on. Let's go,' said Esther. 'I'm cold.' She didn't like me to be the centre of attention.

We took our burgers and milkshakes into the ABC with us and I laughed and clapped when the Giant Marshmallow Man was defeated and the music played.

Afterwards we went down to the amusements again because they had run out of cigarettes and the friend that looked like Madonna had dared Esther to try the cigarette machine. It was even colder now and we hugged ourselves as we walked through the pleasure gardens to the beach. The fat bare trees might have

111

been Marshmallow Men in the dark and the Christmas lights glowed strangely like monsters' eyes.

'Why can't you do it, anyway?' said Esther, who was walking along in front with her hands in her pockets.

'Because we've already been chucked out once tonight.'

'You've got to give me the money, though, if I do it.'

'OK.'

When we got near to the arcade, Esther and her friends sat on the slope that led down to the beach, still discussing tactics. I went on to the sand to look at the sea. I hadn't been on the beach when it was so dark before and it was hard to tell where the sea ended and the beach started. I could feel the darkness on my face as I went closer and I could just make out the cold white edge of the water, coming up the sand towards me. Then the friend with the denim jacket and the heart came up behind me.

'You've got to be lookout. We can't do it because we've already been seen.'

'OK,' I said, but when I got back to where the others were sitting, Esther was arguing with the pink-and-blue-eyed girl.

'I don't think she should do it, because she hasn't done it before,' said Esther.

'I'll be all right,' I said.

'OK, I'll go with you,' said pink and blue friend, ignoring me, 'but if I get caught you're in trouble.'

'Can I still come?' I said. I was eager to prove myself.

'OK, you can come and watch,' said Esther, 'but don't do anything stupid.'

'I'll put the money in,' she said to her friend. 'You keep a look out for the security man.'

We went in. It was suddenly warm as we went inside, like going into an underground cavern with a fire at the centre and people digging. The cigarette machine was in the middle of the wall

112

next to the change booth. We got there without anyone noticing us. Esther put the money in and pressed 'Benson and Hedges', while the friend with the eye shadow stood against the wall and I watched the coloured lights from the machines flashing. Esther's money fell back out again. 'Sold out' rolled across the small screen at the top in square red letters.

'Shit,' she said. She put the money in again and pressed 'Silk Cut'. This time the machine came to life and a packet of Silk Cut fell into the plastic slot at the bottom. The square red letters said 'Thank you'. Esther put her hand inside. I was still watching the lights and wondering what it would be like to win the jackpot.

'Esther,' said the friend.

'What?'

'The security guard.'

Esther had the cigarettes in her hand. I looked up and saw the security man coming towards us past the change booth.

'Come on,' she said, pulling at my sleeve. The friend had already started to move away quickly through the machines, thinking we were behind her.

'You two. Stop,' said the man.

'Come on,' said Esther again. The security man broke into a run, then Esther ran too and I followed her. We went round the fruit machines and the Wild West simulators, and caught up with her friend.

'Where were you?' she said as we tumbled out into the cold Christmas air and down on to the beach. We looked round. The security man hadn't followed us.

'He doesn't care once you've left,' said Esther, and we made our way back over to the others.

'Oh my God, you must have been fast,' said the tall one.

'It was OK, but she slowed us up,' said Esther, waving in my direction.

'Sorry,' I said, but she ignored me after that. We all sat in silence looking out at the sea, shivering and smoking the Silk Cut. Christmas lights shone down at us from the lampposts that ran all the way along the promenade, and just above our heads a red snowman with 'Merry Xmas' written in curly letters underneath it flicked on and off like it was breathing.

Esther got a crimper and more make-up for Christmas, and I got a new pair of jeans and a Depeche Mode record. Then December 1984 turned into January 1985, which was just as cold, with no presents to look forward to.

Persephone

My name is Persephone and I'm looking out at the night waves as they dip and dive out at sea, but there are no signs yet so I'm still waiting. I'm thinking about a long time ago, when I was taken down into the earth by Hades. When I eventually returned, my mum threw a welcome home party for me, with a banner saying 'Many Happy Returns' on the wall. She gets depressed in the winter so she is glad to have me back. But it was no good, I wanted to be in hell with the one I love. Spring comes round again each year, but I can't wait for autumn. I'm still waiting for a sign, so I'm thinking about the story of Esther and Rice. It is a love story and the story starts like this: there were once two girls who lived in a hotel in Bournemouth, which looked over the beach. From the attic room, where the two girls slept, you could look down on the beach as though it was a map. As the seasons changed from green to gold and hot to cold, one of the girls fell in love with the other one (although that's not all that happened). They had been growing together for nearly fourteen years and they didn't know it. For all that time, they had grown up like bindweed that snaps and oozes white sap and has white flowers like bells and is hard to dig up. Its roots go down deep. In 1984, Rice and Esther's paths crossed like two cats and then they wound around each other's places, starting with the day Esther showed Rice the attic room. Rice grew into the hotel like Alice after she ate the cake. She grew up towards the roof and pressed up against the windows until she was far too big ever really to leave.

The story of Hades and me is a love story too. When we got married, my wedding dress was green. Hades looked deep into my eyes, took my hand and slipped a silver ring on to my finger. Then pink flowers, then a kiss. In the world above, apples turned red, leaves turned brown and children cracked open horse chestnuts. Old men sniffed at the mist clouding the windows and women lit fires and talked about the cold. That was the first autumn. It caught people unawares. It caught folk without a sheepskin to wear, and the sound of the slaughtering of thousands of sheep rang up to the heavens. The blood of the surprised sheep flowed into the earth and through the sand and the clay and dripped sullenly through the ceiling of the cold blue bare-light-bulb room where I was marrying Hades. Months passed on the earth, but time in hell passes slowly. I looked up at Hades with my cat-grey eyes and said 'I will.' There was a sound like glass forming, like a million snowflakes falling, like a tree digging its roots in deeper. That was the first winter.

Every year I rise up from hell in blue frost and snowdrop fields, bringing spring rains with me. I am come into the world as guardian of life and death. My home is on the earth in the spring and summer, when I make the plants grow and the flowers blossom, when I leave Hades, the one I love, down below the earth. My home is in the underworld in autumn and winter when the world turns icy and withered and animals die of the cold.

At eleven o'clock at night on 21 September, the day autumn started in 1984, and two days before Rice's fourteenth birthday, I stood by the water's edge and looked towards the horizon. I saw the gates open. It was a rough sea that day and waves were puffing their chests far out to sea. It's deeper than I am, I thought, then I took off my clothes and stood on the sand for a moment longer before going in, the goose bumps rising on my arms. It would get much colder once I was out there where the waves were breaking in excitement, tumbling over themselves to get to the sand. But because I do this every year I know that when the water washes above my head it is calmer and when I am white-faced and with the fish again and my human eyes are no longer seeing, when I sink into the depths, sand under my toes, it is peaceful and I can no longer feel the cold. Still I always hesitate on the sand with my toes in the water, feeling cold, even though I know it will be lovely once I'm in and floating back to hell. At five past eleven on 21 September 1984, I took a step into the water and I could feel autumn beginning around me. I bit my lip hard against the cold, so hard it started to bleed. I clenched my fists, both hands, drew blood with my fingernails and kept walking.

I spent the autumn in hell, watching. Frosts came, winter began, then December ended and 1985 started. In the world of the dead in January, the leaves turn see-through, like skeletons, and the surface of the river turns from watery grey to ice grey. The shadows breathe in the misty air and it turns to clouds of frost inside them and their spirits turn blue with cold. Once Hades started a fire to try to warm the spirits up, and the ghosts that got too close turned into wisps of smoke or were burnt into piles of dust, depending on what they were made of. Some of the burnt spirits wound their way back up to the earth and hung about in corners or rested on fields or in alleyways and when someone passed through they were filled with a sense of sorrow that burrowed into their hearts like a mole and fell asleep there.

In early 1985, I remember looking up from hell to watch Esther and Rice and I smiled secretly to myself. I was looking forward to spring when I could be back in Bournemouth again, but in February the ground was still hard and unforgiving. From the underworld I could see Rice fall for the Water's Edge Hotel like a sycamore seed, windmilling to the ground. As certain as rain falling in silver blades from a heavy sky or a horse chestnut tree throwing its spiky conkers to the ground, Rice was falling and couldn't stop herself. She felt as if she was sinking to the bottom of the sea with a mouthful of salty water, like a stone that's been thrown over the side of a boat. I looked inside her head once when she was dreaming and saw strange glowing seahorses and sandy-coloured starfish. This is a love story that starts with the words: there was once a girl who sank to the bottom of the deepest ocean. Or maybe it should start: once there was a girl whose mother died, so she went to live in a hotel next to the sea, and when she put her face under the water or her head under her pillow she thought of Esther, who was as beautiful and strange as a seahorse.

Later I watched Rice in Room Fifteen, thinking about what it would be like to kiss someone. When I come back from hell in the spring I miss kissing the soft lips of Hades. Sometimes I kiss my hand and close my eyes to remember what it's like. This is a love story, as I told you, because almost everybody in it wants to kiss someone softly on the lips without breaking away too soon.

When I returned from hell for the first time, I didn't get to kiss Hades goodbye. There is a garden in hell with bright pink flowers. The first time, a gardener was standing by the fountain and he handed me a rough fruit. I tore it open. I hadn't eaten since breakfast. It was a pomegranate. As I tore back the soft flesh, I saw that it had six seeds, which I ate. I saw Hades there for a moment, in the first seed. Then I was surrounded by cold waves, but I didn't turn back, I went on up into the water and let the waves carry me. I thought I had drowned, but when I reached

Bournemouth beach, I realised I hadn't. The buds came out on the trees and the flowers woke up and that was the first spring. The next day, I saw a round green oak tree in bud and watched layers of sky growing dark as clouds passed over the sun and I remembered that whenever light fades, Hades is there. Each time I am in hell I have to eat lots of things that I don't want to eat before I find the one that will send me back to start spring again, but I always eat six tasty pomegranate seeds to remind me of the first time.

The Boy from Liverpool

My name is Rice. One day in January 1985, when breakfast had just finished and Esther was putting her coat on, I suddenly felt brave and went and asked her if I could go into town with her.

'No,' she said.

'Why not?'

'I want to go on my own. Anyway. I'm meeting some people.'

Then Beatrice came out from the dining room. 'Can't you two be friends?' she said.

'No,' said Esther.

'Go into town together. Keep each other company,' said Beatrice.

'Mum!'

'Don't argue, just go.' I smiled to myself and ran upstairs to get my coat. We got on the big yellow bus that stopped at the end of the road. Esther tried to ignore me. She sat on the other side of the bus from me and got off so quickly that I had to run to catch up with her. Then she went quickly through the gardens, passed the bandstand, towards the Pier Approach amusements. When we got there, two of her friends were waiting for her: the pink-and-blue-eye-shadow friend from when we went to *Ghostbusters*, who was called Michelle, and a girl I hadn't seen

120

before who had a pink fringe and a Spandau Ballet T-shirt, who turned out to be called Clare. She must have been from a different school. Esther told me to wait over by the railings. It was a lot colder near the sea and the wind was stronger. I pulled my coat around me for protection. Esther went over to her friends.

'Who's that?' said Clare.

'She lives with us,' said Esther.

'Why?'

'She's OK. She's in the third year at our school,' said Michelle.

'What's her name?'

'Her name's Rice,' said Esther.

'Rice? What, like boiled rice?'

'Shut up, Clare,' said Michelle.

'No. That's just her name,' said Esther.

'Or Rice like pasta, noodles or rice?' said Clare, 'Hey, Pasta, why don't you come and talk to us?'

'My name's Rice,' I said, turning to face her and looking at her steadily with my grey eyes.

'Same thing,' she said, and shrugged.

'Leave her alone, Clare, her mum died,' said Michelle, under her breath. 'Let's go in the arcade.'

'Yeah,' said Esther, 'leave her alone.'

When I heard Esther's friend mention my mother, the back of my hands felt like they had pins and needles in them. I gripped my fists until I left nail marks in the centre of my palms. I wanted to say something but in my head I was fighting between a feeling a bit like eating honey because Esther had stood up for me, just for a second, and a feeling like I was so angry I wanted to kick and punch and scream at all of them, and pull their hair and make them pay for making fun of me. I couldn't speak. Instead I turned round and let the wind blow into my face and make my eyes water so I couldn't tell if I was crying or not. When I turned back round, they had gone into the arcade. The security man, the one who had chased us out before, looked me up and down. This time he was wearing a Frankie Says War T-shirt.

'What are you doing?' he said.

'Nothing.'

'I've seen you in here before, messing around.'

'No. I've never been here before,' I lied.

'It's over sixteens only.'

'I am sixteen,' I lied again, 'and anyway, I'm not inside, am I?'

'Yeah right,' said the man, and went back into the dimly lit interior. I could see the lights flickering and hear the cartoon-style music. Then he spotted Esther and her friends and went over to chuck them out. I decided I didn't care and I turned away again.

When Esther re-emerged she was talking to a boy who had spots and a crucifix and looked like he was attempting to grow a moustache. She told me later that he was on holiday for a week from Liverpool. Michelle and Clare were laughing and Clare stuck her fingers up at the man in the Frankie Says War T-shirt, who didn't see. They went down on to the beach without saying anything to me.

A pleasure boat pulled out from the pier, loaded with tourists. There was a sign next to the amusements that said that it left every forty-five minutes and went to Poole and back. I thought I would like to go on the boat to find out what the beach and sea looked like the other way round and to lean over the side and think about how much water there was underneath us. When the boat was so far away I couldn't see the people's faces, I looked over to where Esther was again. She was kissing the boy with the spots and the crucifix. She did it for quite a long time. I had the angry feeling I had had before and couldn't watch any longer. I wished really hard that I was on the pleasure boat with the other people, but

I wasn't, so I turned and walked back the way we had come. Still thinking about the boy with the crucifix, I got on the bus and went back to the hotel by myself.

When I got home, I went straight to Room Fifteen to think. As I went in, I suddenly noticed how musty it smelt in there – dusty and like old things smell in museums – so I used one of Beatrice's boxes to prop the door open. Then I climbed up and lay on top of the mattresses, thinking about the girl with the pink fringe and Esther kissing the boy. I closed my eyes and I felt like there was a stone inside me that was getting bigger and bigger. Soon it would get so big that I would sink to the bottom of the sea. Then I thought about what it must be like to kiss someone. It must be nice, like standing in the sea with your face in the water or burying your feet in the sand. Or maybe it was a bit like when I took a photo of someone and I felt like I had caught all of them in my lens.

When I opened my eyes, there was someone standing in the doorway of Room Fifteen. I thought for a moment that it might be Esther, come to find me to tell me that she didn't like kissing the boy with the moustache and spots and crucifix and that she wanted to lie on the mattresses and talk to me instead, but it was Beatrice.

'I didn't know you were back. Where's Esther?' Beatrice said.

'Still in town.'

'Sandra's gone home with a headache and I'm doing the rooms. Seeing as you're back you can help me.' Beatrice got the cord she used sometimes for a washing line and strung it from the side of the house to the ivy-covered tree in the corner of the garden by the wall. Then I took some of the big white sheets that wouldn't fit in the tumble dryer and I hung them on the line. The sheets smelt good when I pressed my face into them. They were bigger than me and I could hide behind them with only my feet showing at the bottom. Afterwards I sat down on the edge of one of the raised flowerbeds and looked at the sheets blowing in the wind.

I wanted to ask Esther about the boy with the moustache and the crucifix. I had my chance when we were in the kitchen making dinner. It was fish and chips that evening so we were feeding the potatoes into the potato peeling machine together. They went in dirty and still in their jackets and came out naked and clean, ready for Beatrice to push them through the chip slicer and drop them into the hot fat. Beatrice was at the other end of the kitchen and couldn't hear what we were saying. I dropped five dirty potatoes into the chute at the top of the peeler. After a few seconds, the clean potatoes began to bounce out of the funnel at the bottom and into the red washing-up bowl positioned underneath. Esther scooped them out and into a big metal pot.

'I saw you kissing that boy,' I said.

'So?'

'On the beach.'

'Who cares? He's from Liverpool and he's going home tomorrow.'

Beatrice came over to get more clean potatoes for the chip slicer. I dropped some more in the chute and listened to them rumbling inside the machine like it was a monster's stomach.

'What was it like?' I said when Beatrice had gone.

'What?'

'Kissing the boy from Liverpool.'

'I don't know. Same as it usually is,' Esther said. She was waiting for more potatoes to jump out of the funnel.

'Have you done it before?'

'Of course I have. Why, haven't you?'

'Yeah, loads of times,' I said, adding yet more potatoes from the sack, but I went red and I think I had the soft-sand and putting-your-face-in-the-water feeling when I looked at Esther, and I had to look away. Naked potatoes bounced out of the funnel and into the washing-up bowl unheeded. The chip fat started to spit at the other end of the kitchen.

'Esther, can you do the peas?' called Beatrice, and Esther left me to do the potatoes by myself.

I went to see Meredith that week. She had been in Canada and it was the first time I had seen her since she had come back. It was very cold and the trees were still undressed and made silhouettes against the grey January sky.

'Happy nineteen eighty-five,' she said. I sat down on the sofa. Meredith was looking very glamorous, as usual. She was wearing a white blouse with elastic bits that made it puff up in unexpected places and she had new blue jeans on and brown boots. She had painted her nails purple and she had tiny musical notes in her ears, which she played with when she was listening to me.

'Was it cold in Canada?' I asked.

'Very. This is for you,' she said. She delved into a plastic bag with 'Toronto Airport' on the side of it and handed me a small toy moose with soft antlers. It was dark brown and fitted in the palm of my hand like a kitten. Then she gave me three more to take home with me for the others. One red, one grey and one blue.

'I saw Esther kiss a boy.' I said.

'What was his name?'

'I don't know. He was from Liverpool.'

'Right. A holiday romance, I expect.' I liked the way Meredith said 'a holiday romance', because the letters curled on her tongue. They didn't sound like they did when I read them in *Just Seventeen*.

'Meredith?'

'Yes?'

'Have you got a boyfriend?'

125

Meredith picked up her green scarf and wrapped it around her neck. 'No,' she said.

'Me neither.'

When I said that she put her arm round my shoulders and gave me a little squeeze like she was embarrassed in case I didn't want her to, but I didn't mind. It felt for a minute like I was in the Greenham photo on the mantelpiece with her, because in it she had her arm round her friends.

Mr Muscovado

My name is Persephone. It was such a pleasure to be washed up on the beach at Bournemouth in spring 1985, knowing that I would be able to watch Rice and Esther more closely. Sometimes in the underworld I am distracted from the story by the cries of the dead or the mists that flow over the grey fields by the wide river. Sometimes my vision clouds and the rocks and the water make it hard to see for a couple of days, like a badly tuned TV. Other times Hades looks into my eyes and we kiss each other and wrap our legs around each other and spread our palms on each other's backs. We go into each other and out again and under each other like we are diving under water. We mingle with each other like mist. We use tongues and fingers and crawl all over each other. Then I am consumed, like fire consumes, and I forget. I forget for a few seconds that seem like a hundred years because time is different in the dead world. Sometimes I miss days at a time and I ask one of the watching spirits to retell the story for me, but ghosts are unreliable narrators. They twist every word into a haunting melody and the phrases come out smelling of dust and some of them disappear before I've heard them.

Sometimes I collect stories like rainwater and drink them and then I think I know what has happened because the pages, turned to liquid, swim around my stomach. Water is always dripping through the ceiling of the throne room in Hades' palace. But in the spring I can get closer, and although I miss the sex and I miss my spirit narrators and their melancholy voices, I enjoy being able to hear conversations properly and look through walls again. I enjoyed bumping into Esther outside an upstairs bathroom or meeting Rice in the dining room.

In 1985, I ate three spoonfuls of chocolate ice cream and that was enough to send me spiralling back through fire and rock and clay to Bournemouth beach. It was enough to take me away from the one I love for another season. I arrived in time for Easter again, which was chocolate-flavoured and full of daffodils, and soon turned into day after day of summer. Then suddenly the air turned cold and Rice had her fifteenth birthday and two weeks later I had to return to the dark world once more. From the underworld, I watched Esther teaching Rice the secrets of the hotel and I saw Rice invent a story about Esther that ended in them holding hands and running into the sea together. It was the beginning of Esther's last year at school and she started to think about what she wanted to be, and through the rocks I saw Hallowe'en and Bonfire Night at the Water's Edge Hotel happen as they had always happened.

In 1985, it was forty years since the end of World War Two. I knew because it was on the news and we did it at school. The history teacher drew a picture of all the countries in Europe on the board and what happened to them, and we had to copy it into our books and colour it in and make a key at the bottom of the page. I took a long time colouring. I liked maps. I used to look at atlases all the time when I was younger and I liked finding out about the countries, because before my mum was ill she used to bring home brochures

128

of faraway places from work, so that I could cut out the pictures.

My mother loved books about other countries. I think she felt like climbing inside the pages and tearing through the paper to the lands inside, to get away from the ordinary, ill and let-down world she lived in. She would often lose herself in an Indian cookery book, or fight her way through collections about colourful bazaars, or beautiful costumes. At school, my mother used to tell me, she had read all the atlases, encyclopaedias and cookery books and there weren't enough of them to satisfy her. She was very good at geography lessons, because she could feel the mountains and rivers meandering under her fingers like Braille in the books she read. She learnt places off by heart, and made up romances about them and the cold and hot weather and the people who lived there. When she closed her eyes she saw yellow cloth blowing this way and that in pictures of market places. Sometimes the cloth was pink and green and gold too, but mostly it was yellow.

My mother's pills were yellow too. It seemed like they were too small to make her happy, but they were the right colour. Yellow is the colour for happiness – yellow beaches, yellow sunshine, buttercups. Yellow is the colour for sadness too. Sickness, yellow belly, jaundice. According to my mother, on the day she left school, her geography teacher had smiled widely, her white teeth shining, and said that a travel agency was the obvious choice for her, until she found a husband.

'It's almost an obsession,' she said. 'Good luck.'

Beatrice told me that when she first left school, the travel agent's my mother worked in was quite near the old hotel. After she moved away from Bournemouth, my mother worked for Thomas Cook for a while. She arranged tours and weekend breaks and safaris to places she had never been to for people with lots of money. Because of her job, she got discounts on coach trips to places of national interest, so before she was ill, we went on trips at the weekend. One of the first places we went was to the Natural History Museum in London to look at the dinosaur bones.

My mother never told me who my father was and it had never been any other way, so I accepted it, until I got to school and other people had dads. When I asked her where my dad was, my mother would pick a country and say, 'In Italy, probably,' or, 'In Egypt, probably,' or whatever country came into her head. I had a picture of my father behind my eyes. He was roaming the globe, wearing his big striding leather boots, discovering hidden cities, new delicacies, music and treasures and collecting them all in a sack. Perhaps he would bring his sack back one day and lay it at my mother's feet. Aged seven, sitting on the sofa, looking at *The Times Atlas of the World*, I thought that my mother was proudly tracking his course around the globe in her head and waiting for his return when he would bring her shiny jewels, like stars.

'What was his name?' I asked, when I was old enough to know that people's dads had names. I hadn't really thought of him having a name apart from My Dad until then, just like Suzie was My Mum, until I emerged into the bright stinging light of my ninth year, coming out of childhood and heading towards puberty as surely as a train or maybe a submarine plunging the oceans in search of new sea life.

'I don't remember,' Suzie said.

Once I wondered if she had ever written his name down and I searched through her things but I couldn't find any-thing – no letters, bits of paper, diaries, photos, nothing. My birth certificate said 'UNKNOWN' next to 'Father' in neat capital letters, as if he had always been anonymous, an adventurer, intrepid, striding around the continents, nameless and godlike.

I asked her what his name was so many times that she got annoyed and threw a plate on the floor. It splintered and I found pieces of cheap white china in the carpet for two weeks afterwards.

'Go to Brazil and ask him, because that's where he probably is by now,' she said, the next time I asked her. She took me into the bathroom by the elbow and I remember it being really cold because it was tacked on to the end of the house. She pulled me in there and took me over to the toilet, which was white with a black plastic seat and she pointed into it, to where the bits had stuck around the bowl because it hadn't been cleaned.

'Shit,' she said, 'that's what his name is. Now stop bloody asking me.'

But then, back in the lounge, wanting to return to how it was before and the countries and the fantasy of my father striding around the world, I said, 'Where is he now?' and she sat down in an armchair, beer in one hand, and relented.

'Bolivia, probably,' she said, and smiled at me.

I looked all the places up on my atlas and I marked them with the colour stickers my mother bought from the Co-op in an attempt to make hotpot and stew for the freezer and label the meals for us, Monday, Tuesday, Wednesday. She had seen it on a programme, but she only used them once, so I was allowed to have them and I stuck them in the pages of my atlas. I filled in the dates: 'Glasgow, May 1978', 'Miami, July 1980'.

My mother told me that my father was a cook and that he collected recipes wherever he went in a scrapbook. Sometimes I would imagine what my father's scrapbook looked like and what the recipes would be like from the different places. She had a cookery book called *Dishes from Around the World* which we used to look at together, and before she was ill she cooked spaghetti bolognese so many times that the pages got splattered with red drops of sauce. I had left the cookery book behind at the council house and my atlas as well.

Back in the history lesson, I wrote 'Europe at War' in big letters at the top of the page and I tried to think of a good colour for Belgium out of the ones I had left, but instead I started to think about how old Grandma Maggie would have been in 1945. I did the sums in my history book, so it looked like I was working out a complicated formula and when the history teacher came to look, he told me off for scribbling, even though I had finished colouring in Switzerland with my pink pencil and had put green sea around the coast of Norway and France, with little blue fish and grey waves. After he had gone to tell someone else off, I wrapped my arm around my book so no one could see. I worked out that Grandma Maggie would have been twenty-five and that Beatrice was probably very young, though I wasn't sure how young, because she never talked about how old she was.

Because it was a special anniversary, the army base in a little town outside Bournemouth called Wimborne organised a reunion, and soldiers who had been stationed there came back to visit, to see how the town had changed. They even raised money for people from America who couldn't afford to fly over. Wimborne was quite a few miles away, but we did have one guest staying for the reunion. Early in the year, the army sent Beatrice a cheque for his room. There was an envelope with a crest and a letter on headed paper. Beatrice looked at it for a long time without saying anything.

Winter turned to spring and then to summer and back to autumn. First Esther was fifteen, then it was my turn and after that it was pumpkins and fireworks again. I forgot all about the letter from the army until a cold wind blew around the hotel like we were in the three little pigs, and a frail old man in a brown hat and coat emerged from the frosty weather outside. I remember the day when the American guest arrived very well because I checked him in. I came downstairs one morning, still in my pyjamas, and found him by reception.

'I have a reservation,' he said.

Beatrice, Esther and Sandra were all doing breakfasts. I stood up straight and felt important. At last, it was a chance to check someone in all by myself. I went behind reception and opened the blue book. I knew what to say. I had been watching Sandra, Beatrice and Esther do it and had learnt it off by heart.

'Name?' I said.

'Mr Muscovado.'

'Sorry?'

'M-u-s-c-o-v-a-d-o.'

'How long are you staying?'

'A week,' said Mr Muscovado, taking off his hat, slightly confused by my pyjamaed appearance. 'I have a reservation,' he repeated. He had a soft American accent hidden inside his voice.

'Ah yes, I see. Room Nineteen.' I took the key off the peg. 'Will you be having dinner here?'

'Yes.'

'Please choose your dinners from the menu.' I handed him a card. He examined it as if it were a very difficult choice. Inside I was fizzing with excitement. It was going perfectly. I was getting away with it.

'I don't think I can decide on dinner so early in the morning, I'm afraid,' he said, and handed the card back to me. For a moment I hesitated, then I quickly marked him down for cheese salad and apricots and ice cream every day.

'I'll show you up,' I said, coming out from behind the desk, and I grabbed his bag with such momentum that I think he was worried I was going to make off with it and rifle through the contents. He followed me very slowly up the stairs. Eventually we got to Room Nineteen and I let him in.

'Dinner's at eight and breakfast is at nine or something,' I said, getting it wrong, but I don't think he heard me. He looked like his mind was on other things.

I went into the kitchen. Breakfast was halfway through. Esther was still doing toast and Sandra was washing up the frying pans. I was supposed to be drying.

'Someone arrived,' I announced to the kitchen in general, still feeling important, 'Don't worry, I took care of it.'

'What?' said Esther, turning round.

'Who was it, dear?' said Beatrice.

'Mr Someone-Beginning-with-M, who is American and is in Room Nineteen and is having cheese salad. Don't worry,' I repeated, 'I sorted it out.' I was pleased with myself.

'Must have been a shock for him,' said Sandra, looking me up and down. She laughed her smoker's laugh.

'Oh, it was probably Mr Muscovado,' said Beatrice. 'We had a letter about the reunion.' I looked at Esther to see if she was impressed. I had forgotten that I hadn't got dressed yet. She was staring at me.

'I'm surprised he didn't go back to America again,' she said.

'Go and get yourself dressed, dear,' said Beatrice, 'and then you can come and do the drying-up.' I didn't feel as important any more. I went upstairs and put my Duran Duran T-shirt on and my jeans, and then I did the drying-up and thought about Mr Muscovado. He was grey, I thought, and fragile like he would break if you dropped him. His back was curved round, so that maybe he would turn into a circle one day.

134

That night he turned up while Beatrice was at the cash-and-carry, expecting Italian meatballs and macaroni and egg custard tart when he was down for cheese salad, and Sandra told him that it was a good job Room Three had changed her mind at the last minute.

The next day I went to lie on the mattresses in Room Fifteen and I could smell the books that Beatrice kept in some of the boxes. They were musty and reminded me of libraries and the slimy green ghost in *Ghostbusters*. I had the picture of my mother and me outside the Houses of Parliament with me, because I liked to look at it. Then I decided to find Beatrice's atlas so I got up to go. I was coming out of the door, still clutching the Margaret Thatcher photo, when I saw Mr Muscovado walking slowly along the corridor. He stopped and looked at me and his eyes were like marbles.

'The kettle in my room is broken,' he said.

Eyes like he might take them out, I thought, and practise rolling them along the floor, under doors and into new rooms so he could see people without them knowing. He didn't move. I was standing with the door slightly open so he could see some of the boxes and the junk piled up behind me in Room Fifteen.

'This is where your mum keeps stuff, is it?'

'No. My mum's dead. She doesn't keep her stuff anywhere.'

'Oh, I'm sorry,' he said.

'It's OK.'

'Is that a photograph you're holding?'

'Yes. Er, I'll get you another kettle.' I didn't let him see the picture. I held it next to my chest, where the stone was that might make me sink if it got any bigger.

'Thank you.'

I moved away down the corridor and Mr Muscovado followed close behind me. I had the eerie feeling that I got sometimes

135

before I fell asleep when I opened my eyes for a second and I thought I saw something move, like a small ghost with a tail, over by the window of the attic room.

'Thank you,' he said again, when I gave him the kettle from Room Ten, which had no guests in it that week. 'I must get my coat. I'm going out for a walk before dinner.' He leant too close to my face to say it and in my head I thought of Mr Muscovado talking to the small ghost in the attic room. Maybe he did strange things in his room, like ouija boards that we had a talk about at school in assembly by a vicar. That was when you talked to dead people.

I ran all the way back downstairs and into the kitchen, where Beatrice was starting to cook. I sat down at the table, out of breath.

'What's wrong?' she said, and put her head inside a cupboard and retrieved a saucepan like it was a prize.

'I had to get Mr Muscovado a kettle.'

'The one in Nineteen is broken, is it?'

'Yes,' I said. 'I don't like him.' Beatrice got the red spaghetti measurer off the wall and opened a family-sized packet of spaghetti.

'Don't be silly,' she said, and gave me the Parmesan to grate.

Once the guests were eating their dinner and Esther was going round to each table with the Parmesan cheese, I peered through the swing doors of the kitchen at Mr Muscovado, twisting his spaghetti around his fork. He looked like he was in a different place inside his head and I wondered where. Maybe he was thinking about the dead people he had been talking to.

Meredith wasn't away with the orchestra when Mr Muscovado came to stay. I remembered that she had said that her dad was in the army, so when I went round to see her that week, I spoke to her about the reunion. She was moving a shelf in the kitchen when I got there.

'Help me with this,' she said. 'I thought it would look better over the other side, then I can put my cookery books on it.' I held on to the shelf while she unscrewed it and then we positioned it on the wall above the fridge. Meredith made some holes for the screws and then started to fix the shelf into place, while I pressed it against the wall.

'Are your mum and dad coming to the reunion?' I said.

'No. Hold that end up a bit. What reunion?'

'It's nineteen eighty-five. Forty years since the end of the war,' I said, straightening the left end too much so that Meredith had to stop and go to look at it again from the other side of the room.

'Yes. I suppose it is.' Meredith didn't watch television very much. 'Maybe we should have measured it first. I know,' she said, and she went and rummaged in the cupboard under the sink for her spirit level. She balanced the spirit level on top of the shelf and I watched as the little bubble came to rest in the middle.

'Perfect,' she said. 'Hold it there.'

'Beatrice says that there's a reunion at the army base in Wimborne. She got a letter.'

'I didn't know about it.'

'Oh,' I said. She picked up the screwdriver again and pretended not to care but I thought she might be thinking about it at the same time.

'My parents don't like to think about those things too much,' said Meredith. 'Where's the other screw?' I handed it to her. 'Anyway, my dad wasn't stationed at Wimborne. Beatrice's dad was, though.'

'He killed himself.'

137

'Yes. How do you know that?'

'Esther told me.'

'Oh.'

'There's an old soldier from America staying at the hotel. For the reunion.'

'Really?' She looked a bit worried then, but she carried on fixing the shelf in place until the screw was all the way in.

'Yes. The army paid for him to come because he couldn't afford it.' At last the shelf was in place and we stood back and admired our work. Then I helped Meredith arrange her cookery books along it. We put the extra ones on top of the fridge so there were two rows and then we moved a pot plant there too. It looked very good when we had finished.

'How's Beatrice?' she said.

'OK.'

'Maybe I'll give you a lift back and I can come in and say hello.'

'I thought you weren't friends any more.'

'We just had a bit of an argument.'

'It's been going on for a long time,' I said. I looked at Meredith's left hand resting on the top of a book, which was still on the table, because it was too big for the shelf. It was called *Perfect Pasta Sauces*. She had green nail varnish on today.

'Did you wear nail varnish at Greenham Common or weren't you allowed?'

'Of course we were allowed. I can't remember. Why?'

'I just wondered. Are you and Beatrice going to make up then?'

'I think I should stop being silly and go and talk to her.'

'Good,' I said. So after we had eaten cakes and drunk cups of flowery tea and picked out some of our favourite pasta sauces

138

from the book that was too big for the shelf, Meredith gave me a lift back to the hotel. When we got there, we went into the kitchen round the back way, through the door marked 'Private'. Esther was out with a boy from Manchester, Beatrice was washing up in the kitchen with her back to the door and Sandra was drying. Grandma Maggie was in her wheelchair at the end of the long brown table, with half a sandwich in front of her. She had pickle round her mouth and some of it had fallen down her dress, which had big purple roses on it and looked like it was made out of a curtain.

'That man with the moustache is here again,' she said when she saw us.

'Hello,' said Meredith from the doorway.

'Don't forget to write,' said Grandma Maggie, picking up her sandwich.

'Hello,' said Sandra, turning round. 'Haven't seen you in a while.'

'No,' said Meredith.

'Hello,' said Beatrice, turning round.

'Um, I'll go for a smoke, shall I?' said Sandra, folding up her tea towel.

'OK,' said Beatrice. She was still looking at Meredith. Sandra got down her packet of Embassy Number Ones from the teacup shelf that ran around the walls close to the ceiling.

'Come on, Rice,' she said and she pushed me through the door, even though I wanted to stay and listen to Meredith and Beatrice. Then she went back for Grandma Maggie and wheeled her into the guest lounge where we sat and watched the news. They spent so long talking that Sandra had to go in and ask what Beatrice wanted to do about dinners. She came back to say that Meredith was staying for Proper Dinner and that she had volunteered to help with the lasagne and carrots,

139

which meant I didn't have to. I went and lay on my bed to think about Beatrice and Meredith being friends again instead, until about half-past seven when Esther came in from seeing the boy from Manchester.

'Dinner's nearly finished. My mum wants me to do duvet covers in Rooms Six and Seven.'

'Meredith and Beatrice are friends again,' I said, hoping she didn't know so she would be pleased with me for telling her.

'I know,' she said. 'You have to do soap before Proper Dinner.'

So I slipped off the bed and went to get the soap out of the cupboard. I liked the way the After Eight-size bars were wrapped in white paper and said 'Welcome' in gold letters on the front. I made my way along the first floor and then the second. I had almost finished and was halfway through the fire door at the end of the second-floor corridor when I saw Mr Muscovado going into Room Fifteen. I stopped for a minute, half in and half out of the door. Even though I heard Esther's voice in my head calling me stupid for not finishing the soap, I ran all the way back downstairs anyway. There were no guests left in the dining room. Sandra had gone home and Meredith and Beatrice were sitting in the kitchen, drinking coffee.

'Greece till January,' Meredith was saying as I came in, 'then the world tour. I can't wait.'

'I saw Mr Muscovado,' I said.

'He's not that bad, is he?' said Beatrice. Meredith looked a little uneasy.

'I saw him going into Room Fifteen.'

'Really?' said Meredith.

'He probably just got lost,' said Beatrice.

140

'Maybe he was trying to steal something,' I said.

'Don't be silly,' said Beatrice, 'I haven't got anything worth stealing.' We went upstairs together quickly all the same.

Beatrice opened the door of Room Fifteen and there was Mr Muscovado on his knees, looking through one of her boxes. He had some of Beatrice's black-and-white photos in his hand.

'What are you doing?' said Beatrice.

Mr Muscovado turned his eyes towards her and he looked even older than he had done before, and greyer. I thought he might break in half as he tried to struggle to his feet. Meredith had to help him up and Beatrice dusted off an old chair so that he could sit down.

Just then Esther came down the corridor to tell us that she'd finished the duvets. 'What's going on?' she said.

'Mr Muscovado was looking through Beatrice's things,' I told her.

Beatrice took the photos from his hand. 'Were you going to take these?' she said.

Mr Muscovado still hadn't spoken. He shook his head from side to side so much that I hoped it wouldn't fall off. 'I knew Henry in the war,' he said in a shaky voice.

Beatrice looked at him sharply. 'I thought you might have done,' she said.

'Who's Henry?' I whispered to Esther.

'My granddad, stupid,' she said.

'I don't know very much about my father,' said Beatrice. 'He drowned himself.'

'I know,' said the old man, looking at his hands like they might contain an answer or a secret. They were full of lines like an oak tree.

'I don't even have a picture of him, if that's what you were looking for,' said Beatrice.

Mr Muscovado didn't answer straight away. 'Henry and I were very good friends,' he said at last.

'And?' said Meredith.

'I was looking for some pictures of him and that girl . . .'

'My mother?' said Beatrice in her most solemn voice.

'Margaret,' said Mr Muscovado. He talked about Grandma Maggie like a snake spitting poison from a long distance. I wondered if he had seen the new version of her.

'No one knows what happened for sure,' Meredith said.

'That girl and her mother know,' said Mr Muscovado. Beatrice took a step back and looked at Meredith.

'The people you are talking about can't help you,' said Meredith. 'Margaret Tamarack has dementia. And Mrs Tamarack died years ago. In the seventies.'

Mr Muscovado lowered his head further like he might be a flower that was falling asleep. 'I thought some photos might help me understand,' he said.

'Why don't we go into one of the rooms to talk?' said Meredith.

Beatrice took Mr Muscovado by the arm and led him into Room Seventeen. 'Go and make yourselves a drink, girls,' she said to us, closing the door behind the three of them, so Esther and I had to go down to the kitchen to wait.

I looked into my cup of tea and thought about the questions Beatrice would ask Mr Muscovado about her father. What did he look like? What did his voice sound like? Did he bring Grandma Maggie bunches of flowers?

'Esther,' I said.

'What?'

'Have you ever done a ouija board?'

'No.'

'I think Mr Muscovado talks to dead people.' I was expecting Esther to say I was stupid again but she didn't.

'Why?'

'Because I think he's scary.'

'That doesn't mean he talks to dead people,' she said, but she didn't sound convinced. 'He's just mental, that's all,' she added after a pause.

'Did you snog the boy from Manchester?'

'Yeah.'

'What was it like?'

'Why do you want to know?' she said, and I didn't get a proper answer because then Beatrice and Meredith came downstairs.

Beatrice looked very tired. She sat down and let Meredith warm up our lasagne in the microwave, while Esther went to get Grandma Maggie from the guest lounge. Beatrice looked so far away that we didn't ask what had happened. We ate our dinner in silence.

'The reunion's on Sunday. He's staying till then,' Beatrice said suddenly when we'd all finished and the plates were stacked in the sink. 'It's only a couple of days away.' She still had a couple of the photos from upstairs in her pocket. She took them out and put them on the table. 'Some of the soldiers who were here in the war,' she said.

'That's the garden,' I said, looking out of the kitchen window at the herbs and flowers nodding in the moonlight, and then at the photo, where several soldiers were posed round what looked like a runner bean plant.

'Yes, said Beatrice, 'that's right.'

'I've seen it. It's boring,' said Esther, but she looked all the same. This was the kind of photo that made you look at it – it had magnets inside like Esther did. It made you wish that you could talk to the people, who always stood so still and wouldn't answer any questions. In the other picture, there was a young girl, probably four or five. She had a ribbon in her hair and she was playing with a cat.

'That's Grandma Maggie and my grandmother's cat,' said Beatrice, and she smiled. 'It was taken on the landing outside Room Twenty.' I looked at the present Grandma Maggie and then at the little girl with the ribbons in the photo. I turned the picture over and on the back, in black ink and old-fashioned writing, someone had written 'Margaret and Barnabus 1925'.

'Fancy some ice cream, anyone?' said Beatrice, putting on her bright face again.

'Yes please,' I said.

I looked at the photo of the little girl and the cat called Barnabus. I wanted to go and sit on the landing outside Room Twenty and think myself back to when Grandma Maggie was only five. Maybe I would be able to make them out, still sitting together, waiting for the camera to flash. Maybe, if I looked closely enough, I would see Barnabus the cat start to struggle and wriggle free from Margaret's small hands. Then he would come towards me with his back arched and his tail up, wagging it slowly from side to side and, if he let me, I could stroke his fur and ask him about all the things he had done in his nine cat lives. I could whisper softly to Margaret like I did when she was a baby and I rocked her in the kitchen. I could tell her about Beatrice, who would be her daughter one day, and Esther, who would be her granddaughter, but maybe she wouldn't believe me, so I would pick up Barnabus the cat and put him down next to her again. Although he would struggle when I held him, if Margaret stroked him behind the ears he would stay still until the picture could be taken.

'Eat your ice cream, dear,' said Beatrice, taking the photograph out of my hand and passing me the Iced Magic chocolate sauce that turned hard after you poured it. While we ate our ice cream, Beatrice gazed at the photos like they were magic cards and she was looking for one to tell her what would happen next.

Henry Duffle

My name is Persephone and, in 1985, I watched from the underworld as Mr Muscovado fixed his marble eyes on Beatrice and he told her about her father. Once or twice during his stay, I looked up through the earth as he stood on the edge of the beach where the water meets the sand, looking out to sea for his lost friend.

I watched Mrs Brown in Room Twenty, Meredith packing her suitcase and setting off for Greece and Rice learning to do new important jobs, and then at last it was nearly Christmas once more. Hades and I decorated the palace of the underworld with crystal snowflakes, and a grey spirit sang a song. We held hands and watched the light from the holes in the world above shine down on us like stars. Winter solstice ended and 1986 began, cold and frosty and blue, so I listened to the ghost narrators spinning stories as if they were silk spiders and waited for my time to come again.

My name is Persephone, but when I'm in Hades, I am as small as a particle of ice and as big as the November moon and my name is Queen of Winter. Because I am a queen I know the truth about dead people and I also know the truth about Henry Duffle.

In August 1941 there was no dining room, so the guests ate with us in the kitchen. I remember once, early on in his stay, when Henry Duffle was sitting at the long table, in his army officer's uniform. Margaret came in from the garden to serve up the main course. I had just handed out the bowls of soup and had sat down myself. I looked into Margaret's head. His face was red and green like an apple, Margaret was thinking, as she watched Henry Duffle gulp pea soup from his spoon. He held his bowl under his chin and cast his moustache into it like a fishing net. Then he looked at Margaret for the first time, and the first thing he said to her was, 'More bread.' His eyes were about level with her stomach. She pushed the bread basket towards him. Henry sent out a hand to retrieve more bread, but he didn't raise his eyes to meet hers. They remained fixed halfway down Margaret's body, like they were waiting for orders.

Two days later, I had just finished dusting the windowsill and plumping the cushions in the guest lounge, and was about to go to bed, when Henry Duffle put his hot hand on Margaret's cheek and said, 'You are very pretty.'

'Mr Duffle, would you like a cup of hot chocolate?' said Grace, who didn't see because she had only just come into the room.

'Lieutenant,' said Henry, 'Lieutenant Henry Duffle.' And: 'No, thank you, Mrs Tamarack, I won't.'

I was in my room (Room Five) when Margaret went up to bed. I watched through the walls and ceilings as Henry Duffle made his excuses and followed behind her up the stairs (his room was next to hers) and along the corridor to Room Fifteen. He asked if he could come in. She said no, and he went away, but the next day he asked Margaret to show him what was left of the pier and Grace said, 'Why not?' so they walked along the road and down the hill the long way to the pier. Henry told Margaret about the three miles he had swum in the sea. Another time, Grace let Henry Duffle take Margaret out for a ride in his car and he steered one-handed and put the other on her knee.

He followed her up to her room again on the night after the car ride. I watched through the ceiling. I couldn't interfere as the future was about to unfold and I'm in charge of seasons, not history. When he persisted, she tried to open the door and go in by herself, but he pushed his way in and then forced her on to the bed. He lifted her dress up and Margaret said, 'No, I don't want to,' so he had to hold her arms down on the bed with one hand and undo his trousers with the other. Margaret found herself thinking that Jonathan wouldn't have been able to do that because he only had one hand. The Germans had taken the other one. It was businesslike, Margaret thought, and over in a few minutes.

They had sex five times. The last time, they were in a field on a picnic with Grace and some of the guests. The rest of the group had gone for a walk. They had been left on their own because Margaret told Grace that she wanted to go home and Grace said that the lieutenant would take her and looked at Henry Duffle, who said, 'Certainly, Mrs Tamarack.'

Margaret had nettle stings on her legs and later she had little white bumps and a red rash. Maybe I am a witch like Henry says I am, Margaret thought, and these are the signs.

'You little witch,' said Henry Duffle.

'I'm cold. I want to go home,' Margaret said.

'Not yet,' he said, and he put his hand on her leg. After three weeks, Henry Duffle returned to his base in Wimborne, but five times was enough. Soon Margaret was sick in the mornings and soon she was kept away from people.

At the end of September 1941, Thomas Tamarack came back and Grace told Margaret later that he was her saviour. He stayed for a week and walked around the hotel as if it was an old friend that he had come to see one last time and had to say goodbye to for good. He was right because four months later

148

he was dead. Here in Bournemouth, the gateway to hell is as wide and welcoming as a giant's mouth, although after Thomas Tamarack died Grace didn't know where to look for him. Not many people know where the gateway is, just one or two, those who have lost loved ones to the water, who stand at the water's edge and stare for long enough. Sometimes they catch a glimpse, just under the waves, of the doorway. They can never be sure and often think they are dreaming. Sometimes they wade into the water up to their knees to follow the pathway themselves, and then mostly they turn back, unable to locate the strange entrance that was visible for a moment. After he died, Thomas didn't return as a haunting spirit so Grace didn't see him again for thirty-four years.

'Your father was a hero, Margaret Tamarack,' said Grace, when she had read the telegram very early one morning in January 1942, sitting on the edge of her bed, tears rolling down her face and splashing on to the smart purple bedspread. Margaret put her arm round her mother, leant her head on her shoulder and cried too, and their tears got mixed together. Then Margaret left Grace, went out into the garden, and walked across to the gate at the top of the beach steps. She looked down to where the sea was flinging itself on to the sand and at the barbed wire thrown like gigantic streamers all along the beach.

'To stop the invaders,' Grace had said, and Margaret thought that if her father hadn't really died, as she secretly thought, and was trying to swim home, he would be unhappy when he got back and found the beach reduced to an ugly strip of dirt and concrete blocks and nails and barbed wire blocking his way like the brambles around Sleeping Beauty's palace. When she went back into the kitchen Grace said she was going to make bread and that Margaret could help her with the kneading.

'Something to do with our hands,' said Grace, as though their

149

hands might do something dreadful out of grief otherwise. She tied on her apron and dried her face with the corner of it.

After Thomas Tamarack died Grace started to go to church more often and prayed every evening. One night in May 1943, when Beatrice was a year old, her faith was tested. We were sitting at the long table in the kitchen having dinner when we heard the air-raid siren and we all ran out to the communal shelter in the road and listened to the silence in between the bombs crashing into buildings. There were fifty air raids on Bournemouth in total during the war, but that night was one of the worst (although in November 1940 Robert Louis Stevenson's house was destroyed). Hotels and churches and a school all came down. We climbed out of the shelter, Grace holding Beatrice in her arms, not knowing whether the Water's Edge had been hit, but there it stood, proudly intact, as it did through all of those air raids.

'Because of prayer,' said Grace, and Margaret wondered about all the other people who had been bombed and whether they hadn't prayed hard enough.

Although she never saw the ghost of her father (he was too keen to get to the underworld to stop and say goodbye for a second time), soon the ghost of Henry Duffle came to haunt Margaret, even though he wasn't dead yet. Every time she looked in the mirror, there he was, behind her, the tips of his moustache green with pea soup. Three months after Henry Duffle left, when Margaret had already worked out for herself why her periods weren't coming, Grace took Margaret to the doctor's surgery and the doctor pursed his lips, clasped his hands in front of him as if he was praying and rubbed his thumbs together.

'Mrs Tamarack,' he began, addressing Grace, who was wearing her special hat for the occasion, 'your daughter is pregnant.'

The old hotel was big enough to hide in. Grace was proud. She didn't want people touching Margaret's smooth belly and asking

150

when the wedding was. Grace kept her inside Room Fifteen and defended Margaret as if she was a whole new England grown up on the spot and Grace was the British army on her own beaches. Grace wore the grey maternity dress that she'd made when she was carrying Margaret, so that everyone would think that it was she who was pregnant. 'God blessed Mr Tamarack before he went away to war again,' she said to anyone who would listen.

Margaret was stashed away like Rapunzel because she had let down her hair. Room Fifteen was her home for six whole round and heavy months. She took trips to the bathroom at the end of the second-floor corridor to throw up, kneeling by the side of the bath as if in prayer, or to wash, in the middle of the night, in case somebody saw, Grace said. And although her mother told her not to, Margaret still liked to come downstairs to the kitchen very early each morning when no one was around, to look out at the garden and to eat red and yellow apples, one after the other.

The plan of the hotel, which I held in my head like an internal map, had to change because when people shift from one place to another in their thoughts the places they live in start to mean something different. When Beatrice was just a week old, Grace hired a porter to lift suitcases and boxes up the stairs because of the new life she had to look after. I heard Margaret tell her mother that she didn't like the sloping ceiling in Room Fifteen and she and Beatrice packed up their things (with the help of Grace's temporary porter) and moved into Room Four. She was fed up of seeing Henry Duffle's face in the mirror every morning and Jonathan Kagel's face outside the window every evening, when she drew the curtains tight together. Then Grace said she didn't like heights now she was getting older and moved out of the attic room and into Room One, which was the only room downstairs. She may have made her excuses, but the real reason she moved out was because she had seen one too many ghosts looking at the view and didn't want to be kept awake at night any more. For a few years after that, the attic room was used for storing boxes and odd bits of furniture and Room Fifteen first had soldiers and then guests in it again.

Gradually, I watched Beatrice grow up and find out who her parents were, or rather who they weren't, first her mother, then her father, as though she was in a fairytale with a tower, a wolf and a peasant princess. Over the next few summers Beatrice became part of the hotel, like the rocking chair in Room Ten or the dresser in Room Four. She learnt to call Grace Ma, like Margaret did (only the soldiers called her Mrs Tamarack, touching their hats as they did so) but inside Beatrice's two- and three-year-old head I could see that she wondered a silent thought the shape of a starfish, which she didn't say out loud, about Margaret and Grace and which way round they were.

Aged three, with the war nearly fought out, Beatrice would hold Margaret's hand (she was still disguised as a sister) and as I did the gardening they would walk around the garden smelling the lavender and watching the bees darting in and out. If it was raining, they sometimes stood looking up at the clouds with rain on their faces or they would go inside and play games like jumping down the stairs two at a time. And when they went up to the attic, Beatrice liked to clamber on to a box so she could look down at the beach like a bird. Sometimes I went with them to look at the view.

In 1945, Margaret stood next to Beatrice and Grace in the town centre for the victory celebrations. There was a band playing and Beatrice had a little Union Jack to wave. There was a tall man in a hat in front of them so Margaret couldn't see much. Beatrice couldn't see anything at all. She was too small.

'The war is over,' said Grace, grimly, with her arms folded. 'God save the King.'

152

Margaret stood on tiptoe and watched people dancing, but she didn't dare go to join in. Her mother was wearing her special occasion hat and Beatrice was hopping from foot to foot next to her.

'Hold your sister's hand, Beatrice,' said Grace.

But Beatrice just twisted her hair round her finger and said, 'I want to go home.' She didn't want to hold Margaret's hand today.

'Wave your flag, Beatrice,' said Grace as a dog ran past. 'Your father died in the war.' Beatrice tugged on Margaret's arm and when her pretend sister bent down towards her, I heard her say quietly, 'Did he win any medals?'

'He won lots of medals,' Margaret whispered back. Then she crouched down next to Beatrice and made up a story for her. 'He wore them pinned to his chest when he went out to war. One hundred shiny gold medals. And before the war he used to take me out for ice cream and he said I was his princess. He would have said you were a princess too. If he was here now. And when he got home he was going to take us all up to London to see the King and Queen.' She realised she wasn't whispering any more but she couldn't stop. 'When you go to Buckingham Palace for tea, the King says, "Well Done", and shakes your hand and everyone cheers. And then you have cheese and ham sandwiches and cake.'

'Stop talking rubbish, Margaret,' said Grace. 'We're going home.' And she took Beatrice by the hand and Margaret followed, walking quickly behind them through the crowds.

Beatrice's early childhood, age nothing to age three, had been filled with the noise of soldiers' weary feet coming up the stairs, walking steadily along the landing, and making the floorboards sigh under their weight. Sometimes I was caught in a shower of soldiers pouring down the stairs for lunch as I was coming up, Beatrice behind them, holding Margaret's hand, taking one step at a time in those days. So after the war was over and the soldiers had gone I could see that inside Beatrice's three- and four-year-old head she wondered whether they had crept into the walls or had been packed away in the linen cupboard with the pillowcases, because she couldn't find them anywhere when she looked, and she wondered why she hadn't gone with them to wherever they were. And when she was older and jumping down the stairs two at a time by herself, she still thought she heard them striding down the stairs towards her.

Sometimes I would hear her through the walls, talking to the missing soldiers before she went to sleep, and listening to their footsteps in her head. It was as if she was praying, moving her lips without the sound coming out, and Grace said, 'God is Our Father,' and smiled and said 'Amen' for her, even though she hadn't been talking to God at all.

As soon as Beatrice learnt how the hotel fitted together, she became an adventurer who liked to get to the top of the house and into the attic room by herself. Aged six, Beatrice would get up in the middle of the night, open the door to Room Four and the guests (including me; I wasn't a chambermaid any more) would hear her solemn footsteps outside their doors as she went along the corridor and up the two sets of stairs to the attic room, to stand on a box and look out of the window in the moonlight. Often Margaret would find her daughter curled up on the floor of the attic room in the morning.

'Why not let her sleep in my old bed?' I heard Grace say to her daughter, so the attic became Beatrice's room and she stayed there until 1981 when she gave it to her daughter. In 1981, Maggie started to talk to guests that weren't there, which was why Beatrice built a plasterboard wall down the middle of

Room One. She turned Grace's old room into Room One and Room One A, and she and her mother moved downstairs.

'So I can look after you, Mother,' she said.

Mrs Brown

After the Mr Muscovado incident, Beatrice kept the door to Room Fifteen locked, so if I wanted to go in there to lie on the mattresses, I had to make sure I had a magic key with me. For his remaining two evenings at the hotel, Beatrice sat talking to Mr Muscovado in the bar and wouldn't let anyone else in. When he checked out after the reunion, Beatrice gave Mr Muscovado a peck on the cheek and the picture of the soldiers in the garden. I think that she wrote to him after that. Two years later the picture was returned to us with a note saying that Mr Muscovado had died in his sleep.

A couple of weeks after Mr Muscovado left, near the end of November, I was sitting on the old sofa in the attic room, looking through Esther's record collection (which I still wasn't allowed to do) which now numbered sixty-five. Although I was supposed to be doing towels, I had been distracted by a new Wham! single I hadn't seen before lying on top of the record player. I still only had five or six singles myself, plus the album I got for Christmas, and I kept them under the bed because I was embarrassed that I didn't have many. I liked looking at the pictures on the sleeves of Esther's records because it was calming, like shuffling cards or playing dominoes by myself. I did it quite often when Esther wasn't there. I liked to think about Esther taking the records out and touching the black vinyl surfaces. I knew it was a bad habit but I still did it, like people who leave toenail clippings in the bath, which I thought was horrible and one of the worst things you could do.

I spread the records out on the floor so I could look at them all at once. They covered all the space between the bunk beds and the sofa. I was jealous that Esther had so many and that she could remember the names of all the pop stars. I decided to arrange them so that all the pictures of the same people were together. The ones without faces on I put round the edge. When I'd done that I thought I would arrange them by the colour of the sleeve, which looked very good. I secretly hoped that Esther would catch me and see how beautiful they were and then she might let me look at her records and play them when she was around and maybe we would hang out together and eat ice cream for no reason and it wouldn't be embarrassing to take me to the cinema or the amusements any more. Then I tried to arrange them by type of hairstyle, and I was just standing up to put 'Karma Chameleon' next to 'Like a Virgin' when I trod on 'Prince Charming' by Adam and the Ants and broke it in half, with a snap. I went cold slowly, like someone was pouring cold custard over my head, and sat back down on the sofa again hard.

'You're supposed to be doing the towels down here.' It was Esther shouting up to me from the bottom of the stairs. She had come to find out where I was. 'You haven't done any of them, have you?'

'I'm coming,' I said.

'It only takes me ten minutes to do this floor. What's wrong with you?'

'Nothing.' I thought for a moment, then put the records back together in the right order, with Prince Charming still in its sleeve near the top with the other As. I was careful to leave the pile looking exactly like it had before. I picked out the Wham! single, put it back on top of the record player and ran down the wooden stairs, in time to see Esther heading back to her floor with an armful of towels from the linen cupboard opposite our bathroom.

'I've nearly finished mine,' she said, disappearing down round the bend of the stairs. 'I'm not helping with yours just because you're too lazy.'

I went and got a pile of towels for myself, some green and some white, and went along the right-hand corridor, so I could start with Room Sixteen, as usual. I was so busy thinking about Prince Charming that I broke one of Esther's rules without realising (don't walk into an occupied room without knocking). Though I had seen Beatrice check Mr and Mrs Brown into Room Twenty only a couple of days ago, my head was full of Adam Ant swinging on the chandelier in his video. I walked in without knocking, clutching my last towel.

Mrs Brown gave a little yelp like she had just run over her own cat when she saw me. She was naked and lying on her back on the bed. Her feet were resting on the shoulders of the man on top of her, who I thought I knew from somewhere, but it wasn't Mr Brown. Mr Brown had a beard.

I hadn't ever seen two people in bed together before (though I knew that some people in my class had done it and I felt stupid for not knowing what it was like). I had the cold custard feeling for the second time in fifteen minutes, but instead of retreating I panicked and made a run for the bathroom.

'Sorry,' I said from inside, 'just doing towels.'

'What?' said Mrs Brown. 'Can't you knock?' Then she told the man who wasn't Mr Brown to get off her.

158

'Who's she?' said the man, sounding confused. I placed my clean towels on the edge of the bath.

'I don't bloody know. A chambermaid or something.' I picked up the soggy towels from the floor and wondered what to do next. It was safer inside the bathroom, but I was going to have to go back out to get to the door.

'I know her from somewhere.'

'No you bloody don't. Put some clothes on.'

'Yes I do. Her and her friend. At the Amusements.'

'Put your pants on and shut up.' While the man was looking for his Y-fronts, I ran for the door, wet towels in my arms. It wasn't till later that I remembered who the man was – the security guard from the amusement arcade. (His Frankie T-shirt must have been screwed up on the floor.) Now I was bearer of two secrets, one about sex and Mrs Brown, and the other one about Adam Ant. That evening, I stayed at the long wooden table in the kitchen with my head in my hands.

'What's wrong, Rice?' said Beatrice. But I wouldn't say. 'Are you coming down with something?'

'I don't know. Maybe.'

'She's looking a bit peaky,' said Sandra when she saw me. 'Are you feeling sick?'

'No. I'm OK.' And they left me alone after that. I was still waiting for Esther to find out about the record, and I was scared of meeting Mr and Mrs Brown on the stairs. As I sat at the table, I got them mixed up in my head and thought about Mrs Brown swinging on the chandelier in the pop video and Adam Ant putting his pants on and popping out from behind the attic room door and saying, 'I know her from somewhere.'

When Esther and I went upstairs to bed, I stared guiltily at the record pile. I wanted her to find out about the record so I could tell her about the other secret thing. I thought that maybe having

159

two secrets made me important and I could carry them around with me and remember that no one else knew the whole truth. But at the same time it seemed like I had done the two worst things in the world and maybe Mrs Brown would tell Beatrice not to let me stay at the hotel any more.

The next morning, I was on the toilet in Beatrice's downstairs bathroom when I heard Mrs Brown's voice in reception. Sandra was talking to her. I checked that the door was locked and sat very still and listened.

'We've changed our plans,' said Mrs Brown. 'We're leaving early.'

'Why's that then? I had you booked in till Saturday.'

'Like I said, we've changed our plans.'

'Up to you, I guess.'

Then I heard Mr Brown's voice: 'I'm going up for the bags, then I'll come and settle the bill.'

'Right you are.' I heard Sandra strike her lighter. Beatrice wasn't around so she didn't have to pretend she wasn't smoking behind reception. Mr Brown's footsteps got quieter as he climbed the stairs.

'I should really charge you for the last-minute cancellation, love,' Sandra said after a silence in which I could imagine her inhaling deeply, exhaling, and flicking the pages in the big blue book.

'And maybe you should sort out that young chambermaid of yours before you start overcharging your guests,' Mrs Brown hissed at her.

'What young chambermaid? I'm the only chambermaid. Where's that bloody calculator?'

'The young chambermaid who came into my room yesterday to change the towels.'

'We have to change the towels, love.'

160

'I know that.'

'Everything all right dear?' Mr Brown was back with the cases.

'Yes. I'll go and wait in the car.'

I was listening to Mr Brown pay the bill when Esther banged on the door, making me jump so much that I nearly fell off the toilet.

'Have you got the runs or something? You're supposed to be helping with the breakfast washing-up.' So I flushed the toilet, washed my hands and went back into the kitchen, my ears full of what I had just heard, like they were full of ants. I was frightened Sandra would come and ask me questions. The next time I saw her was when Beatrice came back from the cash-and-carry and they both came into the kitchen while we were finishing off the washing-up.

'Mr and Mrs Brown have checked out early,' Sandra said. 'Something about someone changing their towels.'

'What about it?'

'It wasn't me,' said Esther. 'She did their towels. They were Room Twenty.' She pointed at me.

'Made no sense to me,' said Sandra, while I started to dry an already dry frying pan.

'Oh well. Can't please everybody, I suppose,' Beatrice said with a sigh.

'That's true.'

I had to sit down at the kitchen table because I felt strange. The ants in my ears got worse. What if Mrs Brown came back in later and told Beatrice what had happened? Maybe I could go incognito and get my hair cut or start wearing dresses and I would be so different and so glamorous that Mrs Brown wouldn't recognise me. I looked up. I must have gone white. Sandra, Beatrice and Esther were all staring at me.

161

'Are you feeling sick?' said Sandra. 'Get her a glass of water.'

'What did you do to their towels, Rice?' said Esther.

'Be quiet, Esther,' said Beatrice, sitting down next to me and putting her arm round me. Sandra passed me a glass of water and fanned me with the edge of a tea towel. Esther sat down on the other side of the table with her arms folded.

'Ask her what she did with their towels,' she said. 'I bet she messed it up. I bet she left wet towels on the pillows.'

'I said be quiet, Esther.'

'I broke one of Esther's records and I saw Mrs Brown in bed with a man who wasn't Mr Brown,' I said all in a rush into Beatrice's arm.

'What? Which one?' said Esther.

'"Prince Charming". Adam and the Ants.'

'Oh my God.'

Sandra chuckled to herself. 'No wonder she wanted to check out so quickly,' she said.

'What did you do with it?' said Esther.

'Put it back with the others.'

'I doubt if they'll be back in a hurry,' said Sandra.

'Mum! Say something.'

'Esther, it's OK. Rice will get you another one, won't you, Rice?'

'Yes.'

'I told you not to play with my things.'

'I'm sure it was just an accident. Now, who was the man you saw Mrs Brown with?'

'The security man at the arcade.'

Esther smiled. 'Really?' she said.

My heart jumped for a moment. Suddenly I forgot about the ants and I wanted to impress her more. 'I went in to do their towels. I should have knocked,' I said, warming to my subject, 'and

162

they were having sex. And she said, "Why didn't you knock?" or something, but I changed their towels anyway.'

Sandra laughed again and Beatrice patted my hand.

'It's not your fault. Don't worry,' she said.

'I wonder what Mr Brown thinks,' said Sandra.

Esther put her records in a box with 'Do not touch' written on it and put the box at the bottom of her wardrobe, even though I bought her a replacement with my pocket money. But she didn't call me stupid any more. Starting from the day after Mrs Brown left, she let me play my own records when she was in the room, as long as there was nothing she wanted to listen to first.

Meredith had started to get very busy with the orchestra and she began to go away more and more on tours. At the end of November that year she went to Greece and she didn't get back until after Christmas. I went to see her after school the day before she left. I got off the yellow bus in Bournemouth town centre where the Christmas lights were already on and I got very cold waiting at the stop for the red bus. It was dark and misty. The ground was hard and it would have taken me a long time if I had wanted to dig a tunnel right the way through to Australia. I thought that my hands might turn blue and see-through and crumble away to nothing. Over the road from the bus stop, the trees in the pleasure gardens were bare again and looked like they might be strange ghosts turned to stone by the cold. I was imagining the trees coming to life and moving towards me with their arms in the air still, and thick roots for feet, when the big red bus came, shining its headlights along the road like it was searching for drowned people. Maybe the world is dead, I thought, as I shuffled into my seat on the bus, or maybe it's asleep so it doesn't notice the cold.

'You look freezing,' said Meredith, when I got there.

'I am,' I said, rubbing my nose to warm it up.

'Borrow my jumper,' said Meredith. She threw me a thick red sweater. It smelt of her when I put it on.

'Make yourself a Horlicks,' she said. 'I'm in the middle of packing.' I wanted to tell her about the man with the Frankie T-shirt and Mrs Brown, but I went and made myself a drink and then I climbed on to her bed and watched. I sat on her denim jacket with the badges by mistake.

'Sorry about the mess,' she said. 'Pass me that.' I wriggled off the jacket and handed it to her. 'I'm not nearly ready and we've got an early start,' she said. Her room, which was usually neat, was very untidy, like she had been throwing things about. There were clothes on the floor and on the bed, and hairbrushes and money and make-up. The air smelt nice, like she had been spraying perfume.

'A bit warmer now?' she said.

'Yes.'

'Good.'

'Where are you going first?' I said.

'Thessalonica, then Athens, then Corinth, then Rhodes, then Crete, then home,' she said as she folded up her T-shirts and jumpers.

'Wow,' I said. I wished that I was going too.

'Where's my purple scarf?'

'Here,' I said, fishing it out from under a pillow. She folded up a white shirt neatly and laid it on top of the T-shirts and jumpers.

'I'm glad you're here,' she said. 'You can take some of the things out of the fridge home for Beatrice. Now make yourself useful and stand by the cupboard and pass me things.' So I got off the bed and when Meredith wanted the next thing I found it for her.

'Blue jumper,' said Meredith, 'green trousers. Hairdryer.' We kept going until I felt like we were on the *Generation Game* like Larry Grayson and Isla St Clair.

'Have you seen many people with no clothes on?' I said, looking at all the clothes spread out around the room like butter.

Meredith was on the floor looking under the bed for her comfortable shoes. She stopped, sat up and tipped her head on one side for a bit.

'A few,' she said.

'At Greenham Common?' I said.

She smiled. 'One of them,' she said. 'Why?'

'I saw one of the guests.'

'Really? Which one?' She went back to the shoes.

'Mrs Brown.'

'Was she sunbathing?'

'No. She was in her room with the security man from the amusement arcade who Esther doesn't like because he chucked her out.'

'Really? Didn't he have any clothes on either?'

'No.'

'Right. Found the shoes. Now socks. As many as you can find in that drawer.'

'I went in by mistake. But Beatrice said it wasn't my fault.'

'Well, she's right. They should have locked the door.'

'I was just doing towels.'

'Right.' I passed her all the socks I could find in the drawer, even a bright pink pair and a bright yellow pair that I thought she probably wouldn't want to take to Greece with her.

'Some people in my class have got condoms,' I said.

Meredith got up from the floor and sat on the white wicker chair next to the wardrobe, still holding the socks.

'Why don't you sit down for a minute and tell me about it?' she said, so I sat back on the bed again.

I wondered whether this was the same as the time when she talked to me about my mother and I had a guitar lesson, or

165

whether this was different because no one had died, but I tried to explain anyway.

'We did condoms in biology and the teacher had a stick to roll it on,' I said.

'I guess it all looked a bit different when you went into Room Twenty.'

'I didn't see much. I went into the bathroom.'

'Oh. I see.'

'I haven't slept with anyone even though I'm fifteen.'

'Fifteen's still quite young.'

'I told Esther that I had snogged loads of people, but I haven't.'

'Because Esther kissed the boy from Liverpool?'

'And the boy from Manchester.'

'Well, it's OK. You'll find someone nice.'

'One time, I felt like kissing Esther.'

'Just one time?'

'A couple.'

Meredith looked at me for a while. 'I think that means you care about her a lot,' she said at last.

'It was only a couple of times,' I said. I was worried in case I'd told Meredith too much in one go and I thought maybe she wouldn't want me to come to her flat any more.

'Where are my black jeans?' Meredith said cheerfully after she had sat in the white chair for a while, so then I knew she didn't mind. I got them out for her.

'I think that's it,' she said. 'Finished.' She did up her big green suitcase and carried it to the door. Then we had flowery tea, and when I said goodbye she promised to send us a postcard of Mount Olympus and gave me two carrier bags full of things from the fridge.

I got back to the hotel and put the contents of the bags out on the kitchen table for Beatrice and Esther to see. There was chocolate and yoghurt and something in a tub and mushrooms and eggs and milkshake and I felt like I was on the *Generation Game* again. I sat and looked at all the things and thought about Meredith going to Greece.

She travelled so much for the next year or so that we hardly saw anything of her and I was secretly jealous because I wanted to travel the world too. Each time we got a postcard, Beatrice pinned it up behind reception and I closed my eyes and wished I was there with her.

The weekend after Meredith left, I had taken my camera out into the garden early in the morning, when Esther came out with two cups of tea from the kitchen and handed me one. I was surprised but I didn't say anything.

'What was it like?'

'What?'

'Seeing Mrs Brown and the amusement man with no clothes on?' she said.

'Weird.'

'When you first got here, you took my photo by the tree,' Esther said.

A seagull had just landed on the wall. 'Yes,' I said, lifting the camera to my eye again, and focusing on the seagull.

'It's a good picture,' Esther continued, trying to get my attention away from the seagull and back on her.

'I know.'

'Will you take my picture again?'

'OK,' I said, and I lowered my camera and let the seagull fly away. I smiled at her.

'I'm older now, so it'll be different,' said Esther.

'Where do you want it?'

'On the beach,' Esther said, so we went down the beach steps together and I took pictures of her with the green sea behind her. It was sunny on the beach even though it was winter. First she pretended to be a model, with her arms in the air, and her hair tucked behind her ears. Then she tried out different poses, like she was in *Just Seventeen*. When she got bored, she sat down and took off her shoes and socks.

'I'm going paddling,' she said.

'It looks cold.'

'Take my picture now,' she said, and I did, just as the water broke over her feet. She wrinkled up her face and ran back up the sand and said it was almost like ice. Then she said she wanted me to take some more photos of her in the garden, so we went back up the steps and I snapped her up with my camera until I ran out of film.

'I'm going to get more film,' I said, and went inside. When I eventually came down again, I found Esther hopping impatiently from foot to foot in the kitchen, fiddling with the serviettes.

'Why did you take so long?' said Esther. She had already chosen her next pose: by the oven with a saucepan in her hand. Beatrice and Sandra were doing breakfasts around us and I took some pictures of them as well.

'You two are supposed to be helping,' said Sandra, but Beatrice didn't say anything.

'Now me and Grandma Maggie,' Esther said. For most of the day, Esther and I went round the hotel, and she told me what angle to shoot from. Later we stood in the hotel car park and I tried to get the whole hotel in the viewfinder, but I couldn't and in the end I had to cross the road and stand on the wall of the flats opposite. The hotel filled the frame completely. There was no room for anything else.

'Did you get it all in?' said Esther.

'Yes,' I said. I got through two more reels of film. Esther and

Maggie, Esther and Beatrice, Esther on the beach, Esther in our bedroom. And once Esther and I were back in the attic room, and my camera was back in my suitcase, she interrogated me. She lay on the sofa and I lay on the floor.

'Tell me all about yourself,' she said, fixing her eyes on me. 'I want to know some interesting things about you.'

'I've got long brown hair and grey eyes.'

'I know that already. Tell me something else.'

'I like Depeche Mode and Madonna.'

'Anything else?' said Esther.

'I was born in 1970. No brothers or sisters,' I said.

'Me too,' said Esther.

'I like chocolate and I hate pineapple. I have a mole above my belly button. I don't have a boyfriend. Satisfied?'

'No,' she said, 'I knew most of those things.' We both looked up at the ceiling for a while.

'Tomorrow,' I said, when I'd finished making shapes in my head out of the Artex, 'I'll go to the place in town before school and that way I can get the pictures back by the end of the day.'

'Rice?'

'What?'

'Will you teach me to take pictures?'

'Maybe.'

'And to use the camera? Properly?'

'Will you let me play my records whenever I want and play some of yours?' I tried to sound cool like Madonna when she was interviewed on TV, but my words came out too quickly. Esther thought about it for a second.

'If you'll let me do your hair,' she said.

'You can't cut it,' I said, getting braver.

'Washing and styling?' said Esther. She took the negotiations very seriously. 'And you have to keep it like that, even if you don't like it?'

'OK.'

'All right, you can play records, if you let me do your hair and you teach me how to take pictures.' I smiled and closed my eyes. This was the best thing that could have happened to me in the whole world.

When I got my photos developed this time, I bought a scrapbook to put them in because I had run out of space in my photo albums. Esther got annoyed that I wouldn't let her see them straight away, but I ignored her. I got a magic key and wound my way upstairs, letting Esther follow behind impatiently. When we were sitting on boxes in Room Fifteen, I finally took them out. It was cold and I was wearing one of Beatrice's big jumpers which I could pull down over my knees. I handed the photos to Esther after I had inspected each one, while she sighed impatiently (I wouldn't let her snatch them from me) and rubbed her hands to warm them up. Then we spread them out on our laps so we could look at a few at a time and pick the ones we liked best. We decided that Esther in the kitchen holding a saucepan was the winner.

Once we had looked at them all over and over, Esther begun delving into one of Beatrice's boxes. She came up with three black-and-white photos, like the ones Mr Muscovado had tried to steal.

'This is Grandma Grace and Grandpa Tom outside the hotel. And this is Grandma Maggie and my mum when she was little. Apparently it was illegal to get pregnant if you weren't married in those days,' Esther continued, 'but the pill hadn't been invented. They did have condoms but they were made out of sheep's stomachs or something.' Esther had had the proper sex talk by the nurse in biology and had two leaflets under her mattress, one about AIDS, which was blue with a tombstone on the front of it, and the other about different types of sanitary protection.

'If you get thrush, you have to eat yoghurt,' Esther continued. 'I've got a banana-flavoured condom in my bag. Someone had some at school.'

'Grandma Maggie was very beautiful,' I said, looking at the photo.

'She still is beautiful now,' said Esther, as if she had been let in on the secret of old age. Esther wanted to tell me more about who was related to who, so she told me the story of Grandma Maggie, and how Beatrice was born, and illustrated it with black-and-white pictures. I had heard her tell the story before, because she was fond of it, but I listened with my mouth open all the same.

'In 1941, Grandma Maggie fell in love with a man called Henry Duffle who came to stay at the hotel.' She put down the picture of a young-looking Grandma Maggie, as if she were playing patience. 'He had medals. He was an officer on leave from the army. Or something like that. Anyway he was very important. He was tall and handsome and polished his shoes every day. He and Grandma Maggie, who was very beautiful, fell in love.' She put a photo of the hotel in the 1940s on the floor, next to the twenty-one-year-old Maggie. There were no pictures of Henry Duffle. 'Then Grandma Maggie got pregnant with my mum,' she added quickly. She laid down a picture of Beatrice in her baby clothes.

'What happened?' I said.

'My granddad was very ashamed of getting a girl pregnant outside marriage and he couldn't go back to the army because he was so in love with Grandma Maggie.' She paused for dramatic effect. 'So he drowned himself and left his clothes on the beach. His body was never found.' I soaked up every word. 'It was

171

Grandma Maggie that drove him to it,' she said, and picked up Grandma Maggie's photo as if it were the portrait of an old sweetheart and looked at it in admiration.

'When my mum was born,' said Esther, 'Grandma Grace hid her and Grandma Maggie in one of the rooms away from the guests so no one would know about my mum. Grace told people that my mum was her baby.'

'How do you know?'

'My mum told me.'

'Do you like living at the hotel?' I said.

'Yes,' she said, and I told her one of my secrets.

'I have dreams about my mum sometimes. That she's not really dead.'

Then I looked from one picture to another and realised I was looking at a kind of history. Not history like Charles I having his head cut off in a book, but an ordinary type of history. I suddenly had the crowded feeling I had had before, the feeling that people had occupied the place I was sitting in thousands of times before me, millions maybe, if I counted as far back as the dinosaurs.

'When were the dinosaurs?' I asked Esther. She was older than me and I thought she might know.

'What? I don't know. Look it up in the encyclopaedia.' Then I thought about Mr Muscovado.

'Does Beatrice mind you looking at these?'

'Oh, she doesn't care,' she said, and stuffed the pictures in the box and turned her attention back to the new photos. We carefully glued them into place in my scrapbook, and I didn't say anything else because I was secretly thinking that maybe someone would find our photos one day and say how beautiful we looked.

Later Beatrice called us both into the lounge and showed us a postcard from Meredith from Mount Olympus. 'PS. Haven't seen any monsters yet, Rice!' it said on the bottom. I was pleased that she'd written a bit all for me. Then Beatrice said that she needed to drive over to the other side of town to see someone about some crates of wine glasses, as it was nearly Christmas, and that we would have to handle dinner on our own, because Sandra was having the day off. Esther had never been solely in charge of dinner before and I knew it was a great honour. Esther was going to be the cook and head of the hotel. She puffed her chest up with pride. We both knew this was a test. It was the first time I had been a waitress and if we did well this time, Beatrice would let us do dinners on our own again.

'Stick to the menus on the cards and you'll be fine,' Beatrice said, but I could see in Esther's eyes that she was already planning embellishments to the tomato soup and beef stew and apple pie and peaches, and I was right.

Later, when we were getting ready in the attic room, Esther said she'd do my hair for me if I wanted, with her crimpers.

'Put this towel round your shoulders and sit on the chair,' she said and when I was in position she started lifting long clumps of hair up away from my head.

'What you need is body at the back,' she said, and after she had crimped me furiously, making the room smell of burnt hair, she told me to put on black trousers and a white shirt.

'Why?' I said. I knew I would be cold without a jumper.

'So you look like a waitress.'

'You, Sandra and Beatrice don't wear black and white when you do it.' But she wouldn't listen and told me to get changed anyway and she headed downstairs to find an apron and get things ready. After Beatrice had gone, she took out her can opener and spatula, waved them at me and issued decrees, but I didn't care because that evening I was a waitress for the first time.

'You look nice,' she said, as I made my grand entrance. 'Take this prawn cocktail to Fourteen. He doesn't like soup.' Esther wanted to think that she was the chef and that the beef stew was her own special creation. I let her think it. I let her spoon yoghurt decoratively on to the defrosted apple pie, in between the grand opening of the canned peaches and the plunging of teaspoons into the enormous pot of coffee. Esther took her job very seriously and I relished my time in the kitchen with her.

After that, I began to be promoted to more important jobs. I had only been officially allowed to do bins, toilet rolls, towels and soap before, but now I worked alongside Esther. And even though I had seen Sandra do it, I let her show me how to arrange the cups on the side of the saucers and demonstrate how each room got two coffee sachets, two tea bags, one hot chocolate, four sugars, four milks. We spent our weekends stuffing pillows into pillowcases and thumping them till they lay still on the beds, climbing inside duvet covers and rearranging bedspreads. We squeezed Jif round the baths and bleach down the toilet bowls till our hands were pickled. We sprayed air freshener and arranged ashtrays and smoked secret cigarettes together behind net curtains. I did so well that Beatrice allowed Esther to give me an induction in cooking breakfasts, one week when there were hardly any guests in. I balanced wobbly poached eggs on plates with kippers, while Esther poured water on to tea bags and cooked bacon under the grill for the people who didn't like fish.

After Christmas Day, the year felt as stodgy as toffee pudding and lumpy like custard, and we all wanted to get rid of it. We were waiting for 1986 to start, all clean and new, like an unlaid table. Meredith finally came to visit us again on 2 January. We had cold turkey for lunch and salad and cranberry sauce and we pulled crackers because there were a few left, and told jokes. Then there was leftover Christmas pudding and custard or ice cream. Soon after that Meredith left on a world tour and we didn't see her for ages. I had to look up each place we got a postcard from in Beatrice's atlas again in case I forgot where she was.

Poseidon

Esther took every opportunity to try out new things on my hair. It was her last year at school and she had applied to do hair and beauty at college so I felt like I had to keep my side of the bargain and let her practise. She often experimented on me and I would go to school to be received with either sympathy or envy by my classmates because my hair and face had been subjected to the very latest techniques.

Meanwhile, I was taking my promise seriously and had begun to teach Esther to take photographs, in return for being allowed to play my records. I showed her how to look through the viewfinder and turn the lens this way and that till it focused. I could see she was impressed.

When I was teaching her about perspective and aperture and depth of field, we often went out looking for new and interesting subjects. Late one evening just before winter turned to spring that year, Esther went down to the beach on her own and came back looking excited. She said that she had walked for a mile in the direction of Hengistbury Head.

'Tomorrow morning I'll show you something, if it's still there,' said Esther. 'We'll have to get up early.'

At six o'clock the next morning Esther woke me by shaking my shoulders. It was still dark.

'Come on,' she said, and threw me a jumper. 'Let's go.' So I grabbed my camera and we went through the sleeping hotel out into the cold morning air and down to the beach. We counted the steps, two hundred and seventeen, and stood on the wet sand. The air was cold and we were both breathing steam. I pretended to smoke invisible cigarettes and Esther laughed. Then we sat on the steps smoking the real Benson and Hedges she had brought with her, lit under my jacket after several attempts with matches from the hotel kitchen, and watched the day around us get lighter.

'Look,' said Esther, pointing, and the sky was grey and orange, and stretched across the beach like a painting.

'Beautiful,' I said.

Then Esther said, 'It's down there,' and I followed the direction she pointed. Quite a distance away down the beach was a black shape, too big for a bird – a boat maybe, I thought. Esther got up. 'I'll show you,' she said.

We made our way across the sand, Esther walking quickly in front of me so that I nearly stumbled in my effort to catch up with her. When we were nearer to the black object I began to see what it was. The blackened bulk of a Ford Capri.

'See?' said Esther, as if she had proved that she were the bearer of truth in the face of the lies of the world. Perhaps she was going to perform a miracle. I ran up to take a closer look at the car. There were deep grooves in the sand leading from the promenade from where the car had been pushed. There were no wheels, just bare orange metal where they should have been.

'Did anyone die?' It was the only thing I could think of to say.

'No,' said Esther, oracle-like again.

'How do you know?'

177

'There aren't any bodies.' On closer examination of the car we found this to be true.

'Maybe they took them to the crematorium,' I said.

'They take them to the hospital first. To check that they're dead.'

We went round to the other side. The driver's door had fallen off completely and was lying on the sand. We both stood staring in through the absent door for a minute or so, taking in all the burnt parts on the inside. There was a smell like the bottom of scrambled egg pans. The windscreen had shattered and glass had sprayed out on to the sand, on to the passenger seat and into the insides of the car. The gear stick was burnt like a sausage. The mats and drinks holders had melted, and charred cassettes, out of their boxes, littered the floor. Then we took some pictures of the car and some close-ups of the car door until Esther got bored.

'Try driving it,' she said.

'What?'

'Just pretend anyway.'

I had never driven a car, so this was a test. Without saying anything else, I gave Esther the camera and moved towards the car. First I checked for glass. Then I put a hand out to touch the leathery surface of the driver's seat, thinking it might still be hot. Reassured, I slipped into it, gripped the steering wheel with both hands and turned to Esther.

'Go on,' she said, and raised the camera in front of her face. I put my feet on the pedals and turned the steering wheel this way and that. I could see the sea, grey and cold, through the absent windscreen, crashing up the beach. I was driving into it, under the waves, down to the bottom of the deepest ocean.

'You're doing it wrong,' Esther said, camera back round her neck again. Esther, who had once driven Beatrice's car around the hotel car park, clambered in, sat on the edge of the seat, in between my legs, and grabbed the steering wheel herself.

'You have to hold it steady like this,' she said. I peered round her shoulder. 'And sit upright and look into the distance, so you can see danger before it's too late.' Then she put her hands over my hands and held them tightly so that I could feel how to hold the steering wheel myself. I was cold from the beach wind and the salty air in my face. It was a relief to have Esther pressing me back against the burnt car seat. She warmed me up like a moving blanket.

The rear-view mirror was still attached to the roof of the car and in it I could see a man in a big yellow coat staring straight at us.

'Esther,' I said, in her ear. She was still driving. 'Esther, there's a man.'

Esther jumped out of the car and I followed her, putting my hand on the passenger seat to steady myself as I did so and cutting myself on some broken glass from the windscreen. I turned and saw the man in the big yellow coat talking into a walkie-talkie. I ran after Esther, blood running down my sleeve. I ran so fast in the cold air that my chest hurt. Next time I turned round was because I heard an engine running and I thought the car might have come to life, but it was the man in the yellow coat driving his pick-up truck along the promenade towards the wreckage.

When we were back at the bottom of the steps, we both fell back on to the sand, laughing and coughing. Then I sat and picked the glass out of my hand and shook the sand out of my shoes while Esther smoked two cigarettes – 'To keep yours alight for you,' she said. After that I had a scar in the middle of my hand, like someone had taken a knife and cut a little cross on my palm.

That night I closed my eyes and thought about Esther and

179

me in the burnt car seat and how she smelt next to me and what the leather smelt like. I thought about driving under the sea together and what it would be like to hold my breath with my mouth pressed to Esther's ear and hair. I would swim out of the car door and pull her with me and we would swim back up to the surface together, or maybe we would drive along the sea bed and look at the sand and the fish and the things people throw away in the sea. We would be caught in an air bubble so that we wouldn't have to hold our breath after all. I imagined lots of people in the car with us, then just Esther and me again.

Next I thought about the story my mum had once told me about Esther in the Bible, who became Queen after the old Queen upset the King. The old Queen was having a banquet that lasted a week and wouldn't go and see the King when he called because she was having so much fun. Maybe Esther would be a princess one day, or even a queen. I was nearly asleep. I thought about how Esther could wear a crown and how the new cut on my hand would mean that we would always remember each other. It would have been better if she had a cut on her hand too.

I had seen Esther get undressed lots of times since I had been at the old hotel, because we shared a room together, although usually I turned away embarrassed and lifted my T-shirt off quickly, with my pyjama shirt ready to slip over my head. That night after we had got back from the beach she said she was hot and took off her jeans and T-shirt and walked around the room, and I saw her thin arms and legs and her small breasts in the white bra and knickers Beatrice had bought her from Marks and Spencers.

I closed my eyes and hugged my pillow, thinking about her feet and her toes and how the skin creased when her toes curled as she walked and she shifted her weight from one foot to the other. I thought about sleeping curled around her feet and toes and I fell asleep wondering what it would be like to put my feet on her feet, into her feet and to get inside her, like she was inside me already.

The next day we went back down the steps together to see what was left of the car. The beach was completely different. Nearly spring rain had been falling. The sand was wet, right up to the sloping concrete walls that led up to the promenade. Seaweed had blown in during the night and small pebbles formed ridges at the place where the waves met the sand. We walked along the edge of the sea, hunched against the cold, towards the spot where we had practised our driving the day before, but the car was gone. We found a piece of glass but nothing else. I picked it up silently and put it in my pocket.

When we got back, to cheer ourselves up, we made hot chocolate, climbed the stairs to Room Fifteen and went through the bric-a-brac, looking for interesting objects. Esther said we might be able to take the things we found to the *Antiques Roadshow* and they would turn out to be worth a million pounds.

But before we could find anything valuable, Beatrice opened the door and said: 'I thought I'd find you in here. We're going to have to clear out this room.' We both stared at Beatrice in disbelief but she was being serious.

'Why?' said Esther.

'We can't,' I said.

'We're going to have to,' said Beatrice. 'I've just had another Easter booking.'

'What about Room Twenty?' I said, knowing I would lose the argument. 'You can fit three beds in there.'

Beatrice told me not to be silly. She couldn't ask strangers to share a room. Either she had to cancel the booking or we had to clear out Room Fifteen. She didn't know why she hadn't done it before. So Esther and I spent the rest of the day shifting boxes. Once they were all upstairs, wedged against the wall and ceiling on one side of the attic behind the old brown sofa, I went into the room again and it looked like an empty coffin and felt cold and musty. I thought about all the times I had lain on the mattresses with my camera and I felt sad because it would be different from now on. All the people who had ever been in that room were standing there with me, wondering what it would look like when it was finished.

Beatrice said that it could do with a lick of paint and went off to the DIY shop and told Esther to find the paintbrushes. We both changed into pairs of Beatrice's old dungarees and Esther tied my hair up with a piece of material and said I looked like Madonna and started singing 'Like a Virgin' into her brush, and then she tied her hair up too, so we looked almost the same. When Beatrice returned we had covered up the pink carpet with old newspaper and were ready to start.

'Come on,' said Beatrice, lifting up a paint can, and by the end of the day the old Room Fifteen had gone for ever. We had painted it green and blue. I wondered what Grandma Maggie would think if she could see what we'd done to her old room, but she couldn't get up the stairs any more. Later that week, or maybe it was the next day, we dismantled the single bed in Room Ten and reassembled it in the new room. Then Beatrice found a bedside cabinet and we covered it with a too-big tablecloth to hide the stains, and Beatrice brought in a vase of flowers.

'It's not en suite but it's very cute, don't you think?' she said.

Spring 1986 turned into summer and the air was warm again. Esther took her exams and then suddenly it was the summer holidays. The days were long and hot, and when Esther and I weren't working, or taking pictures, we invented other things to do. We laughed at guests in floral dresses and brown suits. We wandered around the town centre looking for Madonna records. We had pillow fights or sat for long afternoons with my camera in crooked rooms with views of the beach. Once we hired boats and went rowing around the pier. We ran down the steps and covered our feet in wet sand and stood in the sea, but we'd always be back in time to make dinner, before the cleaned and tidied guests filed into the dining room with their beach-fresh children held down with hair gel.

My name is Persephone, and in 1986 I ate avocados and honey and ears of corn and cold plums for three days before I felt myself being pulled back to the surface of the earth. It was the plums that did it in the end. There was so much juice, it ran down my chin and my neck and on to my breasts, and when we ate each other for the last time that winter, Hades told me that my nipples tasted sweet. So 1986 was the year of the plums. I ate them until I felt sick, although once I had to eat porridge and that was much worse. I felt my feet lifting and my head swimming and soon I was heading up to the world above again. When I got back, there was, as always, the story of Esther and Rice and the Water's Edge Hotel, near enough to touch again and in colour. I felt the fresh air on my face that I hadn't tasted for six months and it felt good to be there. I came back from the underworld on the day that Rice and Esther stumbled along the beach together and took photos of a car that had been abandoned. Being a goddess, I know how the car got there because I watched it arrive on the sand, before I came through the gateway to start spring.

Poseidon hates to miss my goodbyes, when I leave the spirit world behind. In March 1986 he was conducting the winds and waves and a thunderstorm somewhere near Cape Wrath on the coast of Scotland. He doesn't have to conduct – usually they get on with it by themselves – but he tries to put in an appearance at least once a year.

He was riding the thunder as if it was a skateboard and sliding down the lightning as if it was a ride in an amusement park when he realised that spring was about to start, so he stole a car and drove down to Bournemouth at lightning speed (it was the quickest way; sea and air are more unreliable). He went so fast and spirited the car through so many houses without people knowing he was there that the car got hotter and hotter and by the time it got to Bournemouth beach, near to the gateway to hell, it caught fire and he had to leave it behind and swim the rest of the way. I was pleased to see him again and shared my cold plums with him before I left, and Hades told him to be more careful next time. Or that's how I think it happened, anyway. Sometimes my mind clouds as though it's full of dust and I can't see one thought in front of another or my hand in front of my face. When I got back, there were Esther and Rice, older and closer to each other, still winding their way round the maze of the love story they were telling each other, which has soft petals in it and scrapbooks and other things that love stories have like hearts and kisses.

I stayed until the end of the summer and watched from my hotel room as Beatrice and Sandra planned specials for Mother's Day, Valentine's Day, May Day, Midsummer's Day and Michaelmas. Rice started to lose track of all the different types of days although she had her special day in September when she was sixteen, and by then Esther had left school. Autumn was late starting that year so, before I went, I followed her on her first day at college. Once she had taken only a few steps inside her new classroom she knew she loved it there. There were diagrams of feet for learning reflexology and charts to help with

184

aromatherapy and massage. There were plastic heads for cutting and boxes of different coloured make-up, and a white coat with buttons for Esther to wear. Soon I had to leave Esther and Rice and Beatrice and Grandma Maggie alone again and descend back into Hades because Hallowe'en was coming and it was time for the trees to turn and for sleet to fall and I would be safer under the earth, buried like a seed, ready to return again in spring.

Suzie, Beatrice and Meredith

It was a relief when the hot days of August ended and we felt the cold air of September on our faces again. Esther started college and then it was my sixteenth birthday. Beatrice said that now Esther had left school, she would pay her a wage to work part time at the hotel. Although I had another year to go, I pointed out that it wasn't fair and Beatrice gave in and said she'd pay me too. Soon the September rain turned into October sleet, and on 29 October that year, just before the Hallowe'en guests checked in, Meredith sent us a postcard from Cairo with a picture of a camel on the front.

'Having fun in Egypt,' it said. 'Have been to see the pyramids. Back at the beginning of November. Love M.'

'November?' said Beatrice. 'That's soon.' We were all very excited about Meredith's return. She phoned and said she was arriving on Saturday the eighth to play at a special concert by Boscombe Pier and she would come and meet us afterwards.

On the morning of 8 November, Esther curled Grandma Maggie's hair with her battered pink rollers and then she inspected my long dark ponytail critically from the front and the back. She already thought of herself as a fully qualified hairstylist.

'We'll have to wash it first,' she said, and I knew I wouldn't be able to make any excuses, so I went down to the second-floor

186

bathroom and knelt on the floor with my head over the bath, while Esther tipped jugs of water over my hair and most of the rest of me. Then she rubbed Beatrice's medicated shampoo into my scalp until it felt like there were ants running all over my head.

'Conditioner?' she said, but all she could find was an old bottle of lavender bath oil and I refused.

'It says you can use it on hair,' she said, pouring cold water over me to show she was annoyed.

'Haven't you got any nice stuff from college?' I said.

'I ran out,' she said. 'We get some more in January.' She let me rub my hair dry with a towel and led me back upstairs to the attic room. Then she took her scissors and snipped off my split ends. I wouldn't let her do anything else with her scissors although on more than one occasion she had tried to persuade me.

'Really, you should let me cut it short on top and leave it long at the back,' she said. 'This is the best I can do for now.' She dried my hair with her hairdryer for a few seconds and took out her yellow and red bottle of mousse and began to work on my fringe. Mousse in the palm of one hand, dryer in the other, she gripped handfuls of hair, held them tightly and then blasted them with hot air.

'Scrunching,' she said, when I asked her what she was doing. She sprayed my fringe with hairspray so it went hard. Then she brushed the rest of my hair and plaited it tightly into a French plait all the way down my back.

'Right, what about your make-up?' she said when she had finished. I was enjoying the attention so I let her paint my face and nails pink and blue. Then I was unveiled and allowed to examine the effects from all angles.

Beatrice had said that we all had to get wrapped up warm to go to the fireworks and to watch Meredith play the cello, because it was frosty outside.

187

'Don't put that on,' Esther said as I got out my brown woolly hat.

'Why not?'

'You'll mess up your hair.' I went to put it on anyway and she grabbed it from me. 'I'll do it,' she said, and she coiled my plait close to my head and pulled my hat over it, leaving my fringe sticking out.

After Esther had done my hair and arranged my hat, we both piled on layer after layer of clothes until we were round and soft like two big balls of wool. Esther was making her usual declarations of truth.

'My mum swings both ways,' she said, as I pulled the hat down hard so that I looked like I had no hair at all.

'What?' It was difficult to hear with wool over my ears.

'My mum swings both ways.'

'Oh.' I only had a vague idea what she meant. I pictured Beatrice swinging from tree to tree above a jungle floor, orange like an orang-utan.

'I don't know why I bothered doing your hair,' Esther said, putting a hat on her own head and wrapping a scarf three times around her neck. 'She kissed Meredith when she was at school.'

'Oh,' I said again, and pulled on my coat, which didn't fit because the extra clothes made me fat, and fished in the pockets for my gloves. 'How do you know?' I tried not to sound interested but secretly I was. This gave things a whole new perspective. Meredith had kissed Beatrice the orang-utan on the lips.

'My mum told me. She doesn't mind talking about it. Ask her. It's true.' Beatrice looked like an unlikely orang-utan to me, but after that I regarded her with a new kind of excitement.

When we came downstairs Grandma Maggie was in her wheelchair, tucked up in a tartan blanket. We went out of the front door and walked along the road to the pier instead

188

of taking the beach steps, because we wanted to get into the best position for seeing Meredith. We knew it would be crowded.

'There she is,' said Esther, as soon as we had pushed Grandma Maggie to the front, and we all waved. Then the orchestra began to play and I could see the lines around Meredith's eyes like tiny riverbeds and her mouth tight with concentration as her big hands drew the bow back and forth. I imagined her kissing Beatrice and wondered whether they both felt different afterwards. I would like to kiss Esther, I thought, and maybe I would be different afterwards. Grandma Maggie had her hands over her ears.

'The fireworks haven't started yet, Mum,' Beatrice said to her mother, but Grandma Maggie couldn't hear her.

After the music, Meredith came out from backstage to find us.

Beatrice was dressed in yellow trousers and a jumper with an orange jacket over the top. Meredith was wearing jeans and a green coat and indigo and mauve stripped scarf. I was dressed in brown and white and Esther was pink and green. Together we were multicoloured, like fireworks ourselves.

'I've got presents for you in the car,' Meredith said after she had hugged us all. She reached into her bag. 'These are for now. Here you are.' She handed us some sparklers. Then the fireworks started and we couldn't talk any more. We lit our sparklers and wrote each other's names. Grandma Maggie kept her hands clasped over her ears the whole way through, even though I wrote 'Margaret' for her and I could see the blue writing dancing in front of her eyes.

'It does her good to get out,' said Beatrice on the way back up the cliff.

It was steep so we all took turns pushing the wheelchair. Esther and I pushed together, one on each handle, but Grandma Maggie,

189

still ear clamped, shouted: 'Go faster, you bloody fool.' Then Meredith and Beatrice took over. They pushed harder, Meredith screwing her face up in effort and Beatrice huffing and puffing like a big yellow and orange horse. Grandma Maggie was lulled back into silence again. When we got back, we had hotdogs, chips and beans.

The next day was Sunday and even though it was very cold, Meredith said we should all go on a trip to Brownsea Island because there were peacocks and red squirrels, and she hadn't been for a long time. Esther had been lots of times and she told me secretly that it was boring, but she came anyway. We all wrapped up like balls of wool again and got into a yellow boat at Poole Quay. Esther trailed her hands in the water and Grandma Maggie sat next to Meredith and ate a ginger biscuit. Her wheelchair had been hauled up the ramp to the boat by the boatman, while a queue of tourists waited impatiently behind us. Beatrice was in her anorak and bobble hat, and was feeling queasy, leaning against the cabin in the middle of the deck. I watched her and thought carefully about the orang-utan. I was being so quiet that when we were halfway across, Meredith asked me if I was all right. I looked into her face for a second, and didn't say anything. Instead, I gazed down at the water, which was flinging itself over the side of the boat, as if it were trying to commit suicide. She squeezed my arm but I didn't respond. I was thinking and the thing I was thinking about was hard to work out.

'The last boat leaves at four o'clock,' the captain said in a loud voice when we all shuffled on to the dock at Brownsea. We wandered round the island under the dark leaves of the pine trees and saw the castle but we didn't see any red squirrels.

Then we sat down at a picnic table and had tuna and sweetcorn sandwiches, crisps, cakes with cherries on, apples and left-over non-alcoholic Hallowe'en punch. I still hadn't said much.

190

'What's wrong, Rice?' said Esther.

'Do you still feel seasick from the boat?' said Meredith, but I didn't answer, so Esther let me have her cherry cake because she thought I was feeling ill. Esther's cures for illness usually involved cake or biscuits.

'It'll make you feel better,' she said.

I took some pictures of the peacocks, then Beatrice and Meredith wanted to go for another walk. I didn't feel like going with them. Esther made cigarette-smoking signs behind her mother's head where she couldn't see, so I knew she wanted to stay behind too. We made our excuses, and when they had gone off into the distance with Grandma Maggie we went over to the tiny patch of sand next to the small brown pier where the boats docked. Behind the beach, there was a row of terraced houses for the people who looked after the island to live in. We walked up and down to keep ourselves warm. Esther lit us both a cigarette and we smoked in silence, blowing the smoke through our teeth. Then we went to sit on the edge of the brown pier to wait for the others.

'What's wrong?' said Esther again.

'What you said about Beatrice and Meredith when they were at school.'

'What's it upsetting you for?'

'No reason.'

'So shut up about it then.'

We sat and watched the yellow boat that would take us home approaching from the far side of the bay.

'Esther?'

'What?'

'Have you ever kissed a girl?'

'No. Of course I haven't.' She thought about it for a moment. 'Meredith's different, anyway. Why? Have you?'

'No.' I pulled my knees up to my chest and hugged them and didn't say anything else about it. Soon the boat that had been only a small yellow dot five minutes ago was pulling in beside us, throwing out its ropes and sounding its horn.

'It's nearly four o'clock,' said Esther. 'Where are they?' But Beatrice, Grandma Maggie and Meredith were nowhere in sight. 'I'll go and tell the man to wait,' said Esther, getting up. 'You go and see if you can find them.'

So I got up too and ran off in the direction of the castle and the peacocks. I stood under the pine trees where the path forked to take you one way or the other way around the island, wondering where to look. It was getting dark and it was even darker under the trees. There was a strong smell of pine needles. My feet and my face were cold and I could see my breath, which was white like frost. Then I saw the three of them, Beatrice, Grandma Maggie and Meredith, under a tree about a hundred metres away down the right-hand path. I ran towards to them.

'It's four o'clock,' I called as I ran. 'The boat's going to leave without us.'

But Beatrice and Meredith didn't turn and say anything in reply. Then I noticed that they were standing in front of one another, holding on to each other's gloved hands. I ran up to them.

'We saw a red squirrel,' said Meredith.

'It's November. Aren't they hibernating?' I said. I had done it at school but I couldn't remember if squirrels stayed awake during winter or not.

'This one wasn't,' said Meredith.

'The boat's going to leave,' I said. They let go hands and smiled and I had the strange feeling I sometimes had like my clothes didn't fit. I thought about the orang-utan again.

'OK,' said Beatrice, 'we're coming.'

192

As we left the island on the yellow boat, we heard the peacocks crying out to each other and they sounded like ghosts. I was glad that we didn't have to stay under the pine trees in the dark, even if Meredith and Beatrice had seen a red squirrel and held hands.

We had to have hotdogs and chips again when we got back because Beatrice had ordered too many. I didn't tell Esther what I had seen. I kept it stored up inside my fists, but I decided to ask Beatrice about the orang-utan thing later.

A couple of evenings after the Brownsea Island trip, I was on cleaning out cupboards when Meredith came over to see us again. Beatrice was up to her elbows in the sink, washing Grandma Maggie's underwear. The curtains on the window were drawn because it was very dark outside. Meredith was wearing a pair of trousers and a shirt she had bought in Japan and was sitting at the kitchen table with her guitar, plucking the strings. Esther was doing bins and soap upstairs.

'Beatrice,' I said.

'Yes.'

'Why don't you wash them in the washing machine?'

Beatrice was wearing green trousers and a brown cardigan. Not orange or furry. She was like an upside down tree, chunky and safe.

'Too delicate. Anyway, washing powder makes her itch,' she said, giving Grandma Maggie's knickers a scrub and lifting them out of the water.

'Oh.' I leant right inside the cupboard I was cleaning.

'Why don't you buy her some new knickers that you can wash in the washing machine?' Meredith said. It sounded like she was teasing her. She put one foot up on the chair so she could balance her guitar better and then she started a new tune. It was slower.

'She likes these,' said Beatrice. She gave Grandma Maggie's

underwear a final squeeze and dumped it on the draining board.

'Why didn't you get married?' I said to Beatrice. Meredith looked at me but she carried on plucking the guitar strings. It sounded nice, like rain falling in a pond, I thought.

'Not everyone gets married,' Meredith said.

'I didn't want to,' Beatrice said quickly. She looked at me in a worried kind of way that I didn't understand, but I had something else to ask. I felt brave now.

'I saw you hold hands on Brownsea Island and Esther said you kissed each other on the lips.' Meredith stopped playing her guitar.

Beatrice looked at her. 'We were very young,' said Beatrice.

'It was my first kiss,' said Meredith.

'And mine,' said Beatrice, half to herself. She smiled her lopsided smile at the big red spaghetti measurer, which was hanging on the wall next to the window. 'Are you shocked?' She looked at me.

'No,' I said, but I was a bit. In my head Beatrice and Meredith swung through the trees in a green jungle.

'I love Beatrice a lot,' said Meredith, putting her fingers on her guitar again.

Beatrice turned back to the sink and pulled out the plug. 'Hot chocolate?' she said.

'Yes, please,' I said, and backed out of the cupboard I was cleaning. I took my hot chocolate into the guest lounge and watched TV with Grandma Maggie.

'Mind that cat,' she said as I went in, but the cat was only in her head. Beatrice and Meredith stayed in the kitchen by themselves for fifteen minutes before they came in and watched *Family Fortunes* with us.

*   *   *

My name is Persephone and I'm still on the sand at Bournemouth beach watching for ghosts. When Beatrice was a teenager, I used to look into her head and I could see what had happened to her. I was there to witness some of it, during the summer seasons. The rest I could watch through the rocks and clay from down below in Hades. I catch up on what I missed by reading her mind patterns, that sing and dance like waterfalls.

In September 1953, just after I went back to Hades for the autumn, and two years after Winston Churchill became Prime Minister for the second time, Beatrice, Meredith and Suzie started a new school together. I watched through the clay and rocks as they got ready for their first day. They were all shiny as pins, washed and scrubbed by proud mothers who thought that they were becoming women now they had sanitary towels with loops and blue knickers and new school uniforms. Throughout their time at school, I kept a careful watch over them (after all, Beatrice was to become guardian of the hotel and keeper of the herald of spring). They were the closest of friends. It was always the three of them and, when I looked into Beatrice's head, I could see she thought it would never be any different. Meredith, who Beatrice thought had a name like laughter, was very clever and had been sent to grammar school early. She was a year younger than her two friends. She was born in Wales and had travelled around a lot in her early childhood because her father was in the army, but they had decided to settle in Dorset.

The old hotel was a silent watcher, like me. It was where they met most frequently. I watched each year from behind a newspaper as they spent the summer holidays together on the beach below the steps, or sitting in the hotel garden. They had sleepovers, and I would listen to Grandma Grace tell them stories about the ghosts she had seen or about guests who had been strange or suspicious, while Maggie cooked hot dinners and made the kitchen smell of boiled potatoes.

On Saturdays, if Beatrice had to help with the cleaning, I would sometimes come downstairs to see the others standing at the front door, complaining, until they were roped in to help too, and I'd watch Meredith set to work, duster in hand, and Suzie lie on the beds after Beatrice had made them and talk about being a film star and travelling to different countries. Then Suzie would clean the windows and mirrors in every room till they shone, but she wouldn't do pillowcases because the feathers made her sneeze, or bathrooms, because they were full of 'other people's hair and muck'. The three schoolgirls (who were young women by now) stayed best friends until 1970 when Suzie and Beatrice fell out so badly that they lost contact with each other.

I could tell that Beatrice thought Meredith was very beautiful from the moment she saw her. She thought Meredith was like a princess. Meredith didn't care what anyone thought of her. They spent a lot of time in the sea. Often when Suzie didn't want to come with them, they would leave her sitting lazily in the hotel garden, and go down the steps to swim up and down, riding the waves and ducking under them, shocked by the salt water in their mouths. When I look into Beatrice's memories I can see that once, in the summer after Beatrice was fourteen, Meredith held Beatrice's hand as they went running into the sea and Beatrice felt her run through her body like an electric shock. She looked at her friend in surprise but she didn't say anything. Later, when they were changing out of their bathing suits, she saw how round Meredith's breasts were getting and she hid under her towel in embarrassment, because hers were still small as frightened mice. That year, on Christmas Eve 1956, eleven months before Laika the dog was shot into space on board Sputnik II, Meredith kissed Beatrice on the lips at the bottom of the beach steps. They thought no one was watching.

In 1963 Valentina Tereshkova became the first woman to go up in a space ship. All the while Margaret was cooking dinner for the guests and then, three years later, Grace Tamarack bought a television for the guest lounge.

'In time for the World Cup final,' I heard her say to Margaret, and she hung a Union Jack up on the wall behind the new television. She was taking an interest in the World Cup now that England were doing so well.

Grace had just hired a chef, because it was too much for Margaret on her own, she said. He was called Timothy Mackintosh and he had a wonderful flick of the whisk and made pancakes so light that Grace said they melted on her tongue when she tried them. Everyone was watching the cup final in the guest lounge (I was there too) when Timothy Mackintosh came in and sat next to Beatrice. When England won, we all stood up and cheered and Timothy Mackintosh lifted Beatrice off her feet and into the air. Afterwards, he got out his new camera and took a photo of the guests with their flags, although I made my excuses because I don't like having my picture taken. I heard Grace tell Margaret later that she thought the television was a great success. On the next Saturday after that, Timothy cooked Beatrice her favourite dishes when she had finished work for the day (I watched through the ceiling from my room) and kissed her on the lips, while she sat at the long wooden table in the kitchen. Then he told Beatrice all about the recipes he liked to cook and spoke to her in bits of different languages, which he'd picked up on trains and in bus stations.

Timothy Mackintosh was good with herbs and spices. He and Beatrice Tamarack were sweethearts from 1966 to 1970. Beatrice thought she was in love with Timothy Mackintosh, even though

197

he believed in alternative ways of living. Timothy Mackintosh was an artist and a traveller as well as a cook. He had been to Iceland and Mexico, and right round the world twice in different directions, collecting recipes wherever he went, and working in restaurants to pay his way. He was chef-ing in Bournemouth to raise money for his next trip, he said. He thought he was a knight in shining armour and sandals coming home from battle, and he liked Beatrice to wear flowing dresses so that she could be his lady and he could wear her colours on his lance and his shield. Each summer I heard him say that next year he would set off around the world again and then suddenly he did.

Esther was a month old when he left. When I look into Esther's head now, I can see that she still thinks of him in watercolour memories made up from the bedtime stories Beatrice told her, in which Timothy Mackintosh always played the hero. He had long brown hair, blue eyes and a beard. His voice was musical. Once his paintings were exhibited in London. Beatrice went with him to the opening and drank champagne and orange juice.

'He was a very good cook,' Beatrice told Esther, 'because he had been to so many different countries.'

'Where did Timothy Mackintosh go?' Esther would say just before it was time to sleep and Beatrice stopped being the storyteller and turned into Beatrice the mother again.

'Don't ask so many questions,' she said in reply, turning out the light.

Before Esther was born, I often overheard them talking about children up in the attic room where they slept. I listened with my ear to the wall. Although Timothy Mackintosh liked to sleep with as many women as possible, and sometimes he was gone for days at a time, he wanted Beatrice to have his baby, because, he said, she was his special one. But she wasn't so sure. The thought of giving birth scared her to death, but she didn't tell him. I heard her tell Meredith that she had signed up for the pill instead.

'Why aren't you pregnant?' said Timothy to her once.

'I don't want to have children yet,' she said.

'Don't be silly, all women want to have children.' He played with her nose.

'Stop it, Tim.'

'We've been trying hard enough.'

'When the time's right, it'll happen,' Beatrice said. I think she was trying to sound mother-like and holy. It worked.

'There's no need to put on a brave face,' he said. 'I know you want a kid just as much as I do. We'll keep on trying.'

'OK.'

'OK.' He kissed her and I could tell that she felt a thrill running up her spine at the mischief she had got away with.

On 21 July 1969, the day Neil Armstrong landed on the moon, Grandma Grace got sick and took to her bed, and a month later Timothy, Beatrice, Meredith and Suzie went to a music festival on the Isle of Wight. They all went over on the ferry, with beads round their necks and flowers in their hair. I went too and pitched my tent next to theirs. I wore dark glasses and a poncho and stayed out of sight, making bracelets out of multicoloured cotton most of the time, although once I heard Meredith say: 'Isn't that one of the guests from the hotel?' But before Beatrice could look closely I was gone back under canvas. Beatrice, Meredith and Suzie brought bags of clothes and a guitar and Timothy Mackintosh brought his camera and hash cakes and acid, and they tripped their way through the weekend. Beatrice danced topless one night and he was too high to notice, or maybe he was too busy taking photos of his favourite bands and showing Suzie how to use his camera.

Acid messes with your head enough to make you forget to

take the pill. Timothy came into the tent in the dark. Beatrice heard the zip of the tent but she couldn't see him. She could feel him, though, and smell him above her and she was tripped out and stuffed up and Esther was begun inside her.

'Better get married before it's too late,' I heard Grandma Grace say, when they told her the news. She was sitting up in bed, her arms folded grimly under her bosom, and I was watching from the dining room.

'Too late for what?' said Timothy Mackintosh. 'Of course we're not getting married.' Grandma Grace lay down again and turned her back to him. 'I knew it was a mistake taking you on, Timothy Mackintosh.'

'But I'm such a good cook,' he said, and patted Beatrice's stomach.

'Make sure it's a biblical name,' Grace said.

'Esther is pretty,' said Beatrice, in Poole General Hospital, after her baby was born, on 10 May 1970. She smiled into Esther's new face. It was five days after Beatrice's twenty-eighth birthday. Esther was a few weeks early. Beatrice told me all about it when I went to see them on the maternity ward with a bunch of flowers.

For a month after Esther came, the three of them lived together in the attic room on the top floor and when Beatrice wasn't cleaning rooms, and he wasn't cooking, Beatrice and Timothy smoked marijuana in a pipe and stroked each other's hair, but in June 1970, Timothy dumped Beatrice high and dry on an island, like Ariadne. He told her he was coming back, but he never did. I think he was scared that Esther and Beatrice would eat him up and his life would end there as a chef in the Water's Edge with the baby girl he had wanted so much that he used to cry out for her in his sleep.

After he left, Beatrice crept further inside the hotel to get over

200

him, turned into a spider, spun a web around herself. For a while, she was vicious, poisonous, with eight legs and a hundred eyes roaming around the hotel into every room, and Esther developed arachnophobia because her mother was forever being spider-like and angry.

For a year and a day after he left, Beatrice remembered Timothy Mackintosh every morning when his brown hair and blue eyes weren't on the pillow next to her, and every evening when she looked into Grandma Grace's crisscross-wrinkled face, as she brought in hot chocolate, and watched her slurping from the cup, painting herself a chocolate moustache.

Later that year, Suzie had a baby girl and called her Rice. Beatrice didn't go to see her, though Meredith did, and she came to tell Beatrice that Suzie's daughter smelt as lovely as new bread.

Beatrice saw Suzie again only once, at Sandra's wedding, in 1973. (I secured myself an invitation too.) Sandra didn't see why she should give up chambermaiding after she got married. Maggie had caused a stir by agreeing with her and saying that she could keep her job, because, after all, she knew the Water's Edge better than anyone. (Maggie didn't know about me and my disguises.)

The congregation was full of the small history of the hotel, some of the favourite guests and the people from Sandra's life. Grace had got out of her bed for the occasion and had a blanket over her knees and two walking sticks to lean on when she walked. She had her hat on and was sitting next to Maggie. It was a Church of England wedding and Grace was smiling at the vicar, keeping her opinions on believers' baptism hidden under her skirt for the occasion. Her dress was voluptuous like her face. She had enjoyed discussing the flowers and commenting on the candles, acting as the bride's mother, because Sandra's mum had died when her

201

hotel was bombed in the war. She had to do something to help, Grace said, because she had known the poor woman before the bombs came. On the other side of Grace was Meredith. She had claimed political objection on account of her feminism, but she had come none the less and was scowling at Grandma Grace, who turned to her before the service began and told her to read Genesis chapter two and find herself a husband.

There was Beatrice, hippie child, hair plaited down her back, feet in sandals. Next to her was Esther, three years old, a miniature of her mother, with a curled nose, her brown hair in a plait. Esther was hopping from foot to foot, touching her nose with her tongue, twisting her hair in her fingers, swinging her arms and flicking the pages of the hymn books. Rice and Suzie were on the other side of the church.

I could see inside Beatrice's head that she wasn't concentrating on the wedding service. She was thinking about 1966, the year she first met Timothy Mackintosh. Sandra was walking down the aisle but Beatrice was daydreaming about blue eyes and brown hair, and the last time she had been to this church, when one of the regular guests had a baby and wanted to have it christened in Bournemouth. Esther hadn't been christened, because she was born out of wedlock and because her father was a non-believer, although Timothy Mackintosh had come with her to the christening service in 1966, as it was just after they had got together and they couldn't bear to be parted from one another. When I looked into Beatrice's head, I could see that Timothy was wearing a gleaming white suit for the occasion. White flares, white jacket, white shirt.

'Listen to the words of the Lord,' the vicar at the 1966 christning had said. '"Unless a person is born again he cannot ever see the kingdom of God."' Then he had tipped water over the baby's head and said its name – Beatrice couldn't remember

202

what it was called, or even if it was a boy or a girl come to that –
'Something something, I baptise you in the Name of the Father,
and of the Son and of the Holy Ghost. Amen.'

'Living in sin?' the 1966 vicar had said to Timothy and Beatrice
as they left the church and he had frowned at them. But Timothy
Mackintosh had taken the vicar's hand, bowed slightly, and
smiled his most gentlemanly smile.

That was the last time. Back at Sandra's wedding in 1973,
the vicar was different and now the vows were spoken and the
service was over. The bride was leaving the church full of smiles
and confetti. Esther could not wait to dive out of the church
after Sandra. The pagan that was growing inside her could not
bear it any longer. She ran headfirst through the doors, nearly
knocking over the vicar, out into the sunlight.

Sandra didn't want the reception at the hotel, although Maggie
had offered. She said it wasn't romantic enough, seeing as she
worked there, and she had the reception in The King's Head in
the little village of Corfe Castle. There was a sit-down dinner
at tables. It was mushrooms in filo baskets, followed by boeuf
orange and lemon torte.

'Just because it's in French doesn't mean it's not out of a
packet,' Grace said to Maggie in a loud voice that made Sandra
laugh into her champagne. Beatrice and Meredith were on a
separate table from Suzie.

'I don't want any trouble between you two,' Sandra had said
to Beatrice when she had shown her the seating plan.

Beatrice looked sadly over to where Rice was sitting on Suzie's
lap, and thought about how the three of them, Meredith, Beatrice
and Suzie, had sat in the hotel garden together when they
were teenagers. Meredith went to speak to her, but Beatrice
refused.

'She's moving Up North,' Meredith said to Beatrice as she sat down again for the cheese and biscuits. But to Beatrice that could have been so many different places, because from Bournemouth, almost everywhere was Up North.

Daniel and Joshua

Esther hadn't been herself through most of the autumn, which I put down to her starting college and having a lot of work to do. It was a while before I found out the real reason.

She started to smile a bit more at the beginning of the Christmas holidays, because all the rooms were full and there was lots of special food to cook and the Christmas tree was set up in the corner of the hallway. Then Beatrice said that everyone, including the guests, had to get dressed up on Christmas Eve for dinner. Even though we had done all our Christmas shopping, Beatrice gave us some money as early presents so on the twenty-fourth Esther and I went out to look for something to wear that evening. We climbed up the hill that winds past Bournemouth town centre and went into John Menzies and Our Price. Then we wandered around the huddles of winter tourists, looking in the clothes shop windows.

'That's nice,' I said, pointing to a shop dummy wearing a red dress, standing next to a man dummy in a tuxedo. Underneath the display it said on a small sign that was decorated with holly: 'Perfect for Christmas'. 'I wonder how much it is.'

'A lot, probably,' said Esther. She wasn't showing much interest. She was daydreaming again.

'What are you going to wear?' I asked.

'I don't know,' she said. For the rest of the morning, the two of us sloped around the shops, eyeing up shop assistants, feeling skirts in Dorothy Perkins and comparing bags in Debenhams, but in the end I went back and bought a red dress and Esther bought some white trousers as well as another pair of very sharp hair scissors for college. When we got back we tried on our new clothes again.

'Do they suit me?' she said anxiously, looking at herself in the mirror.

'Yes. What do you think of the dress?'

'Lovely,' said Esther, without really looking. She was trying on tops to go with her trousers.

'Will you do my hair?' I said.

'OK,' she said after a pause, 'in a minute.' She turned her back and began to rummage through a college folder that said 'The Anatomy of the Face' on it in black letters. She had drawn cartoon flowers and stars on the front and a love heart with E 4 D inside, with crosses for kisses. I wondered who D was. She sat down on the brown sofa and began to study two bits of paper she'd found in the folder. One of them was a diagram of the skin and the muscles of the face. She began to mutter something about the epidermis.

'Is that homework?' I said.

'No, it's independent study. You don't get homework at college.'

'Oh.' She held up the second piece of paper, which was a picture of a woman's face with instructions for how to do the make-up and hair.

'Can I do this on you?' she said, cheering up a bit.

'OK,' I said, 'if you think it will look all right.' So I sat down and Esther brushed my hair and wound it about my head and pinned it until I felt like a princess. She followed the picture very carefully and applied brown and white eye shadow and blusher and pink lipstick. I looked like the wind had changed and my face had stuck. Then she went and found my camera and took my photo.

'We have to have evidence to prove that we did it,' she said, and after the photo she did her face to match mine.

'I didn't know hair and beauty was so hard,' I said, looking at the picture Esther was following.

'There's a lot to learn,' she said seriously. 'We've got a massage and reflexology exam as well.

'We're both ready now,' she said when she had finished, and we looked at ourselves in the mirror for a while before going downstairs.

After that we got tangled up in Christmas. The guests expected extras like sauces, crackers, Father Christmas napkins and snowmen candles, so we had to work hard and I forgot about Esther acting strange.

The year died suddenly and another one sprung up to take its place like a daffodil. Esther went to a college party on New Year's Eve. At midnight she rang up when the guests were in the bar singing 'Auld Lang Syne' with Sandra conducting, and we could hear her friends in the background.

'Happy nineteen eighty-seven, Esther,' I said into the phone when Beatrice passed it to me, but I couldn't hear much because of all the singing. A week later Esther went back to college and seemed to be her old self again, so I didn't worry about the folder and the hearts and kisses again until Easter, when Meredith was just back from a two-week concert run in Verona.

On Easter Saturday, 1987, I was supposed to be on reception, but instead I was in the dining room making some special table decorations. I was very proud of them. They had daffodils in the middle and stones I had collected from the beach around the outside. Esther had told me earlier that she didn't have time to help and that they were babyish, and I had got annoyed with her. She was being moody again, like she had been before Christmas, and I was angry that she wouldn't tell me the reason.

Beatrice came back from the cash-and-carry just as I was beginning to wonder where Esther was and whether I should go and look for her. I hadn't seen her since our argument and I knew she hadn't been helping with the rooms because I had heard Sandra complaining when I went to show an early guest upstairs.

I went out to help with the shopping. Beatrice had got some tiny Easter eggs wrapped in shiny foil for me to add to my decorations.

'They're wonderful,' I said.

'Meredith phoned just before I left,' said Beatrice.

'Oh. Where was I?'

'Upstairs doing Room Twenty with Sandra. Sorry. I was in a rush to get to the shops. Anyway. She's back from Italy.'

'At last,' I said, 'We haven't seen her for ages.' I picked up as many bags as I could, pushed the door with my shoulder and waited for Beatrice so I could hold it open for her.

'She's here for a while this time,' Beatrice said, and she couldn't help the smile creeping across her face like the sun. 'I've invited her for Proper Dinner tomorrow.'

'Lovely,' I said. We went back out to get the last of the bags, a catering-size tin of peaches and a gigantic plastic bag full of toilet rolls.

'Do you know where Esther's gone?' I asked, when we were back inside.

'She couldn't wait. She went over to see Meredith as soon as she phoned.'

'She didn't say anything to me,' I said, and I remembered that I was still annoyed with her.

'I know. She's being very secretive. She said she wanted to talk to her about something.' I wondered what Esther's secret was that couldn't wait till tomorrow.

'Do you want a hot cross bun when we've put these away?' said Beatrice, manoeuvring some of the bags through the swing doors. 'I've got loads left over from breakfast.'

'OK. I'll make the hot chocolate,' I said, and we went into the kitchen together to unpack the bags, which I always thought was like unwrapping presents, especially when someone else had done the shopping.

Esther got back in time for lunch but she hardly said anything while we were making the mushroom omelettes and chips. We were very busy because we were fully booked, but I had a chance to talk to her later. That afternoon there was non-alcoholic fruit punch in the bar and Beatrice and Sandra were busy making spring lamb with rosemary and sauté potatoes for dinner. As the guests were drinking their punch, I helped Esther with one last check of all the rooms. In each one there was a little basket of flowers and two chocolates in gold wrappers. We checked them one after the other, ashtray, bin, soap, toilet roll, pillows, windows, flowers, chocolates, like we were looking for clues in a murder mystery.

'How's Meredith?'

'OK,' she said uneasily.

'Can you pass me another ashtray?' Esther gave me a little glass one and I positioned it next to the bed to cover a stain in the wood.

'She brought us back some eggs but you can't have yours till tomorrow when she gets here. They're made with good chocolate.'

'Have you eaten yours?'

'Only half of it.'

'Why did you go and see her and not tell me?' I said, trying to sound annoyed.

'I wanted to go on my own.'

'Why?' I said, but she turned away.

The next day, for Easter Sunday, Beatrice had organised a special interest trip to Purbeck Pottery in the afternoon to get the guests out of the way. Sandra was in charge of tickets and she went with them, while we stayed behind to tidy up. The guests had had a big roast chicken lunch and there were five tiny Easter eggs on each of their serviettes, so we almost had to stuff them into the seats on the minibus, they had grown so fat. We had all had sandwiches because we were saving ourselves for Proper Dinner with Meredith. Later the guests came back smiling, shaking Sandra by the hand and clutching their souvenir dolphins. I helped Beatrice with the spring blossom ham salad and summer pudding, while Sandra and Esther dished out sherry and more hot cross buns in the bar.

We were doing the guests' dinner early so that we'd have time to get ready. At last it was over, the washing-up done and the dining room was empty. Beatrice and I had been extra busy because while we were making the ham salad we had been organising Proper Dinner as well. We had been cooking our own roast chicken and roast potatoes, and carrots and peas and gravy. When we had set it all out on the long wooden table in the kitchen, I put one of my special decorations in the middle. By everyone's place mat was a small Easter egg parcel covered in green and silver paper. There were two extra places: one for Sandra and one for Meredith.

When Meredith arrived I went out to meet her and gave her a hug.

210

'Hello,' said Beatrice. She hugged her for a long time and looked at her carefully, just to check that she hadn't changed.

Then we went inside and Meredith got her Easter eggs out of her bag so we had two each. As soon as we were all sitting around the table, Esther helped Grandma Maggie tear the wrappers off hers.

'Happy Easter,' said Grandma Maggie suddenly, when she saw what was inside. Beatrice put a plate down in front of Meredith, then Sandra, then me, then Esther, and then herself, and she chopped up a special serving for Grandma Maggie and gave her a spoon. Sandra passed round the leftovers of the non-alcoholic fruit punch and we all chinked our glasses and took a sip. It tasted sweet like raspberries and liquorice. I looked at Meredith. She was new and exciting again after all her time away and I was full of things I could hardly wait to ask her, but Beatrice wasn't leaving any gaps in between her own questions.

'Esther wants to tell you about someone,' said Meredith when she had finished describing Italy and the Tower of Pisa and the Grand Canal in Venice.

'OK,' said Esther suddenly, 'he's called Daniel.' Everyone stared at her.

'Who's Daniel?' said Sandra, smiling and glancing sideways at Beatrice.

'My boyfriend,' said Esther, just as I took a mouthful of peas. I had to spit some of them back on to my plate to stop myself from choking. I couldn't believe she hadn't told me. Meredith smiled sweetly like she knew all about it, so I could see that Esther had talked to her about Daniel the day before.

'Lucky old Daniel,' said Sandra, and chuckled to herself.

'Oh,' said Beatrice. 'Where did you meet him?' I thought maybe she was going to say he was from Liverpool and she'd

211

met him on the beach. Then I remembered the hearts and kisses on the folder.

'At college,' she said.

'How long has he been your boyfriend?' said Beatrice.

'A few days,' said Esther, starting to enjoy the attention. 'I liked him for a long time but he was going out with someone else and, anyway, he split up with her and I asked him out.' She looked relieved after she had said that, because she found it difficult to keep things secret. I had managed to swallow the rest of my peas.

'Why didn't you tell us?' I said. I tried not to sound upset, but I felt suddenly cold inside, like when you drink milk straight from the fridge.

'I'm telling you now, anyway,' she said, and started to cut up her chicken violently like she was frightened it wasn't dead yet.

'I think Esther thought you might not like him,' said Meredith putting her hand on Esther's arm.

Beatrice looked pleased. 'Well. You'll have to bring him over and then we can decide,' she said. Esther stopped cutting up her chicken and looked round the table at us all doubtfully.

'Dust and tea should do it,' said Grandma Maggie cheerfully, and she waved her spoon in the air.

'Ice cream, anyone?' said Beatrice.

The next day there was an Easter party instead of dinner for the guests who hadn't already gone home. Meredith came round again to help out. She was wearing a blue trouser suit and sunglasses, which she had bought in Milan and which made her look like an Italian film star. Unusually, Esther didn't come down to meet her and to eat leftover hot cross buns in the guest lounge with the rest of us. At four o'clock, after I'd eaten so many buns I felt like an elephant, I was on bathrooms. I went upstairs to the attic room to put on my jogging bottoms and my old Sisters of Mercy T-shirt that I didn't mind getting dirty. I found Esther trying out a new eye-shadow technique, following instructions from a textbook.

'Meredith's here,' I said.

'Do I look all right?' she said. 'I'm meeting Daniel.'

'Where are you going?'

'Bowling.'

'I've got to do the bathrooms.'

'Well, I don't have to help anyway, because I did breakfast on my own.' Esther had put on her best jeans and her fluffy green off-the-shoulder jumper with a little pink vest top underneath, and had brushed her hair very straight so that it didn't curl up at the edges like it usually did.

'Aren't you coming to the party?'

'No.'

'You look nice,' I said.

'Good. See you later.'

'Have a good time,' I said, not sure if I meant it. She picked up her purse and went out of the door and I heard her footsteps fading on the stairs. I stood and looked at Esther's textbook for a while, which was called *The Role of Make-up in Beauty Techniques*. Then I went downstairs to find the others.

Meredith, Beatrice, Sandra and I put on our aprons. We stood around the kitchen table and made egg sandwiches, cheese and pineapple on sticks, party sausages, canapés, fairy cakes, spicy twist, custard tarts, crackers with cream cheese and chives and fruit salad. We also made some punch, with vodka in it this time, in big bowls.

Before the party started, Beatrice put on a new pair of brown trousers and an orange jumper and helped Grandma Maggie into her green dress with red roses on it, with lace round the

213

neck and sleeves, so that she looked beautiful when she sat in the corner by the bar. I wore my red Christmas dress.

We took some big tables from the dining room into the bar and laid out the food and the plates and cutlery and put two big ladles next to the punch. Beatrice brought in the old record player and got out some records that Grandma Maggie had bought in the seventies. Then Meredith fiddled with the record player until it was working again. The guests loved Grandma Maggie's records and sang along and danced all evening.

Sandra handed round the punch and supervised the food. She was wearing a party outfit with animal prints on it and a gold chain around her neck and she had piled her hair up on top of her head in a way that Esther would not have approved of, but Esther wasn't there. Up until that evening Esther had always put the hotel first before anything else, but now it was different. The party went on till late and as most of the guests were checking out early in the morning, we decided to leave the tidying up until the next day. Esther still wasn't back when it was over.

'I hope she's OK,' said Beatrice.

'She'll be fine,' said Meredith.

'She's nearly seventeen,' said Sandra. 'When I was seventeen ...' she began, but then she saw Beatrice's worried face and we never found out what Sandra got up to when she was Esther's age. Meredith persuaded Beatrice not to wait up for her so we all went to bed.

When I woke up the next day at ten o'clock, Esther's bed was empty. I went downstairs to start clearing up to find Esther sitting in the kitchen drinking coffee with a boy with brown hair and all the tidying already done.

'Rice, this is Daniel,' said Esther. 'Daniel, this is Rice. Do you want a coffee?'

'Yes, please,' I said, looking at Daniel suspiciously.

'Hello,' said Daniel. 'That's a funny name.'

'No it's not,' said Esther. 'Daniel's a funny name.'

'Who tidied up?' I said, feeling pleased that Esther stuck up for me and jealous at the same time.

'Me and Daniel did it.'

'Oh. Where's Beatrice?'

'Still in bed, I think.' She passed me a coffee.

'Did you come back last night?'

'No.'

'You're in trouble,' I said.

'I know.'

Eventually Beatrice got out of bed and came into the kitchen in her nightie, looking worried and like she hadn't had much sleep. Meredith followed her. She had her red pyjamas on.

'I was worried about you,' said Beatrice.

'We tidied up,' said Esther, awkwardly. 'This is my mum and this is Meredith.'

'Beatrice,' said Beatrice, shaking hands.

'Pleased to meet you,' said Meredith.

'Hello.'

Then Sandra, who had slept in Room Four for the night, and was still wearing her animal print dress, tottered into the kitchen. She grinned when she saw Daniel and went right up to him and pinched his cheek.

'Ow,' he said.

'This is Sandra,' said Esther.

'Pleased to meet you. I think Esther and her mum want to have a chat now,' said Sandra, looking at Beatrice. She poured herself a coffee and then ushered Daniel and me outside and into the garden. Meredith stayed where she was. It was a bright spring day and the daffodils were dancing to themselves, but the wind, coming in sudden blasts from the sea, was cold like fingers.

215

'God, it's cold,' said Sandra, as soon as we stepped outside. 'Rice, be a love and go and get me my cardi.' I ran back into the kitchen and grabbed Sandra's white mohair cardigan. Meredith, Beatrice and Esther had sat down at the table.

'I hope you used a condom,' I heard Beatrice say.

'We didn't have sex,' said Esther, sounding shocked.

'Well, make sure you're prepared,' said Beatrice, as I dashed back out of the door again.

Sandra and Daniel were standing looking over the gate at the top of the beach steps.

'There are two hundred and seventeen steps,' Sandra said. She had taken her cigarettes out of her pocket. I gave her the cardigan and she put it round her shoulders. I was annoyed at her for giving away one of the hotel's secrets.

'Two hundred and seventeen,' he said. 'It's a long way down.' And when he said that I suddenly felt like watching Daniel curl up into a ball and roly-poly down the steps like a hedgehog until he got to the bottom. Sandra lit a cigarette.

'How did you get to be called Rice?' he said.

'I don't know,' I said. 'My parents called me it.'

'People get called lots of funny things,' said Sandra, pulling her cardigan closer round her. 'I know someone who was named after a whole football team.'

'How did you get to be called Daniel?' I said.

'My parents go to church,' he said. 'They like the story of Belshazzar's banquet and Daniel and the lions' den.'

'Oh.' Sandra saw me glaring at him.

'Now how I got to be called Sandra is an interesting story,' she said. 'My mum used to own a B. and B. in Brighton where there are stones on the beach and she was always nagging my dad to move to Bournemouth where it was sandy.' She sucked on her cigarette. 'Just before I was born, they finally moved and my

216

mum wanted to call me Sandy, because you could see the beach from the top bedroom, but my dad said, "You can't call her Sandy, it'll have to be Sandra." So that's what I was called.'

'Really?' I said.

'Well, that's what I like to tell people,' said Sandra, carefully stubbing out her cigarette end on the gatepost. 'Shall we go back inside? I'm bloody freezing.'

We went back in but as I went I noticed the first blossom on two of the saplings Beatrice had planted and how it danced in time with the daffodils. As I watched, some of the pink petals jumped off the branches and flew around the garden. The others had finished talking. Meredith saw me looking at the trees and came out to join me.

'It's definitely spring now,' she said.

Esther got me to take a photo of Daniel and her in the garden next to the pink blossom and I had to have two copies done. One for him and one for her. She showed me the silver frames she bought from W H Smith's for them. I stopped acting annoyed when she did that and told her that I thought they looked very nice together, even though I didn't mean it. Once or twice Esther stayed over at his house and they went on lots of dates together.

None of us had been to see *Top Gun* yet and Esther had a big poster of Tom Cruise and Kelly McGillis, which she had put up on the wall of the attic room. She had wanted to see it for ages, so we all went together and sat in the front row.

'What did you bring her for?' Daniel said to Esther as I opened my popcorn loudly.

'Because I wanted to,' she said. I looked sideways at them during the film while I was stuffing popcorn in my mouth and not offering Daniel any on purpose, and they were holding hands. My stomach did a pancake flip, even though I had seen

217

them do it before. It still shocked me every time. We got chips from the Wimpy afterwards and Daniel got a hamburger. Then we walked down to the beach, next to where the amusements are. It was a warm evening and it felt like spring down by the water's edge.

'It was good when the plane went upside down,' I said, 'and it's funny when he sticks his finger up.' Then I noticed that Esther and Daniel weren't listening, because they were snogging, with tongues it looked like, like Tom Cruise and Kelly McGillis. Esther was leaning against the railings by the beach. It was dark and the air smelt of salt. I went and sat down on the edge of the promenade with my legs dangling over the side and waited for them to stop.

I was in my last year at school and was revising for my exams. I had studied the college prospectus very carefully and chosen a photography and art course, which would mean I could apply for art college in London when I'd finished it. Esther and I both spent a lot of time studying in the attic room, sitting on the brown sofa. I was trying to memorise the subjects she had stuffed into her head the year before and had forgotten about now, because she would either be staring at make-up colour wheels and fashion magazines or trying to remember human anatomy for her aromatherapy massage practise.

One day in May, I went up to the attic room to try to learn French verbs and equations and found Esther crying on the brown sofa instead of looking at her hair and beauty textbooks.

'What's wrong?' I said.

'Nothing,' she said, wiping her hand across her face.

'Tell me,' I said.

She sniffed and picked up the photo of her and Daniel from the arm of the sofa, only now it wasn't one photo, it was two: one of him and one of her, because she had torn it in half.

'We split up,' she said.

I put my arm round her shoulders and she started sobbing again so in the end I had to go and find a tissue for her to blow her nose.

'What happened?' I said.

'We only had sex a few times,' she said, and blew her nose again. I felt cold inside my chest when she said that, but I didn't say anything. 'Then he said I wasn't doing it properly because I had to take my bra off and I said no and then he said he didn't want to have sex if I didn't take my bra off and so I said I didn't want to do it anyway and then we split up.'

'You don't have to take your bra off if you don't want to,' I said, not sure if I was right or not. 'He's a pig.'

'Yes,' said Esther, sniffing loudly, 'a pig.'

I was pleased that I had Esther back to myself again for a while and, although she went to one or two more parties that year with boys from college, she didn't bring them back to the hotel to meet Sandra and Beatrice and me.

One day on the edge of summer, we went down the steps very early before the beach got full of tourists. We had our swimming costumes on already under our clothes and we took off our T-shirts and shorts and sat on our towels on the sand, looking out to sea. Then Esther took hold of my hand like she had with Daniel in the cinema, only maybe not exactly the same, and we sat there for a few seconds, just like that, without saying anything.

'Ready?' she said.

'Yes.'

'Come on then.' She stood up and pulled me with her and we ran into the sea together, and even though it was cold I knew it would be all right once we were in and most of us was under the surface. Our feet made splashes as we ran and once we were in up to our waists, Esther let go of my hand and we both dived under the water and swam, and when we came up we looked like we had been baptised and the sea had told us what our names were again. Then Esther held on to my hands and spun me round and round until I was dizzy and I fell backwards. A wave went over my head and I came up coughing and laughing.

When we were back on the sand, shaking like dogs, and rubbing ourselves with our towels, Esther turned to face me and I stopped rubbing my hair and stood and faced her too. She picked up my right hand and looked at it and pretended she was the palm reader on the pier. She pointed at my life line.

'This means we will live in the Water's Edge Hotel for ever,' she said, 'and never leave it, and when my mum and Sandra and Grandma Maggie die we can be in charge of the hotel and we'll be so rich that we'll be able to pay a chef and lots of chambermaids to cook and clean for us.'

'What about when you're a beautician?' I said doubtfully, 'Or what if you get married to one of the boys from college?'

'I'll open a boutique in Room Eighteen,' said Esther, 'and the guests with lots of money can come in and pay extra to have their hair and make-up done.'

'And for massages and that feet thing?' I said.

'Reflexology.'

'Yes.'

It was nearly a year later before I could try out kissing for myself. In March 1988, it was spring again and I started going out with a boy I had met at college, but it didn't work out. Although Esther gave me advice on condoms, I wasn't in love. Not with him, anyway. I finished it after two months. We were in bed together in Room Eleven at the time. Or rather he was sitting on the edge of the bed, with his knees hunched up to his chest, a cigarette in his hand, and I was lying on top of the covers.

'What's your name?' I said.

'Don't be stupid.'

'I know you're called J. But were you named after a letter or a bird or is it short for something? And is it short for John or Joseph, or Jeremiah, or are you just called plain J. It's important.'

'My name is Joshua. I was named after my granddad,' he said. 'He was a policeman.'

'Oh.'

'I've got something to show you,' he said, lowering his eyelids. He paused. He wanted a response, as if this were to be a momentous revelation, like the Statue of Liberty or the Eiffel Tower.

'What?' I half expected a present. Or maybe I expected more sex. I've got something to show you. My body. Here it is. Like you haven't seen it a hundred times before. White and flabby, spotty, hairy, biological. Here it is. My dick. Like you'd never noticed it. Surprise body parts. But no, I thought, leaving him waiting, hunched on the side of the bed, cigarette-clad, it couldn't be body parts. He was already naked. Legs to his chest on the edge of his bed, like he was embarrassed in case I saw his balls. I was undressed too, but in order to see me naked now, he'd have to peel off my skin. I was like a banana. There wasn't anything else to take off, not a shoe. Nothing.

'I said, I've got something to show you.' And he unveiled it. I thought there was nothing left to show but there it was, in the middle of his hand, like a stigma. He made a poor Christ figure – like he had just come down off his cross, all confused, not knowing how to die any more but desperately wanting to. It was an engagement ring.

I looked out of the hotel window. There was a view of the car park from Room Eleven. It was seven o'clock in the morning and the early sun was shining on the windscreens of the cars.

'What are you talking about?' I laughed. 'I can't marry you. I don't love you.'

'Oh, I thought . . .' he said. He clenched his fist again, like a tragic hero ready to bear his downfall.

I pulled him back on to the bed, climbed on to his lap, and stroked his face with my hand and said: 'It's all right. We've only been going out for two months.' And then I thought to myself, I'm in love with Esther, anyway, and as soon as I thought it I realised that it was true and I remember thinking how good it sounded. 'Look, maybe we should split up,' I said. I pulled on my big All About Eve T-shirt so I wasn't undressed anymore.

It was a Saturday morning that day when I finished with the boy from college and realised I was in love. Soon it was ten o'clock and time to start chambermaiding.

'Where shall we start today?' Esther said.

'I could start at the top of your head,' I thought. The idea didn't surprise me this time. Esther was bigger and more powerful than anyone I had ever had in my head before. She took up all the room until there was none left, no room for other thoughts. Esther was red too, like the hotel. Like a giant red monkey she had grown, elbows nudging, knees nudging the skin round my head. She was all there was inside me. She put her feet down into my body and kicked around somewhere between my legs, inside. But although I didn't know it yet, we didn't have much longer at the old hotel together.

My name is Persephone. The journey back from Hades is hard

and cold. In the millennia before the hotels came, I would have to lie still for days while I recovered and then find a cave or a hut or a smuggler's cottage to stay in further inland, depending on which century I was in. Over the years, I watched the cliffs form, the grasses grow and the beach nestle in the folds of the cliff, like a small yellow egg. Then in the last two hundred years people came. Mostly ill people at first, because it was so convenient for the underworld.

At last holidaymakers arrived and sat on the beach and hotels grew up like sudden daffodils. The owner of the Water's Edge Hotel stood outside proudly, shook hands with the mayor and had his photo taken. After that, when I came back in the spring, I brought a towel in a suitcase and dried off quickly in a beach hut, which my mother had reserved for me, and then went and checked in. I first stayed at the Water's Edge eighty years ago. I used to like to stand at the top of the two hundred and seventeen steps that led to the beach from the hotel garden and look down towards the sea. Sometimes I stood at the top of the beach steps and I felt as if I was falling, tumbling over and over, like I do when I am too keen to get back to Hades, when I go through the gate too quickly, lose my footing, and tumble through rocks and clay and fire to be with the one I love.

In the spring of 1987, I went for long walks on the beach and sat in deck chairs and waited. I like to watch the budding trees, and the birds with twigs in their beaks building nests, and the eggs opening with naked hatchlings inside them. I had seen Esther watching Daniel from the world below, but when I returned in March that year I got to see the colour of his hair properly and found that it was milk-chocolate brown and that Esther thought he was very good-looking. I looked into Rice's head and saw that she wished he would disappear in a puff of smoke so that it could be her and Esther again. But

223

their story had twisted around and about like pink and yellow marshmallow twists and the story was still a love story, because in love stories the people are attached by thin cords that won't undo, wherever they go.

Soon autumn began again and I went back to the underworld. Rice started at college too and, although she felt new on the first day, there were people in her class who hadn't used a camera before. Soon Rice was seventeen and feeling grown up, and she showed the other students in her class how to focus and they came up and asked her questions and she felt more important than she ever had done before. I was back with Hades, waiting for the frost to turn us all blue and silver.

I am guardian of the seasons and of the story they tell about life and death and the afterlife. Winter 1987 turned cold and white and became 1988. The trees lifted up their arms like statues or like frozen worshippers. Then there were Christmas presents as usual and we took the slow journey from January to the beginning of February when the first signs of hope arrive. In March, I was spat out on the beach and spring came. The leaves turned yellowy green and it rained so much that Beatrice thought she might have to turn the old hotel into an ark and sail away in it. Hot days followed and the water dried up, and the garden had to be watered twice a day, once in the morning, once in the evening, when the sky was at its coolest. In the spring of 1988, I watched while Rice went out with a boy called Joshua and then Esther left college and Meredith's friend Ian (who is a hairstylist) got her a job in a beauty salon in Wimborne. Esther did well in her job and was soon in charge of manicures and pedicures.

Rice's relationship ended with the beginning of summer. She told Esther she was waiting for the right person to come along but, deep inside her head, Rice thought that she already had (although the story turned out to be more complicated than that). Eventually autumn came and I went back into the earth again. Then it was winter once more and the year turned into a snowflake, all sharp and frozen, until it snapped, and then it was 1989 and the decade was nearly over.

I watched Esther and Rice carefully from Hades, looking up through the rocks and sand and clay. On 1 January 1989, they made their resolutions on scraps of paper as usual. Esther's were: This year I will go swimming once a week, give up smoking and lose a stone. And one that she didn't show Beatrice: I will not have any more one-night stands. Rice's was: Save up and buy a new camera. She had already given up smoking and was so thin Beatrice was worried about her and kept trying to feed her cake.

Esther did stop having one-night stands and by the time I returned in the spring of '89 she was going out with Meredith's friend Ian, who was gay but hadn't realised it yet. He lived above the salon where they worked. Rice secretly thought it might be a career move on Esther's part. She thought about it with a smile as she washed her paintbrushes at college and looked forward to going to Proper Art College in London in the autumn to do a degree in photography.

My name will always be Persephone but in 1989 I pretended I was called Daphne. Having the gift of prophecy, I knew what was going to happen and I thought I might be closer to the hotel's stories if I came back as a seasonal chambermaid for one last time. So, just as I did in the 1940s, I got Demeter to send in my curriculum vitae and to make sure the other applicants went down with colds and on 21 March I presented myself to Beatrice, who said: 'We'll need you down at six tomorrow morning, I'm afraid, to help with breakfasts, but you might as well settle in till then,' as she handed me the key to my room.

225

A few things had changed at the old hotel. Steve the Saturday boy had left in 1986 to train to be a nurse. He was married with two children already and had been replaced by Lizzy the Saturday girl, and Beatrice had had Room Twenty painted pink, but soon things would change so much that they would never go back to how they were.

Daphne

M y name is Rice and 1989 turned out to be the year of the fire, the year I was in hospital and the year I had sex with a woman for the first time, but first of all it was the year of the ants. In April, ants invaded our kitchen at the Water's Edge. Small red ones – not those bright red kind; these were more browny red. They refused to die, even after the poison and the man with a mask and the ant gun. Once I drank some juice from a mug and didn't look and there was an ant in my mouth. I hated them. However many you squashed with your fingernail, tomorrow they were back, crawling on the washing-up that Esther and I were too tired to do the night before. I should have known they were a sign. It was spring. The ants had just arrived and I had just finished college when my life changed all over again.

It happened two days after Esther's nineteenth birthday, a week after Beatrice was forty-seven and just over ten years since Margaret Thatcher had become Prime Minister. We had a joint birthday party for Beatrice and Esther on the Sunday before, with nice food set out on the kitchen table, and Meredith came and some of our friends from college and some people from where Esther worked. It was a late spring day and fresh-smelling rain fell on the lavender outside the kitchen window and the gate swung on its hinges. As we watched the light got thinner and

227

by the time we had finished the food it was dark and the shapes outside were like strange statues. If we had stood by the gate we would have seen that the horizon was pink and white, but we didn't. We didn't know it but we were heading towards the end of the week like fireworks shooting into the spring twilight and over the sea.

It was 12 May 1989. I woke up and the air smelt dusty. I called out to Esther but she wasn't in her bed. It turned out she was in the bathroom on the second floor when it happened. I think it was about one o'clock in the morning. Then I saw smoke coming from under the door, a little bit at first, then great big handfuls of smoke. That's all I remember of the fire, because then I started to dream. I dreamt that my throat had been cut but I was taking a long time to die.

Next I was on a hospital trolley. I didn't know if I was still dreaming or not, though I could feel the trolley moving. Brown signs clung to the walls like monkeys, with explanations underneath in case I couldn't understand them. Orthopaedic (Teeth) Pathology (Madness) Geriatric (Suicide) Haematology (Death by water) Radiography (Electrocution) Paediatric (Death by fire). A nurse looked down at me as the trolley moved quickly along the corridor and the ceiling zoomed past.

'My name is Rice,' I said. I was wearing a plastic mask so she couldn't hear me, though she smiled because she saw I was awake. I tried to move the mask from my face so I could speak, but the nurse shook her head and put her hand out to stop me.

Much later, I think it was the next day, I was on a hospital ward. The mask was gone and the same nurse was leaning over me, writing my name in marker pen on a notice board behind the bed. I think I said, 'What happened?' and the nurse said, 'I'm sorry,' and I felt the words inside my legs, inside my hands, in my throat, like someone was skinning me alive with a blunt

228

knife, but it was a good feeling because I wanted to get out of my skin and run away.

Those were same words that the nurse said to me in the hospital in 1984 when I had come in with Auntie Something in the morning as usual to see my mother. She had taken me into a small yellow office with a frosted-glass door. I can still remember the 1984 nurse's eyes, which were deep brown, and inside my head I can see her words, worn thin to a frayed string with use. I hear them over and over, when I make a cup of tea or pick up baked beans in the supermarket. 'I'm sorry.' So the 1989 nurse said 'I'm sorry,' (she had brown eyes too) and sat on the edge of the bed and said that I was in Poole Hospital and that there had been a fire at the hotel where I had been living and that Beatrice would come in and see me soon. I didn't know what time of day it was, but I was worried in case it was night-time and I should have been asleep.

'I can't sleep,' I said to the nurse, but she had gone to tell another patient about burnt hotels and didn't hear me. Later – I don't know how much later, a minute or an hour maybe – the nurse came back and gave me an injection in my stomach and two white pills.

'To make you feel calmer,' she said.

'My name is Rice,' I said to her again, in case she hadn't heard me the first time, but she must have done because she had written my name on the board behind my bed. Then I fell asleep, wondering how bad the fire had been. I dreamt that I was the manager of the hotel and that the insides were plated with gold from top to bottom, like I was Midas. I had to keep them clean all the time, but we had so many guests that I couldn't keep up. Then there was a crowd of guests with blank faces at the end of a seesaw and I was the only one on the other end and I was still too heavy. Then my skin began to stink. Everyone on the other end of the seesaw was clean, but I was dirty. And then someone came to set me on fire. 'To make you clean again,' the fire starter said.

When I woke up next time I thought maybe I had dreamt up the fire at the hotel too and I looked down and noticed I was wearing a white nightgown, and wondered where my clothes had gone. There was a plastic band around my wrist that said Rice Parker 23.9.70, and there was a machine to take my piss away next to the bed.

'Because you can't walk very well at the moment,' said the nurse, when I asked her about it. 'It saves us worrying about bedpans.'

The next time I opened my eyes, Beatrice was by the bed.

'Hello, Rice,' Beatrice said. 'How are you feeling?' She looked exhausted. There were red circles around her eyes.

'Bad,' I said.

I tried to sit up but there was something that felt like a stone in the middle of my chest. I managed to hunch myself up on my elbows so I could look at her properly.

'What happened?' I asked again, and Beatrice told me about the fire.

'The hotel is burnt to a crisp, like burnt toffee,' she said (or I think that's what she said).

I sunk back down into the pillow. I hadn't dreamt it after all.

'I know. The nurse told me,' I said, looking up at the green-tiled ceiling, which seemed to have been specially designed to make ill people feel worse. She went over to the window and looked out.

'It's a lovely day outside,' she said, 'very warm for May.' Then she came back over to the bed and sat down again. 'You have smoke inhalation, your lungs are a little bit damaged.'

'Is everyone OK?'

'Esther's fine. The guests are fine. We got off luckier than you did, I'm afraid.' I looked at her.

'Grandma Maggie?' I said.

'She died in the fire, Rice,' Beatrice said, and patted my hand and I could see there were tears in her eyes. She carried on talking anyway. 'Of course, we'll get the insurance on the hotel. Esther and I are staying with Meredith until it's sorted out. She's cancelled Austria and Greece for us. We'll have to go to the estate agent. Now try to get some more sleep.' She stood up.

I wondered if Beatrice was really going to leave and not take me with her.

'I've got to,' said Beatrice. 'It's ten past eight. Visiting time is up.' I realised I was holding on to her arm, so I let go.

'You didn't stay long,' I said.

'We've been here all day,' said Beatrice. 'You were asleep. Esther and Meredith were here too, but they've gone back to the flat. Esther's very tired.'

'Oh,' I said. I was already half asleep again.

'See you tomorrow,' said Beatrice, and she left.

The pills and injections made me feel odd. I think they were painkillers but they made my head feel like it was full of water. I remember thinking the next morning that I should lie very still and not move and that I had to keep my hands under the covers in case my arms grew too long, like a monkey's arms, and I started to swing from the lights.

When I woke up, I noticed that Daphne, the seasonal chamber-maid, was in the hospital with me. She was in the bed opposite, although I hadn't noticed her before, and when she saw me looking at her, she waved. She was sitting up in bed reading a magazine, her knees hunched up under her blanket. After I had had so many weird dreams, I thought that maybe I was going mad but I knew I wasn't the maddest one in the hospital, because Daphne the chambermaid thought she was a goddess. Or maybe she thought she was a devil, because an old woman at the end of our bay started talking in a loud voice about what strange weather we were having and how she had heard the weathermen predicting a heatwave that was going to last until November.

Daphne said: 'Yes I know, but when I get back to hell I'll sort it all out.' Then she told me in a stage whisper that people who worked in hospitals were vampires and they were planning to kill us all. It was the shock of being in the fire, I thought. She was only making up a story because the blood sample woman had been round earlier with her needles and her trolley of tiny labelled bottles, like vials of red perfume. About a hour later, Daphne got out of bed, got dressed and went and discharged herself.

'See you at the funeral,' she said to me before she left.

'OK,' I said. I wondered if she was still mad, or whether it was just temporary. When Beatrice came in at visiting time, I asked her whether you could be mad for a limited period only and when she asked me why, I told her what had happened to Daphne.

'Maybe you were imagining it, dear,' she said. 'I don't remember them bringing Daphne in. In fact, she called Meredith this morning. She said her mum had found her somewhere to stay and she asked her when the funeral was. Seemed like a pretty sane conversation.'

'That must have been after she left here.'

'Honestly, Rice, you were the only one who was hurt, apart from Grandma Maggie, of course. Maybe she just looked like Daphne.'

'But it said Daphne on the board above her bed,' I insisted, although when I looked now there was someone new in the bed and a different name on the board, and when I asked the nurse later she said that they hadn't had anyone in called Daphne, not in the whole time she had worked there.

'Sometimes the pills give you bad dreams,' she said. All the same, I slept that night with my blanket pulled up under my chin, just in case there really were vampires.

'Hallucinations and crying are normal,' said the nurse, and went to lift the woman next to me off her bedpan.

When Beatrice and Esther came the next day, they brought me puzzle books and a novel, but I couldn't concentrate on them. The days and nights started merging into each other. I think it was down to the pills again. I remember being frightened of the things around me, of the colour green and of the sound of the nurses and doctors walking. I think I cried when I thought about Grandma Maggie and the hotel, and the nurse came and said, 'Shh! Shh!' in a kind voice and gave me two more white pills. Sometimes someone gave me a drink. Once someone fed me fish. I can remember the smell. I got shit on the sheets on the third night and hands lifted me to my feet and the sheet fell away under me. It was replaced by a new sheet and I was put back and everything was the same again.

Beatrice, Esther and Meredith came to see me every day. They sat on grey chairs near the bed and talked about how the policeman had told Beatrice that the fire was started by accident, probably faulty wiring combined with gas from the oven. He had said that the whole place was a tinder box waiting to go up and that it was amazing it hadn't happened years ago. They talked about where Grandma Maggie would be cremated and what colour the flowers would be, but their words buzzed round my head like wasps and I didn't reply, because they sounded like they were a long way away and I wasn't sure they would be able to hear me.

Also, I remember that there was a sign saying something hanging over my bed. It sat just above my head like a sword dangling, and though I wanted to ask them what it said, I couldn't form the question in my head, so I made up words for it instead: nil by mouth, radioactive for twenty-four hours, diabetic, psychiatric, don't feed the animals, pigeons are pests, dogs must be carried, don't ride on the pavements. Then a doctor came and leant over me and pressed my cheek with one thumb.

'We're going to ease up on the medication now,' I heard her say, and after that there was only one white pill and no more injections and they took away the machine for piss and trusted me to walk to the toilet. Things started to come into focus again and on the fifth day I was allowed to sit in an armchair, tucked in like I was in an upright bed.

'I think you're coming back to us now,' said Beatrice, smiling and pulling up a chair.

'How long have I been in here?' I said.

'Ages,' said Esther, unwrapping the chocolate she had brought me and breaking it into pieces so she could have some too.

'Nearly a week,' said Beatrice.

'It feels like years.' I noticed how striking Meredith looked in contrast to the drabness of Poole Hospital, with her big hands and short blonde hair and blue eyes.

'How do you feel?' she said.

'OK.'

'No you don't. You feel terrible.'

'Why did you ask then?'

'We've rescued some stuff from the hotel,' said Esther.

'It's all in storage at the moment,' said Beatrice.

'We had to help the guests find other hotels,' said Esther. 'Most of them got their stuff back.'

Then they talked about staying in Meredith's flat and how small it was compared to the hotel, and the view of Poole Harbour and the nice weather. When Beatrice and Esther went to get a cup of tea, Meredith told me how Beatrice hadn't been up to organising

234

the death so she had stepped in, making phone calls and speaking to lawyers.

'The funeral's on Friday,' she said. 'You've got to get out of this place. It's terrible,' she added, glancing around at the occupants of the other beds. 'Have they told you when you can leave?'

'No.'

'You can probably get out in a couple of days. I'll have a word with them.'

After they'd gone, I sat still in my armchair and thought about the space that was left now Grandma Maggie had gone and all the stories that had left with her that she would never tell. Even if there was a big book where all the ordinary stories were written down, it would take too long to read, I thought, and then I began to fall asleep and a nurse came and helped me back into bed, where I dreamt that Grandma Maggie hadn't died in the fire after all and then she came and sat on my bed and told me all her stories, until they were ringing in my ears like bells.

Grandma Maggie's Ghost

My name is Persephone. Rice was in hospital and her thoughts were all mixed up like clothes at a jumble sale. That night, she lay very still and thought about arriving at the hotel for the first time as a grey-eyed stranger with long brown untidy hair and no mother. She dreamt that Esther sat next to her and said, 'I had never seen anyone like you before.' She thought about how Beatrice set her tasks to do around the hotel and made her happy again using her magic books and potions.

Meanwhile, the hotel's ghosts and monsters, who usually hid in dusty corners and cupboards, had been disturbed by the fire. They looked around the hotel and the damp and darkened corridors and inspected the burnt wood in order to piece together what had happened.

This is how Grandma Maggie died. (I watched through the walls with my fingers in my ears, but I couldn't save her. I can't interfere with events or the passage of time.) It was nearly midnight when she heard a noise and sat up in bed. There was a sound like a cat scratching at her door, but it was probably just the wind, whipping up leaves outside her window. (She often dreamt about cats.)

She was annoyed with her daughter for giving her sleeping pills, so on that day she had hidden them under her pillow. What she really needed to help her sleep was a mug of hot chocolate. She would have to make it herself, she thought, because Beatrice was snoring in the next room (although Beatrice heard Grandma Maggie in the kitchen and woke up just in time). Grandma Maggie got out of bed, reached for her sticks, stood for a while to get her balance and caught her darkened night reflection in the mirror. There was Henry Duffle standing behind her, with his drooping moustache and his arm in a sling. He watched her silently. She ignored him, turned and went into the kitchen. She was fed up of that man with the broken arm following her around. She could hear him a few paces behind her as she went along the passageway and down towards the staff door to the kitchen. She found the light, switched it on and glanced over her shoulder. There he was in the corner, leaning against the wall, watching her, his green eyes shining. Grandma Maggie concentrated on the saucepans. Then the milk. Then the cocoa. She turned on the gas and waited, imagining his fingers around her throat although when she turned he was still in the corner. Why the milk was taking so long to heat she didn't understand. It was probably that man in the corner of the kitchen watching her, she thought, stopping it from getting hot. Ghosts make everything around them frosty and cold, and there was that cat around his legs, so she hadn't dreamt it at all. She turned up the gas a little more.

When she looked round again he was right behind her although the cat had disappeared.

'Where's my baby girl, Margaret?' he said.

'I told you, she's grown up. She's not a baby now.'

'You're hiding her from me.' And then he stroked her soft face with the palm of his hand and offered her a box of matches. 'Try these,' he said.

'Thank you,' she said, and struck a match. There was a big

bang (the start of creation) and Grandma Maggie was in the middle of it.

Esther couldn't sleep on the night of the fire, because it felt like there was a thunderstorm in the air. Rice was asleep so she didn't wake her, even though she wanted to. Esther had been worried that she might be pregnant, although she wasn't that first time. She was sitting on the toilet in the middle of the night feeling relieved because her period had started at last. She was the first to see the smoke and she rang the fire alarm and shouted up at Rice to wake up. Thinking Rice had heard her, she ran downstairs. Beatrice was already awake and was trying to get into the kitchen where the fire was coming from, but she couldn't see. There was too much smoke. The guests came downstairs and were pouring out of the door like water. Esther thought Rice was with them. She thought she saw the back of her head. She thought she saw a cat too, but she told herself that they didn't have a cat and that she must have been seeing things.

'Where's Grandma Maggie?' Esther said.

'I've called nine-nine-nine. Go outside,' said Beatrice. I made my way out of the front door with Esther and the guests and let an ambulance driver in a green jumpsuit put a silver blanket round my shoulders.

'Daphne,' I said, when he asked me my name.

Maggie fitted in easily with the dead people that lived at the Water's Edge already. She haunted the darkest corners, mingled with the smell of dust and burning that lingered in the corridors and whispered the story of her life into the walls. She felt like she was keeping it alive with her ghosting of it, with her silent weightless walking through the empty rooms. Under her breath she repeated her story like a mantra, because she knew that ghosts can't exist on the earth for ever, only as long as someone remembers them. The hotel remembered everything it heard,

238

even now it was burnt and bruised, but she told it her story over and over just to make sure. She wanted to take her time getting to the doors of hell.

Grandma Maggie is dead and there's nothing she can do about it. I am the Queen of the dead, so I should know. She was the mother figure, Mrs Riding Hood, the woman who lived in a shoe. Before her, there was Grandma Grace and Thomas Tamarack. After Grandma Maggie died, she looked for her mother and father's ghosts everywhere. That's weird, she thought, when she couldn't find them.

Then she thought that maybe Grace and Tom had sunk into the sand on Bournemouth beach or been carried away by the waves and dissolved into a stream of soulless particles. She'd heard it could happen, but she carried on looking all the same. She didn't want to believe that they were in the world below or that they had been taken down to Hades through the gateway that lies just under the surface of the sea, next to Boscombe Pier. Thomas Tamarack has been there since 1942, for longer than he was alive, and he can't remember what the world was like, before it was grey and Elysian. Grace went in willingly. She was tired. But Grandma Maggie was reluctant to go. She wanted to stay in Bournemouth for a while, to bide her time. Sometimes she practised her dancing in the charcoal remains of the dining room, marking out the waltz with ghostly footsteps. The walls were no longer a barrier.

It's strange how humans imagine ghosts to look like a living body. They want to forget about the rotting and the burning. This is what Margaret looked like now she was dead: misty, like a children's book illustration, musty, like the dust in libraries, golden, like Midas in the rain, salty, mouth salty, rock salty, like Lot's wife. And like Lot's wife, she never got to say goodbye to her daughter. Is there something that's all about Maggie and no

239

one else? She does have one secret. The other night she dreamt that two women pulled her skin away. Starting with a small cut on her finger, they uncovered her and pulled her skin over her head, until they had stripped it all away. When she woke up she realised that her skin had already gone; what wasn't burnt at the hotel would be burnt at the crematorium.

Sometimes Grandma Maggie's ghost sat and thought about when she was in charge of the hotel, after her mother got ill, and the ice-cream man she danced with when she was sane and not mad. When she was thinking she shone yellow like a candle from the memory. I watched her as she shone and I smiled. Then I turned over what had happened in my head and remembered Margaret's time as queen of the hotel too.

Almost three years after England won the World Cup, Grace stopped getting out of her bed in Room One every day and Margaret Tamarack took charge of the hotel. It was March, and I was spending lots of time in a deck chair that year, but I watched Margaret take over with interest. The first thing she did was to tell Beatrice and Sandra to give every room a spring clean. Then she discovered that her mother had put some money by each month in the hotel account, so she ordered some paint and covered each room, one after the other, in dustsheets, while Beatrice and Sandra gave them a new coat of paint.

Maggie presided over the cleaning of the rooms every Saturday at check-out time like a queen on her throne. She introduced inspections, so that Sandra stopped sitting on the bed in Room Nineteen on her cigarette break in case Maggie came in and asked her why the room still smelt of tobacco when the guests had been gone since ten o'clock and the new guests were due at four.

'Have you run out of air freshener?' I heard her say to her once, so after that Sandra had her cigarette break in the guest lounge and secretly approved of Maggie taking charge so efficiently.

When Maggie went into a bathroom that Sandra had cleaned she wouldn't find bathroom cleaner smeared along the sides of the bath and not rinsed properly and there were no brown marks around Sandra's plugholes. Sandra didn't see the point of moving the chairs when she hoovered or checking behind the bedside cabinet for fluff, but what people could see was clean and tidy.

Beatrice and Sandra took half the rooms each until Beatrice was too pregnant to work any more and then Meredith came to work for a while, although she spent too much time dreaming for Maggie's liking, and too much time on each room. For Meredith everything had to be just so, the ashtray in the right place and the curtains hanging right.

In 1960, two years before Marilyn Monroe was found dead in Brentwood, California, Grandma Grace had had part of the kitchen and the hallway partitioned to make a dining room, because, she said, in a modern hotel people liked to mind their own business, but Maggie said now it was time to build walls and put up wallpaper and put in doors and do it properly, so she and Beatrice drew up plans for a new dining room and Maggie called a builder. Then Maggie asked him to build a wall down the middle of the guest lounge and to make them a bar and she applied for her licence and went out and bought big bottles of whisky and wine and beer.

By Christmas 1969, when Beatrice was four months pregnant, the hotel had a new look. I watched it from Hades. It stood up straight as if it was wearing new clothes. Maggie bought a big tree for the guest lounge and hung fairy lights on it and brought her mother in to see it.

There were twenty guests staying for the festive season. On Christmas morning, Maggie played a record of carols and the guests had stockings full of little presents with their breakfast of English muffins, cooked on the premises by Timothy Mackintosh who had a way with dough. Timothy Mackintosh also cooked a wonderful Christmas dinner with turkey and bread sauce and peas and sprouts and sausages wrapped in bacon. All the guests had crackers by their plates.

'I've never seen anything like it,' said Grace as she chewed her turkey and stuffing.

That afternoon Beatrice organised games for the guests and Maggie stood behind the bar and sold Christmas drinks. Grandma Grace fell asleep in the guest lounge after she had opened her presents: a new cardigan from Beatrice, a new hat from Timothy, and slippers from Maggie.

'Do I look cold?' she said, but she was pleased nevertheless, and put on her new cardigan and slippers and kept her hat folded in her hands.

On New Year's Eve, Maggie got Grace out of bed again and opened a bottle of buck's fizz, and everyone sang 'Auld Lang Syne' and counted down to midnight.

'A new decade,' said Maggie to Beatrice, who had red cheeks, like an apple. 'I had a craving for apples when I had you,' Maggie said. 'Happy New Year,' and she kissed her on the cheek. 'Happy New Year, Mother.' She kissed Grandma Grace too.

Maggie had an eye for business and in spring 1970, just after I had returned again and just before the Beatles split up, she phoned the tutor who ran the ballroom dancing classes in town and asked if her new dining room would be big enough for lessons, if she cleared the chairs and tables away once a week. So soon there was an advert in the *Bournemouth Evening Echo* inviting people to learn the charleston and the rumba at the Water's Edge Hotel in Boscombe. Maggie even organised an intensive weekend course with food and accommodation included. I didn't join in, but I sat in the dining room and spectated and I looked through the wall into Room One and into Grandma Grace's head so that I could watch her dreams.

'Why ballroom dancing?' said Beatrice, when Maggie told her about the idea.

'I've always wanted to learn to dance,' said Maggie, picking up one of the records she had just bought so that she could examine the sleeve.

When it was time for the first class, it was a beautiful spring day outside, warm and fresh, with a breeze coming in across the beach so it smelt of sand and fish. There were daffodils in the garden – like ladies in Easter bonnets, Maggie thought. Fifteen couples arrived, and sat gingerly around the edge of the dining room on the chairs that Maggie had put out, while Grandma Grace shifted painfully on to her other side in bed and listened to the waltzes and the cha-cha-chas coming through her bedroom wall, and the sound of feet moving in time, and let the rhythms rock her to sleep.

She dreamt she was on a ship with Thomas Tamarack and that they were dancing around the deck. The stars were out and Grace was nineteen years old and wearing her blue dress. Then Thomas Tamarack ran to the side of the ship and jumped over and she wanted to shout 'Man overboard!' but she couldn't because her feet wouldn't stop dancing and her lips couldn't stop humming the tune she was listening to.

Meanwhile, Maggie waltzed her way around her new dining room with the ice-cream salesman, who was a whiz on the dance floor and was seen a week later (by Timothy Mackintosh) in the corridor outside Room Four with a toothbrush, heading for the bathroom. I looked up through the ceiling to where Beatrice and Timothy Mackintosh sat in the attic room, laughing and shaking their heads. Later, after the class had finished, Beatrice found

Maggie and the ice-cream salesman practising their steps in the guest lounge.

'It keeps you fit,' said Maggie when Beatrice asked her about it afterwards.

'Who was he?' said Beatrice.

'No one special,' said Maggie.

When Grace woke up later that night, she thought she heard a noise outside her room and that maybe it was the ghost of her old cat, Barnabus, chasing mice or killing spiders. 'Don't kill spiders, Barnabus. It's bad luck,' Grace said into her pillow as she fell asleep again.

I was watching through the walls in July 1974, on the day that Chris Evert won Wimbledon for the first time, when Grandma Grace turned over in her sleep, felt like she was having a bad dream and died. I was still watching three years later, in 1977, when Voyager Two was flung into space, Elvis was found dead and the Queen had her Silver Jubilee. Beatrice and Meredith took Esther, age seven, to see *Star Wars* and to wave her flag in Bournemouth town centre when the Queen came to visit on her whistle-stop tour of the country.

In the same year, Maggie ordered duvets with tasteful floral patterns for every room of the hotel. Six years later (two years after Voyager flew by Jupiter and a year before Rice arrived at the old hotel) Meredith went to Greenham Common with her tent and a guitar and she stayed for six months, until the orchestra gave her an ultimatum and said if she didn't come back they would find another cellist.

But that all happened after July 1974 which, at the Water's Edge, was about tennis and death. We all went to church again to say goodbye to Grandma Grace (of course I invited myself, although Maggie wondered why), a different church this time, with a different vicar. Beatrice held Esther's hand because she didn't understand where her great-grandmother had gone. Suzie and Rice weren't there because they had already moved Up North and no one had heard from them, not even Meredith, who had just been to her audition with the Bournemouth Philharmonic. After Grandma Grace's funeral, Maggie changed her name to Grandma Maggie straight away.

Meredith took her Beatrice's hand and squeezed it at the hotel afterwards. Then she stood next to her and listened as she said: 'My grandma had a good life,' to everyone who asked her over the sandwiches and coffee cake. There were lots of old guests there, as Grace had been very popular, and even the odd soldier and his wife who had stayed at the hotel during the war came to say goodbye. (Fifteen years later there would be another funeral, this time for Grace Tamarack's daughter.)

Grandma Maggie's ghost shone green like a sea monster as she thought about the things that went on at the Water's Edge Hotel. She told some of her stories to the spirits who still lingered on the landings, which were black like burnt toast, until it was time for her to go and find Meredith's flat.

I discharged myself from hospital and went to stay in our beach hut at the bottom of the steps up to the old hotel. The beach hut smells of crabs and children's wet feet and it's cold at night. It wasn't very comfortable, and I had to go to the fish-and-chip café for breakfast, so I could to go to the toilet, but I didn't have anywhere else to go (Demeter was somewhere off in the mists of time again and I couldn't get her on the phone). I didn't want to stay in a different hotel.

Meredith had told me when the funeral was, so a few days later I went round to her flat to meet up with the people from the hotel beforehand. Grandma Maggie was there too, not mad any more, although no one else could see her. Beatrice made us all tea and Grandma Maggie's ghost walked into the kitchen behind us and

245

sat down at the kitchen table wishing that she could breathe in mouthfuls of the perfumed steam like we did before driving to the church in Meredith's red Ford Fiesta. Maggie got in the back, squeezed in between Rice and Esther and me. Lizzy the Saturday girl went on Sandra's moped.

The sun was shining when we got to the church. Sandra whispered to Rice that it was the same church she had got married in, and had another cigarette outside before she went in. Grandma Maggie's body was in her coffin next to the altar. I sat next to Lizzy and Sandra, and the others filed in at the front. Meredith stood with her hands on the pew in front of her, staring at a stained-glass window through her sunglasses. Rice was looking at the coffin and remembering her mother. Esther was crying loudly and blowing her nose and Beatrice was also crying but silently, tears running down her cheeks like she hadn't noticed them at all. The ghost of Grandma Maggie sat down in the pew next to her daughter. Beatrice couldn't see her but I wondered if she could feel her there, like a cold wind in the stuffy church. The vicar had had heaters put in under the seats. He said the Twenty-Third Psalm and the ghost of Grandma Maggie joined in, hoping that Beatrice could hear her, whispering the words she remembered: 'Green pastures, still waters, forsaketh me.'

There were no tea and cakes after this service. Instead we all drove to the crematorium. It was hot in the chapel, which was painted red and orange with white flowers. We watched the coffin disappear behind the curtains into another fire. After the funeral, Maggie went back to haunt the hotel for a while longer. Meredith drove Esther, Rice and Beatrice home, and Lizzy and Sandra went off on the moped, leaving me to stand in the crematorium car park waiting for a bus back to Boscombe.

My name was still Rice, but after the fire I felt like a different

246

person. When I left the hospital I went to stay with Esther and Beatrice at Meredith's flat.

'How are you feeling, Rice?' said Meredith when she and Beatrice came to pick me up in her red Ford Fiesta. I was getting out just in time for Grandma Maggie's appointment at the crematorium. It was 21 May.

'Summer already,' said Beatrice, on the way back to her flat.

'Thunderstorm weather,' said Meredith.

Esther was sitting on a beanbag and said 'Hello' in a strange voice when I came in, and there were the three chambermaids from the old hotel, Sandra, Lizzy and Daphne, looking out of place on Meredith's small white sofa. Sandra was smoking, which sent Meredith into a flurry of opening windows and fetching ashtrays.

'I don't normally let people, but seeing as it's today . . .' she said. Sandra nodded and flicked ash into the ashtray. I wanted to ask Daphne about whether it really was her at the hospital, but somehow I forgot.

'I'm making lemon and ginger tea,' Beatrice said, putting her head round the door. 'Come into the kitchen.' So we all went and sat down at the table.

My surname is Parker, but what's in a name after all? After the crematorium, I was tucked into the sofa with a duvet because I was still officially ill and Esther went out for a walk down by the flat sands at Whitley Bay by Poole Harbour to watch the sea going out. The day was heating up like an oven and soon I threw off my duvet. We couldn't think what to do so Meredith turned on the TV and *King Kong* was on so we watched that. Then she put her arm round Beatrice's shoulders and told her it was OK, and kept it there, even after Beatrice had stopped crying. Beatrice seemed to like it and even leant her head on Meredith's chest and fell asleep.

I felt a bit awkward, sitting on the sofa with my duvet at my feet, and wanted Esther to come back. I was relieved when *King Kong* was over and Esther came through the door and Meredith told her to put Beatrice to bed. Meredith didn't say anything about Beatrice being asleep on her chest all afternoon, so I didn't either. That night there was a thunderstorm and I stood inside the window blind and watched the purple lightning flash across the bay, until Esther and Meredith got up and said they couldn't sleep either, so the three of us sat in the kitchen and drank more of Meredith's herbal tea, listening to the thunder.

Meredith's flat seemed so small after living at the old hotel that it took a while to get used to it. I found it strange that there were no guests to bump into or to serve bacon and eggs to in the mornings. Beatrice slept in Meredith's room and Esther and I slept in the lounge. We unfolded the futon every evening and remade it each morning after we had drunk big cups of camomile tea and eaten hot buttered toast in the kitchen.

As well as extra people, there were extra things in the flat too, including a box full of photos brought over from the lockup where the furniture and the teapots from the hotel were being stored. (Later Beatrice raised a bit of money from an auction, but for now it was all still locked away.) Beatrice's photos were on top. Some of them were black round the edges, but I could still see the pictures.

'We managed to save most of them,' said Esther.

I rummaged through the box, under Beatrice's pictures, and I found my own, some of them in albums, some of them loose but all still intact. The one of me and my mother outside the Houses of Parliament was brown in one corner, like someone had held a match underneath it, but it didn't matter.

'Look what else we found,' said Meredith, taking something out of a plastic bag.

248

'My camera,' I said. I inspected it. 'I don't think it will work.' I opened the back and found I was right. The film had melted on to the insides. I pulled it out, and tried to remember what it was of, but I couldn't. Then I tried putting in new film and from the sofa I focused through the window on one of the little boats enjoying the early summer sun in Whitley Bay, but I couldn't even press the shutter release down properly.

'It's definitely broken,' I said, and sadly put the camera back in its case.

'The *Echo* want a picture of the hotel for the paper,' said Beatrice. 'They're doing a special story about it.' There had already been an article about the fire, with a picture of a fireman, but this was going to be a two-page piece about the history of the hotel, Beatrice told us. So we looked through the photos, trying to find the best one. When we got to the one of Grandma Maggie, aged five, with the cat, Beatrice took the photo from me and caressed it and told us the story of the picture even though we had heard it before.

'I'll get this one framed,' she said, and I noticed Meredith rubbing Beatrice's elbow backwards and forwards like she was smoothing her down with sandpaper.

Steve and the Estate Agent

We never did choose a photo for the paper. None of us wanted to talk about it, because it was like admitting that the hotel wasn't there any more, but each time we looked through the box we pretended that that's what we were doing. Soon Esther went back to work at the beauty salon and, after Beatrice had spent a lot of time on the phone to estate agents, property developers bought the land where the hotel stood.

I had a lot of time to think after I came out of hospital. The days stretched out and became longer and hotter and smelt of apples, and we ate a lot of ice cream. Often my thoughts were accompanied by the piano or the cello because Meredith was still teaching young musicians with school uniforms and round glasses. She had to do it, she told me. Because of the fire, she wasn't going away with the orchestra on their summer tour any more. Beatrice usually went out to the shops or to the beach to put her toes in the water when they arrived, but because I was still supposed to be ill, I stayed indoors and made tea for the mums or dads, just as I'd done many times before. And they waited at the kitchen table, treating the whole thing like a visit to the dentist.

One of the musical children's dads was Steve, who used to be a Saturday boy at the old hotel and had just trained to be a nurse at Poole Hospital. I hadn't seen him while I was there.

He was in Geriatrics, he said. His eldest son, Peter, was four and was learning the violin.

Steve told me how when he trained to be a nurse he was the only man and that some of the people on his ward still called him doctor, even though he had told them that his name was Steven.

After a few sessions of chatting about the lovely weather and hospitals and the hotel and his children and art college and cameras, he suddenly said: 'Do you need money for college?' and I thought for a moment he was going to pass over a handful of notes. Instead he said: 'Because I'd like a picture of Peter with his violin.'

'I can't,' I said.

'Why not?'

'I haven't got a camera.'

'I've got one at home,' he said. 'It's very old – my granddad gave it to me – but I think it works. You can borrow it if you can figure out how to use it.' I handed him another cup of tea.

'What flavour is this one?' he said, looking at it uncertainly.

'Strawberry and nettle.'

Meredith had overheard the conversation and after she had packed up and closed the lid of her piano and we had said goodbye to Peter and Steve, she came into the kitchen to talk to me about it.

'It's a good idea,' she said.

'I'm not sure,' I said, but I let Meredith convince me. So Steve the nurse lent me his battered old camera with its wobbly tripod and I took some pictures of him and Peter holding the violin next to Meredith's piano. They came out well.

'How much do you want?' said Steve, getting out his cheque book.

'It's free,' I said, 'in return for letting me use your camera for a bit longer.'

'Sounds fair,' said Steve.

Then some of the other mums and dads heard about the photo and asked me to take their young musicians' portraits too. Taking pictures of the children and their parents gave me something to do while I waited at the flat for summer to end and for autumn to come so that I could go to London and start all over again. By the time I went away to college, I had taken lots of pictures of flautists and pianists and cellists and guitarists with one or two of their smiling parents in the background. Sometimes their grandparents came as well.

When I could persuade Meredith and Beatrice that I wasn't too ill to go on my own, I walked to Branksome Chine because I wanted to stroll on the beach again. I went out in the summer rain once, even though Beatrice told me off. I shielded Steve's camera under my coat and took pictures of my footprints in the water at the edge of the sea, but when I got the pictures developed, I couldn't see the footprints any more.

That summer, after the cheque from the insurance company came through the door in a brown envelope, we always seemed to be driving to the estate agent's office and sitting in the uncomfortable red chairs. The first time was in June when it was hot and we were all wearing our T-shirts and fanning ourselves with our hands. Beatrice and Meredith sat down when we got there and I stood and looked at the large green pot plants, which must have been smaller when they were brought in through the door and had now grown to the size of beanstalks. I wondered if Jack was at the top, fighting giants. Esther looked at the pictures around the walls of the houses and flats that were for sale, with the prices underneath. In the corner there was a special section with a handful of hotels and guesthouses.

'I spoke to you on the phone,' said Beatrice. 'My name is Beatrice Tamarack.' The man behind the desk nodded and handed Beatrice a black-and-white photocopy of the pictures of the guesthouses and hotels on the wall.

'I think I have a few places I can show you,' he said, pointing them out on the photocopy, so we all squeezed into the estate agent's Ford Escort, Beatrice in the front, Esther, Meredith and me in the back. The car was sticky and the heat outside made the tarmac in front of us shine like the road to heaven. I wriggled impatiently and wished we were on the beach, letting ice cream drip on to our swimming costumes instead.

'The first place is vacant at the moment,' he said, changing gear and heading off towards the town centre. When we got there we burst out of the hot car like seeds. I wanted to put my head under a tap and be cool again or stand under a hose pipe while Esther watered the hotel garden, but then I remembered there wasn't a proper hotel garden to water now, and followed the others up the driveway.

This hotel was higgledy-piggledy, and sandy-coloured on the outside. The inside was completely empty. All the carpets, curtains, light bulbs, chairs and tables had gone. Esther and I went and stood in the middle of the dining room, which was a big echoey white hall with wooden tiles on the floor. At first it was a relief because it was cool inside, like a hospital, but soon it started to feel very strange. We went into the kitchen, which had dull metallic surfaces and a big electric cooker, but no utensils on the wall, and no saucepans or teapots. Upstairs, the bedrooms were the same: completely empty and clinical.

I felt like I was inside a bad dream and that I'd come back to the old hotel but none of it was the same and none of our things were there. Someone had stolen the Hoovers and the brochures and the white tables in the bar and the spoons and the beds.

253

'It's unusual because the owner has got rid of the inventory,' the estate agent said as we came back down the stairs. I wondered for a moment if he was talking about men on horseback riding into battle, with their bayonets ready, and I imagined them charging through the dining room and out into the hall, where there were no light bulbs and no lampshades.

'It would take a lot of work,' said Meredith.

'It's too big,' said Beatrice, so we got back into the car, where the seats were almost melting and we thought about lemonade and ice. We had to go on to the next place instead, which was neat and compact and smelt of roses. The owner was there this time and she showed us round. There were six guest rooms, built as an extension on to the side of a squat white house. It was cool inside the owners' part and it had a brown roof and a big garden, where there were children and a dog in the sun. When we got there, the dog ran up to us, jumped up at Esther and barked.

'It's lovely,' I heard Beatrice whisper to Meredith as we went round. Then we went to look at the guest accommodation, as the owner called it. Downstairs there was a yellow tiled kitchen and a small dining room. Upstairs the beds all had bedspreads on them which were white with pink, blue and green flowers and embroidered edging. There were cushions resting in the armchairs, which took up the same pattern, and the sinks were perched on top of pine cabinets, with brass taps that said 'hot' and 'cold' on little enamel buttons on the top of them. On the wall above the beds in each room was a large print in a frame. One was a painting of two women in a yellow rowing boat and it said 'Renoir' in big letters underneath the picture, but I knew that already, because I had done it at college. We looked inside cupboards and under desks and the stairs but we didn't find any dust or dirt anywhere.

'I like to keep a clean house,' said the owner proudly, and

Beatrice took her hand and said thank you but on the way back out into the hot June day she shook her head and said, 'It's too small. Ten would be nice. Not six.'

'I might be able to arrange some appointments for tomorrow,' said the estate agent.

We went home feeling sweaty and tired and I felt like a traitor to the old hotel, which I hadn't been back to visit since the fire like the others had, because I was frightened that seeing it would ruin the picture I had of it in my head.

Martha Kagel

My name is Persephone. From the water's edge where I am
sitting with my knees hunched up under my chin, if I turn
my head round, I can see my beach hut. Someone has painted it
green and yellow. It is the same beach hut I have always used
and the one where I lived in 1989 after Maggie turned into a
ghost and stopped being mad. Watching the beach hut makes
me think of the past again and the bits of the story that I've left
out up till now, pieces of jigsaw to do with Grace and Jonathan
Kagel and Margaret and Henry Duffle and Beatrice and me.

It was almost the end of March 1942. I had just arrived and
told Grace that I was Delilah's sister, Dorcas, and had started
work as a chambermaid again. I have the gift of prophecy and I
knew what was going to happen so I sat upright in bed waiting,
watching through the floorboards for Jonathan Kagel to come
back from Wales, intent on asking Margaret to marry him.

Margaret was in the kitchen on one of her early-morning
adventures. I could see that her fingers were wrinkled from
the washing-up water. It was six o'clock and Grace was asleep.
Margaret was feeling queasy from morning sickness, so she had
eaten an apple and made herself a cup of peppermint tea, with
the mint from Grace's herb garden, to make herself feel better.
If Grace had caught her in the kitchen, she would have chased

her back upstairs in case one of the soldiers saw her swollen stomach. But Grace never did catch her and never mentioned the jobs that were done mysteriously in the early morning, because Margaret was always back in her room by the time the soldiers came looking for sausages.

I watched as she stopped scrubbing the pots and looked out of the window (I could see right inside her head). She looked past the things Grace kept on the windowsill, the different coloured sand in a jar and the pot of spoons. The garden was littered with leftovers from her mother's gardening adventures – plant pots, old bits of wood, and a spade lying on its side on the path. The washing line was strung loosely from the side of the house and tied to the stumpy ivy-covered tree in the corner by the wall. It was curved against the grey sky.

'Pregnant like me,' Margaret thought.

She wiped off the sauce stuck around a fork, and the tomato at the bottom of a pan. Then she carefully selected her cup of hot tea from the five or six that were waiting to be cleaned. She gulped at it, getting soap bubbles round the handle. There was a wet patch on her thighs from the water that had escaped from the sink. 'Maybe the baby is crying,' she thought.

'If you are a boy you'll be called Thomas Tamarack,' she said, inside her head, to the baby, stirring the dirty water this way and that. 'If you are a girl you'll be called Margaret Tamarack after me.' She wondered what it would be like to have her baby and how much blood there would be.

'It's suffering sent from God,' Grace had said. 'Punishment for the apple in the garden of Eden.'

The sun came out from hiding but the sky still looked cold. It's more like autumn than spring, she thought. Daffodils sat shyly under the windowsill. The buds were still a timid green colour, like the eyes of a dead animal. Margaret closed her own

257

eyes and remembered walking along the beach in the hot sun before the war.

It was a Sunday. Later Grace would put her hat on and go to church to tell lies. She would wear her maternity dress and ask the congregation to pray for her daughter, who was ill and couldn't come to church.

'We're so grateful it wasn't TB,' she would say. 'And no, please don't feel like you have to visit; we are frightened it might spread.'

Margaret dropped a plate into the water and it splashed her. Then she reached for the last cup, when suddenly, the kitchen door opened and Jonathan Kagel came in. Moving swiftly across the kitchen, he put his hand over her eyes and said, 'Guess who?' and then when she didn't respond: 'I'm back, Margaret.'

She realised who it was but she didn't want to turn round because then he would see her stomach. She felt his warm hand on her face and smelt his skin, tobacco and, somewhere underneath lots of other smells, there was lavender. Instead of turning round she asked questions. It surprised him. He had expected her to be pleased to see him. He took his hand away from her face. She was still up to her elbows in water.

'How did you get in?' she said.

'Through the front door.'

'What are you doing here?'

'I thought I'd surprise you, while your mother isn't about.'

Then Margaret turned round. He smiled and then the smile fell off his face like a child falling out of a tree.

'You're pregnant.'

'Yes.'

'Who's the father?'

'A soldier.'

Then Margaret lied to Jonathan Kagel. She wanted him to see

into her head and understand that she was lying, but instead he listened to the fantasy she had created while she was looking out of the window in Room Fifteen and while she was counting the lines on each of her fingers, and he believed her.

'He took me out to a restaurant overlooking the sea and there was a band there with someone playing a cello and a trumpet,' Margaret said, with her back against the sink. 'And he gave me flowers and said I was his princess and lots of things.'

'Are you getting married?'

'No.' Margaret started crying quietly to herself and Jonathan turned round and went back out through the kitchen door and she heard the front door closing snap behind him. She didn't see him again for seven years.

The sun went back into hiding behind the clouds and Margaret went back upstairs to Room Fifteen and lay on her bed with her face to the wall, so there was no wedding, although Margaret kept the photograph of her and Jonathan Kagel with her during her six months in hiding. She got through the sickness and got over her cravings, for apples mainly, and blossomed like a tree. Her cheeks were red, her breasts were full, and she sat in her hideaway room, waiting for her time to come. On warm days, she kept the window open, and through it she could see the beach lit up in the sunlight, and smell the salty air.

Beatrice was born on 5 May 1942. Grace swore that she was hers when people who weren't convinced by the grey maternity dress whispered that the girl had got herself into trouble. Grace said that Margaret should name her baby girl Beatrice, after her own mother who had died in 1918, and she brought out her old perambulator and said, to anyone that asked, 'One life ends and another one begins. Mr Tamarack has left me a new baby girl.'

One summer, about four years after the end of the war,

Jonathan Kagel came to stay. The beach had been cleaned up and the guests had started coming back. He was dressed in civilian clothes so that Margaret didn't recognise him at first. His hair was parted in a different style too, she noticed as he took off his hat. He left the place where his right hand should have been inside his coat pocket, making him look slightly untidy in the cleaned and dusted reception area of the Water's Edge Hotel.

'Jonathan Kagel,' said Margaret. His face looked whiter than before but his eyes were still like two streaks of blue paint, and they darted across Margaret's face.

'We're nearly full,' said Grace to Margaret, coming out from the kitchen and into the hallway to meet the new guest, who had arrived out of the dark night like an apparition. Then she realised who the ghost-faced young man was and said: 'Mr Kagel, we're very pleased to have you back,' shaking his hand up and down like a seesaw. Then in through the front door came a small woman, wobbling slightly. People who stopped to look at her wondered how she managed to carry a baby inside her which seemed almost as big as she was, but not many people looked at her, because she was so small and seemed to fade into the wallpaper. She had short wavy blonde hair, which sat close to her head, too nervous to stray any further. She was wearing a blue cardigan and she had big blue eyes, like blue balloons, which cast about the hotel reception, looking for something to rest on.

'This is my wife, Martha,' said Jonathan Kagel, looking at the floor. 'Mrs Tamarack, Miss Tamarack, Mrs Kagel.' They nodded at one another.

'Pleased to meet you,' said Mrs Kagel.

'We're here on holiday. We thought we'd stop by to see if you had a room,' said Jonathan. To Margaret he seemed older and more anxious, although his face had softened. Then Beatrice ran in and nearly collided with Martha Kagel, whose eyes settled on Beatrice's head like an unhappy butterfly trapped in a flowerless room. Jonathan opened and closed his mouth, not knowing what to say to the new arrival.

'Beatrice, be polite,' said Grace.

'Sorry, Ma,' said Beatrice, who was learning to write stories at school and who had ridden a bicycle in the playground only two days before.

'I want to drive a train,' she had told her teacher, and wrote a story about a train that went from Bournemouth all the way up to Cape Wrath in Scotland but it didn't stop and went into the sea and ended up in Iceland. All the passengers had to go fishing so they would have something for their tea. Her teacher had given her a silver star but she made her write out her spelling corrections three times.

'I want to drive a train,' Beatrice said proudly to Jonathan and Martha Kagel, who were standing in the hotel reception with their coats still on.

'This is my daughter Beatrice,' said Grace, looking at Margaret. 'I see you're expecting a little one, Mrs Kagel.'

'Yes,' said Jonathan, 'we have one already, about Beatrice's age.'

'A bit younger,' said Martha Kagel.

'She's staying with her grandfather,' said Jonathan. 'We're hoping for a boy this time.'

'Room Fourteen, Margaret,' said Grace. 'Take them up so the poor woman can sit down. You look exhausted. Would you like some tea bringing up?'

Jonathan and Martha declined the kind offer of tea and Margaret showed them up to Room Fourteen. She had opened the window earlier and when she pushed the door she saw the curtains flutter and she could feel the cool breeze on her face,

261

which smelt of salt because it had come up from the sea. Martha Kagel went inside and sat down heavily on the bed.

'My feet,' she said, and wriggled free of her shoes.

Jonathan hung back in the corridor. He closed the door on his wife.

'Hello, Margaret,' he said. 'How's the garden?'

'Got to get on,' she said.

'See you later then,' said Jonathan, his blue eyes darting between Margaret's small nose and her dark brown eyebrows.

It was a hot day. Margaret was in the garden, thinking of going down to the water's edge and putting her feet in the salty water, when Jonathan Kagel came out to smoke. She tried to go back into the kitchen but he held on to her arm.

'Wait,' he said. 'I'd like you to show me how the garden's changed.'

'Mother's put in some more runner beans over there. The tree in the corner died, but we haven't chopped it down because the ivy growing up the trunk is pretty. We planted some daffodils and there were lots of them in the spring. You should have seen them. And tulips.'

'Flowers,' said Jonathan, and touched the white faces of the dog roses and smelt the sun-coloured honeysuckle.

'Where is Mrs Kagel?' Margaret said.

'Sleeping,' said Jonathan. 'Shall we go down to the beach?' Margaret followed him over to the gate and they undid the latch and walked down the beach steps. They both took off their shoes and socks, and the sea came up the beach and covered their feet. The water was so cold it was shocking, so they retreated and sat down on the sand.

Jonathan spoke softly and said, 'Martha and I are in love.' Margaret felt the words creeping over her toes like the sea water had done. 'When I came and found you that time in the kitchen,

I was going to ask you to marry me. Things would have been different.'

'Yes.'

'The army gave me a permanent job in Wales.'

'I know.'

'Beatrice is a pretty name.'

'My mother chose it. My grandmother was called Beatrice.'

'Where is Beatrice's father?'

'Dead.'

'I'm sorry.'

'Don't be.'

'Were you going to get married?'

'No.'

'Beatrice calls Grace Ma,' Jonathan said. Margaret played in the sand with her toes. 'Grace told me Beatrice was her daughter, but Beatrice is your daughter.'

'You're the only person who knows,' said Margaret, 'only because you saw me. You and the doctor.'

'Beatrice doesn't know?'

'She's only seven. Ma says we'll tell her when she's older.'

Maybe this isn't exactly how it happened; sometimes my memory clouds – something to do with the salt water getting in my ears when I go back to Hades. Funny how I can remember some things like shiny crystals and others are misty as bath water. This is how Beatrice remembers it anyway, when I look into her head.

Beatrice, aged seven, went to play on the beach with Mr and Mrs Kagel who said they would look after her for the afternoon and buy her ice cream, because it was so hot. Grace was grateful to them for their kindness. Margaret was lying on her bed again, facing the wall, and had said she couldn't do anything today because she was probably coming down with something.

263

Beatrice played at the edge of the water, collecting shells, while Martha Kagel sat in a deck chair and looked as though she wouldn't ever be able to get up again. Then Beatrice made a sandcastle and Martha watched her and smiled with one hand on her stomach.

Jonathan went for a walk along the wet part of the sand, holding his shoes, and when he came back he had stashed fish and chips under his jacket to keep them warm and they ate them quickly, burning their tongues and crunching the sand that had got mixed in with the chips.

'Do you want to come and paddle, Beatrice?' said Jonathan, and they set off along the edge of the beach together, making disappearing footprints in the water. Martha watched them, her hand shading her eyes. After they had walked in silence for a while, splashing their legs with each step, Jonathan suddenly stopped and crouched down next to Beatrice and said, 'Beatrice, do you know who your grandma is?'

'She died,' said Beatrice. 'She was called Beatrice, like me.'

'No,' Jonathan said, 'she's still alive. She lives with you in the hotel.'

Beatrice thought of her Sunday school teacher. 'Like Jesus?' she said, looking into Jonathan's kind blue eyes.

'What's your mother's name, Beatrice?'

'My mother is called Grace Tamarack. She lives at the Water's Edge Hotel, in Bournemouth, England.'

'No, Mrs Tamarack is your grandma. Margaret Tamarack is your mother.' Beatrice opened her mouth in an O shape. Then she spread out her hand like a starfish and put it under the water to find out what it would do.

'Who's my daddy, Mr Kagel?' she said then, because Jonathan Kagel knew lots of things about mummies and maybe he knew about that too.

'He was a soldier,' said Jonathan.

'Mr Thomas Tamarack,' said Beatrice. 'He died in the war. Hitler shot him.'

'No. Thomas Tamarack was your granddad. Your daddy was another soldier. But he's gone now.'

Beatrice was confused. 'Where has he gone, Mr Kagel?'

'I don't know.' He couldn't explain different types of death to Beatrice Tamarack, aged seven. Beatrice went skipping into the water so it was just above her ankles and danced along, making splashes that got her dress wet. She kept this new information safe inside her fist as she went back up the beach steps with Jonathan and Martha Kagel. It was interesting, mothers and fathers, and who belonged to who, and she decided to think about it later, and maybe put the pieces together like a big puzzle.

'Your dress is wet,' said Grace, when they got back to the kitchen and Beatrice thought, you're not my mother so you can't say, but she didn't shout it out loud like she wanted to; she kept it safe instead, because she had found out that she was special and she didn't want her secret to fly away from her like a bird and maybe get squashed if it fell off a branch or get eaten by a ginger cat.

Jonathan and Martha went on a trip to Poole the next day, as one final excursion. Before they checked out, Jonathan told Grace that he liked Poole very much and would move there if it wasn't for the army, and that they would be back again on holiday next year. They took with them some cuttings from the garden and promised to write to Grace and tell her how heavy the baby was and how their plants were faring.

Grace called the sixteen-year-old Beatrice into the guest lounge in July 1958. Margaret was sitting in an armchair, next to her mother, and was falling into it, folded into it like a cushion, Beatrice thought. Grace told her that Margaret her sister was really her mother and that they had been trying to protect her but it was time that she knew, now she was sixteen and had grown into a Christian woman with periods, and that her father was called Henry and had killed himself by walking into the sea.

When Grace had told Beatrice all this, she said, calmly, 'I know,' like a girl who has already slept with three men before her mother tells her to wait until you really love him.

'I know,' said Beatrice to Grace, who folded her hands in her lap and looked at the floor. This wasn't what she had expected but, after all, Beatrice had always been a difficult child. Exactly seven days after she was born she started crying and didn't stop until she was three years old, Grace thought to herself, and then she ran around everywhere, laughing all day, to make up for all that crying, getting under the feet of the guests, banging on doors. Now she was difficult again.

'What do you know, Beatrice?' said Grace.

'I knew you were pretending.'

'How did you know?'

'Jonathan Kagel told me. On the beach. We were paddling.'

Beatrice had had the secret inside her fist, like a dead butterfly, for nine years.

'We were trying to protect you,' said Grace. 'Don't have relations with a man until you are married.'

'Do you want me to call you Mother?' Beatrice said to Margaret, who had started to cry, tears running down her face like little rivers. Margaret got up, wiped her face with the back of her hand and ran out of the room.

'You can call me Ma, like you always have done,' said Grace, folding her arms under her chest. 'If you want to call Margaret Mother then you'd better let her get used to it.' But soon, however much she protested, Grace became Grandma Grace, and sixteen years later she was dead and Margaret became Grandma Maggie in her place.

Joshua Lyal

I was working at the hotel in June 1942 when Henry Duffle fell down the steps to the cellar. (Beatrice was a month old.) It was late at night, about half-past eleven, and I watched it all happen through the ceiling of the room I was staying in, with my goddess eyes. The door to the cellar was open, as it often was, because Grace stored tin cans and sacks of potatoes down there, along with other rations, and vegetables that she grew in the hotel garden, and hung from the ceiling. He should have watched where he was going, but he was drunk and angry, so he fell in backwards, surprised as Goliath. Grace wouldn't let him see Beatrice, his daughter, who was upstairs and sleeping. He had heard rumours about her amongst the soldiers at his base and he had come back to find out if it was true and if she had a nose like his. Grace wouldn't have a drunk man in her house.

'You're drunk, Henry Duffle,' she said, and grabbed her broom and tried to shoo him away.

Margaret had her hands over her ears. She was sitting at the long wooden table in the kitchen. Her mother was trying to get him out of the back door, but he wouldn't go. He was edging round the kitchen towards Margaret, so Grace jabbed at him with her broom. He lunged forward and tried to grab it from her, lost his balance and fell backwards. Grace ran quickly down the cellar stairs after him. Margaret took her hands away from her ears and went to stand at the top of the steps. She saw his body lying awkwardly on the cold floor, leaking from the mouth and bladder, and her mother bending over him. There was a sweet smell, urine mixed with beer, that made her retch and she had to run to the sink in case she was sick. The curtains in the window twitched and she felt the chill night air coming in through the cracks.

Grace couldn't find a pulse and thought, mistakenly, that he was dead. She climbed back up the stairs, leaving the cellar door open, and sat opposite her daughter at the table. The kitchen was silent. The sweet dusty smell and the cold of the cellar was winding its way up the stairs towards them. The two women, mother and daughter, sat at the table for a long time, half an hour, maybe an hour. Grace was the first to speak.

'We've broken one of the commandments, but your father killed other men for Mr Churchill,' she said, and stood up. Then Grace descended once more towards the inert body of Henry Duffle. Stepping carefully round him, she brought up the tin cans first, then the vegetables, the carrots she had grown lovingly from seed, the parsnips, turnips, pumpkins and onions, then the big sacks of potatoes. After that she closed the cellar door (there was no lock but she didn't expect him to get out) and told Margaret to go to bed.

Next morning, the event hung in the air between Grace and her daughter like dancing particles of dust. Grace grimly cooked breakfast for the soldiers, standing next to the gas oven. After the soldiers had left, full of home-made scones (because there were no sausages that day) and coffee, she sat down at the table, her apron still on, and told her daughter that something had to be done, so without opening the cellar door again, Grace and Margaret went to get the big boards of wood that Thomas Tamarack had been saving to fashion into a cupboard before he went off to the war. Grace made sure the curtains were tight shut and took up the hammer and nails.

'Bang them in hard, Mother,' said Margaret. 'We don't want him to get out.'

'There's no danger of that,' said Grace, hitting the last nail with her hammer.

They used some spare wallpaper to paper over the cracks. Then Grace said it looked a little too new, so they rubbed the patch with cold tea on a cloth and dirt from the dustpan.

The next day, a policeman came to the door of the Water's Edge Hotel, while Beatrice was asleep in Room Four. I was dusting upstairs with Margaret when she looked through the window, and saw him coming up the drive way. She ran to tell her mother. I carried on dusting and watched through the floorboards.

'Mrs Tamarack, how are you?' said the policeman. 'Sorry to hear about Mr Tamarack.'

'Hello, Joshua.' Grace recognised the policeman straight away. His name was Joshua Lyal. He was a nice boy. When he was a youngster, Grace used to give him ginger biscuits to fatten him up, and tea when the weather was cold. She baked the biscuits until they went crispy at the edges in the old gas oven.

'You better come in,' said Grace, opening the door. Joshua Lyal spent sometime talking to the serious men in Room Nineteen, while Grace walked up and down in the kitchen below and Margaret sat at the table with her hands flat in front of her. Then he came downstairs again.

'I've got to ask you some questions,' Joshua said.

'Now, what's this all about?' said Grace.

'I've got to ask you about an officer who was staying here a while back,' said Joshua, 'a Lieutenant Duffle.' Margaret looked down at the table and then at the door to the cellar, just to make sure it was still hidden under the wallpaper.

'He was here late last summer,' she said.

'Tea?' said Grace. 'Ginger biscuit?'

'No, thank you all the same,' said Joshua. Grace helped herself to a cup of tea from the pot and a ginger biscuit from the tin on the side.

'Some of Lieutenant Duffle's clothes have been found on the beach,' Joshua continued. Grace and Margaret turned and looked at him in surprise. 'We are treating it as a suicide,' he said.

'Oh.' Grace sunk into a chair next to her daughter, who had turned pale. Now Grace looked at the space where the cellar door had been. Grace believed in ghosts (who else could walk through walls?) but this was still a surprise.

'Is something wrong, Mrs Tamarack?' said Joshua after a minute had passed.

'It's just such a shock,' she said, coming back to her senses again. Margaret didn't say anything, but she gripped the edge of the table with her hands to stop herself from falling.

'He had no family to speak of,' said Joshua.

'This is all so upsetting,' said Grace. 'He never behaved strangely while he was here.'

'Right. Some of the boys down at the base said that Margaret and him were friends,' he said, looking directly at Margaret for the first time.

She looked back at him steadily and said: 'We weren't friends.'

Then Grace took a sip of her tea and said, 'I have just lost my husband and I have a new baby to look after.'

Joshua walked over to the door. 'Very good, Mrs Tamarack,' he said. 'Probably best not to spread it around. Bad for morale and all.'

Later that year Joshua started a relationship with Sammy, the

271

other chambermaid, and a few years later they were married and Grace went to the wedding, leaving Margaret and Beatrice behind at the hotel.

Although Margaret asked her to three times, Grace wouldn't uncover the cellar door again in case her superstitious heart was right and the body of Henry Duffle still lay at the bottom of the stairs, decomposing. It was more than she could bear, to think of tearing off the newly laid wallpaper and opening the door to find that the dead thing remained there. Perhaps it was his ghost who had stripped his body of its clothes and left them on the sand, she thought to herself. But the ghost of Henry Duffle never visited Grace Tamarack. For the rest of her life, just before she went to sleep, she worried that he might and she kept the cellar hidden for fear that she would disturb his spirit.

Margaret guessed what had really happened, turning it over and over in her head. She realised that he hadn't been dead from the fall, that he had climbed out and escaped to the beach in the night. He had drowned, by accident probably, she thought, because he was so drunk. But she was secretly haunted by the memory of his face, above her in Room Fifteen, and at the bottom of the cellar stairs. She wanted to uncover the cellar so that she could see an empty space where he had fallen and remember that instead, but her mother wouldn't do it and by the time Margaret took charge of the hotel herself, she didn't want to disturb the memory of him, where it lay hidden underneath all the other things inside her head.

This is what happened to Henry Duffle on 5 June 1942, after Grace and Margaret had gone to bed. Joshua Lyal knew nothing about it. With my goddess ears I heard Henry Duffle, not dead yet, but still drunk, wake up at the bottom of the cellar steps. With my goddess eyes, I could see into his head and I could read his thoughts, and I knew he had a bad pain in his arm and in his head. When he tried his arm it didn't work so he thought it might be broken. He climbed unsteadily up into the kitchen, opened the back door and went out into the garden, feeling like he needed some fresh air because he couldn't remember everything that had happened. The cold air on his face was good, and looking down towards the beach he thought that maybe he would like to go for a swim – he had once won a prize in the army, swimming for three miles in salty water, although then the sea was calm, unlike on 5 June 1942, when it was wild and thrashing about like a monster. He didn't know about the mouth of Hades, full and gaping and ready for him. He unlocked the gate, went down the steps and had to climb out on to the cliff to get round the barbed wire, nearly falling as he did so, dragging his bad arm behind him. He swore under his breath and at last he was on the beach.

Standing at the window of my room, I could see the figure of Henry Duffle, swaggering along the seafront. I decided to go for a closer look, so I went out of the hotel and down the long way to the beach by the road, not wanting to climb on to the cliff to avoid the barbed wire at the bottom of the beach steps myself. There was no light because of the blackout, and the air wrapped itself around me like a cloak. I walked as far as the pier and then down to the beach. The sea was getting choppier and with my special night vision I could make out the anti-tank blocks and the jagged shapes of the rest of the obstacle course that had been left on the sand for the enemy to fall over. The sand itself looked dirty and grey when I bent to pick some of it up and sift it through my fingers. I crept down to where the pier had been detached from the land and stood next to one of the pillars, so that I was hidden inside its shape. Then I saw Henry again. He was taking off his clothes at the water's edge, shirt, trousers, shoes, socks, vest, pants, and stood there naked in the wind for a second, before walking into the sea. I saw him swimming purposefully backwards and forwards, dragging one arm behind him, until he was out of his depth, and then hell's mouth opened up and took him in a single bite like a Venus flytrap and he went under the waves. I didn't see him again until I went back to Hades in the autumn, and there he was a ghost of his former self, his arm in a sling, still broken.

I went back to the hotel and watched through the walls as I cleaned the carpets the next day as Grace and Margaret sealed up the cellar door, thinking there was a body at the bottom of the steps. And the day after that, I watched through the walls as I did the dusting, when Joshua the policeman came to call and said that Henry Duffle's clothes had been found that morning by a routine patrol.

Laina

Just after we began looking for a new hotel, I had an introductory session at the Proper Art College in London about what sort of camera equipment to buy before October, so I got on the train at Bournemouth station.

'This train will call at Southampton Central, Southampton Airport Parkway, Basingstoke, Clapham Junction and London Waterloo,' said the ticket inspector over the intercom. I sat and watched through the window as Bournemouth disappeared behind me and I sipped a cup of tea I had bought from the Lemon Tree Café on the platform. It tasted reassuringly of sterilised milk and almost completely unlike tea, which is a taste I have associated with train journeys since the weekend trips I used to take with my mother to see interesting places. Because of the tea, I started thinking about the time we went to Stonehenge and we stood together wondering how the stones had got there, and watching the sun go down, so that, without even noticing the time, I found I had daydreamt my way to Southampton.

Once we went to a stately home where some of the ceilings were made of gold and there were four-poster beds and big tapestries on the wall, and there was a maze in the garden. My mother and I had wandered around the maze for ages. I think she might have been scared, but then she said, 'I know,' like she had worked it out in her head and she led us straight to the exit and bought us both an ice cream as a reward for finding our way out.

I sat on the train to London wondering what it would be like to turn the stately home with the maze into a big hotel and whether people would want to spend the night in the rooms with the gold ceilings or whether it would stop them sleeping and the hotel would have to be called the Insomniac's Hotel. Once I saw a programme about a woman who believed that she floated out of her body at night and up to the ceiling of her bedroom, where she slept. The programme makers illustrated the story with a moodily lit but ordinary-looking bedroom with a boring white ceiling. They had set up an experiment where the floating woman would have to read a hidden number from the ceiling in her sleep and disclose it the next morning, to prove what she said was true. The floating woman ran away the next day. What would she have made of the ceiling in the stately home my mother had taken me to? Perhaps she could get work as a supernatural chambermaid and clean off the cobwebs as she slept. I found that I had dreamt myself all the way to Basingstoke.

The view outside the window was becoming greyer now, as if the train was trying to prepare us for London. There was a man on the same programme who believed that every night a small green witch came and sat on his chest and paralysed him. Then a scientist came on and explained that our brain paralyses us in our sleep so that we don't act out our dreams. But that made me feel worse. How did the man get the green witch off his chest if he couldn't move?

The Proper Art College was a modern-looking building with concrete walls, and the talk was in a room on the sixth floor. Before it started, I looked out of the window and I could see London down below with red buses and taxis and cars and people hurrying by. Then the room started to fill up with the other photographers on my course. The chairs were set out in a circle and we sat down. When the circle was almost full, the door opened and we all looked up because we thought it might be our tutor, but instead it was another student. It was a woman with very dark curly hair in a bob, wearing a black leather jacket, a white shirt, black jeans and a silver chain around her neck. There was one chair free, opposite me. She sat down and took off her jacket so I could see that her shirt was sleeveless. I was looking at her brown arms and her black tattoo when she turned, looked straight at me and smiled. She had dark brown eyes, the same colour as her hair. Then the tutor arrived and I didn't have time to find out what her name was. The tutor welcomed us to the course and talked about the merits of buying this and that piece of equipment until I felt like I had cotton wool in my head.

After a while I stopped listening and I looked over at the woman with the silver chain and invented names for her instead. Wendy or Rose or Josephine or Carrie. I decided on Rose although it turned out I was wrong. I looked at the way her curly hair was tucked behind her ear and the way her face turned into her neck in a smooth curve and the way her neck turned into her shoulders and her shoulders turned into her arms and her breasts and her back. Her brown skin was beautiful, and she had long thin fingers. She saw me looking at her and smiled at me again and I held eye contact with her for a second. Her eyes were so brown I nearly fell into them. When she asked the tutor a question, she had an accent which I thought was Australian, although I was wrong again, because she was from New Zealand. I listened to her voice and thought about how when I was a child I wanted to dig and dig right through the world and see where I would come out.

'Australia, probably,' said my mother, when I asked her.

I remember being surprised by the feeling the woman with the

277

silver chain gave me in the back of my hand and in the middle of my chest. I didn't know what the feeling was. When I started at art college in the autumn, I found out, and I found out lots of other things about her too. Her name was Laina. Like Elaina but without the E. She was my first true love. True because I buried myself inside her and then dug myself up again. Love because I put my hand into her like a lucky dip and found it, love, like a present. From October to March we fell into each other and over each other and I loved her like waves on the beach over and over again.

That all happened later. I didn't even speak to her that day. After the talk, I did my journey to London backwards, although I thought of different things this time. Mostly, I thought about the woman with the silver chain and her brown skin and her brown eyes. I watched as the view out of the window became softer and greener, as I left Big Ben behind. Soon Christchurch Priory came into view over the fields.

I got the bus back from the train station to the flat and at five thirty, when I walked in, I found Beatrice and Meredith kissing on the sofa. I remember thinking it was nice because they were holding hands at the same time and kissing each other gently. I was a bit jealous too, because they were kissing each other like they knew about each other's stories and histories, like their stories were passing between them on their tongues. I wanted to know someone that well too, so that I could kiss them holding hands and sitting upright on the sofa in Meredith's flat. They realised I was there and Beatrice blushed. I had never seen her blush before.

They both smiled and Meredith said, 'Hello, Rice. You're back soon. I could have picked you up.' She was still holding Beatrice's hand. I sat down on a chair and read them the list of things I had to buy for art college.

'Standard (manual) SLR, with lens attachments.'

'Don't they have them for you to borrow?' said Beatrice.

'We have to have our own. Colour and black-and-white film, different speeds. Sketch books and pens and pencils, 2B to 8B. Putty eraser.'

'Do you do drawing as well?' said Beatrice.

'I think so.'

'That's a good idea,' said Beatrice.

'Developing tray. Collapsible tripod.'

'I wish I could draw,' said Meredith. 'Beatrice and I are going out for dinner, do you want to come?'

'No.' I said, and they went to get ready in Meredith's room.

'You need a rest after being in London all day, anyway,' said Beatrice, because to her London was a strange and distant place and strange and distant things always make you feel tired. I went into the kitchen to make myself a banana sandwich, then I turned the TV on. It was *Neighbours* and I didn't usually watch it but I did anyway that day, because I wanted to go over what I had just seen and staring at the screen helped me think about it.

'How do we look?' Meredith said, as the credits started and they both walked back into the lounge. Meredith was wearing a blue silk shirt that went with her eyes and a green jacket and Levis, and Beatrice had on her cords and a cream-coloured jumper.

'Great,' I said.

'Make yourself some dinner,' said Meredith.

'OK,' I said, and turned the TV off. When Esther came in from work, I smiled at her and went and made her a cup of normal tea (we could only have normal tea when Meredith was out. I had to smuggle the tea bags in under my coat).

'How was work?' I hadn't stopped smiling.

'Fine. Why are you so happy?'

'I saw your mum and Meredith snogging on the sofa,' I said,

and sat down right next to her, with my own mug of tea in my hand.

'I thought they would,' said Esther, and we didn't say anything for a bit. Then I put my hand on her knee and left it there. Esther looked at me. 'What are you doing that for?' she said.

'Oh, sorry,' I said. I took my hand away.

'Do you want to watch TV?' Esther said, picking up the remote control.

'OK.'

'What happened in London?'

'Nothing much. They gave us a list of things to buy.'

Esther flicked the TV on. The news was halfway through. Something about Mrs Thatcher being Prime Minister for ten years.

'What did you do at work?'

'A few trims and a blue rinse,' she said, and showed me the tips she'd made.

The Four Seasons

'This is a bit far,' said Beatrice doubtfully as we all headed out in the estate agent's car again that weekend. It was another sticky day.

'Wait until you see it,' said the estate agent. After a couple of miles, we pulled into the drive, which was lined by rhododendron bushes and fir trees. The guesthouse we had come to look at stood at the end of a pathway through some more trees and past a small pond that might once have had frogs and ducks. The house itself was painted yellow and white on the outside and looked a bit like a gingerbread cottage, although it wasn't a cottage and it wasn't really made of gingerbread. When the estate agent opened the door I thought it might be a haunted house instead, because it smelt of dust and cobwebs and the door creaked, though it seemed like the ghosts might have got bored and left, because no one had lived there for years.

'It needs a bit of work,' said the estate agent, 'but it's structurally sound and it has got ten bedrooms.'

'No, thank you,' said Beatrice to the estate agent after we had all peered into each of the dusty bedrooms, some of which still had beds in them. 'I want somewhere that doesn't need too many alterations.'

Then we went to see somewhere that turned out to be a shop,

with fake wood finishing and orange lampshades, and not a bed and breakfast at all. So we were feeling hot and tired and weren't expecting to find the new hotel when we actually found it.

'It's got ten bedrooms,' said Beatrice, as we went up the drive. The gate had trees either side of it and the outside of the building was painted black and white. I liked it straight away. Inside it was painted blue, and there were blue and red luxury carpets and thick curtains.

'One of the selling points,' said Beatrice, looking at the estate agent's leaflet and smiling, so I could see she liked it too. It was all so new there were no ghosts there yet, like the leftovers from yesterday's guests, or things that happened there left inside the walls or under the carpet, although maybe there were some in the furniture.

All the rooms had en-suite bathrooms, with tiny glass shower units, toilets and sinks behind wooden doors with floral yellow and white tiles, and there was a big cast-iron bath and curly taps in the shared bathroom on the landing. Esther loved the owner's apartment with its separate white and blue kitchen. There was a utility room off the main kitchen, which had new white units and a dishwasher, a small dining room and an even smaller garden for the guests to sit in and read the papers. There was just enough space for a couple of sun loungers and some flowers in pots, and no steps leading down to anywhere.

'It's almost perfect,' said Meredith on the way back.

'It is decorated OK,' said Beatrice, 'but the furniture doesn't go.' They talked about what they could do with it all the way home and we knew that this was the place. When it was decided, we went out to an Italian restaurant to celebrate and I ate lots of garlic bread and spaghetti bolognese, and zabaglione for pudding.

We carried on living at Meredith's flat while we did the

decorating but we spent a lot of time getting the new place ready. At weekends, we travelled to different car boot sales and second-hand furniture shops. Usually we came back hot and excited, with our eyes shining and our heads full of the bargains we had hunted out together. We bought velvety blue duvet covers and some red ones too to go with the carpets and the curtains and new soft towels and trays with handles.

'In case they want breakfast in bed,' Meredith said, and Beatrice put a heart-shaped bath pillow on the side of the bath with some aromatherapy oils from Esther's salon.

'Guests expect to be pampered these days,' she said. Soon we had handles and cupboards and tables and chairs and pictures to hang on the wall, and material for cushion covers that Meredith made on her sewing machine.

On my birthday, 23 September, the decorating was nearly finished. I had my birthday lunch in the owner's apartment and Sandra was there too.

'I'm still going to come in and help,' she said. 'You can't get rid of me that easily.'

When Sandra brought out the cake and ice cream, Beatrice announced that she had decided to open for a Hallowe'en and Bonfire Night Special at the end of October, but she said we needed to think of a name. We all shouted out names but there weren't any that stuck in our heads. Sandra said it should be called 'The Seaview' like her mum's hotel in Brighton, but we couldn't call it that because you can't see the sea from the new hotel. Esther said it should be called B's B. and B. but then I looked into Meredith's face and she went quiet and sat down on the new blue sofa and I kicked Esther under the table and she said, 'Ow.'

'You could just call it The New Bed-and-Breakfast,' I said.

'No, it won't be new for ever,' said Beatrice.

'The Four Seasons Bed and Breakfast,' said Esther suddenly, looking out of the window at the golden leaves that had fallen from the trees on to the road outside. I wondered then if she was thinking of running about in them and making patterns or standing in the wind until the leaves stuck to her hair.

'The Four Seasons Guesthouse,' said Meredith. We nodded our heads. It was a name we all liked.

'Perfect,' said Beatrice.

'I'm moving into the bed and breakfast with Beatrice,' said Meredith, suddenly.

'What will you do with the flat?' I said.

'Someone from the orchestra will probably rent it from me.'

'Oh.' I was worried for a moment. I suddenly had a picture of Meredith cooking and cleaning the toilets in the new hotel instead of playing her cello. 'Is it so you can help with the rooms?' I said, to find out if the picture was made up or not.

'Of course not. I've got a very busy schedule coming up. I'm leaving for Vienna in a few weeks,' she said. 'I've got to rehearse.'

'That's my job, anyway,' said Sandra, crossing her legs.

After I left for college, Meredith moved to the new hotel and Esther moved into the flat above the beauty salon in Wimborne with her boyfriend, Ian the hairstylist, so we were all somewhere different.

Back at my birthday dinner, Meredith picked up a catalogue from the floor and passed it round for us to look at. It was full of different hotel signs.

'We're going to get one made,' she said, 'with the name and the phone number. It lights up at night.'

'I'm only doing continental breakfasts,' Beatrice said, sitting down next to Meredith and tucking her arm neatly round her waist like a belt, 'muffins and orange juice, croissants and coffee or tea and toast. And no dinners. So there's not much cooking. Just beds and bathrooms really.'

'Good,' said Sandra, 'less work for me. There you go, love.' She handed me a birthday present. I unwrapped it. It was a framed photo of all of us, including Grandma Maggie in her wheelchair, outside the old hotel. 'So you don't forget about us while you're up in London,' she said.

'Thanks, Sandra,' I said, and kissed her on her fake tan cheek, and she smelt of cocoa oil and nicotine. Then I looked at the photo and said, 'I don't remember who took that one.'

'One of the guests, probably,' said Esther.

'Go on,' said Meredith to Beatrice, nudging her with her elbow.

'This is from Esther and Meredith and me,' said Beatrice, and she picked up a parcel from the sideboard. 'Happy birthday.'

I unwrapped it and then I looked from Beatrice to Esther to Meredith in disbelief. It was a shiny new camera, in a case with lenses and filters and everything.

'Many happy returns,' said Beatrice, and kissed me on the cheek.

'Happy birthday, Rice,' said Esther and Meredith together.

'It's amazing,' I said. 'Thank you.' And then there was another long thin parcel, wrapped in the same paper, and it was a tripod. Everybody clapped and then Sandra lit the nineteen candles on my cake with her silver cigarette lighter and I blew them out.

Beatrice wanted me to take some photos for her brochures with my new camera so Esther, Sandra and I spent the rest of the day picking positions and camera angles. I had to cram myself into the corner of each room to try to get everything in.

Suzie Parker

A rose by any other name would smell as sweet? I'm not so sure. I think I would smell different with a different name. On 23 September 1989, I took my feet from the wooden ledge that ran around the beach-hut walls and stood up and stretched. I was glad there wasn't long till autumn. It was uncomfortable, sleeping in the beach hut every night. I pushed my face against the window and I could see the not-quite-summer sun shining round like an egg through the clouds and on to the flat beach, which was wet and had long furrows and ridges in it as if it had been ploughed. I pushed my face against the window everyday for the next week and watched the weather. I saw summer dwindle and it was nearly time to leave. The beach was different then, looking out from the beach-hut window eleven years ago, from how it is tonight. The beach is always different and I am still waiting. Tonight the clouds are big, like giant's breath, and the sky looks bigger than the sea or as if the sea doesn't stop and carries on up into the air. I don't feel cold from the rain any more. I feel like a fish must feel, safe and wet. Rice is still by the pier under her umbrella and we are both still remembering.

The day before she left for London, it was time to go to meet Rice again. I had something to deliver, which I had kept safe for a long time, all through the seventies and all through the eighties, but I wanted to give it to her before she went away, now she was ready to understand. I put the present in my pocket and left the beach hut. It was a hot day so I took off my shoes and walked along the sand for an hour and a half until I got to Branksome Chine, which is the name of the beach where it changes from Bournemouth into Poole, where the sand seems whiter and the ice creams taste different. When I got there I bought some candy floss from the café and sat down and waited by the white pavilion. Gradually, the tourists went home for their teas and the dog walkers started to come and go along the beach. A few children played cricket with a plastic tennis bat in the distance and shouted at each other when the ball went into the sea and they had to wade in after it, and the sun started to go down.

Then there was Rice, thinking no one was around, lying on her stomach, focusing her lens on things that had been left behind on the sand, a bottle of suntan lotion, a white bottle top, a hat. I finished my candy floss, got up and walked towards her.

'Daphne,' said Rice. She stood up. She was surprised to see me, but I'm glad she remembered my name.

'Hello,' I said. 'Taking photos?'

'Yes.'

'Can I buy you a lemonade?'

We went and sat in the café inside the pavilion with the plastic tables and chairs, and when I had finished my drink I gave her the secret thing I had in my pocket. She looked shocked.

'Good luck at art college,' I said. I smiled at her before I left and retraced my footprints back to the beach hut.

Here I am by the pier, and now I'm thinking about names again, like I did when I was younger, when I used to wish that I could choose my own name. When I lived at the hotel, I played a game with the names of the guests, and put my name in front of theirs

287

to hear what it would sound like. And sometimes I would wonder, if I was called Rice Tamarack instead of Rice Parker, would I look different in the mirror and in photographs?

I had gone down to the beach for one last time before I went away, when I saw Daphne, the seasonal chambermaid, again. It was the end of a warm almost-autumn afternoon. I had returned Steve's camera because now I had a new camera all of my own and I had been practising with it. She walked up to me like she'd been waiting for me, like she knew I was going to be there and she just smiled at me for a long time, as if she was a long-lost friend. I offered to take her picture but she said no and asked me if I'd like a lemonade.

'Where are you staying?' I asked her. I wasn't convinced that she was sane again. Her smile had madness hidden in it.

'My mother's found me a place till I go home.'

'That's nice.' I sipped my drink. Then after a pause I asked the question I had wanted to ask on the day of the funeral. 'Was it you in the hospital with me? Beatrice thinks I was making it up.'

'Of course it was me,' she said.

'Oh.'

'Only minor burns, nothing serious.'

'Do you remember that stuff about vampires and hospitals?' I tried to laugh. 'You must have been in shock or something. Are you OK now?'

'Oh, I wasn't in shock,' she said. 'That was all true. I should know, after all.' She winked at me and I shifted uneasily in my chair.

'This is for you,' she said. She reached into her pocket, got out a film canister and put it on the table between us. I looked at her uncertainly.

'What's it of?' It was the only thing I could think of to ask.

'Have them developed when you get to art college. Don't take them to the shop. They might not come out,' she said, and winked at me again. 'I've been meaning to give them to you for some time. Good luck in London,' she said. 'Oh. And happy birthday.'

'What?' I said, but she got up and left without saying anything else. I sat and stared after her for a while until I couldn't see her any more and I started to wonder if I was still unwell myself and had daydreamed the last ten minutes, but when I looked back at the table, there was the film waiting for me. I picked it up and put it in the bag with the camera and trudged back up the hill to Meredith's flat. I didn't tell the others what had happened. I wanted to find out what the photos were first.

I didn't take the film to the chemist's. Like Daphne had said, I waited till I got to college, although it looked just like an ordinary film to me. When I learnt how to use the darkroom, I mixed up the chemicals carefully in the red light and developed the film myself. As the pictures emerged under the water, I felt something hot like a flame in my stomach. There were twelve photos and they were of my mother and me when I was just born. I felt special, because I hadn't had any baby photos before. The person who took them was good with the camera, I thought to myself. I hung them up to dry and meant to ask Beatrice for Daphne's phone number so I could ask her where they came from, but the thought went out of my head like a flame breaking away from the rest of the fire in a fireplace and shooting up a chimney.

It was 2 October and time for me to leave my beach hut behind and go back to hell. Next year would be different because I would come back and stay at the Four Seasons Guesthouse with the sign that lit up. But first of all, I went to watch Rice get on to her train at Bournemouth station, and in the Lemon Tree Café, hiding behind a newspaper, I listened to Meredith tell Rice the story that she had been keeping hidden inside her

289

for nearly twenty years, which I had known about since the beginning.

It was 1970, the year that Peter Shilton got his first cap for England and the year the Equal Pay Act was read in the Palace of Westminster. Six years later, the Viking spacecraft tested for signs of life on Mars, but could find no conclusive evidence.

I was eager to follow what was happening between Timothy Mackintosh and Beatrice, and I watched carefully from my throne in the garden of the lost souls below the earth. In January 1970, Timothy Mackintosh left Beatrice, who was four months pregnant, at the hotel, and went up the road and round the corner to Suzie Parker's house. Suzie had a passion for interesting things and Timothy Mackintosh was one of them. Suzie laughed and kicked her shoes off and tossed her hair back. She was wearing a brown flowery dress that buttoned up the front.

'What took you so long? Playing mummies and daddies?' she said. She had a joint already neatly rolled and a bottle of red wine uncorked, and she took a swig and lit the joint with the matches Timothy Mackintosh gave her.

'Beatrice knows I experiment,' he said, taking the wine bottle himself.

'With her best friend?'

'You're not her best friend, Suzie. She likes Meredith more.'

'How do you know?'

'She told me she wants to sleep with her.'

'And who do you want to sleep with, Timothy Mackintosh?' she said, blowing smoke rings into his face. He smiled and pulled her dress open.

When they had finished, he lay naked on the floor of the lounge, the feather on a string still around his neck, and looked up at the Artexed ceiling, with his arms behind his head. Suzie was asleep on the sofa, dress unbuttoned but still on, as if someone had got halfway through skinning her to make a coat.

When Timothy Mackintosh came into her life I could see Suzie thought he was her Messiah, God incarnate descending from heaven to save her. Timothy Mackintosh tasted of coconut and spices and he promised to take her to places that were holy and eccentric. When they were alone together, although she laughed and pretended not to care, Suzie would close her eyes and pray sometimes, put her hands on his face and imagine she was touching the places he had been to, eating the food he had eaten, like rice and pork or soft dough and raw fish. She imagined that she had spoken to the people he'd spoken to, in bits of different languages, switching from one to the other with ease, the same way that he fucked her, easily, slipping from one place to another. I looked inside Suzie's head and I could see, right inside her most intimate memories, that when they had sex, he would come quickly, withdraw and roll over. He would sleep and dream of banquets he had created, leaving Suzie wet and wanting to gorge herself on his other places.

Later, I saw Timothy go back to the hotel and climb into bed next to Beatrice. Beatrice was asleep but she could smell her friend on his body and under his breath.

It was June of the same year and I was back in Bournemouth again when Timothy Mackintosh got up and cooked one of his tastiest breakfasts ever. The guests loved him and often sent messages of congratulations. To celebrate, he rolled a joint and took a bottle of Jack Daniel's down to the beach. When he came back up the beach steps he was drunk. I went and sat in the garden to watch. Maggie was in the kitchen; I could see her through the window, making lunch in his absence. She was muttering about men with children to look after. Beatrice was over the other side of the garden with her pram. Esther was inside. She was one month old. I tuned in my ears so I could hear what they were saying.

'I'm going to stay with Suzie,' he said.

'Are you coming back?' she said.

He swayed drunkenly. 'You know I like to make love to lots of women. Don't try to tie me down.'

'I said, are you coming back?'

He looked at Esther. 'I wouldn't leave my daughter behind.' He smiled and tried to kiss her, but Beatrice moved her baby's face away from his bristly whisky-flavoured mouth.

Timothy Mackintosh never came back. He left Beatrice with Esther, who was new and clean and sleepy, and went round to Suzie's house. I followed close behind him and hid myself behind a lamppost to watch. When he got there he found all her cookery books and books about other countries swept to the floor and her glasses smashed and her little wooden chairs knocked over and Suzie throwing up into the bath.

'I thought you were on the pill,' he said, lighting a cigarette and passing it to Suzie, once she had calmed down and was surveying the damage she had done.

'Pills mess up your body,' she said, taking a drag of the cigarette.

'I'm leaving,' said Timothy Mackintosh.

'Take me with you,' said Suzie, looking him in the face.

'You're carrying my son,' he said. 'What if you caught malaria? I'll be back before he's born. Can you get me some tickets?'

Suzie did get him some tickets printed on the sly at the travel agent where she worked, but he didn't come back and Suzie had a girl, not a boy, and named her Rice, in honour of her father who was a wonderful cook and liked to make the recipes he had practised in India and China, Mexico and

Iceland, Australia and Egypt. And after long nights waiting for Timothy Mackintosh to come back, Suzie Parker packed up her new daughter and the rest of her things and moved Up North.

Rice and Esther

It was suddenly cold and misty, and I wondered where summer had gone. All the lazy warmth of August and early September had deserted us and we stamped our feet to keep warm whenever we went out. Autumn meant the start of something new, and on 2 October, it was time to go to art college and leave Bournemouth behind. Meredith drove me to the train station. We sat in the Lemon Tree Café on platform two, and that's when she told me a story that I hadn't heard before, not even from my mother.

'We should have told you years ago,' she said afterwards, 'but Beatrice didn't want to upset you. Or Esther. She says she doesn't mind me telling you now.'

'Does Esther know?' I said, after I'd heard it.

'She knows some of it, about her and Beatrice, but not the ending about you and Suzie. Beatrice says she'll tell her soon.'

'OK,' I said.

Rice is an unusual name, and it turned out I was named for my father, who was unusual like me. Meredith and I sat in the Lemon Tree Café and she told me the story about why Beatrice and my mother had fallen out and how Esther and I were half-sisters and how my father was Timothy Mackintosh too, and how he used to take photos like me. I gave her a hug and said that I had to go. I picked up my suitcase. My train was already waiting by the platform.

'I'm glad that you told me,' I said, and hugged her again. 'Thanks for everything. See you soon.' I got on to my train. When I turned round to wave, Meredith waved back. Then I watched as Bournemouth slowly disappeared.

The first time I came back to Bournemouth after leaving for college was on a Thursday. It was nearly the end of October 1989. Beatrice had phoned and said she had just found out that the old hotel was being demolished at the weekend. I got on a train down straight away. Meredith was back from Austria and she came to pick me up.

'Beatrice has got lots of guests in,' she said. 'We're almost full. People come at all times of the year these days.' She paused. 'Esther's upset about the hotel.' I wanted to ask Meredith if Beatrice had told Esther the story she had told me on Bournemouth station, but I couldn't, because we pulled into the drive and there was the smart new sign that said 'Four Seasons Guesthouse', and Beatrice ran out to say hello and to pick up my suitcase before I could stop her.

'I'm afraid you'll have to have the smallest room,' she said, showing me into Room Five, which just had enough room for the bed. 'All the others are taken.'

'This is fine,' I said. 'Is Esther here?'

'She's at work, but she's coming over later.'

'I think I'll go and find her,' I said. 'Are you going to come and watch at the weekend?'

'No. I don't think I could bear it,' said Beatrice, and Meredith agreed with her and said she didn't want to watch either but maybe I should take some pictures.

I hadn't been back to the old hotel since the fire and it was months since I had seen it. I was still frightened but I wanted to go on my own to say goodbye, so before I went to find Esther, I went to look at it, standing lopsided on the cliff top. I remember thinking that I would make an interesting colour picture, staring up at the cliff top like that. I could hear the autumn sea tossing like chopped cabbage behind me, as I looked up at the remains of the old hotel, with my hair blowing in the wind. My stomach filled with smoke, just from looking. What had been a tall red brick building now looked like a corpse with empty eye sockets. The fire had run its fingers seductively around the walls and windows, leaving a black trail behind it. The pipes and metal stairs and windowledges looked like its veins and nerves, crawling over the outside of the building, trying to escape. I remember thinking that the fire had stripped the old hotel naked or turned it inside out. I walked in through each black window with my eyes before making up my mind. Then, before I could talk myself out of it, I hurried up the beach steps. I got to where the garden used to be and kept walking until I reached the back door, which was so rotten it opened with a gentle push. I went inside and, moving slowly in the dark, I went into the kitchen, then the dining room, guest lounge and bar. They were exactly where they used to be. Then I climbed up the stairs, which smelt like dog piss and blackberry bushes. I kept going up and climbed the next set of stairs. The door to the attic room was still intact. I stopped outside and pressed my hands and face against the door and shut my eyes, thinking of the first time I had opened that door and hearing Beatrice's voice again calling to Esther that tea was ready and had she checked the sink in Room Ten. Then I walked down the corridors, and went from bedroom to bedroom looking into each one.

I walked into the hairdresser's.

'Hello,' Esther said as if I'd never been away, as if I had

just come out of Room Nineteen with a yellow basketful of pillowcases. 'I can't talk now. I've got some hair extensions and a perm waiting.'

'Esther . . .' I said, trying to bring her back to her senses. I could see she was upset.

'I'll meet you after work, five thirty. Café next door,' Esther said.

'OK.'

I wondered vaguely for a moment why she didn't invite me upstairs to her flat, or for lunch at least, but thought maybe she was too upset, so I left, with the doorbell ringing behind me, a bell Esther must have listened to a hundred times a day, six days a week. She must hear bells in her sleep, I thought. I wandered around Wimborne Minster, slowly, because it was cold outside and when it got to half-past five, I went and sat in the café next door to the hairdresser's and waited, thinking about the colour of my coffee as I stirred it too much and ate a doughnut with jam in the middle. Suddenly, there was Esther sitting down opposite me.

'Our receptionist was off sick and I've had highlights and perms and extensions all day. No one wants a trim any more. How's art college?'

'Good.'

Then Esther told me that Ian had left her for a man with blond streaks and a goatee, and she had moved out of the flat, which had brown wallpaper and smelt of mushrooms, so she didn't like it anyway.

'We're still friends,' she said, receiving a cup of tea from the waitress. The man with the goatee had a small flat by the river and he was letting her rent it.

'We kind of swapped.' she said. 'He couldn't afford it any more and I make a lot of money on tips. I'm applying for another job, though, so he might have to get someone else.' She sat up straight and there was a little bit of shininess back in her eyes.

'You haven't been working here long.'

'Over a year.'

'Where is the new job?'

'In a hotel in Bournemouth town centre.'

'Which one?'

'The Royal Winchester. It's five star and the staff live in. They want someone for the hair salon.'

'Perfect,' I said, and laughed.

'Yes, only, I think I might be pregnant,' she said, and her eyes looked worried again. I looked at her in surprise. She had always been the one telling me about condoms.

'Does Beatrice know?'

'I'm not sure myself yet.'

'Don't worry,' I said, and although I wanted to ask her about the half-sister thing and whether Beatrice had told her, when I looked into her green eyes, I thought that, yes, she did know and we would have lots of time to talk about it, but for now we had to think about the hotel and whether Esther had a silent invader growing inside her.

On Saturday Esther and I stood on the beach together. Though I had my camera with me, I only used it afterwards. I wanted to watch. It was windy but the diggers and the crane didn't seem to care, perched like giant vultures on the cliff top. It seemed like we'd waited for a long time. Then a man got into the crane cab, which had a dangerous metal ball on the end of its chain. Esther put her arm around me for protection. The wind was making her eyes water and was whipping my hair around my face. The first blow was the worst. I felt like Houdini being punched in the stomach. The wall above the kitchen crumbled, and I could see right into Room Sixteen, and the space where I had stood so many times to make the bed was now in mid-air. It was like there were still lots of Rices standing there and, as I watched, each one tumbled through the broken floorboards on to the pile of rubble below and lay there bruised and dying. For a moment the hotel looked like someone had taken a huge bite out of the side. Then the ball hit it again and this time we could see into the kitchen and the dining room. Esther turned her face into my shoulder and cried until there were rivers of water running down my T-shirt. Then we both turned round and looked out to sea, the noise of the execution going on behind us mixing with the noise of the October waves crashing up the beach.

My name is Persephone and my story is nearly over. I knew that it was a love story when I first started, and I tried to think of all the things that make up a love story so that I would get it right, because even though it is an unusual kind of love story, it is one all the same, like most stories are. In a love story there is a pink carpet and ice cream and roses and sweet smells and walks on the beach. There is music too, and white lace, laughing, rocking chairs and fires. A love story has slightly yellowing pages, pages that have been read in the bath before you put two fingers inside yourself. A love story has different coloured sand in a jar. People get old. Someone dies and people hold hands. A love story has leaves that the wind blows in someone's hair. There is a scar on someone's hand and the blood runs down her wrist. Bubblegum and hearts with two names inside them. Crosses for kisses, tongues. Small flowers. Cartoon stars. Travelling, on a train maybe, on a day out. Curled toes, rowing, getting salt water in your mouth and laughing. Watching the waves. The white-crowned king waves come up the beach, sigh, go back, return again. A love story has candles, velvet and hairbrushes. This is a love story because it is about two people who fall over each other, who get inside each

299

other and crack each other open like eggs, or fall off the wall like Humpty and get mixed in with each other. Not just two people, lots of people, all the people who ever lived at the old hotel, all running together like egg yolk, after they collided.

Sometimes people can run along the water's edge, down by the sea, where the tourists are in the summer. People can run towards each other and get their feet wet, stretch their arms out and miss each other and then maybe they run into the sea and swim with all their clothes on. A love story is like hot buttered toast, like leaves somersaulting over each other in the autumn. A love story tastes of rice paper when you eat it, because the pages dissolve on your tongue. You eat them one after another and you can't stop. You eat them over and over like eating history, like swallowing the days of the year, one at a time. They all taste slightly of rice, slightly of cherries and make you feel thirsty. A love story has lines like the lines on your hand; when you look at them they are a map telling you which way to go. A love story is like that.

I closed my eyes once before I went to sleep and imagined a big book of stories, so big that I couldn't lift it, and when the pages opened by themselves I was nearly squashed under the weight of them. Then I found out that inside all stories are two things. There is a case of buried treasure and a bunch of nettles. The nettles are green and sharp and hurt when you touch them. The case of buried treasure snaps shut when you look inside and swallows you, just like it did to Pandora after she lost her hope and she died like people who are swallowed by sharks die. In a love story things happen. People come in and out of rooms. People look at each other with wide eyes and laugh. People go to bed with each other, kiss each other and shout at each other.

After the fire things were different. The fire was the place where everything began, a mini universe creating itself from its own ashes, expanding and contracting over and over again, like the path that runs from my thighs up into my body. There was the love story at the heart of the fire, inside the peach kernel, inside Esther's hand, inside Grandma Maggie's fist, deep inside the stomachs of the people at the hotel that night, and in their smoke-filled eyes there was the love story, which was where they all started. The love story is a bit like one of those puzzles where you have to slot the numbers into place in the right order or like a Rubik's cube. It is like being at the centre of a maze or at the bottom of the sea and trying to find your way out or up to the surface. Being inside the love story was like being Abednego at the centre of the fire, or like being in hell or like being at the centre of the earth or being in that film where they go inside someone's body and through their heart.

The fire is like a body made up of everlasting circles that are opening and closing. It is like Demeter, who creates and destroys, and the blood that comes from between her thighs. The fire left bits behind, hanging in the air, things that had happened in the hotel's spaces. And it made a hole, like a scar, where all these things are still remembered. There are ghosts telling stories to keep themselves warm. There are the hotel guests and suitcases. There are things that will happen in the hotel spaces in the future. People will stand here pegging out washing or talking idly to one another. People who aren't alive yet will die in the spaces. The stories will hang in the air around them and stay there.

The fire was the thing that changed the story. It burnt the hotel people inside out, twisted them around and shifted them as though they were pieces in a game of chess. The hotel people turned from red into blue into yellow like the flames. Bits of them were left scarred for ever and other parts woke up and saw the bright light of the fire and those parts knew what was at the heart of it. The hottest place of the fire was like the hottest place inside Esther and Rice and Beatrice and Maggie, the silent part of them, where their stories were.

My name is Rice. I have left the beach and have driven to the Four Seasons Guesthouse. It's 22 September 2000 and in just an hour it will turn midnight and I will be thirty years old. I got here half an hour ago and everyone came out to greet me: Esther and Meredith and Beatrice and Esther's little boy (my nephew) Thomas, who is ten. She named him after her great-grandfather. I think the first Thomas Tamarack is very proud of him. I like to think of him watching from the centre of the earth as his great-great-grandson grows like an apple tree.

Esther is experienced in being thirty so she has been giving me advice about it on the phone.

'It's not as bad as you think,' she said. 'I've started yoga and I'm doing M. and B.'s garden for them.' Esther is the Senior Beauty Consultant and Stylist at the Royal Winchester Hotel (five stars) in the centre of Bournemouth. She and Thomas live in. Ian, who is Thomas's father, comes round to visit at the weekends, although Esther has been going out with the breakfast manager since 1995.

When I arrived, I kissed them all on the cheek and Esther handed me the present that she couldn't wait till the morning to give me. It's a big book made out of sugar paper with sheets of tissue between the pages, and it's got a thin black ribbon tying it together. Inside she's made a scrapbook. She's written the story of how we found out about each other and all about how we are proper sisters now. My eyes filled with salt water when I saw it and turned the pages. My very own book, that's mine and no one else's. Beatrice and Meredith and Thomas and Esther have all written 'Happy Birthday' and 'Many Happy Returns' underneath photos of themselves. Here's a bit of what it says:

302

Dear Rice,

This is a birthday present. Your thirtieth birthday scrap-book. It's all for you. The idea is that this is a reminder of what it was like at the hotel and of the things we did together. Anyway, you know all of this already, it's just that it's important to write it down. There are some odd things I could find in it, like a bus ticket from the school bus which I found inside an old maths book. Happy birthday, Rice. I hope you like the scrapbook and that you'll carry on adding things to the pages.

I saw you for the first time at Sandra's wedding, in August 1973, when I was three and you were still two. I only remember it from the pictures. You were sitting next to your mother. I was on Beatrice's knee. When I was a bit older, I liked to count things. I used to count up how old I was and how many days I'd been alive. I counted the people in the pictures and I counted how many were smiling. Each year as I grew up, I looked into the photos and invented names for the people. I wondered who the only other little girl at the wedding was and where she was now. Once I made up a conversation that we would have when we met and I imagined us both wearing the ballgowns from my Ladybird *Cinderella* book.

'That's Rice,' Beatrice would say, and she wouldn't tell me any more.

'Rice is a silly name,' I said when I was eight. I thought I knew about all the sensible names that people could have, and later, when my mum was sitting in the guest lounge with a cup of tea, I tried to find out more about you.

'Where is Rice now?' I said.

'She moved a long way away,' said Beatrice.

'Why?' Then when I didn't get an answer: 'What school does she go to?'

'I don't know. Go and count if there's enough soap in the stock cupboard.' That's how I started my apprenticeship at the hotel, by counting things. I counted toilet rolls, tea bags, bottles of Jif, cans of soup, whenever I asked a difficult question. I loved lining up the tins so I could count them properly. I made towers out of custard cans and cartons of washing powder. Then I would report back exact amounts. Sometimes I would count just for myself. Number of plates to be washed up. Number of pairs of knickers and socks in my laundry basket. I grew out of it. Right after I grew past the top of the measuring tape with a giraffe on it that used to be stuck to the wall of my bedroom. I wasn't good at counting things at school. Red bricks and yellow bricks weren't interesting enough. I grew out of it right after I grew out of asking questions about the people at the wedding and you, the other little girl, who looked like she was only a few months younger than me. After that I started accepting the pictures and the people in them because they had always been that way, inside the pictures and nowhere else. Even my mother and I were different people in strange clothes. I gave up counting and took on new responsibilities around the hotel.

When you started at my school, I told my friends I would fight anyone who teased you for not having a mother and I didn't know why I said it then because I thought I hated you, but when we got to school together I felt like I had to protect you. Like you were a bit of the hotel that I had brought into school with me. Sometimes my friends asked me who my father was and I told them: 'Timothy Mackintosh, I've got a picture at home,' and if one of them said, 'What kind of a stupid name is Timothy Mackintosh?', I'd pull her hair or slap her hard on the arm so she cried out and got into trouble. When I told my friends that you didn't have a mother, they asked me if you had a father and I said that I didn't think so and someone would say, 'Don't be stupid, everyone has a father. Did he die too?' I said yes because I didn't know. Once I got into a big fight with a thin girl called Jenny who said that it wasn't normal not to have a father and it was even weirder not to have a mother or a father and that God must hate me and he must hate you even more. I pulled her arm behind her back and told her to say it again so I could hear it, but she kicked me in the shins and spun round and bent my hand back till it felt like it would snap off. Then she said I was a weirdo and that you were too so I pinned her head down on the desk and pulled her hair until the teacher came in. You didn't know about any of this. I got into trouble and had to stay behind after school for a week and I told Beatrice I was trying out for the school football team and tore up the letter the teacher sent her saying how she wouldn't tolerate fighting.

Sometimes, when we were in a classroom together, which wasn't very often, only if Beatrice was picking us up from school, a teacher who was new and didn't know about us would say to me before you came, 'Are you waiting for your sister?' and I would say: 'I don't have a sister,' and when you arrived we would leave together, our bags swung over our shoulders and our black shoes clicking on the floor. Once in an English lesson the teacher said, 'You look like your sister, don't you?' and everyone laughed behind their hands.

I didn't know that Timothy Mackintosh was your father too until Beatrice told me. I only knew it in my fingers, which are a lot like yours. When I first saw you I think you might have wanted to press your hands against mine to see if they were the same size, but I was an ugly half-sister at first. I didn't like you from the start and I don't think you liked me either, but sisters don't like each other. They are supposed to fight and pull in different directions so we were living out the sister rules although not on purpose.

Eventually, I don't really know when it started, we began to like each other, and we would walk along the beach smoking or go into town. We worked in the hotel together and we became partners. We were better at it together than apart. You went from sitting lazily in armchairs to knowing exactly what to do and where to start, so that we could clean a room in fifteen minutes, including the bathroom and bed, without speaking to each other.

Sometimes, just after the fire, I dreamt that I went back into the burnt hotel and down into the foundations and that I found a body there amongst the rubble and concrete. When I looked up, there was Grandma Maggie again, just about to turn on the old gas oven, and just about to cook Hansel for her tea.

We were sisters underneath our skin. After I split up with my first proper boyfriend, I sat on the sofa in our room and cried and when you came upstairs I told you what had happened. You put your arm round me and it felt warm and I put my head on your shoulder and you put your head on top of mine. You said it didn't matter because I'd find someone better, on a white horse, you said, with armour on like in 'The Lady of Shalott' that you were doing in English and I said that the Lady of Shalott died and you said yes like that but not the dying bit. It was me that told you about condoms when you went out with a boy from college. It was sisterly advice, although I didn't know it. But

I hated him and I didn't want to speak to you because I was jealous that your attention was divided. Eventually it was too much effort and I gave in and we laughed in relief and made chips in my mum's biggest frying pan and ate them in the kitchen with vinegar.

I love you, Rice. I didn't always love you, or I didn't know I loved you. I love you because you brought a bit of me that I didn't know was missing, not aged nearly fourteen I didn't know it. I hated you, or I thought I hated you, coming into the hotel with your bags, wanting to share my spaces. Now we are both thirty years old and proper sisters, I can write down the words I love you, like a tattoo but on the page, and I can look at the words and see that they go right back to the day when my half-sister arrived at the old hotel, with her hair in a mess, and sat on the edge of the sofa in the guest lounge and watched us all with big eyes and her mouth in a straight line.

Rice and Persephone

My name is Persephone. It is time to go back into the sea, under the paper waves to the place where the grey spirits live. I am looking forward to seeing Hades again. She misses me in the summer like she misses the rain and the sun on her face. She hasn't visited the earth since she first swept me off my feet. I stand up and walk into the salty green and blue water and slowly, autumn begins around me. But I have never seen the leaves turning brown in the first breath of the new season. I never look back at the frost forming or the sky turning a different shade, because that's when I'm tunnelling under the water and through the earth to find the one I love.

My name is Rice and I'm sitting in my room now, looking at the book Esther gave me. My other present is a voucher for a free makeover, hairstyle and pedicure at the Royal Winchester Hotel.

'That's worth a lot of money,' Esther said, when she gave it to me. I said they were lovely presents and then I ate the sausages, mashed potato and beans and the rhubarb crumble that Beatrice had saved for me.

'Because you've been up in London – you need to build up your strength,' she said.

'Beatrice, I live in London,' I said, but I couldn't convince her. Beatrice considered London to be somewhere that drained the energy out of anyone who went there so much that they need feeding up when they returned. I've been in London for ten years and haven't wasted away to nothing yet.

'But it's such a big place,' she said.

It was good to eat something hot because I had got very cold on the beach. It was so dark just before I left that I could no longer make out the space where the old hotel used to be and when I looked across the beach, the woman in the green dress had gone. She must have got cold and gone home, I thought. I wonder why she wanted to come to the beach, and I went to get into my car, but as I started up the engine, I was sure I caught a glimpse of the woman in the green dress walking steadily into the sea, as if she was on her way to somewhere. I thought I saw a green light shining around her head like a halo but I could have been seeing things. When I stopped the car again and got out to look she wasn't there.